Division One: Definition and Alignment

by Stephanie Osborn

Chromosphere Press

Huntsville, AL

CHROMOSPHERE
PRESS

Definition and Alignment
© 2018 Stephanie Osborn

ISBN 978-1-947530-04-1 (print)
ISBN 978-1-947530-03-4 (ebook)
Cover art © 2018 Darrell Osborn
Fiction

First electronic edition 2018

This is a work of fiction. All concepts, characters and events portrayed in this book are used fictitiously and any resemblance to real people or events is purely coincidental.

Chromosphere Press
www.chromospherepress.com

Table of Contents

Chapter 1

"...Yes, that's right," Fox noted, as he stood in the Alpha Line Room, talking to that department's chief and assistant chief. "The Software department has been working on that upgrade as their top priority for months, now—ever since last Christmas, when the whole mess with the doppelganger shape-shifter went down. And it's finally in place and operational."

"Well, it makes sense," Echo decided. "I thought the memo was pretty explanatory of the changes. Swapping to genetic scans from visual, limited A.I., full voice activation capability, voice response..."

"Exactly. Software folded several updates they'd been working on into one release, but the security identification aspect was the main driver. I wanted that out—well, the Ennead did; those orders were coming from on high, but I fully agreed—as soon as they could shove it through beta testing, and they delivered."

"So, um, they decided to go with genetic scan patterns, rather than visual?" Omega queried, and both men realized she seemed a bit diffident about the matter...and understood the probable reason. Fox and Echo exchanged concerned, surreptitious glances, but neither man said anything; Omega was justifiably sensitive about the forced genetic 'enhancements' that had been performed upon her as a child, and which had only been discovered the year before. "What, uh, I mean, how...detailed...?"

"Not that much, Omega," Fox attempted to soothe. "Detailed genetic scans take nearly an hour just to gather the data, and days to weeks to analyze. That's useless for purposes of nigh-immediate identification of the personnel. It would make using it for security purposes moot. You have nothing to worry about, tekhter; no one outside of the appropriate persons is going to know about..." Fox shrugged, then glanced around, ensuring no other Alpha Line Agents were about to enter unexpectedly. "About the cold cases and the like which your, ah, genetic modifications, helped us to close last fall."

"Oh, okay," she decided, seeming relieved. "Well...good."

"Also, Echo, I wanted to tag up with you about it so I could pass on a few personal matters," Fox added. "Software wanted to make sure you knew that they transferred all of your special coded commands into the new system."

1

"Great. I was gonna ask about that."

"Not to worry. All those special codes you have for security and drek will still work. Also, per your—and one or two others'—request, a scaled-down version of the Autonomous Technology Lifestyle And Security System has been pushed through to certain, ah, 'personal holdings,' shall we say? Only you should call it A.T.L.A.S.S. Junior there. It still uses the old voice you had installed, though, so you might want to upgrade that at some point, too."

"Okay, that's good. I appreciate that."

"Zebra and I did, too."

"Oh, so you had it installed at your private getaway, too?"

"We did. The security of certain...personnel...were deemed high-priority, most especially the Director and his designated successor. Other facilities are being upgraded as Software gets to 'em. Safehouses and other Offices are highest priority, of course. And there are a few, such as the Ranch, where the system will be upgraded but not to the full-on A.T.L.A.S.S. coding; there was some concern that the civilian guests at the Ranch, for instance, might get a little freaked out at a talking security system. After all, it IS supposed to be a dude ranch these days."

"Good point," Omega murmured, then addressed her partner and department chief with an affectionate nickname. "Ace, we need to sit down at some time or other and talk about the in-house security. You mentioned something to me the other day about hidden corridor escapes and whatnot, and now I wanna know about those special codes you have in the housekeeping computer, too."

"We can do that, Meg," Echo agreed, using his own nickname for the female Agent. "Maybe later tonight, if you want to. Over dinner or something."

"That sounds good."

"You're just now filling her in on all of that, Echo?" Fox wondered, surprised.

"Yeah," a sheepish Echo admitted. "To be honest, since it never gets used and hasn't in...what, years?—I completely forgot to tell her about the escape routes; it just doesn't enter my thought any more unless there's a potential emergency where they'd NEED to be used. Which, I admit, is way the hell too late for Meg." He shrugged, then threw Omega an apologetic glance. "One of the down sides to having been here as long as the organization has existed, I guess. Sorry, Meg."

"Not a problem, hon," Omega said, offering a soft smile in return. "I can see where stuff like that can fall through the cracks. I'm just glad you thought to start telling me about 'em before we had a real need to know about 'em!'"

"True," Fox agreed. "No harm, no foul, as Romeo is wont to say." He glanced at his wrist chronometer. "Damn. I suppose I'd best get back to it. It was nice to get away from my office for a few minutes, though."

"You're always welcome to pop by, Fox, if you need to stretch your legs—or your mind—for a minute," Echo said. "As long as we've known each other—"

"Since the beginning," Omega added with a grin.

"...It isn't like we need to stand on formality with each other. And Meg won't ever take advantage of our friendship."

"Never mind that she is part of the 'family,'" Fox chuckled. "Omega?"

"Yeah, Fox?"

"I...wanted to thank you...for putting together this little 'family,' this mishpokhe we seem to have developed," Fox murmured. "I don't often express such, but I expect I speak not only for myself, but for Echo, Romeo, and India—I know for a fact that I speak for Zebra—"

"And Dihl," Echo interjected, referencing his birth mother, a skilled nurse who had recently been recruited to the Division One Agency, after discovering—to her shock and delight—that her only son was still alive and working in it.

"And Dihl," Fox reiterated. "So I think I speak for all of us when I say that your little mishpokhe has made this a warmer, more welcoming place... for all of us."

"I think it's made a difference in the feel of Headquarters overall, and the Agency in general, Boss," Echo decided. "It spills over, I've observed. Alpha Line is becoming more like an extended family for us," he gestured to Omega and himself, "and I've always known the Agency was like 'Fox's Kids,' especially given the whole age thing and how much you were involved in developing it to its present state, but it's...more so, now. Especially Headquarters."

"I'm working on expanding the concept to the other Offices—figuring

3

out how, rather; but...yes, I would have to agree," Fox said, considering. "And that's generally a good thing, I suspect. It means the, uh, 'imports' also find it a warmer, more welcoming place. We've even gotten some positive feedback to that effect."

"We have? That's cool!" Echo exclaimed. "Meg, baby, you done good. It's a better place because you're here. How 'bout that, huh?"

"I'm...glad," Omega said with a smile.

* * *

After a more cheerful Fox headed back to his office, Omega stood.

"Echo, I think I'm gonna run get something outta the break room to eat," she decided.

"You hungry, baby?"

"Starving, to be honest."

"Well, we have been training pretty hard on some of that Alpha One/Alpha Two team-up stuff," Echo realized; her artificially-altered genetics—an atrocity that had been performed upon her as a child by a psychotic alien criminal, a particular old enemy of Echo's, who had been the target of those alterations—had boosted her metabolism. That, in turn, tended to mean she needed a lot of fuel, though this had only been discovered a couple of months prior; but now that they knew that fact, Echo tried to encourage his partner to eat more, and more often. So he threw her a mischievous glance to ensure her mood stayed positive and added, "It's probably causing that souped-up metabolism of yours to burn fuel like a nebular hypernova."

"HA!" she exclaimed, pointing. "You've been reading my research paper notes!"

"Caught," he admitted, and grinned. "I'm starting to understand more and more of your research—well, I always understood it, to some degree, only now I'm understanding what you're driving at—as you use me as your guinea pig, developing those astronomy course concepts for Division One University."

"Good," she declared. "I'm doing something right, then."

"Yeah, and I'm getting a lot out of it. Listen," Echo said, glancing at his wrist chronometer, "it's almost time for first lunch, anyway. I'm just about finished with the paperwork for the latest department applicants; if you can wait about half an hour, maybe forty-five minutes, we can go out and grab something together. If you can't, why don't you run to the deli down the

4

street and get take-out for both of us?"

"That'll work, and—" Omega broke off as her belly let out a loud, and prolonged, rumble. It finished with a quirky burbling noise. Echo and Omega both stared at her talkative abdomen for a moment, then Omega flushed. "Um..."

"Go," Echo said, laughing. "Get take-out. We'll eat when you get back."

"Gone!" Omega said with a grin, heading for the door.

* * *

Tare peeped in the door of the Alpha Line Room about five minutes after Omega headed out to get lunch for Alpha One. So Echo was alone at his desk when a self-conscious Tare cleared his throat. Echo looked up from his interminable paperwork.

"Oh, hey, Tare, come on in," the department chief invited. "Where's Yankee?"

"He's, um, back in his quarters," Tare noted. "It's our day off, an' I told him I needed to run a couple errands. He wanted to watch the game, so I managed to get out...alone...for a few."

"This sounds important," Echo decided, brows drawing together in concern.

"It is. Could I maybe get with you and, and Fox, for a few minutes?"

* * *

"...And I think it's getting worse," Tare finished his explanation. "I'm... not sure what to do any more."

"That fits with what I've seen, Fox," Echo agreed. "Meg has asked me to try to stay hands-off as much as possible, unless he becomes downright insubordinate, and I've tried, but damn, Boss."

"I know, zun; I've seen it, too," Fox confirmed. "Tare, let me ask you something."

"Shoot, Fox."

"How do YOU feel about Omega?"

"Oh, geez, Fox, she's a damn impressive lady," Tare declared. "She's like, I dunno, the female version of you or Echo. I respect the hell out of her. But..."

"But? Go on, zun. I'm not going to bite. I'm trying to understand."

"You'll both be disgusted with me as an Agent if I tell you."

5

"I don't think we can be more disgusted than we are with Yankee of late," Echo noted.

"Well...Omega intimidates the hell outta me," Tare confessed. "I... think I handled it more or less okay until earlier this summer, when she took that rattler bite and not only lived to tell about it, but kinda brushed it off as no big deal." He shook his head. "She's like, I dunno. Like if Superman was one 'a your colleagues or something. It's...hard for me to explain."

"That...makes some of the things I've seen make a great deal more sense," Fox decided.

"Yeah, Fox, I'd agree," Echo noted. "Tare, just so you know, Meg brushes off stuff like that ONLY when she's talking to somebody else other than me, or maybe Fox, or her doctors. She knows it's 'weird,' as she calls it, and she doesn't want to draw attention to it. The truth of the matter is, she was sick as a dog for pretty much the entire day, after that rattlesnake bit her. I honestly don't know how she even managed to stay in the saddle, let alone trailing perps."

"Were you there with her? Why didn't you take her to help?" Tare wondered.

"No, I was only with her for the last couple of hours of her...whatever you wanna call it," Echo said, sighing. "I had to head back to the Ranch and notify Fox of what was going down, and pick up some equipment I'd brought along just in case, and it was while I was gone that Meg got bit. But I know about it, because I had to trail her, and I could see that at times her horse was walking unevenly—"

"Which meant the horse's load was uneven, which means Omega really WAS having trouble staying in the saddle," Tare realized.

"Exactly. Not to mention the patch I came through where there was vomit just everywhere. As far as I could tell, she completely purged her gut from the saddle," Echo told them. "And when I finally caught up to her, she had all the classic symptoms of Mojave green envenomation—unfocused eyes, drooping eyelids, labored breathing, rapid heartbeat but low blood pressure, difficulty speaking, a leg that was so badly swollen it was at least as big around as mine, all that shit. And damn, she was so deep in shock from the hemotoxic effects that I thought she was gonna turn into a popsicle. Do you know, I had to wrap her up in a blanket, her sleeping bag, MY sleeping bag, AND pull her into my lap to provide my body heat? In

6

90-plus degree weather?"

"Oh damn," Tare murmured, horrified. "So about the only thing it DIDN'T do was kill her."

"Pretty much," Echo agreed. "Even she admitted to me that it was 'rough,' as she put it. Which...was her typical understatement."

"Then how did she manage...?"

"She's just that determined, Tare," Echo observed, shrugging. "Yes, she's different—but she USES it! Meg busts her ASS to find ways to make what she considers a disability, what she considers a CURSE, actually WORK for her as an Agent! You may not know it, because she rarely talks about it, but Meg...she hates what was done to her. She hates what she IS. Despises it—all of it. Maybe even despises herself, at least at times. I'm not sure why, but sometimes she seems to view herself as...less of a person, or something, because of it; I dunno."

A stunned Tare rocked back in his chair; Fox closed his eyes, a knowing expression on his face.

"...So when you, and Yankee, and a few others—mostly not in Alpha Line—react like she's a pariah, like she's some sort of inhuman THING, it's only reinforcing that attitude!" Echo continued his rant, almost snarling as months of annoyance and irritation exploded. "Why the hell do you think she was willing to risk biting it under the Cortians' ion drive to save me?? Because she considered herself EXPENDABLE, Tare! Stop and think about that, dammit! The best friend I've ever had in my LIFE thought she was unimportant cannon fodder, because I'm the department chief and she's an inhuman creature!"

Echo practically leaped to his feet and began to pace the room, as Tare gaped in horror.

"The more things we find that Slug tinkered with, the worse that attitude gets!" Echo went on. "And every time you, or Yankee, or Chelovek, or Nagoya No Ta, or any of the rest, makes a crack, or a joke at her expense, or recoils from her? Then the more she doubles down, trying to prove she's USEFUL, that she's a good Agent! That she's WORTH our trust! And the harder it gets for me to keep her from jumping in where angels fear to tread, and ensure she comes back from each mission BESIDE me, instead of in a pine box...assuming we can find enough pieces!"

"It's...I...I'm sorry, Echo! I didn't know!" Tare murmured, shocked.

"I...had no idea! I swear! She always seems so, so strong, so sure, so on top of things!"

"Yeah, well...now you know," Echo grumbled.

"As for the, ah, little incident last Christmas, the one that seems to have cemented Yankee's attitude toward her," Fox noted, watching Echo carefully in some concern, "I believe that to have been a case of mistaken expectations. The shapeshifter which had infiltrated our ranks was putting forward the notion that Omega was far more 'loose,' shall we say, than she really is. Yankee, therefore, saw her behavior in the light of that image, and approached her in kind—when, in fact, she is actually very old-fashioned, reserved, and genteel, where morals are concerned. I strongly suspect, had Yankee approached her more...traditionally, perhaps by waiting for her under that farshiltn sprig of mistletoe, he likely would have gotten his kiss, with an affectionate laugh and hug thrown in for good measure. Am I not correct, Echo?"

"You nailed it, Fox," Echo agreed. "I think she got almost her whole Agency family that night; she'd have gotten me, too, if the Grendel hadn't gotten the mistletoe first. Anyway, yeah, she's reserved and even a little shy about that kinda thing. I call her 'our old-fashioned Southern belle' when I want to tease her about it."

"And I believe I am correct in saying that she usually retaliates by calling you Rhett Butler, am I not?"

"Yup. A bit of a rascal when I need to be, but completely capable of behaving myself when the situation calls for it." Echo grinned. Fox relaxed upon seeing his expression.

"You like her," Tare observed. "I mean, you weren't kidding when you called her your best friend."

"Not at all," Echo averred, "and yes, I do. I also respect the hell out of her."

"And it shows," Fox added. "All around."

"Yeah. It's..." Echo broke off, and sighed. "I know I have this reputation as 'Mr. Badass,' as Meg puts it—the toughest Agent in Division One. And I can be, when I need to be. But in some ways, Meg...is so much tougher than I ever thought of being...and all because she doesn't have a choice. She now REMEMBERS everything Slug did to her, guys. How the hell she deals with that on a daily basis, I don't have a clue."

"What-all did he do to her?" Tare wondered, showing genuine concern. "I've never heard her say."

"Nobody has," Echo said, "because she won't talk about it. I don't know of anybody, except the Deltiri that deprogrammed her, that has more than a minuscule clue what she went through."

"What?! YOU don't even know??"

"No," Echo admitted. "I've tried to get her to open up, to talk to me about it, but she won't. All she'll really say is..." And suddenly Echo and Fox became a Greek chorus, quoting in unison, "'Nobody else needs that in their heads.'" Both men sighed.

"Oh wow," Tare breathed, perturbed. "Oh, damn."

"I can tell you this," Fox added. "If you have read your Alpha Line handbook, you will know about my personal history, and how I came to be in the Agency."

"I, um..."

"Aha. Well, it is somewhat different from the standard agent handbook; it might be worth a look to determine how," Fox said in some amusement. "It is NOT for general dissemination, however. For the purposes of this discussion, let us simply say that I am a good deal older than I look, and that I have firsthand knowledge of the inside of the Nazi concentration camps. And the Nazis who ran them. And Tare, as nearly as I can tell, Omega is the only human in history ever to have survived that kind of...all-encompassing...experimentation. For the simple reason that it was intended that she should."

Fox's office was silent for a long time.

"Okay," Tare said, squaring his shoulders. "I already respected her. Now I respect the hell outta her. And I'll do my damnedest to keep the intimidation hidden as much as I can."

"Good," Fox murmured.

"Thanks," Echo said, sincere.

"But...what are we gonna do about Yankee? I dunno that we can even get him to listen to what you just told me, not any more." Tare shook his head. "We need to do SOMEthing. He's gonna get himself in trouble, big trouble, if this keeps up."

"My hands are kinda tied," Echo noted. "I've already had several long talks with Meg about this very thing, and she refuses to file any sort of complaint. She's the assistant department chief, so her refusal has some clout. Plus, she's my partner, and I gotta live with her, so I don't wanna blow off her wishes on something this important. And this is HER personal business. It doesn't affect her work, except in the ways I already laid out; it makes her push that much harder, trying to prove herself to y'all, so I can hardly complain about THAT aspect. And Yankee hasn't gotten himself in trouble... YET...that I can do anything about without Meg's go-forth."

"Fox?" Tare turned to the Director, seeming desperate. "I'm tryin' to stop my best friend from doing something dumb, here. Help me. Please."

Fox raked a hand through salt-and-pepper hair.

"I'm sorry, zun; I'm in much the same boat as Echo. If Omega had chosen to press a complaint against him last Christmas over the whole kiss thing, I might have been able to do more now. But Echo and I have asked and asked if she wants anything done...about ANY of it...and she turns us down, every time. And as Echo points out, while Yankee has skirted the thin edge of insubordination, he hasn't crossed the line...yet. I have nothing actionable to go forward with." He shook his head. "If you, as his partner, have a matter on which you can file a complaint, do so, and we'll try to buffer his reaction for you."

"I...got nothin'. He and I get along like bread an' butter. About everything except this."

"Tare...is Yankee your best bud, the way Meg is mine?" Echo wondered, keeping his voice soft.

"Yeah," Tare murmured, shoulders slumping in despair. "I've tried and tried to get him to ease up, but he's got a chip the size of Pikes Peak on his shoulder, and it's getting bigger with every Alpha Line department meeting. He always comes away finding some new way to gripe about Omega. Sooner or later, all that resentment is going to build to a boiling point, and something's gonna blow. And...damn, I don't wanna be there to see it, when it does..." Tare's voice cracked. He put his face in his hands; soft gasps emerged from between his fingers, which quickly grew damp.

Echo and Fox looked at each other, then at Tare, dumbfounded.

* * *

"I dunno what I expected, but it wasn't that," Echo breathed to his boss and surrogate father-figure, as they stood near the door of the Director's office and watched Tare in deep concern. "The poor guy is breaking down, he's so torn over what to do."

"I think this has been bottled up...probably since last Christmas. Let me talk to him and try to see what can be worked out, Echo," Fox murmured to his department chief. "I'll let you know what we decide to do, so you can do whatever you need to do in response."

"Okay, Fox," Echo agreed. "Do you know what you're gonna recommend?"

"Well, I'm going to try to talk to Yankee at some point. But as upset as Tare is at this juncture, especially after certain revelations we made about your assistant chief today, I think I'm going to recommend he take some time off, starting immediately, or at least in the next couple of days, before he loses it at a bad time. He needs to work through all this stuff in his head. Maybe we'll get a better Agent back for it."

"Well, our department gets the toughest missions," Echo admitted, "and not even Meg and I can keep at it indefinitely without needing a break. So I get it."

"Good. I'm glad you're being understanding, zun. You head back to your office, and I'll take care of this."

"Okay, Fox. Later."

Echo slipped out, and Fox moved to Tare's side, seating himself in the chair Echo had vacated.

* * *

"Son," Fox murmured, laying a hand on the younger man's shoulder. "Are you going to be all right?"

"I'm...I'm sorry, Fox," Tare murmured, refusing to look up or lower the hands that hid his face. "I knew Yankee was being unfair to Omega, but...I didn't know it was that bad for her. And I...don't know what to do. She shouldn't have to put up with that shit, but I don't wanna see anything bad happen to Yank, either. He's my buddy. He's...the nearest thing I have to an other half."

"Tare," Fox queried, keeping his voice soft, "are the two of you...more than just partners?"

"You mean— oh! N-no, it-it isn't like that," Tare decided, finally raising his head, but still trying to hide the tracks of tears down his cheeks. Quickly he scrubbed his hands over his face, trying to erase the damp marks. "But I never was much into the dating scene, in any sort of way." He

11

shrugged. "Yank is the nearest thing I got to family any more, Fox. In that, I understand Omega's feelings...probably way better than he does. Please... is there some way we can fix this, before things go too far?"

"Let me think on that, Tare," Fox said, considering. "I understand about family within the Agency; you see, quite aside from the fact that I more or less consider the entire Agency to be 'my kids,' Omega seems to have gathered a sort of family around her, and I appear to have fallen into the father-figure role. It's a bit meshuginah, our little family, but it works. And...it is making a difference, in our lives and in the lives of others. So I understand how you feel, and I will do my best to try to come up with a solution before matters...reach a head, and pass the 'do not cross' line."

"O-okay. Thanks."

"Meanwhile, might it be good if you took a little bit of a vacation, zun? Echo's reports in recent weeks have indicated that Alpha Seven has had a pretty intense series of back-to-back-to-back missions recently, and that, combined with the stress of the personality conflict, has probably worn you out."

"I...I did mention the idea to Yank...but he thrives on the adrenaline. He wasn't ready for a vacation."

"That doesn't mean you can't go on one by yourself," Fox noted. "I know we have a policy that partners travel together for safety reasons, but it sounds like you need a break, and some time to work things out in your own mind and heart."

"Well...I do. Yeah, that would be...good, I think," Tare decided. "Kind of a sabbatical, sorta."

"This can be arranged," Fox agreed. "I can see to it that you are sent somewhere safe, where the policy can be waived, and you can relax and get your head together, as Omega likes to say."

Tare suddenly winced.

"Yank isn't gonna like it if I go off by myself," he realized.

"Don't worry about that. I'll do my best to smooth any rough bumps this causes." Fox reached across his desk and grabbed his tablet, which was currently linked to his virtual desktop. "Now let's figure out where you can go, and when..."

* * *

"Good workout, guys," a certain tall, cool, seasoned Agent told his

12

three colleagues as they exited the Alpha Line training area in Division One Headquarters later that day. "This new combat room is really improving our teamwork. I can't believe you got the idea from a comic book, Romeo—great idea! And that was a really smooth bit of work in there, India, the way you took out the battle 'bot," Echo congratulated the lovely Afro-Asian woman, who smiled at her department chief's praise. "Romeo, I want you to work with Omega tomorrow," he told the handsome young black man. "With your experience in the Middle East, I figure you can probably give Meg a couple pointers on street confrontation. She's probably not had the benefit—if you can really call it that—of some of the...shit...you and I have had to face."

"Gotcha," Romeo replied.

"I'd like to be in on that, too," India added. "I didn't do as well as I would've liked."

"Okay. Romeo? Meg? Heartburn with that?" Echo asked.

"Naw. Shit, Echo, my partner c'n go anywhere I do, as far as I'm concerned," Romeo responded, and the statuesque platinum blonde with the long French braid, standing beside Echo, nodded agreement.

* * *

"Echo?" Omega asked softly, Southern accent drawing out her partner's name, as Romeo and India headed for the dressing rooms.

"Hm?" Echo grabbed the corner of the towel around Omega's neck and wiped his face. "What's up, Meg?"

"Um, well, I just wanted to say, uh, I'm sorry I hosed up the scenario in there." Omega studied the toes of her black athletic shoes as they wandered slowly toward the dressing rooms. Echo looked down at the top of the silver-white head with warm eyes.

"You didn't. You just had a bad day."

"That's an understatement. I got myself 'killed.' I'd call that a definite bad day," she responded, subdued. "I'm the other half of Alpha One. I'm the assistant division chief. I can't afford to have 'a bad day'. Besides, I'm supposed to be better than that. I'm supposed to be one of the top Agents in the Division."

"It's a training session, Meg. Mistakes are allowed. That's the point," Echo soothed his partner. "Besides, it's probably as much my fault as yours. Frankly, I just forgot you hadn't ever been in a situation like that when I

13

set up the scenario. I didn't properly prepare you for it, and I shoulda done. We'll make sure we fix that tomorrow." Echo clapped Omega lightly on the back. "After all, I'd kinda like to keep my partner around for a while longer, if that's all right with you."

Omega grinned then, and Echo smiled, satisfied that he'd gotten her out of her blue funk.

"I take it, if I bought the farm—"

"I thought you already owned a farm," Echo interjected, straight-faced.

"—That I wouldn't be the only one having a bad day?"

"Well," Echo hedged, "let's just say I'd be actively considering getting out on the other side of the bed the next day." *The hell you say,* he thought to himself, hiding a wince at the notion. The senior Agent in the Alpha One partnership—the premier team in the Agency—had realized months prior that he had fallen for his partner, but he was still trying to feel out her attitude toward a possible romance with him. And until he ascertained that it wouldn't risk breaking up that premier partnership, he had had to be satisfied with gentle nudges and mild almost-flirtations, here and there. But the notion of losing her did not leave him unfazed, in the least—especially since they had come close to that very thing a couple of times already. *Still, until she gets her head on straight after all of Slug's machinations, I better not say how I feel,* he'd decided long since.

"Ooo," Omega said, giving him a lopsided grin, "that smarts. Guess I know where I stand."

Echo shot a swift, concerned glance at his partner, saw the grin, and relaxed.

"If you bite it," he deadpanned, "I don't think 'standing' is an issue any more."

Omega whipped the towel from around her neck and popped it smartly in the direction of Echo's posterior, and he dodged nimbly out of the way with a grin.

"Go hit the shower before you get hit," she laughed, and they both ducked into the dressing rooms.

* * *

The next morning, Alpha One and Alpha Two met first thing in the training room, and Romeo spent an hour teaching Omega, and to a lesser extent India, all about street confrontation—what to watch for, how to ana-

14

lyze what they saw, and how best to react to various scenarios. Echo assisted Romeo in the teaching session as needed, but generally stood back and watched as the younger man skillfully took the two female Agents—both of whom were sharp and capable, but neither of whom had had street experience—through the specific training.

"Okay, if y'all get that set in y'r heads," Romeo finally noted, "then put in a little practice, y' oughta be good f'r anything that comes up. You're both sharp as tacks, analyze like computers, an' got eagle eyes, so I expect you'll do great."

"I agree," Echo said, pushing away from the wall on which he'd been leaning, mostly watching. "What do you think, Meg, India? Did you take all that in?"

"Yeah. Makes good sense to me," India said with a shrug.

"I think I see where it's all coming from," Omega decided after a moment to mull over it all. "I've seen some of that behavior on the streets during our patrols, Echo, and it's making me reassess some of our subsequent little adventures..."

"That's good, then," Romeo said. "It means you're startin' t' see what I was talkin' 'bout."

"You two maybe feel like trying one or two basic scenarios, and see if you can put it into practice?" Echo wondered. "Don't feel like you're being tested; Romeo and I'll have your backs to point stuff out as we run through it. I just want you to have a chance to see it happening, so you can start practicing it while it's all fresh in your heads."

The two women looked at each other.

"Let's do it," Omega declared.

"I'm with you," India determined.

"Okay. Let's start with yesterday's scenario," Echo decided, going to the control panel near the room's entrance and entering a code sequence. "If that doesn't fly, we can try something a little more basic. If you handle that okay, we'll go with something tougher."

* * *

Since both female Agents had had time to mull over the previous day's scenario, the benefit of Romeo's teaching tended to combine with their prior analyses, and rather to the men's surprise, the women stepped out, taking the lead in the simulated confrontation. In moments, they had analyzed and responded to the threat, and no less than four programmed androids had been neutralized and taken into custody by the two distaff Agents, with no need for Echo and Romeo to do anything save stand back and watch in mild amazement.

"Uh," Romeo said, when the scenario ended scant moments later. "Echo, man, I think we need ta put in somethin' a little harder."

"We can do that," Echo agreed, moving back to the control panel near the door of the room. "This one's a little more complicated, y'all. Pay attention, and you'll do fine. Romeo and I have your backs."

But Romeo was right—both India and Omega were smart and observant, and now that they knew what to look for and how to respond to it, throwing an entire gang of some dozen multiple-offworlder S.M.M. banger replicas at them didn't faze them in the least. It only took a little longer, because of the additional bodies. Inside ten minutes, the android simulacra were on the floor, safely restrained...without either Agent so much as having to ask Echo or Romeo for assistance applying force cuffs.

"Ho-lee shit," an impressed Romeo breathed to Echo, standing next to him, as they watched their partners mopping up. "We done created a couple monsters, dude. They are moppin' up th' damn floor."

"They are awesome, all right," Echo agreed, sotto voce. "Damn. From zero to warp in, like, six-tenths of a second."

"Pretty much, yeah. Wanna try one 'a those Klydonian invasion scenarios we been workin' on? Th' ones based on th' actual shit we did, couple-three years back?"

"Yeah, I'm thinkin' so," Echo decided. "And if they can handle that, we got some damn amazing partners. Not that we didn't know that already."

"True."

* * *

They did handle it. But Echo had set that scenario to keep ramping up to a designated maximum; he wanted to get in some action himself, and so did Romeo. So the opponent numbers began to increase, until both men had to join in the fray.

It took a little over half an hour, but Alpha One and Alpha Two working together managed to take down an entire platoon of simulated Klydonian warriors, though they wisely resorted to their weapons partway through, scattering 'body parts' over the training room. Finally the last 'Klydonian'

16

went down, and Echo called, "End simulation!"

The room's equipment went into standby mode, and four Alpha Line Agents moved to the center of the room, panting.

"Was that better, Ace?" Omega wondered.

"Damn straight, baby," Echo averred. "That was one helluva workout, but you and India impressed the hell outta me an' Romeo."

"What he said," Romeo agreed. "Like 'e said after th' second scenario, we got some damn amazing partners, like we didn't already know."

"Yup," Echo confirmed. "I'd say my objective for today's training session was achieved and exceeded, ladies and gentleman. Let's go hit the showers and get cleaned up, then hit the real streets."

* * *

As Echo exited the shower and headed for his locker to get dressed, he found Romeo waiting in the empty room.

"Echo? C'n I ask you a personal question?"

"Depends." Echo opened his locker, toweling off. He reached for his boxers. "How personal?"

"Well," Romeo said hesitantly, "you know how India an' I are...more 'n just partners?"

"Yeah. Y'all put in and got approved for a life partnership a while back, didn't you?"

"Uh-huh, we did," Romeo confirmed, as Echo donned his Suit trousers. "An' pretty damn happy 'bout it, too, though we kinda want ta do more. Do th' ceremony an' all, ya know."

"Okay. So?"

"Um, well, you an' Meg have been partners f'r goin' on a couple years now, an'...an' I know you two are real close friends and all...and she's one more pretty lady..."

"No, hot shot."

"No? As in, 'No, you can't ask that question,' or as in, 'No, Meg an' I aren't—'"

"Yes."

"Which?"

"Neither—if it's any of your business."

"C'mon, man. You gonna try an' tell me you never think about it?" Romeo eyed his ex-partner, skeptical. "With a gorgeous lady like that beside ya all th' time?"

"What I think I told you was that it was none of your business."

"Hey—Echo," Romeo said in protest. "C'mon, man. Don't be like that. You an' Meg 're both friends. More 'n that—you're family."

"I know, junior," Echo said quietly, with a sigh. He turned and sat down on the bench, buttoning his shirt, before reaching for socks and shoes. "Look, Romeo. You know about Chase. You know I took a sabbatical from Division One. You know I'm back. You know I have no plans to leave again. You can probably guess why, assuming you haven't already. You know Meg and I are at least as close as I was with X-ray..."

"Yeah. And closer than you an' I ever got."

"I...didn't mean for that to happen that way..." Echo paused, and looked up at the other man, allowing the concern to show on his face. "I hope you know that, too."

"Naw, man. Don't sweat it. I'm sorry; I didn't mean it like that. You were still grievin' X-ray, an' I knew it. I gave you plenty o' slack t' do just that, or at least I tried to. I been there; I know what it feels like to lose a close buddy in a battle. We'd 'a got there, eventually, you an' me, if we'd stuck with it. 'Sides, it wasn't your fault that India an' I hit it off b'fore you could get done with th' grieving."

"It...doesn't bother you?"

"Nah. You an' me, we're good, Echo. Buddies an' brothers."

"All right."

"Keep goin', man. 'Bout you an' Meg."

"Aw, c'mon. You're a bright dude. Figure it out." Echo stood and began tucking in his shirt. "Besides, you know Meg: She's an old-fashioned, Southern lady—with strong beliefs that she tries to live by. What does that say about her attitude toward a relationship?"

"She wants the 'C' word, I s'pose," Romeo replied, shrugging. "Commitment. Ring on th' finger an' all that. Same as India did an' does, only... more so, kinda."

"Right. Have you and India checked out the Division One charter on 'all that' yet?"

"Yeah," Romeo answered quietly. "Seems like nobody thought about it when they set up the Agency. 'S why India an' me are stuck with a 'life partnership' instead of a full-out marriage, like we wanted t' do. We did th' best we could manage, anyhow."

"Exactly. And we don't exist outside of the Pan-Galactic Coalition bu-
reaucracies, and offworld marriages aren't legal here. So what have I got
to offer?" Echo asked, unusually frank. He spread his hands in a *laying out
the cards* gesture.

"Love," Romeo said simply. "Same as me an' India."

Echo glanced upward, shaking his head, willing the other man to understand before he was forced to say something he wasn't ready to say...
at least, to anyone but the woman under discussion. *And the timing hasn't
worked out right for that yet,* he thought. *But I don't wanna come out and
say it to anybody else until I've had a chance to actually tell HER.* So he
tried a different tack.

"Romeo—the lady in question has never given me any indication she
wants anything but friendship. And she already has that. In spades." Echo
put the finishing touches on his tie and reached for his jacket.

"You sure?" Romeo pressed.

"I'm sure."

"All right. I had to find out."

"Why?"

"That Secret Service agent Meg recruited some time ago?" Romeo
grinned. "Agent Mu?"

"Yeah?"

"He thinks Meg's a hot lady. But he didn't want to go steppin' on your
turf, so he asked me if you an' she 'uz an item. You two 're so close, I
wadn't sure myself, so I figured I'd ask. Now I c'n tell 'im the coast is
clear." Romeo clapped Echo on the back and exited the locker room.

A shocked Echo turned and sat down abruptly on the bench, staring
blankly into space.

* * *

"Yeah, he's going to spend some time in the Treehouse, up in the Pacific Northwest," Fox told Echo on a private call between their respective
offices, that afternoon.

"Oh. That's a nice spot," Echo observed. "Safe, remote, good place for
introspecting."

"You should know, zun; you've done enough of it in your life."

"Well, yeah. That's just me, though. When is he leaving? I need to

19

make sure I keep Alpha Seven clear of assignments until he gets back. Uh, and how long will he be gone?"

"He's leaving in the next day or two," Fox said, "as soon as he can get everything together and slip away. I'll meet with Yankee once he's gone and let him know that Tare needed a mental health break. And he'll be gone at least a month, maybe more. I talked with Zebra last night, and we're making this a true medical sabbatical. She's as concerned for him as we are."

"Okay, got it. So I'll file it as extended sick leave."

"Exactly."

Echo brought up a screen on his computer, then filled out the fields. "There we go," he said, entering the form. "All taken care of from my end."

"Excellent. Yes, there's the form on my desktop. Annnd...approved. All right, that's done. Oh, by the way, he specifically said to tell you that A: if you needed him back, just call or text his cell, but once he leaves, he's blocking everyone but you, me, and Omega for the time being, we three being his supervisors; and B: he's taking what you said about your partner to heart, and if you can find a way to apologize to her on his behalf, he'd be forever grateful. Or words to that effect."

"Right. I'm not seeing anything that would require us calling him back, though that sorta thing tends to always blindside ya. Anyway, that oughta be okay. And I'll see what I can manage with Meg. To tell the truth, I think she always understood where Tare was coming from, more so than Yankee."

"Probably. Your partner is incredibly sensitive and understanding of other people, for someone who can be such a fierce fighter."

"It's because she cares about the people around her that she IS a fierce fighter, Fox."

"I think I know what you mean, but elaborate, if you don't mind, zun."

"I remember realizing it on our first real mission as Alpha One, Fox— do you remember the Antarctic mission?" Echo reminisced.

"Oh. Yes, I think I do. The attempted assassination of my friend from Ke!enda!ar, when Omega got frostbitten half to death, thanks to a woefully insufficient supplied wardrobe?"

"Yeah, that's the one."

"All right; what did you realize, essentially right off the bat?"

"It's like this: Meg is a mama bear. Mama bears are very affectionate and take good care of their cubs, but don't get between her and them, or you'll get your head ripped off and handed to you."

There was laughter on the other end of the line.

"Ha! Yes! That is really a very excellent description of her attitude, zun! I hadn't stopped to think of it like that, but I believe you are exactly right! We are her family, and she 'loves us to pieces,' as you Southerners like to say. But woe be it to anyone who threatens us! Especially you."

"Well," Echo murmured, feeling his face heat. "I kinda hope so, anyhow."

"I take it she isn't in the office with you at the moment."

"No, she's not. Evidently she'd been clamping down on her appetite this whole time, for fear of getting fat and out of shape, when this job needs us to be lean and mean fighting machines—and she knows it," Echo explained. "But now that she knows her metabolism has been tinkered-with along with everything else, and she NEEDS that fuel, she goes and gets food when she gets hungry. She's careful not to eat too much junk food, though; she told me, a couple weeks back, that a souped-up metabolism might be good in that regard, but she didn't think it justified knocking back a whole bag of chips, say, when she might have had a well-balanced meal... unless, I guess, that's all she can get her hands on, to refuel. Anyway, she stepped out about twenty minutes ago to fetch us a...well, I guess it's kind of a third snack, as it were. I think she was walking down to the deli again, but I'm not sure. I have to say, I think the increased calories and nutrition have improved her overall musculature and tone. She's stronger, too, I think. By my estimate, her one-rep maxes in the gym have gone up by maybe ten or twelve percent. And after Romeo put her and India through some street confrontation training first thing today, damn, Fox! Those two fairly mopped up in the training simulator this morning. I swear, Romeo and I didn't have to do much but stand back and stare at 'em."

"Then that...is a good thing."

"Yeah, it is."

"All right. Keep me posted on Yankee's behavior, and I will see if I can catch him right after Tare slips away on his medical leave, to explain WHY Tare took medical leave."

"Roger that, Boss."

"Fox out."

"Echo out."

21

* * *

As Echo and Omega walked back to their adjoining quarters from the gym later that day—the training session with Alpha Two having taken up their usual morning workout time—they heard a call behind them. Turning, the couple saw Mu running up. "Hi, guys! Wait up a minute!"

Echo nodded a cool greeting to the former Secret Service man as Omega said warmly, "Hi, Mu! How's it going?"

"Fine, Meg," Mu responded in a familiar fashion, and Echo raised an eyebrow at his presumption. "You?"

"Considering I 'died' big time in the combat room yesterday morning during the training session, I'm doin' okay, I guess." Omega pulled a face. Echo raised an eyebrow, quirked his lips, and gave her a *Come on now, ease up on yourself* look, and she chuckled wryly.

"Don't give me—" Echo began, about to remind her of how she and India kicked ass that morning. But he didn't get that far.

"Ow," Mu interrupted, and grinned at her. "Listen Echo, I hope you don't mind if I talk to your partner in private for a minute?"

"You don't waste much time, do you?" Echo muttered. "It was just this morning..."

"Nope," Mu's grin got wider, and he winked at the other man. "Not when there's a...prize...to be won."

"...All right. Meg, I'll have dinner ready in about forty-five minutes." Echo turned and headed for his apartment alone, stifling a sigh.

"I'll be there," Omega called after him.

* * *

Well, that majorly sucks, Echo thought, as he headed for his quarters. *Here I am, trying to give Meg plenty of time to get her head together, and Mu comes waltzing in, and cuts in on my dance. And gets the benefit of all the effort I've put in, trying to help Meg come to grips with it all.*

If she's happy being with him, if it's what she wants, I'll step aside. I want her to be happy. But damn, I just want the chance to at least TRY.

I suppose she might turn him down. It's selfish, but I really hope she does. I don't know if I can stand being partnered with a woman I'm crazy in love with, while she ends up in a romantic relationship with another man. I guess...if it comes to that, I'll have to look at dissolving the 'defined partnership' anyway, so she can have a life partnership with Mu. Oh damn. And gronk and abdab, as Fox likes to say. *God, just gimme a chance.*

He sighed as he reached his front door.

* * *

Inside, a certain medtech was waiting for him.

"Wha? Ma?" Echo wondered, as his mother rose from the sofa to meet him, smiling. "Did you use the, um, 'special' passages to get in here?"

"Of course," Dihl said, and her smile morphed into a grin. "You showed them to me partly so I could come and go between my quarters and yours and Omega's with no one else the wiser."

"Yeah, you just hadn't done it before. I wasn't expecting it."

"Well, I waited until I had an opportunity to discuss it with Zebra and Fox," Dihl noted. "I know you said it was all right, but I rather wanted Fox to 'buy off' on it, as you like to say."

"Okay. That makes sense. But I'd already checked it with him."

"Yes, but I had not. By the way, Omega does know about them, doesn't she? I mentioned it the other day, just in passing, and she looked...blank."

"Well, she knows now, but I messed up. That shoulda been done when she got made assistant department chief at the latest, but what with the whole crash landing during the training run, and trying to get two Humpty Dumptys put back together again afterward, I think that slipped through the cracks. I'd intended doing that once we got back from the training run, see, but Meg's noggin was still outta commission, and...well. I've told her, but I haven't showed her around 'em yet."

"Put it on your to-do list, son, and make it high priority. I think that's an important one."

"All right. What's up?"

"I was about to ask you the same thing, son," Dihl said, concern writ large on her face. "You look...downhearted."

"Aw, I got a rival," Echo grumbled.

"For?"

"Meg, of course. There's not really anything or anybody else to compete over."

"What has happened?"

"Remember that Secret Service agent that got recruited back during the whole Presidential assassination thing?"

"Yes?"

23

"Turns out, he likes Meg. Romeo came in the locker room this morning after our training session, asking me if Meg and me were an item, while I was cleaning up and getting ready to hit the streets with Meg on patrol. We're not—yet—so of course I told him NO. I kinda don't wanna admit I'm interested, until MEG knows, you know?"

"Oh. And it turns out that he was asking for this newly-recruited agent?"

"Yup."

"Oh dear. And?"

"And...so he barely waited until the end of the shift, and didn't even wait until she got home after getting off duty! He came running after us as we were leaving the gym this evening, basically told me 'three's a crowd,' and to go away, so he could ask Meg out." Echo flung himself into his recliner, morose. "I tried to be patient, and I'm getting cut out, instead."

"You don't know that."

"No. But he's a good-looking guy, and he'll flatter the hell outta Meg, which she needs right now, and which I've been trying to do, but I've had to be subtle...and he doesn't."

"Then maybe it is time to make your move, son. Start letting her know that she's special to you, that you're interested, that you want to be with her ALL the time." She eyed the Agent that was her son. "Are they going out tonight?"

"I doubt it; Meg promised she'd be home in time for dinner."

"Then start with dinner tonight. Get in your kitchen and pull out the stops. I'll set the table quickly, while you cook."

"Oh. Okay," Echo agreed, getting up and removing his Suit jacket and tie, and draping them over the back of the couch. Then he headed for the kitchen, rolling up his sleeves as he went. "In that case, make it kinda formal, if you wouldn't mind, Ma."

"I can do that," she said, dimpling as she smiled. "I'll run back to my quarters and bring your grandmother's china, if you want me to. What about candles? You could have a lovely candlelight dinner..."

"Uh, that might be pushin' it, quite yet," Echo decided, studying the contents of his refrigerator as he planned a menu. "Feel free to trim a couple of stargazer lilies off the plant in the corner, an' stick 'em in a vase, though."

"Consider it done, son."

24

"Why did you come over? Is everything okay?" he wondered, pulling out ingredients and setting a sauté pan on the stove.

"Oh, that! I wanted to let you know that I'll be away from Headquarters for a little while."

"How long? What's up?"

"I'm not sure yet. It seems that the medic at the Ranch, Angamar...well, you know how she was on her homeworld when we were there in June?"

"Yeah. Joe said her dad got hurt or something."

"Exactly. It seems it was worse than anyone thought; he never healed properly, complications set in, and now he is dying. Angamar has to go back home, but no one knows for how long, her least of all. And Zebra says I am now ready to 'solo.' So, since I'm already intimately familiar with the Ranch, I was the logical person to send there to fill in for her while she is away. For...however long it takes."

"Oh. That makes sense. We'll miss you—*I'll* miss you—though."

"I know, son, and the feeling is mutual. Please apologize to Omega for me, and tell her I'm sorry I won't be here to help her try to recreate some more family recipes on your next day off?"

"I'll do that, Ma, no problem. And she'll understand. She always understands."

"I know. You have a wonderfully unique and very special partner, son. And I'm NOT talking about her...'modifications.' I...hope she becomes more than a partner for you, and without much in the way of outside interference, if you understand me."

"Boy, do I," Echo grumbled, putting olive oil into the hot pan, then adding fresh minced garlic. "How's the table coming?"

"All done," Dihl declared, setting a small bud vase, containing two lilies, in the center. "See what you think."

Echo stuck his head out of the kitchen and surveyed his dining area.

"Oh, that's great, Mom!" he exclaimed, pleased. "That looks as good as any fancy restaurant, here in the Big Apple."

"Good. Have a nice, semi-formal dinner with her, then. And to that end, let me slip back to my quarters, so it can be just the two of you. I couldn't stay long anyway; my maglev train leaves in an hour and a half, and I haven't finished packing."

"Thanks, Ma," Echo said, coming to his mother and dropping a kiss on her forehead as he hugged her.

"You are more than welcome, son," she told him. "Good luck, and blessings on you both."

She returned hug and kiss, then headed for his bedroom and the door to the super-secret warp tunnels, intended for clandestine and emergency situations, hidden in the back of his closet.

* * *

"Hi, Echo," Omega called as she entered her apartment, some fifteen or twenty minutes later. "I'm here."

"Hi," Echo's voice floated through the 'back door' connecting their quarters. "Dinner's almost ready. C'mon in. What did Mu want?"

"Now there's a mind-boggler," Omega responded, walking into Echo's living area, where she removed her Suit jacket and draped it across Echo's couch beside his jacket, before loosening her tie and collar. "He asked me out."

"...You gonna go?" Echo asked from the kitchen.

"I...don't know." She glanced wistfully toward the kitchen door. *I wish it was Echo asking me out, instead,* she thought. *I'd go in a heartbeat, no hesitation, if he did.*

"Why not? Do you...like him?"

And there's my answer to THAT, she decided. Omega's sky-blue eyes blinked sadly, but she replied in a normal tone. "Oh, yeah, he's a nice guy. I hadn't thought about it, really, to be honest. But I don't know if I should. It's not fair to him. I don't think Mu...knows about me."

* * *

"You mean about your recombinant DNA?" Echo asked, bringing a garnished platter of chicken Marengo from the kitchen and putting it in the center of his dining table.

"Yeah. I don't think he knows I'm...not exactly human."

"He doesn't know you're an enhanced human," Echo corrected.

"Whatever."

"Dinner's ready." Echo waved his partner to the table. "Meg, if...he loves you, it won't matter to him."

"Whoa, whoa, waitaminit," she declared, and grinned. "He's only just asked me out, and I haven't said I'd go yet. The 'L' word hasn't even come into play." Omega glanced at the rather formally-set table, Echo's tastefully-presented dish taking center stage. "Wow. Somebody was feeling like a culinary artist tonight. That looks good. And it's pretty, too."

"I was in a...creative...mood, I guess," Echo shrugged and made excuse. "Sometimes I like a formal, sit-down dinner for just us two, we eat on the go so much. Since I had time, I kinda thought I'd make one."

The truth of the matter was, as his mother had suggested, he wanted Omega to have a sense that his time spent with her was important to him... and maybe, just maybe, make it feel like the date he wanted it to be. He had even re-donned his tie, deciding he wanted that added touch of formality.

"What's it called? The dish, I mean."

"Well, it's a version of chicken Marengo. It's supposed to have crayfish, but I didn't have any, so it's got everything but."

"It looks delish!"

"I've got a pretty good feel for your tastes by now; I think you'll like it, baby." He paused, then added, "You might think this sounds...odd, but I think this dish is sexy as hell, in the good kinda way."

"No, I don't think it sounds odd. I get where you're coming from. Some dishes are, like, decadent."

"Exactly."

They sat down at the table together, and Echo watched casually as an intrigued Omega sampled the unfamiliar dish.

"Mmm. Oh, wow. Good job, Echo. You're still just fulla surprises, Ace."

"Thanks," he responded nonchalantly, starting on his own meal. "But listen, Meg, I was serious a bit ago. If Mu really cares about you, he won't care about the DNA. I don't. Neither do Romeo and India."

"Sure you do, Echo," Omega told him, offhanded, digging into her dinner with enthusiasm.

"How do you figure that?!" Echo looked up from his plate, badly startled. Omega paused and laid her flatware down.

"Echo," she said softly, dropping into a formal technical discourse, "as a scientist, I am aware that a species is defined by its basic genetics. Now, there are individual variations, true, but not in the fundamental chromosome structure. Change these basic structures even slightly, and you get a different species. My genetics are, as a result of deliberate manipulation by an interstellar criminal, radically—not just slightly—different from that of

27

any other human. We're talking as much as multiple percentage points of variation in some areas of the chromosome, according to my understanding. And then Slug forced it to express, despite my already being prepubescent at the time of the manipulation. I am now, therefore, a completely different species from the one into which I was born. I am not human. It's a simple syllogism. Yet, every time I state that fact, you vehemently insist it's wrong. The only conclusion I can reach, Ace, is that it does matter to you."

Echo stared at her, at a loss to know how to respond, and worried that he'd screwed up for the entire lifetime of their partnership. *And if that's the case,* he realized, *I may have hosed any chance I had with her, from the get-go. Long before I ever realized I was in love with her.* Finally he ventured an answer.

"Meg, I...I know it's caused you pain—in the past, at any rate—and I..."

"You're trying to make me feel better about myself. I know," Omega finished for him, a tired, almost sad, kind of half-smile on her face. "But you're trying so hard to make me into something I'm not, something I can never be again. Wouldn't it be better to say, 'Meg, you're fine the way you are'?"

Echo sat gazing across the table at Omega, his brows drawn together as he puzzled how to answer. *I love her exactly the way she is,* he thought. *It really doesn't matter to me. And I disagree with her—I DO think she's still human, just with some mods—so I can't say...but then, if I press it, she'll... shit.*

"I...don't know what to say," he eventually responded in a low voice. "You ARE fine the way you are, of course, but...I just...disagree...with your conclusions."

"Oh, Ace, I'm not trying to make you feel bad, or put you on the spot," Omega said, somewhat contritely. "You're my...my best friend, my partner, and you want me to feel accepted—and I do, because you accept me. And I know it, even if you don't say it like that, so don't worry about THAT. But I want you to accept the truth, too. I am my own species, Echo. There's nobody else like me. I. Am. Not. Human."

"I guess...maybe you define it different than I do, Meg," Echo remarked, thoughtful. *I gotta word this just right,* he realized, *so she'll understand where I'm coming from. At least she already knows I accept her 'as*

28

is,' thank the good Lord.

"Oh? How do you define it, then?" she asked, cocking her head to the side.

"I get what you're saying, baby, though I'm not sure I agree, even on that. I mean, I'm no scientist, but Zebra is, and I know she doesn't agree. But that's all neither here nor there. See, I couldn't care less about what's in individual cells, anyway," Echo told her, as sincere as he knew how to be. "I look at what's here—" he tapped his temple, "and here—" Echo touched his breastbone. "And according to that definition, you're all human, Meg. And you can't say that about any other species, not even Klack, who's from Earth—and the offworlders are even more different in those ways. It's simple, really. Humans think and, and feel, you know, emote, like humans, baby. And so by that definition, you're human. A hundred and two percent."

Omega's gaze defocused as she lost herself in thought, considering Echo's statement.

"Okay," she murmured after a moment, "I can see it. Philosophic rather than scientific, I suppose. Well, no; more like...maybe psychological? Emotional and mental? I dunno what to call it, but I see what you're saying. I never thought about it like that before. I guess it's a good thing we finally hashed it out. All this time, we were coming at it from completely different directions."

"Yeah."

"I'm sorry, Echo. I misjudged you."

He waved a dismissing hand.

"I can see why. It's okay. It's not like it happens very often any more. Except about this, I guess."

"Us talking about it?"

"Us misunderstanding each other." They smiled, and resumed eating in a companionable fashion.

"Echo...this stuff is just fantastic," Omega said a few minutes later, gesturing at her plate—which was rapidly emptying—with her fork. "Where'd you learn to make it? And can I get the recipe??"

"You always have loved my cooking."

"Yup. 'Cause you're really good! And I know that your mom taught you a lot of it, but then you come up with something like this, and at this point I KNOW it didn't come from your mom's kitchen, 'cause we've all been cooking together so much, and it blows me away."

"Oh, that makes me think—lemme tell you, while it's in my head, that Dihl won't be joining us on our next day off, to cook with us and try to reproduce some of your family recipes, Meg. Angamar, the medic at the Ranch—I dunno if you remember, but her dad was injured right before we vacationed there, and she had to go back to the homeworld?"

"Oh! Yeah, I remember..."

"Well, it turns out evidently her dad didn't do so well after all. He's dying, and Angamar has gone back home to be there for him at the end, and for the...funeral equivalent, I guess. I pinged Joe after Ma told me, to get all the particulars, and also send Alpha One's condolences. Angamar had already left, of course, but he said he'd forward our message. She was pretty upset, according to Joe. Aside from her filial affections, her dad was the clan patriarch or something. The funeral-thing is gonna be a big deal, too. And she was dreading it, because as the eldest offspring, she's gotta take a big role..."

"Aw."

"Yeah. Anyway, given Ma's extreme familiarity with that particular facility," Echo said with a grin, and Omega grinned back, "there was a quick discussion amongst Medical, and it was decided she'd be the perfect fill-in, while Angamar was off-planet. And she wasn't about to disagree."

"Oh. So Dihl is stationed at the Ranch for the time being?"

"Yeah, she is. And just between us, it wouldn't surprise me if she either asked to make it permanent, or maybe to split her time between Headquarters and the Ranch. I guess part of it depends on what Angamar decides to do, once her dad is gone. I'm not sure what the homeworld rules and traditions are, let alone the line of succession, but Angamar could end up the family matriarch, in her dad's place."

"Oh, I see. That works, I guess," Omega decided. "If I had a vote in that, which I know I don't, but if I did, I'd like it if Dihl could split her time, though. I kinda like our 'family nights,' as it were. I dunno if it's the Glu'gu'ik spliced genetics or what, but sometimes I swear I can almost feel your dad and granddad there with us. Especially when we're all in the kitchen, cooking."

"Really? Cool."

"Yeah. And I like it; it feels...well, it reminds me of my own family.

Which members, for some reason, I do NOT feel." She sighed. "So...I know it's selfish of me, but I'd really like her to stay at Headquarters, at least part of the time."

"Me too, and I agree with you. But it's her call. I'm not even going to put my oar in on that one."

"I understand."

The pair were silent for long moments.

"So where did you get the recipe?" Omega finally returned to her original query, jabbing her fork at her plate by way of antecedent.

"Well, believe it or not, one of X-ray's hobbies was gourmet cooking," he told her, and grinned, remembering. "I picked up a few things from him over the years. This is one of 'em. I'd give you the recipe if I could, but just like your mom's and grandmom's cooking, there isn't one—X-ray taught me to...eyeball it, I guess you could say. He normally used recipes, at least as a base for starting the dish, but this one is something he put together by trial and error, based on us having had it on a mission—he was trying to reproduce the flavors and textures. I was his guinea pig, while he worked on fine-tuning the combos. He did a damn fine job, I gotta tell you. And I've never seen just exactly the same ingredients in any cookbook, either. I suppose between us, we can manage to codify it and get it written down, if you'd like. Anyway, I'll be happy to teach you how to make it, if you want me to. It's not hard."

"I want you to! I want you to!" Omega exclaimed enthusiastically, and Echo chuckled.

"Okay. Next day off. Want some dessert?"

"Did you make that, too?"

"Yep."

"Ooo, yeah, I—"

Omega was interrupted by Echo's cell phone in the living area. Echo got up from the dining table and hurried over to answer it.

"Echo here...oh, hi, Fox." Echo listened for a long moment, then exclaimed, "What?! Shit, you can't be serious. Yeah, she's right here. We were just finishing dinner. Yeah, we'll be there in a couple minutes." Echo closed the cell phone. "Dessert will have to wait. Let's go."

"What's up?" Omega asked as they grabbed their Suit jackets and headed out Echo's front door toward the Core, adjusting collars and ties as they went.

"A couple of agents just brought in a civilian, a...Mark Wright, I think Fox said," Echo answered. "Does that name ring a bell with you?"

"No. Should it?"

"Well, see if these characteristics do: He doesn't respond to the brain-bleacher, he disappeared for approximately twenty-four hours in his mid-to late teens, and, judging by India's medscanner readings, he has human/alien recombinant DNA."

"You're kidding." Omega caught her breath. "You've got to be."

"No," Echo said, and shook his head. "Meg, maybe you're not as unique as we thought..."

Chapter 2

When they entered Fox's office, Romeo and India were there, as well as two agents that Omega and Echo didn't recognize, from one of the West Coast offices. An engaging, sandy-haired man of average build, looking to be in his late thirties or—just possibly—early forties, stood beside Fox.

"There you are," Fox remarked as Alpha One entered. "Mark, these are Agents Echo and Omega. Omega is the Agent we were telling you about. She's another one of Romeo's 'cream of the crop.' So is Echo. Delta Four," Fox added, "you're dismissed. Thank you." The two unfamiliar agents left.

"Thanks, Fox," Omega responded warmly to the Director's praise, as Echo stepped forward and shook Wright's hand. Omega offered her hand to the civilian in turn, saying, "Hi, Mark. Looks like I've finally got somebody to compare notes...with...now..." her voice trailed off as Wright grasped her hand, and both of them abruptly became rigid, eyes defocusing.

"What the hell?!" Echo muttered, as the other Agents stared, startled.

"Looks like another one o' those telepathic links, like she had back durin' all th' Cortian shit," Romeo observed in a soft tone. "Meg's all stiff and starin' into space..."

"Mm. You have a good point, zun," Fox murmured, reaching for the phone. "I'll get one of the Arcturan embassage down here." He quietly issued orders into the phone as the others watched the silent tableau.

* * *

When a full five minutes had passed with no change and no ambassador, an impatient—and very concerned—Echo reached out and laid a light hand on his partner's cheek, intending to try entering the link to check on her.

"Echo, wait for Tt'l'k," Fox began, but suddenly Echo was slammed across the room and into the far wall. He slid down the wall to the floor, lying in a crumpled heap, and India ran to the semi-conscious man, initiating a medscan with the portable scanner she pulled from her pocket. Echo sat up, rubbing his temple, as India completed the scan and the others gaped.

"Slow down," she cautioned. "You're all right, but that was quite a jolt."

33

"No shit," Echo muttered.

"What happened?" Fox demanded. Echo gestured at Mark as he got to his feet.

"He sensed me trying to reach Meg, and knocked me away. Hard." A determined Echo headed for his partner again, but Romeo and Fox restrained him.

"Echo, let a trained telepath handle this," Fox urged quietly. "I know you're concerned, but half of Alpha One is already incapacitated. We don't need the other half taken out."

"But..."

"ECHO. If you won't listen to reason, zun, think about your partner. OMEGA doesn't need you taken out."

That gave Echo pause.

* * *

Just then, a faint noise from Omega drew their attention. The dumbfounded Division One Agents emitted a collective gasp: Wright had drawn their colleague close against him and was now kissing her passionately, tugging at her Suit jacket as if to remove it. But the pair's eyes were still glazed, incongruously wide open.

Suddenly Omega jerked, blinked, then began struggling. She broke the kiss, and seconds later, the embrace, backing away from the entranced man, who resumed a stiff, unblinking posture.

"No...NO!" Omega whispered in horror, dragging the back of her hand across her violated mouth.

"Meg?? What the hell is happening?!" Echo exclaimed, and Omega glanced at him. Their eyes met, and a shocked Echo read emotions in the blue eyes he'd never seen there before. Horror, panic, fear—and something else—Echo saw, just before his partner turned and bolted, running headlong through the Core in her flight, right past a startled Tt'l'k.

"Echo—go get her!" Fox commanded, but Echo was already out the office door, sprinting after his companion.

As Tt'l'k entered the office, they all watched Echo disappearing down a corridor, hard after Omega. Romeo, glancing at the enigmatic and unmoving figure of Mark Wright, summed up the situation.

"This ain't good..."

* * *

34

Echo caught up to Omega in her astronomer's refuge, up on the roof. But when he spotted her, she was standing on the wall, looking down at the street several stories below.

"MEG!!" he yelled, scrambling to her side and yanking her down to the roof level. "What the hell are you doing?!"

"I...I don't know," a white-faced Omega stammered. "Echo, please... leave me alone."

"No."

"Echo...you don't understand..." She pushed away from him.

"Then explain."

"GO AWAY!!" Omega shouted, desperate, and Echo blinked in surprise, then clenched his jaw in stubborn tenacity.

"Meg, I'm not going anywhere. A friend of mine needs my help. You."

To his shock, Omega hung her head in patent humiliation and shame. Her face flushed, and her expression crumpled. Tears filled her eyes, but did not overflow...yet.

"Echo," she whispered, deeply unhappy, "I'm not your friend. At most, I'm...a pet."

"What?!" Echo exclaimed, confused. "Meg, talk to me! What the hell are you talking about?! What's going on??"

His partner sank to the rooftop in despair, and Echo knelt in front of her, holding her shoulders in a light grip, offering gentle encouragement.

"Talk to me, baby," he urged. "I'm here. I swear, I'm here for you. I wanna help. But you gotta tell me what's wrong."

Omega nodded, keeping her gaze cast down, apparently unable to meet his eyes.

"You were right, Echo: Mark Wright is another one of Slug's little genetic experiments, just like me," Omega sighed then. "But...but...it's not random, and it's definitely no accident he's here now."

"Programming? Brainwashing?"

She nodded.

"So I should watch my back?"

"I...I'm not sure. Maybe. But you're not the main reason he's here."

"Then what IS the reason?" Echo asked, puzzled.

"Who. No...no, I guess you had it right. What." She sighed again. Echo just stared at her, waiting for an explanation. She shook her head, then

35

added, "I'm the reason."

"I don't get it," a grim Echo muttered, noting her change of personal pronoun. *And I can't help thinking that bodes ill,* he decided.

"I was telepathically programmed to assassinate you, Echo," Omega reminded him. "Y'all thwarted the programming—thank God—and my 'mission' failed. Mark is part of Slug's backup plan. The next generation of Slug's 'tools' will be genetically programmed to kill you." Her voice was low. Echo knit his brows in thought.

"Next gen—" he broke off, remembering Omega in Wright's arms, and his eyes narrowed in horror as understanding struck. "Oh, no..."

Omega nodded, ashamed.

"That's right, Echo. Mark is the man Slug chose for my...my mate. That's his primary programming. I'm..." she chuckled bitterly, face aflame with embarrassment and humiliation, "breeding stock. I'm not human. I'm not even alien. I'm an animal."

Echo stared at her blankly, as the ramifications sank in. Then, heart aching for the woman he loved, he instinctively drew her against his chest to comfort her.

"No, you're not," he breathed in her ear. "Just because somebody treats you like an animal doesn't make you one."

"You still don't understand." Omega gently pushed away. Her voice was so low Echo had to lean forward to hear. "When I touched Mark, it triggered a telepathic link. That's how I know all this."

"Yeah. I saw that."

"That's not all it did."

"What else did it do, then?"

"Echo, it...it triggered...biochemical changes...in me..."

"Wha—? Wait. You...you're in—" Echo felt the blood drain from his face, as the significance hit him.

"Yes," she whispered, utterly miserable. "So now you understand, Echo. I can't be a friend to you. Instead, I'm a pet. Slug's pet. A highly-trained, very dangerous...animal. And...it's mating season."

* * *

As they entered the Core together, Omega hung back. "Echo...don't make me go back in there. Into Fox's office. Please. Let me go to the Alpha Line Room, and you...well, just try to preserve what little dignity I have left, when you explain..."

"Meg, we've got to work this all out," Echo said, voice quiet but firm. "I'll be right beside you the whole time, I swear I will. Now let's go, baby."

"Heel, girl," she muttered under her breath.

Echo heard. Indignation flared, and he reacted with vehemence.

"Stop it!" he snapped, spinning to face her. Then he broke off, coming to a dead stop as he saw the look of agony on his partner's face. "No, baby. Don't go there. Just...don't. I don't let anyone talk about my closest friend like that, Meg—not even you," he said in a gentler tone. "Don't put yourself down like that, and for God's sake, don't make jokes about it. It isn't funny."

"Would you prefer that I have a nervous breakdown?" Omega said in a low voice. Echo studied her with a concerned gaze.

"Not handling this well, huh?"

"Not handling this AT ALL. You have no idea. Damn, Echo," Omega said, the curse nearly as harsh as when they had the dogfight with the Cortians, "I've lost control of my own body. Lost all sense of myself as a person. Do you have any idea what I'm going through right now?"

"...No," he admitted, keeping his voice as soft as he knew how to make it. "But I know this: The sooner we figure out what the hell is going on, the sooner we can end it. And the answers are in there." Echo nodded at Fox's office.

"...All right. 'Lay on, MacDuff,'" Omega sighed. "'Once more unto the breach, dear friend,' an' all that shit."

"That's my gal," Echo encouraged. They walked in lock-step across the Core, then Echo paused outside the door of Fox's office and turned back to face her. "Omega," Echo said seriously, in a tone meant only for her, "I'm...this sounds damn stupid, not to mention disgustingly like Romeo's whole 'sensitive emoting' thing he's gotten into lately, but...I'm here for you, baby. This has gotta be hell. I understand that much. But, to use your personal motto, if I can help, I will. Whatever you need—whatever you want me to do. I'm here. Into hell, and out the other side, if need be. Just like you did for me with the Cortians."

"Thanks, Echo," Omega whispered. The finely-featured face was a mask of carefully-controlled impassivity. But the look of gratitude deep in her eyes cut through Echo like a blue laser. "Sometimes I don't know what

I'd do without ya, Ace."

"Well, you wouldn't be going through this, for one thing." Echo looked away, guilt-ridden. Omega was left with no reply.

* * *

Fox and Alpha Two awaited Alpha One in Fox's office; Wright was now gone, but Tt'l'k had taken his place.

"Well?" Fox demanded, expectant, as the pair entered and moved to the two empty visitor chairs.

Omega averted her face as she sat down, but said nothing.

"Omega—I'm waiting," Fox reiterated, becoming stern.

Omega blinked several times, but still said nothing.

This...is not good, Fox decided, studying the female Agent. *She's traumatized, almost as badly as she was after the first programming triggered. Almost? No. That face looks worse. I thought Zz'r'p took care of all the deprogramming, but apparently she was right at the time; there's still programming in action. And I need to know what, if I'm going to protect my people. Especially my designated successor, who also happens to be her partner...and Slug's target. I have to know what just happened.*

So Fox raised an eyebrow and turned to Alpha Line's chief.

* * *

Echo sat down next to the woman he loved, the woman who needed him, holding out his hand, palm up, without looking, and Omega wordlessly laid her hand in his. He promptly wrapped his fingers around that hand, holding it firm in his gentle grip.

"Echo—" Fox began.

"Don't go there, Fox," Echo interrupted. "Don't put me in that position."

"All right, Echo," Fox said slowly, evidently considering, and Alpha Two watched the confrontation in amazement. "Tt'l'k? If you please?"

"NO!!" Omega cried, lunging forward, and Echo felt her fingers dig into his hand. "I've got my block up—"

"True," Tt'l'k said, "but you did not when you entered. Nor does Agent Echo possess a telepathic block."

"Damn," Echo whispered, horrified, as Omega began to plead.

"Tt'l'k, please don't! Please!"

Romeo and India looked on in shock.

"The Director requires the information, Agent," the thin blue alien responded, indifferent to her entreaties. She turned to Fox, desperate.

"Fox? Please—?"

"Fox," Echo interjected quietly, "all you'll do is embarrass and humiliate Meg. Let me handle this."

"I'm sorry, Echo, Omega, but after what happened with Omega and her original programming, I have to know what's happening now," Fox replied, firm and unswaying. "Echo, I'd think you'd understand, of all people; I'm trying to protect you, zun."

Omega doubled over and buried her face in her hands.

* * *

Once Tt'l'k got started, however, it proved impossible to stop him. It didn't take long before a shocked and dismayed Fox had put together the entire picture; he quickly told Tt'l'k the information already provided was sufficient. But Tt'l'k refused to cease the telepathic interrogation, picking Echo's brain with ease, and forcing his way past Omega's block...thanks in large part to her disordered, confused mental state in the wake of the unexpected and highly unwelcome revelation.

"No, Director, it is my considered opinion that you need the fullest, most detailed debrief of the situation possible," Tt'l'k responded, his objective immovable, "especially given the event of both Agents having refused a direct order. Insubordination of this nature must not be tolerated."

"It wasn't insubordination!" India protested. "It's a medical matter, and it should go through medical channels!"

"They both refused a direct order from the Director, Agent India," Tt'l'k reiterated. "It was, in my considered opinion, the worst kind of insubordination. I will not be party to it."

"Dude, jus' shut up! Can't you see you're doin' a number on Omega?!" Romeo cried, waving his hands at the female Agent, now huddled in her chair, face white to the lips, eyes dilated, gaze distant and fixed.

"India is correct, Tt'l'k," Fox noted. "This level of detail is not necessary. I understand what happened. The medical personnel can handle any additional details, and brief me as they find it necessary."

"I respectfully disagree, Director," Tt'l'k declared, seeming almost... pleased. "I saw such an incident take place on Xemlona some five of your years ago, and it was the predecessor to a successful coup. I will not be

39

party to such a thing here..."

* * *

By the time Tt'l'k had finished dispassionately summarizing the total situation in excruciating detail, Omega was curled in a tight fetal ball on the floor of Fox's office, completely unresponsive to any of them. Worried, Echo and India knelt over her as India examined her, and Romeo and Fox watched in pity. Tt'l'k stood back and...smiled.

"Basically, I think she's just retreated into herself," India eventually told the others. "Semi-catatonic, sort of, but not. Meg's finally found the psychological limits of what she can take."

"Nervous breakdown?" Fox asked, concerned.

"I...don't think so," India answered, sounding uncertain. "Not yet, anyway. There's no telling where this will push her, though. This is not a situation I'd want happening to me."

"I told you to let it go, Fox," Echo said, cool verging on cold. "I said I'd handle it; I'd planned on grabbing India and Meg and going straight to Zebra, after letting you know that there was a situation that warranted it. Zebra would then have briefed you with whatever was appropriate for you to know. We came back here only to obtain more info on Wright. And you," he glanced in accusation at the alien telepath, "could have shown a little more sympathy. You went way over what Fox asked for. Your superior, Zz'r'p, would never have handled this the way you did. You might try learning a few things from him. I'll see to it he knows exactly what you're deficient in, diplomatically-speaking. Never mind two probable charges of mind-rape." At that, the tall blue alien finally showed evidence of an emotion: worry. Echo turned back to India. "What do we do now?"

"It's really late anyway." India exhaled thoughtfully. "Let's take Meg home, and put her to bed. Give her some much-needed privacy. Maybe rest and some time to get her perspective back will help. She's had a helluva shock. And even more embarrassment. I'll fill in Zebra when we're done with that...maybe with Fox's assistance."

"Of course," Fox murmured. "I'll do all I can to help."

"All right. Fox, where's Wright?" Echo asked as he gently gathered Omega's limp form into his arms to carry her back to her quarters.

"He's in the medlab-secure area of Confinement, under observation," Fox responded, very quiet. "We thought it best to put him there, under the

40

circumstances."

"Good. Keep him out of Meg's sight," a curt, angry Echo said, by that point uncaring that it sounded like an order to the Director, and Fox nodded silently before the four Agents—one unconscious—trailed out of his office.

* * *

India exited Omega's bedroom to find their worried partners standing in the living area. "She's conscious now, and in bed," India told them. "We had a little girl-chat, and I got a good feel for her state of mind."

"And?" Echo asked.

"Well...she wants to speak with us. All of us—or, well, as many of us as are here; I gather Dihl is off on a temporary assignment. But Fox is on his way, with Zebra."

"What about?" Romeo asked, curious.

"That's for her to say, honey."

* * *

A knock sounded at the front door then, and Fox entered, Zebra close behind.

"We're here, and I've filled in Zebra on that whole fershlugina drek from earlier—in private, this time, as Director to physician." He shook his head, then sighed.

"And admitted that he screwed up," Zebra noted, crisp, her eyebrow raised. Fox added another sigh into the mix, then nodded acknowledgement.

"What's this about?" he wondered.

"Meg wants to talk to us, Fox," Echo told him, as India ducked into the bedroom to notify Omega of the arrivals. Moments later, she poked her head out the door again.

"Come on in, guys." India waved them through the door.

* * *

As they filed into her bedroom, the Division One Agents saw a pale, almost childlike Omega sitting in the middle of the bed, covers drawn up to her shoulders, propped against pillows, gleaming white-blonde hair brushed by India and spilling loose over her shoulders and across the pillows. Nervous, she stared down at the blanket, tracing patterns on it with her fingertips.

"What's up, Meg?" Echo asked softly.

Without looking up, Omega spoke in a husky tone.

"The...the people in this room—um, plus one, I guess, given Dihl isn't here—are the closest thing I've had to...a family...since Slug killed my parents and grandmother years ago. Now I need to know something..."

"What do you need to know, baby?"

"I need to know if...if Slug's killed this one, too."

"What do you mean, Omega?" a puzzled Fox queried.

Pained by her inquiry, and fully understanding its import immediately, Echo closed his eyes and drew a deep breath. Then he interpreted for the others.

"She's asking if we still accept her 'as is,' Fox," Echo answered for his partner. "Or if what went down in your office has permanently changed the way we see her, the way we...feel about her."

Still angered by the recollection of those events, Echo stood aloof, folded his arms, and watched the others as they assessed themselves and their friend.

* * *

Romeo, characteristically, spoke first.

"Hey, pretty lady," he said softly, "you can't help what that bastard did to ya. Damn, I'm glad he's dead. I jus' wish he'd stop comin' back to haunt us. To haunt YOU." Romeo paused as Omega choked. "Not jus' no, but hell no, Meg. You're still my second-best girl—India bein' my first, of course." Romeo grinned, and Omega smiled up at him, a suspiciously moist look around her eyes.

* * *

India, who had stepped aside to give Echo room to stand near his partner, moved to the right side of the bed and sat down on its edge.

"Remember this, Meg?" she asked, pulling a gold charm out of her sleeve. "It's the 'sister' bracelet you gave me back during your first Christmas with the Agency. Sisters are forever, girlfriend. No matter what." The two women embraced, then Omega dragged a hand across her eyes.

* * *

"Omega," Fox began in turn, "I have always considered you an excellent agent, an honorable person, and a fine woman, in the old-world sense of 'gentlewoman.' I have yet to see anything that would cause me to change my opinion. More, in the time that you have been with us, I have come to view you as...yes, as part of my own family, as well. I have no biological children...yet," he offered a fond glance at Zebra, "but you are, nevertheless, the closest thing I have ever had to a daughter, and your siblings are the others in this room."

"Except me," Zebra noted. "I guess I'm the stepmom, since—while I'm older than you four—I'm not quite old enough to be your mom. And I'm good with that. Especially if it gets me this lot as my 'kids.'"

"Well said, bubeleh. Romeo is right, Omega, tekhter. You can't help what has happened to you. Why, therefore, should it affect my opinion of you? I'll see to it that you are discreetly provided with whatever help you need to get through this with...no more embarrassment than...you've already endured." Fox glanced away for a very brief moment. "And please, forgive me for that. You and Echo both. I...had no idea. I thought it was more mental programming...in YOU. Like you were afraid of, last year." He sighed, and crouched beside the bed, to look into Omega's face. "I should have trusted you both, should have listened...but I know how close the two of you are, and...I thought perhaps Echo was trying to, I don't know, help you work past the programming, just the two of you, willing to put himself at risk to help you. I'm...sorry, child." Fox sighed again, standing. "I hope you can forgive me. I...sincerely only wanted to help. BOTH of you."

Then he turned and looked at Echo as well; that worthy nodded his head, accepting the apology—both spoken, and unspoken—directed his way.

"Thank you, Fox," Omega whispered; Echo noted she had surreptitiously watched the wordless part of the exchange from behind a curtain of platinum hair. "Coming from you, that means a lot to me. All of that. And...I never blamed you; there's no need to ask forgiveness. You have the hardest job in the whole Agency, and you were just trying to do it."

* * *

"Tt't'lk didn' help that sitch at all," Romeo noted, angry. "Dude went way th' hell overboard on readin' Meg. An' Echo, too, I guess."

"From what I heard, he sure did," Zebra agreed. "Did he really force his way past your telepathic block to do it, though, Omega?"

The others were silent, waiting for Omega's response. She continued to stare down at the blanket for a long moment, then finally nodded affirmation.

"Not that it was real hard," she said, in a voice so low they almost couldn't hear it. "I was so shaken up by what had just happened, it might as well have been tissue paper."

"Damn, baby," Echo breathed, perturbed. "That was as big a violation as anything that's happened to you."

"What he said. Okay, on to my answer to your question. Meg, as your principal physician AND as a friend and," Zebra chuckled, a wry sound, "a reasonable approximation to a step-mom, I'm here for you, honey. Nothing's changed, as far as I'm concerned. Just let me know what you need, and I'll try to provide it. And if I can't do it myself, I'll find the best person who can."

Omega nodded.

* * *

"What...what about...Dihl?" she whispered then.

"It won't make a bit of difference to her, baby," Echo told Omega, voice soft. "I don't know if you're aware of it, but...Ma has been working on your case."

An already-pale Omega blanched until the others thought she might pass out.

"No, no, no, baby. It's okay," an alarmed Echo declared, throwing out a hand. "Calm down, baby. I swear it's all right. She asked Zebra if she might be the specific medtech assigned to your case, because she wants to help. She wants to help YOU."

"But...how much has she told you?" Omega breathed, looking horrified.

"If I know Dihl, not a word," Zebra observed. "The woman is as professional as ever I have seen. Not to mention, and no offense, Echo, but your mother makes the 'inscrutable Indian' stereotype look like an understatement."

Echo laughed.

"Yeah, that's Ma, all over," he agreed. "And no, Meg. I understand that there are things you aren't ready to talk about...may never be ready to talk about. And I'm not going to pry. Ma hasn't said a word to me about it, except that I know she's working on it, as hard as she can around her other duties."

"True words," Zebra affirmed.

44

"Baby, she's gonna do her damnedest to take what care of you she can; see, when she told you at the Ranch that you were part of the family now, she meant it—every word." Echo met his partner's troubled gaze, his own steady and calm. "As if she wasn't already convinced of it, the fact that you saw Shiitsooyee was the capper on that one."

"She met your grandfather, Echo?" Fox wondered. "But I didn't think Omega was in Texas a decade ago. I didn't think she was even out of graduate school at that point."

"I wasn't," Omega noted with a sigh.

"But...he died ten years ago, according to what Fox has told me," Zebra said, confused.

"He did," Echo said, "but Meg saw Shiitsooyee FIVE years ago, while she was doing an observing run on the southern end of the Ranch, with Gonzo's permission. Years before Meg and I ever met. And then positively identified his photos in one of our family albums. BEFORE Dihl or I could point him out."

The room erupted in confusion. Omega flinched, then began to tremble at the noise. India spotted the fact and stood, raising her hands.

"SHUSH!" India cried. "Everybody calm down! You're upsetting Meg! And she's already had enough for one day. Everybody just settle down and let's let Echo and Meg explain this."

The others silenced immediately, shocked and worried for their stressed colleague, and India sat back down on the bed, taking one of Omega's hands in hers and holding it, shushing the anxious Agent in a motherly fashion.

"There, Meg. It's okay, honey. I know you're on edge. It's fine," the Alpha Line medic murmured. "Everything is gonna be okay. We didn't mean to scare you."

"I'm...I'm all right," Omega whispered, once the room was quiet once more. "Well, I'm not all right, but...you know what I mean. Um, Echo, can...can you take a stab at, at answering their questions? Then I'll fill in... whatever."

"Uh, okay. The truth is, we can't quite explain it," Echo noted. "According to Meg, my grandfather showed up one morning to teach Meg how to take care of herself in the brush, after a close call with a rattler, the evening before. All I can say is that it doesn't go against Lipan—or most Christian—beliefs, that someone who had already passed on might show up to a family member as a guardian of sorts, which is basically what Shiit-sooyee did. And that right there is why Ma views it as confirmed that Meg is supposed to be considered part of the family. And she's unswerving on that." Echo smiled. "And I'm good with it, too."

"But scientifically..." Zebra murmured.

"I have no scientific explanation," Echo said, holding up both hands, "though I think Meg has been working on one." They all turned toward Omega, who blinked.

"Um," she said, then swallowed hard. "I don't have a...a whole lot to go on. But...we know I have enough Glu'gu'ik, specifically Hou'd'ni, spliced into my genetics that the F'al recognized me as its new caretaker—as the Last Caretaker. So, um, I sorta figured that...gave me some access to the, uh, the quantum foam phenomena, kinda like what Ke'ri Gla'd's did, back at Halloween. Only, well, I didn't exactly call him...but I DID sorta call for help when the snake struck. I mean, I vaguely remember yelling, 'Oh God, help me!' or something like that, when it happened; I was kinda busy dodging, so I don't recollect for sure exactly WHAT I said. But the intent was definitely there, whatever I said. I was asking for help beyond me."

"So Meg figures maybe that passed for the 'séance' part of the whole deal," Echo added. "There seemed to be a time delay, in that the snake attacked that night, and Shiitsooyee showed up early the next morning...but that might have just been when Meg first saw him. There's nothing to say he wasn't there all night, standing guard while she observed, in response to her request. There's six or seven different kinds of rattlers around that part of Texas. And other nasty critters around that area besides rattlers—copperheads, water moccasins, scorpions, couple different kinds of spiders... you get that picture."

"And neither Echo nor I have any sort of theological problem with it," Omega said with a shrug. "We even talked it over with Father Papa one time. He thought it was fascinating...but didn't have a problem with it, theologically."

"In fact, he came up with some interesting passages in Scripture to support it," Echo added.

"Whoa," Romeo murmured. "That's...cool an'...sorta scary, like."

"That's the only time it's happened, though," Omega pointed out. "So...I'm not sure."

"And she hasn't felt like testing it," Echo pointed out, offering his partner a gentle, teasing grin.

"Nope." she averred, succinct. "No tellin' who...or what...would show up. Not goin' there. Nope nope nope."

"Anyway, Ma thinks of Meg as part of our family, and in her turn, she's been happy to be considered as part of the bigger family Meg has gathered around herself, the rest of whose members are here right now," Echo concluded. "And that's not gonna change, not with Ma. No matter what."

The room fell quiet, as the others pondered the revelation, and Omega's role in it.

* * *

After a silent moment, Omega glanced at Echo. The expression on her face said, *What about you? How do YOU feel about me now?*

"Do you even need to ask?" he murmured in response to that look.

"No. But I...need to hear," Omega replied, looking down at her fingers pleating the blankets as if they belonged to another person.

"All right." Echo moved to the side of the bed opposite India and sat. "I've already told you earlier tonight that what's important is what's here—" Teasing gently, Echo tapped his index finger directly between Omega's eyebrows, crossing her eyes and eliciting a weak grin, "and here." He tapped the top of her breastbone lightly. "Now, you tell me: Has any of that changed because your biochem has gone wonky?"

Vulnerable blue eyes met a smoky brown gaze, then Omega slowly shook her head.

"No," she whispered. "No, it hasn't."

"I would have been surprised if it had," Echo murmured. "So if you haven't really changed, and I haven't changed, our relationship can't have changed." He smiled slightly. "A pal of mine told me it was called a syllogism. Right, pal?"

Omega smiled back, a single tear spilling over as she said, "Right, Ace."

"That's better," Echo said, ruffling the platinum blonde halo briefly, then wiping the tear off her cheek.

"Looks t' me like the 'family' made it through, Meg," Romeo remarked with a smile.

"Except we haven't heard how Omega feels about all this," Fox point-

47

ed out.

"Good point, Fox," India agreed. "Meg? Honey?"

* * *

The room was silent for a long time. Omega kept her eyes cast down at the bed covers, thinking—wondering exactly how she DID feel—and working on wording.

"Well...um..." Omega said at last, rousing herself, "I was raised in a... kind of a reserved home. Not repressed, just...reserved. I learned to think that...some topics simply aren't for public discussion."

"Like raging hormones and your sex life," India said frankly, and Omega blushed painfully.

"Exactly. And in a couple decades of adult life, nothing's ever changed that fundamental way of thinking for me. Now, not only is it public knowledge, but...I feel like I'm in one of those nightmares where you're married to somebody you either don't know or can't stand..." She sighed, a painful sound.

"Meg, I wouldn't exactly call six people knowing, 'public knowledge,'" Echo offered consolation. "Especially given who five of the six are." He gestured to the room's occupants.

"Echo, everybody saw you carry me through the Core, pretty much a limp dishrag in your arms. And they're gonna know you brought me home, not to the medlab. What do you suppose they think? Besides, we've gotta try to deprogram Mark, and get him—and me—back to some semblance of normal, hormonally-speaking in particular. That means telepaths and doctors. How many more have to know?" Omega asked, quiet.

"We'll try to be as discreet as possible, Omega," Fox reiterated. "I learned my lesson earlier this evening, and I'll do better, I swear to you. I'll get on this right away and try to have something arranged by the time you come on duty tomorrow."

"And I'll help," Zebra added.

"Me, too," India agreed.

"Thanks, y'all," Omega mumbled. "Anyway, this is about as...I mean, it's just...oh, I don't know what to do..." For the first time since they had entered, she raised her head and glanced around the room, as if seeking an answer.

"And it's not easy to talk about, even with us, is it?" India asked, sympathetic.

"...No."

"Are you askin' f'r help, Meg?" Romeo wondered.

"I..." Omega dropped her head. Her shoulders slumped in defeat. "Yeah."

"What do you want us to do?" Echo asked, beside her.

"I...don't know. I can't get through this alone. But I don't know how to ask for help. I don't know WHAT to ask for help! I don't know of anything y'all can really do, anyway."

"Well, if you do think of something, let us know," Fox said. "I think I speak for everyone here, Omega, when I tell you we're behind you and we'll support you. However you need us to." The others nodded. "Why don't you get some sleep, my dear girl? Alpha One was already off duty, and I called you back in when Wright was brought to me; it's late, and you're overdue for some rest. We'll work on this in the morning."

"All right, Fox," Omega responded, not bothering to hide her exhaustion, sliding down in bed and pulling the covers up. "Thanks, y'all—for... everything."

"Take it easy, girlfriend," India said, as she, Romeo, Zebra, and Fox exited Omega's bedroom. "If we can do anything, let us know."

"Wilco."

"Meg, I'm going to bed now, too," Echo told his partner. "Yell if it gets to you. I'll get dressed—or grab my robe an' house shoes, at least—and come over. Good night, baby."

"Good night, Ace. Thanks."

* * *

The next morning, Alpha One and Alpha Two met in the Director's office. "How are you this morning, Omega?" a solicitous Fox asked.

"I'm fine, Fox," Omega said, setting her jaw firmly. "The people I care the most about are behind me on this, so I'm gonna make it." The room's occupants smiled.

"Meg," India asked, "are you up to going over to the medical portion of Confinement and seeing Mark Wright again? The medic—singular—assigned to the case has requested it. She wants to see how Wright will react to you."

"Wait," Echo demanded. "Zebra isn't doing this?"

"No," Fox noted. "Not for this. Zebra is very good at emergency medicine, like India, here, but Bet came from the military and has a specialty in psychological warfare and PTSD that Zebra and Zarnix felt might serve the purpose better than anything either of them could do. And," he added, "she has already been read in on the delicacy of the matter, and the need for... privacy. She has promised to safeguard the entire matter."

* * *

At the suggestion, Omega closed her eyes for a moment, shaken at the thought and not yet ready to face another confrontation with the strange man to whom she was tied so intimately and unwantedly. Then gentle male fingers touched her spine—a familiar touch at once soothing and surreptitious, feathering along her back, somehow seeming to add strength to her very being. Omega opened her eyes.

"All right. Let's go," she told India.

Echo followed his partner out, his hand still on her back, encouraging.

* * *

"Hi, Bet," India greeted the freckled, redheaded medic as Alpha One and -Two entered the secure area. "Here's Meg."

"Hello, everyone," Bet responded cheerfully. "Omega, Fox and Zebra both have discussed the situation with me, and I understand the delicate nature, and your feelings about matters. I'll do everything I can to help, and make you as comfortable as I can at the same time."

"Thank you."

"Mr. Wright has remained in a catatonic, trance-like state since you left yesterday. I've gotten complete data scans on him. Now I'd like to see how he responds when you come near him."

"Not too close," Echo warned. "Under the circumstances..."

"Of course," Bet responded, leading the Agents toward a confinement cell, scanner in hand. "That much is understood. I won't let her fall into the grasp of his programming. For now, we'll keep her outside the confinement fields. I don't actually have any plans of bringing her closer than that, anyway."

Inside the cell, which had three solid walls, solid floor and ceiling, and one double-force-field wall between them and its interior, Mark Wright stood stiff, staring blankly. As Omega approached, however, he turned to face her, extending a hand toward her. Instinctively, Omega retreated a step;

a protective Echo moved in front of her.

* * *

"That's...interesting," Bet murmured, studying the scanner.

"What is?" India asked, coming over.

"Look." The two doctors bent over the scanner, mulling the readout for a moment. Then India looked up at Wright.

"Wow. Interesting? Well, that's one way to put it, I guess."

"What?" Romeo asked, curious.

"Let's just say, if you reacted that strongly to me every time you even saw me, we'd have a hard time getting any work done," India murmured. Omega's eyes grew wide; Echo blinked, startled at the implications.

"Woo! Hot mama," Romeo chuckled. Omega blushed deeply, and Echo frowned.

"He definitely knows I'm here, all right," Omega agreed.

"How could he not?!" Romeo expostulated. "Eyes wide open like that. Ow. He don't even blink!"

"No, Romeo, I mean he...KNOWS...I'm here. Watch," Omega said, stepping just around the corner, out of Wright's field of view. The sandy-haired man nevertheless turned to face her, as if the intervening opaque, and very solid, wall didn't exist.

"Telepathic?" Bet asked, and Omega nodded. "Can you reach him?"

"Yes," she answered. "I found that out last night—the hard way."

"So to speak," Romeo remarked with a grin, and Omega blushed scarlet again.

* * *

"Romeo," Echo muttered to the other man under his breath, delivering his patented Yellowstone glare, "if you don't shut your damn mouth and quit embarrassing her, I'll shut it for you. This is hard enough for Meg as it is, without your cute little innuendoes."

"Sorry, Echo," Romeo murmured, subsiding.

"Try reaching out to him," Bet told Omega.

"NO." The emphatic syllable came from Echo.

"Why not?" the medic asked.

"That's way the hell too dangerous."

"Echo," Omega said, considering, "I think it'll be okay. There's a field barrier between us."

51

"Not between your heads," Echo told her. "He slammed me across Fox's office yesterday, before I even had a chance to completely ENTER your damned link! I don't trust him. We'll find some other way to do it."

"After what he did yesterday, I don't trust Tt'l'k, and I don't want him involved," Omega said firmly. "And Zz'r'p isn't available, per both Fox's information, and my attempts to reach him this morning. And, like you insisted yesterday, we need answers."

"Wright doesn't seem to be very verbal," India observed.

"No, it's the programming," Omega agreed. "He can't respond. That's why I have to...go in."

"Okay, take me along, this time," Echo volunteered. "Do you think you can, baby?"

"I...dunno. Maybe. Are you sure you want to try?" she asked, uncertain.

"Funny, I was gonna ask you that."

"No. But I have to," Omega sighed.

"Here we go, then. Guys, keep an eye on us," Echo told Romeo and India.

"You got it," Romeo said.

"Ready, Echo?" Omega asked.

"Do it."

* * *

Echo dropped his mental defenses as Omega lightly brushed his temple with sensitive fingertips, and his eyes defocused.

Huh. I seem to be getting better at this, Ace.

Hi, Meg. Easier than usual.

Yeah. Comfortable?

Uh-huh, Echo replied. *You're always careful to put up blocks to guard my privacy, Meg. And I appreciate that.*

I'll never do to you—or anyone—what's been done to me, Echo. Omega's very thought was guarded. *This is too easy. I think something about this situation must be boosting my ability.*

Could be, Echo responded thoughtfully. *We'll know when it's all over, maybe. If things stay ramped up, then you've developed as a telepath. If not, then something in the link with Wright triggered it. And it's entirely possible that it'll end up being a little of both. Or that the link ends up permanently boosting your ability, even over and above what you've developed.*

Yeah, that all makes sense. Ready?

Yep.

Here we go...Mark?

Megan! came the response. *I hear you, sweetheart. You've come to me! Are you ready now?*

It's 'Omega' these days, she replied, with glacial levels of cool. *And I'm not your sweetheart. I don't even know you.*

I...I know, Mark stammered, confused. *I can't help it. I don't understand any of this. I'm crazy for a woman I've never met before. I don't want this, Megan. Not like this, anyway. I—wait! Who else is here?!*

Me, Echo said.

You!!

Unexpectedly, Echo felt himself mentally yanked away from Omega.

Stay away from her! She's mine!! Mark shouted at Echo.

I think that's my line, Echo replied, calm. *Or something to that effect. She's my partner.*

She's my mate!!

I think the lady might have a say in that.

She has no choice!!

She does, if I have anything to do with it. Echo felt a chill run through him as he realized the implications of the programmed statement.

You had your chance. You ignored it. The thought was vicious, pointed, and Echo reeled back mentally.

Damn you!! Let Meg alone! She doesn't want you!

I don't care!—I...I do care...It doesn't matter...It...I...Megan, HELP ME!!

Suddenly, Omega's presence surged between that of the two men.

There you are! Echo, I thought I'd lost you!

Megan, help me! Mark pleaded. *You and your partner—Echo?—help me! I don't want to hurt you, but I don't know how to stop...*

* * *

That sounds familiar, Echo. Omega's thought was pained. *When my programming triggered, I couldn't stop either. So when Alpha Two burst in, I was mentally begging India to kill me before I killed you. Not that she could hear me, but still.* She sensed Echo's shock. *Why are you surprised?*

What would you NOT have been willing to do to stop, if the situation had been reversed? She waited for Echo to respond; his reply was not verbal, but Omega sensed his slow, thoughtful mental nod. *Mark doesn't want this any more than I wanted to kill you, Echo.*

That's...not exactly true, Megan, Mark admitted. *If I weren't naturally attracted to you, this would be easier to fight, I think. You're beautiful. Intelligent. Witty. Strong. Brave...*

* * *

Both men sensed Omega's stupefaction at Wright's unabashed praise. *Where on earth did you get that idea?* she wondered. *Beautiful? Brave? Strong?*

When I first met you, I read it all through the link that popped up between us, Mark told her. *Plus what your co-workers had already told me. And I'm not blind.*

Meg, a curious Echo interrupted, *how do you see yourself?*

*Well...*and hesitantly, an image formed in the minds of the two men of a nondescript woman with average build, pale, colorless face, washed-out blue eyes, and a somewhat mousy blonde braid, timid and shy, so colorless she was practically invisible. They watched as the woman, trembling lightly as if in fear of some nameless threat, stood to the right of, but slightly behind, a tall, attractive, imposing, dark-haired man in a black Suit, both wielding Mark IV Tachyon Splitter Rifles.

Damn, Mark responded. *I recognize your partner, but is that supposed to be you, Megan?*

Hm. I didn't recognize either one, Echo said. *Look, Meg. Let me show you something.*

* * *

She watched as Echo formed an image of a tall, beautiful, athletic woman in a black Suit and goggle-glasses, arms akimbo, fists on her hips, shining platinum-blonde braid hanging down her back, smiling.

That's the first time you ever wore the Suit, Meg, Echo told her.

That's a memory?! Omega asked Echo, stunned. *That's what I look like to you?*

That's what you look like, Mark agreed. *Except for the sunglasses, that's what I saw yesterday when we met. You...you're...I want...*

* * *

Both Agents sensed the man struggling to overcome his programming, and losing. Omega instinctively retreated, and Echo felt the wave of anguish and self-loathing that washed over her at Wright's reaction to her presence.

Mark—do you remember Slug? Echo asked, changing the subject, hoping to divert his partner's thoughts.

Yes! Hate emanated from Wright. *Well, I do now, anyway. I didn't remember any of it until I touched Megan. And I'm not sure I would, even so, except SHE remembers him. Because of that, it's like her memories... released...mine, I guess you could say.*

What did he do to you? Echo pressed.

Abruptly, Echo experienced a kind of explosion of agony as Mark, helter-skelter, projected his memories of his abduction and forced modification. Echo heard Omega's mental shriek...

...Then everything went black.

* * *

When Echo awoke, he was on the floor outside the confinement cell; India, Bet, Zebra and Omega were bending over him, and Fox was standing beside Romeo, having been summoned by India's emergency call. Omega was white to the lips and trembling as she responded to a question.

"...I-I don't know, Bet. I'm afraid to try. Mark's memories brought all mine front and center. If I try to reach Echo to wake him, I may make things worse."

"Nnh...no-no need," Echo murmured, pushing up on one elbow. "I'm... all right."

"Echo, I'm sorry, I'm so, so sorry," Omega apologized, deeply upset. "I didn't see it coming. I swear, I didn't see it coming."

"It's not your fault," he said, sitting up and shrugging. "I asked him what happened. He showed me. Damn. It was like some sort of mental tsunami or something. It felt like I was getting ripped apart."

"Kinda, yeah. In an orderly, surgical fashion. And then put back together, but different." She shrugged. "If I'd been prepared, I could have blocked it, I think. At least filtered it. You...didn't need to know all that."

* * *

Echo waved his hand in dismissal, then reviewed the memories that had been forced into his brain, his still-too-pale face drawn in pain. Omega

55

studied his face, realizing what he was doing.

"Echo, stop, hon," Omega said, laying a light hand on his arm. "Please, just stop. Let it go."

"I'm looking for a clue, Meg."

"I can do that. I'm used to dealing with it. You're not."

Echo's breath caught. The other four Division One Agents stopped and stared at Omega, as did Zebra and Bet.

* * *

"What...do you mean by that, Meg?" Echo asked slowly, afraid he already knew the answer. She shrugged again.

"I deal with the abduction memories every day of my life," she told them. "I'm...used to it."

"Omega," Fox said, shocked, "do you mean that Wright's abduction memories, the ones that were so powerful as to have just rendered Echo unconscious, are fundamentally the same as yours? And you deal with them continually? Every moment of every day of your life?"

Omega nodded.

"Damn, Meg," an appalled Echo whispered, his apprehensions confirmed. "I knew it had to be bad, but—"

"Echo, let me get rid of them for you, Mark's memories," Omega said quietly, pulling out her brain-bleacher. "There's no need for you to—"

Echo pushed her hand aside, then swiftly put his fingertips to her temples, opening up and reaching out...

* * *

The spacecraft that soared over the northern Alabama field was silent, barely rustling the leaves of the trees as it passed close overhead, then paused. Echo sensed the delight and excitement in the curious young mind as a twelve-year-old Megan McAllister spotted the craft when it came into her field of view, slowing to a stationary hover, directly over her. A hatch opened; a seven-foot-long, iridescent green, slug-like being appeared in the opening.

Greetings, young Terran, *a telepathic voice said.*

Adrenaline surged through the young body as an excited Megan McAllister tried to sit up and respond with a smile. Excitement turned to anxiety as she discovered she was unable to move.

What's going on? *she thought.* Why can't I move?

Because I have need of you, *the alien replied.* You will become my hands, you see.

But I don't want to! I want to go get the grown-ups, so they can do this 'first contact' thing right!

This is no first contact, child. Now be silent.

Please stop! You're scaring me!

Shut up.

The giant green slug vanished from the hatchway, retreating deeper into the ship.

A faint yellow-orange beam shot down from the spacecraft, and Megan began to float into the air, up toward the saucer's hatch. Out of the corner of her eye, she could just see the blanket on which she lay, drifting skyward below her. The yellow-orange glow of what the adult Echo recognized as a tractor beam flickered, its focus adjusting, and the blanket fell to the ground in a crumpled heap, even as Megan passed through the hatch opening.

Echo felt the panic rise in the girl who would grow up to become his partner, as she realized her body no longer obeyed her will. She floated aboard the spacecraft and hovered in midair, immobile, as her young, almost-adolescent form was stripped naked and placed on an examination table. Scanners detailed every aspect of her being, down to the molecular level. Probes examined every square inch of her nude body.

At last. A perfect candidate, *Slug told his computer system.* Commence metamorphosis.

Echo felt the pain as hypodermics were inserted deep into various organs of the girl's body, disgorging a highly specialized, bioengineered DNA soup. Megan was unable even to scream at the agony of the molecular restructuring, as her body was forced to accept and incorporate alien biology. Like some perverted extraterrestrial Nazi physician, the alien being opened up young Megan's abdominal and cranial cavities and began extensive work with no consideration of sensation, even dissecting and reassembling her eyes and heart.

* * *

Instinct kicking in, an overwhelmed Echo, in deep pain, almost broke the link with his partner then. But he clenched his teeth and held on, determined to know—and share—what had happened to her.

Echo sensed a soft sob from somewhere outside the memory, and realized that Omega was agonized, torn between her intense sense of responsibility to her partner, and the desperate need to finally be able to share the experience with a trusted friend, someone capable of helping her carry the dreadful burden she had shouldered alone for so long.

It's all right, baby, Echo told her. *I wasn't prepared when Mark hit me with his memories. But I made sure I was ready for this, before I touched you. Show me. Let me share this with you. That way, you have someone to talk to about it. You don't have to keep it bottled up any more.*

But...I don't want you to have to...to deal with this. You've already had to deal with the whole 'getting torched under the Trindak's *ion drive' shit.*

Yeah, and I got that under control now. If I can handle that, I can handle this. Let me, baby. I've wanted to help you with this for so long. Let me do it.

He sensed her reluctant yet relieved acquiescence, and their joint attention returned to the memory of young Megan's torture at the hands of Echo's old enemy, as she was transformed slowly and excruciatingly into an instrument of revenge.

Damn, Meg, honey, the thought was wrenched from Echo as he watched various body parts removed, disassembled, modified, reconstructed, and replaced, *he nearly killed you—literally.*

Yes. There's no part of me he didn't rework. And I swear, it just went on and on and on; he never stopped, never paused. I never had a moment's respite until he was finished. I'm blocking most of the pain memories for you. No sense dredging it all up.

What?! Echo was shocked; the sensation of remembered pain that filtered through to him was already horribly, incredibly intense. He spiraled back into the universe of Omega's memory.

* * *

But this time, the mental and emotional distance was greater; Echo realized then that Omega had sensed his instinctive reaction, his near-withdrawal only moments before, and had increased the thickness of the screen between him and her memories.

She's protecting me, by only letting me feel a small part of the hell she lived through, he grasped. *And even that much is horrible. My poor baby.*

* * *

Echo watched in horror, a passive, intensely interested, invisible ob-

server piggybacking on Omega's memory, as Megan's eyes and ears were dissected and reassembled; nanites 'rewired' her brain and nervous system and then were extracted; her metabolism and systems were restructured to maximum performance and efficiency. Then the telepathic programming began as the incisions in her body were closed without—visible—scarring.

The young Megan was programmed using both standard brainwashing techniques and sophisticated telepathic thought-insertion. Then, after a full twenty-four hours of abuse, Megan was left in the woods nearby, all memory of the ordeal carefully suppressed—until the trigger that would, years later, set off the deadly assassin program within her.

* * *

The images faded, and Echo felt Omega shudder mentally.

Meg—are you...all right?

After what you've just experienced, Echo, you tell me: Will I ever be 'all right'?

I meant—

I know. It's...I'm...yes, I'm all right, Echo. I promised you I'd tell you one day. I just never knew how. As you can see, words aren't exactly adequate. She chuckled without mirth, then sobered. *But you know now. I...I wanted you to know, to understand, why I...react the way I do sometimes. That's why I didn't stop your establishing the link. Maybe I should have.*

No. No, I do. I understand better now. A lot better. Um...now what? Back outside?

Okay.

* * *

Omega still knelt beside Echo on the floor as they emerged from the link, and Echo dropped his hands from her temples, but their gazes held for a long time. Echo searched her eyes thoughtfully, and an uncertain Omega suffered the scrutiny patiently, waiting for his reaction, as the others watched in silence. Finally Echo spoke.

"Meg, you are one damn tough lady." The tone was quiet and filled with respect. Omega chuckled; it was a shaky sound.

"Well, when your options are deal with it or go insane..." She shrugged. "You just deal."

"Go insane?!" Fox reiterated.

"I believe it," Echo told the Director. "Especially now." He turned back

59

to his partner. "Meg, I wonder why you don't wake me up every night screaming from the nightmares."

"I...don't have 'em as often as I used to," she admitted. "And I don't scream even when I do. The dreams replay the actual events, and like you saw, I couldn't scream then—I couldn't move, couldn't speak, couldn't do anything. At times, he wouldn't even let me think. So...no. I don't scream, when I dream about it. Besides, I...didn't want to wake you."

* * *

"Aw, hell, Meg," Echo responded, chagrined, as the others listened, shocked. "You've been dealing with this all alone for way over a year, keeping it from me because you didn't wanna wake me?!"

"What could you have done?" Omega asked simply. "At least one of us was sleeping well."

"Meg," India interjected, "he could have gotten you counseling."

"And what could the counselor have done? Suppressed the memories? No. Stopped the dreams? No. Gone back in time and stopped it from happening? I wouldn't have let him, even if he could have; after some of the missions we've handled, people—including Echo, including you guys— might very well be dead if I weren't...what I am. No. All a counselor could have done is tell me how to deal with it. And I already know how to do that," Omega replied. The others were silent.

"Are you both okay now?" Zebra asked then, very quiet.

Echo nodded; Omega shrugged again. It was a reaction that Echo was beginning to think had become her standard response to the subject. *And, like I told Tare,* he considered, *it's her way of blowing it off, of making light of it, in front of the others. She's not lying; she's just not letting them know everything. I dunno how you put something like that into words, anyway.*

"Okeydoke. Bet, are you ready to get back to it?" Zebra wondered.

"Yes, Zebra. But let's...try a different angle. Omega, will you come with me to the medlab? I want to run some tests..."

Omega sighed.

* * *

Omega spent the rest of the day having medical tests run. Echo stuck close by and kept her company when the testing was such that privacy wasn't required, a thing that Omega deeply appreciated. Fox, meanwhile, had recalled the West Coast agents that encountered Mark Wright, and he and Romeo went off to interview them in more detail. India assisted Bet in analyzing Omega's test results, so that no one else needed to be involved.

For the most part, Omega remained quiet; but during one lull in the interminable testing, she turned to the man sitting beside her.

"Sometimes I get so tired of this..." she murmured in a low voice, shoulders slumped in dejection. "Even my annual physical is a little like this. They always find something new."

"I don't blame you," Echo replied, more sympathetic than she had ever known him, which was saying a good bit, since he had always shown a certain level of caring, a compassion for her—even when she had been his trainee, even before she had passed Alpha Line testing. "It really dredges up the memories, huh?"

"Oh, yeah."

"Anything I can do, baby?"

"Not really. Nothing more than you're already doing, anyway."

* * *

"But...I'm not doing anything," Echo protested, at a loss.

"Yes, you are," Omega told him. "The person I care most about on the whole planet, my best friend and my partner, is sitting right here talking to me, sharing it all with me, keeping my spirits up, helping me get through this. I couldn't do it without you, Echo. Not...not this time."

Echo blinked, startled at his normally-reserved partner's unusually frank affection, watching her. Her cheeks flushed slightly, as she noticed his stare.

"Uh, listen, Echo," she said, seeming hesitant, "don't pay any attention to my, uh, hyper-sentimentality right now. Not only are...are the hormones... runnin' wild, I'm rather...um...this situation has kinda...kinda blasted away all my...my defenses. And y'all—especially you—know 'way more about me now than...than I ever expected you would..."

* * *

"Does it bother you? That I—that we—know?" The brown eyes studied Omega's face intently, and she tried to meet that laser-like gaze.

"No, I don't guess so," Omega replied with yet another shrug. "I trust you. I trust all of you. It's just that...blast it, Echo, it's being forced out of me, rather than my being able to...to confide in you in my—and your—own time." Omega paused. "And I don't expect to get out of this with very much in the way of privacy left intact."

"And as reserved and private as you are..."

* * *

"That's what I was fixin' to say about you, Ace," Omega said with a rueful grin. "This has gotta be makin' you uncomfortable. I just wanted to say I'm sorry. I wish—"

"Meg," India leaned through the door of the room, "time for the next round, girlfriend."

Without another word, Omega stood and exited the room.

Behind her, Echo sat in astonishment, staring after the impressive woman who, in the midst of her own agony and humiliation, still sought to protect his comfort.

* * *

"Welcome back, gentlemen," Fox said from behind his desk as the Delta Four team returned. "You remember Romeo."

"Yes, sir."

"We called you back to have you tell us the circumstances behind your encounter with Mark Wright. We seem to have developed...some difficulties...with him." Fox paused. "Gimel, could you describe the events? Iota, feel free to add anything you think is pertinent."

"Well," Gimel began, "it was a normal unauthorized-territory retrieval until Wright showed up. We were trying to catch up to our favorite 'starship captain,' who was outside his designated zone in L.A.—"

"Riding around the countryside, as usual," Iota added.

"—when Wright simply...walks into the middle of our collar. Like, right in the middle! Between us and him. He almost made us lose him."

"Was he doin' anything strange before the collar?" Romeo asked. "Wright, I mean."

"No," Gimel replied. "I never even noticed him until he walked between us and our target."

"...Yeah, now that you mention it, it was kinda strange," Iota remarked, thoughtful.

"What was?" Fox responded, jumping on the response immediately.

"Well, I remember seeing Wright off to one side when I scanned the area before we moved in," Iota explained. "Then, when he looked up and noticed us, it was like he...stiffened, froze up for a split-second. He got this really odd look on his face, almost like...like he recognized us. Only we've never met, and I did some quick research since we found him, and he's never even been brain-bleached before! Nobody in the Agency has ever encountered him, that I could find, anywhere."

"That's good to know," Fox commented, jotting notes on his electronic tablet. "What happened next?"

"Well, it all went down with our target, the way we expected. Then I lost track of Wright, because we were on the 'Captain,'" Iota finished. "Next thing I know, he's marching right up to us, between us and the 'Captain'—and we couldn't brain-bleach him."

Fox and Romeo glanced at each other.

"Anything else?" Romeo asked.

"Yeah," Gimel said. "He kept saying, 'It's time.'"

"Over and over," Iota added. "He nearly drove us crazy with it. It was like he was hypnotized, an' trying to hypnotize us, too."

"We knew that there was another agent that had come into the Agency in a similar fashion," Gimel tag-teamed his partner, "so we went back to the L.A. Office and did some basic research. We learned she was stationed at Headquarters..."

"So we told our supervisor, and she said we should bring him here right away. We headed out with Wright immediately," Iota continued the story.

"He snapped back to normal as soon as we entered the Headquarters building," Gimel finished.

"For which we were both thankful," Iota agreed.

"Hmm..." Fox murmured, considering. "Think carefully, gentlemen. Can you remember anything else that might be unusual? What was he doing at the time? Where exactly were you?"

"Riding horseback in the desert southeast of L.A., like a few dozen others in the area," Gimel said. Iota nodded agreement.

"All right, Iota, Gimel," Fox replied. "Thank you very much. You can return to L.A. at your convenience. You've been a big help."

Delta Four departed again. Romeo looked at Fox and shrugged.

"Looks like the programmin' musta kicked in when he saw 'em."

"Yes. There must have been some internal timer to sensitize him. Then when Delta Four ran across him, they were the trigger," Fox remarked. "Probably some sort of loose psychic link to Omega occurred when her own programming kicked in, and that started the countdown clock." He sighed. "Dead end here."

"Yep. Gotta go tell Echo."

"I'll handle it, Romeo," Fox replied. "Don't worry about it."

"Okay. Glad it's your job."

"Indeed. I hate to tell him we have no leads."

* * *

First lunch had passed unobserved, along with second lunch and snacks; dinner had passed, the end of the shift had long since passed, and it was getting very late, but still Bet and India ran tests on their colleague.

"Guys, I'm tired, y'all. An' hungry. It's getting late," Omega protested quietly as the two indefatigable doctors set up yet another test.

"Just a couple more, Omega, and we'll be done for today," Bet said, in an effort to soothe the tired, ravenous Agent.

"No." The male voice came from the doorway. The three women turned. Echo leaned in the lab door, watching. "Meg's had more than enough for one day. You can finish tomorrow. Come on, Meg." Echo held out his arm. "We're going home now. You need food, and you need rest."

Without question or hesitation, a thankful Omega moved to her partner, who put his arm across her shoulders and steered her out of the medlab.

Behind them, the two physicians gaped for a moment, then shrugged, and began planning the next day's testing.

* * *

As he guided her down various corridors toward their quarters, Echo realized just how drained Omega had grown: She had no clue where she was, depending entirely on Echo to keep her on track. Her eyes were half-closed, her shoulders sagged beneath the weight of his arm, and she stumbled as she walked.

"Damn, Meg, you're wiped, baby," he murmured, and she nodded. "Want me to carry you?"

"N-no," she responded, trying to straighten her shoulders. "If people saw you doing that again, the rumor mill would fly. I'll...be okay."

"You're about to fall asleep standing up, Meg."

"I'll be fine. We're almost home."

"You think."

"Huh?"

"Do you even know where we are at the moment?"

"Uhm..." Omega's eyes opened a little wider and she looked around. "I think..."

"The answer is, 'No, I don't,' and 'Around the corner and down three doors.'"

"Oh."

They turned the corner and walked down to Omega's front door, entering their connected quarters through her apartment. Inside, a considerate—and no little sympathetic; it was the first time he had ever seen the kind of medical testing to which Omega was regularly submitted, and he had had no real grasp of how extensive it truly was—Echo turned to his partner.

"Go get in bed, Meg. Don't worry about anything else; I'll take care of things tonight. You're probably starved, too, 'cause you haven't eaten since breakfast, and that with your hyped metabolism, so I'll bring you something to eat before you crash. Bedtime snack."

"No argument." Omega disappeared into her bedroom as Echo went through the back door. In his kitchen, he put together a small tray of snack-type food calculated to help his partner sleep as well as fill her belly—sliced sharp Cheddar and smoked Gouda cheeses, some whole-grain crackers, a couple of grape clusters, a banana that he sliced into sections, a few ounces of walnuts, and a small handful of sweet baby carrots. Given he hadn't eaten either, he grazed as he went, deciding based on his own belly that this would do for his partner as well. As an afterthought, he threw several of her favorite pre-packaged oatmeal cookies onto the tray, in addition.

A few minutes later, he knocked on her bedroom door with the tray. The door was only partly closed, due to a relatively recent agreement the duo had made—since Echo's PTSD over the Cortian incident the previous winter, Omega tended to leave the door at least partway open, if Echo was welcome to relieve a nightmare by checking on her. Given their closeness and relative comfort with each other's presence, not uncommonly it was wide open. *Evidently she didn't get it all the way open after changing into her pajamas,* Echo decided. *The poor baby was all but sleepwalking anyway. I wonder if she slept okay last night, or if the whole telepathic thing was causing dreams an' shit, like Slug's original attack did.*

When there was no answer to his knock, Echo carefully pushed open the door, calling softly, "Meg?"

The white-blonde hair spilled across the pillow, the covers were pulled up to her shoulders, and the blue eyes were closed; Omega was sound asleep. Echo set the tray on one of the bedside tables in case she woke up hungry. Then he eased an unopened book out of the limp fingers, turned off the lamp, and slipped out, as silent as any ninja.

Chapter 3

Later that night Echo was, himself, sound asleep and dreaming about Alpha Line's second serious mission—Slug's attack.

He found himself reliving the scream from Omega that had awakened him from a sound sleep. His dream-self ran into her bedroom, as he had done then, to find her in agony, under telepathic attack, as Slug baited him. Her cries of pain haunted his dream.

"Echo!"

He ran to Omega's bedside and knelt.

"Meg! Tell me, what's wrong?"

She sat up and reached for him, desperate.

"Echo! Help me! Oh, dear God! Help me!!"

Echo scrambled for the cell phone on Omega's dresser, then stopped, confused. "That's...not right...not the way it..."

"ECHOOOO!! HELP! Oh God, please help!" There was a note of horrified desperation in the shriek, and suddenly, an aghast Echo was wide awake in the dark, listening to the sounds of a struggle coming through the open back door from the apartment next to his own.

* * *

Omega looked past the naked shoulder of her assailant and saw her trouser-clad partner appear in the bedroom door. She was pinned beneath the attacker, but had managed to keep her right leg from being trapped, and she fought with all her might against the blond man who had crept into her bed while she slept.

Suddenly she was free as an enraged Echo, spouting curses and epithets in multiple languages—most of which were not Earth-based—grabbed Wright and flung him bodily across the room, where the intruder smashed into the wall and slid to the carpeted floor.

A nude Omega scrambled for the sheet to cover herself as a blank-faced Wright came to his feet.

* * *

Unheeding of anything save his target, Wright lunged forward, toward Omega, and Echo body-checked the unclothed man, slamming into

67

him with all the strength he could muster, knowing he was fighting against alien-enhanced genetics and programmed strength.

Wright staggered back, but then lashed out with a backhanded fist that sent Echo stumbling backward in turn, hard into the wall. The seasoned Agent staggered and fell to the floor.

* * *

As soon as Echo was out of his way, Wright resumed his seemingly-inexorable progress toward the bed, effectively negating Omega's only escape route by blocking the path to the door.

Damn damn damn! she thought, nearing unaccustomed panic. *These quarters need some sorta escape hatch or something. Wait! The warp passages! Echo said they had 'em in here, and showed me the schematics the other day...where...? I don't remember! Shit!*

She looked around frantically for something that would approximate a likely weapon, but there was nothing within reach; only the small bedside lamp, the alarm clock, and the now-empty plastic tray whose contents she had awakened to polish off earlier, then gone back to sleep.

My Winchester & Tesla! she thought. *It's on the dresser. I gotta get to it. But...I can't kill him. He can't help it. Hand to hand, I guess, but that sure puts me in harm's way—without a stitch of clothes on either of us! Dear Lord, what do I do?!*

A commotion rose outside in the living area as Echo, back on his feet, suddenly made a flying tackle from the side, taking Wright down hard. Enraged, the tall, dark-haired man in the black trousers literally sat on the shorter, nude, blond male and beat him into unconsciousness as India, Romeo, and Fox ran into the room. A shocked and surprised Omega thrashed in the bed with every blow Echo gave Wright.

* * *

"Echo! Stop!!" India grabbed Echo's fist in midair as he raised it to strike again. "He's out of it! Meg's safe. You can stop."

Echo froze as the red veil covering his vision faded, and gradually, he lowered his arm as the nigh-berserker rage that had filled him drained away. *Damn,* he thought, shaken. *I think...I think I was ready to kill him. All because he attacked Meg...while under programming. That...whoa. I need to get a grip.*

He stood slowly, letting Romeo and India restrain the unconscious

Wright even as India began treating Wright's bruises, but he himself turned toward his partner's bed. Fox already stood there, cell phone in one hand; the other hand held the tattered pajama top that Wright had ripped off Omega's body and flung aside.

A panting, gasping Omega lay tangled in the sheets, trying desperately both to remain covered and to maintain control. Only then did Echo realize his partner was completely naked. *Oh no,* he thought in horror, as comprehension hit. *Oh, Lord God, not that. Please, not that.*

"Meg?" an anxious Echo whispered, looking at the wide blue eyes stark in the white face, and feeling something in his gut clench tight.

"He...he tried...he tried..." she stammered, voice breaking.

"Meg...did I get here in time??"

"I...I..." She buried her face in the pillows.

"Oh, dear God," Echo said in a low, strangled voice, as his worst fear in those moments lay before him in the bed. "Meg...I'm sorry...baby, I'm so sorry..."

"You two get out of here and help Romeo with Wright," India said quietly from behind, laying a hand on Echo's bare shoulder. "Let me check Meg."

Echo and Fox filed out into the living area, where Romeo had managed to partially-clothe Wright from the pile of garments Wright had left on the floor outside the bedroom. Echo rounded on Fox.

"How the hell did he get in her damn bedroom?!"

"We're not sure, Echo," Fox answered, shaking his head, deeply worried. "It seems our specialist on the case is tenacious and untiring, which was fortunate: Bet went over to Confinement to run some more tests and found Wright missing. Given the nature of his programming, we knew where to come looking."

"But how did he get out of confinement? And how did he get in here? The computer security system is only authorized to let you and me in here without Meg's express—VOCALIZED—permission," Echo wondered.

"India said she had an idea," Romeo volunteered, "but she didn' say what."

"Did you two get anything useful out of the West Coast team that found Wright?" Echo asked then.

"No, Echo," Fox replied. "Everything went down in a very similar fashion to how you encountered Omega, with the exception that Wright ran across them, not them across him, like you did Omega. Probably it was all part of his programming. Some event initiates a timer, and when the timer counts down, he seeks out the nearest Division One agent and makes contact; they'd lead him to Omega. I suspect the 'some event' was likely Omega's own programming triggering; if a loose, temporary telepathic link flashed up at that point, it could have started the countdown in Wright's programming without Omega's even being aware of it. But the Arcturans say it's too risky to all parties to attempt deprogramming while the programming is...in full effect. And no, that information didn't come from Tt'l'k."

"But they did it wit' Meg," Romeo noted.

"Not really," Fox elaborated. "You and India managed to confuse Omega's programming and temporarily 'lock it up,' remember?"

"Yeah, she was frozen in place, sorta," Echo remembered. "Unlike now..."

All three men stole worried glances at the closed bedroom door.

"Damn," Echo groaned then, dropping into Omega's recliner and resting his forehead in his hand, "if I wasn't quick enough...if I didn't get here in time..."

"You did," India's soft voice floated from the bedroom door as she exited.

"Thank HaShem," Fox said, fervent, and Echo relaxed marginally.

"What he said," he murmured, feeling a megatsunami of relief wash through him.

"How's the pretty lady, hon'?" a still-worried Romeo asked then.

"Bruised, scratched, badly shaken. Why she isn't in hysterics, I don't know," India answered, shaking her head, concerned.

"I do," Echo said in a low tone. "What she showed me Slug did...damn, y'all have no idea. You know, actual sexual rape may be the only type of violation Meg hasn't already had to deal with."

"Well, Wright didn't rape her. This time," India qualified.

"This time?" Echo queried.

"Yeah. The only reason he didn't succeed was because she managed to keep one leg free and kneed him in the groin—quite a few times, I have it to understand—while screaming bloody murder, whereupon you showed up, Echo, and flung him across the room, according to her."

"Uh, yeah, pretty much."

70

"So...like I said, not this time."

"We need t' ensure there ain't a 'next time,'" Romeo declared, incensed.

"Amein," Fox agreed. Echo stood and turned to India.

"Romeo said you had an idea how Wright got in here."

"Yes. If I'm correct, it'll explain how he made it all the way through the security systems," India said. "But I need to test it, and I'll need you guys' help."

"Whatchu want us to do?" Romeo asked.

"You and Echo take Wright into Echo's quarters," India ordered. "Grab a cell phone."

"Gotcha." Romeo and Echo assisted the zombie-like Wright, none too gently, through the back door.

"Close the door, Echo," India said, and Echo complied. India pulled her cell phone and hit the speed dial for Romeo's phone. "Okay, stand by, guys. Fox, put a secure lock on the door."

"Housekeeping security computer A.T.L.A.S.S., this is Director Fox. Place a Director-level emergency maximum security lock on quarters designated Alpha-One-Omega," Fox spoke into the air. "No trespassers. Entry privileges: Omega, Echo, Fox. Voice authorization: Fox. Confirm, please."

"Orders. Received. Director. Fox. A.T.L.A.S.S. Will. Comply," the artificial voice stated.

A soft series of clicks and relay switches came from various parts of the apartment, then a soft, confirming beep sounded.

"Alpha. One. Omega. Quarters. Secure," came the verification.

"Okay, guys," India spoke into the cell phone. "Let Wright go."

Only a few seconds had elapsed before another series of clicks sounded at the back door, and Wright opened it and walked through, unhindered. A bemused Echo and Romeo followed, and stopped the glazed-eyed man a few feet from Fox and India.

"What the hell?!" Fox remarked, shocked.

"Fox, ask the security computer who just came through," India said.

"This is Director Fox. A.T.L.A.S.S., please identify all entities passing from quarters designated Alpha One-Echo to Alpha One-Omega in the last five minutes."

"Entities. Identified. Alpha. Two. Romeo. Known. Visitor. Accompanying. Alpha. One. Echo. Occupant. Alpha. One. Omega. Occupant." The electronic voice floated in mid-air.

"Shit!" Echo exclaimed, as the explanation dawned on him. "Their tinkered genetics are so close, the security sensors can't tell the difference."

* * *

"Well, it isn't like the sensors are Glu'gu'ik level," Fox pointed out, as the three Alpha Line Agents quickly conclaved with the Director over the revelation, while keeping several hawk eyes on Wright. Echo even ducked back into his quarters and emerged seconds later with several sets of force cuffs, tethering Wright's wrist to one leg of Omega's dining table and hobbling his ankles, thereby ensuring he couldn't go anywhere. "That's currently beyond the level of anyone in the Coalition, and has been, for several decades. There's a technological barrier there that nobody's been able to break through; it's on a par with lightspeed travel, in that it'll be huge once the breakthrough occurs, only it's gonna take a bit of a paradigm shift to figure out how to do it. But evidently Slug knew that—anticipated the lack of development in that area, even. And his genetic skills and knowledge were sufficient to be able to take this poor bastard and make him look like Omega's identical twin, to the security sensors."

"That's...not good," Romeo noted.

"No shit," Echo agreed. "What I wanna know is how the sensors aren't reading the difference in Meg's obviously female body and Wright's obviously male one."

"Genetically, I can't begin to tell you," India said. "I don't have any knowledge of the security system's coding, so I dunno how that was done. But Fox, correct me if I'm wrong—currently the security uses ONLY the genetic recognition system, because the software gurus thought that would be way more able to differentiate between individuals, right?"

"Exactly, India," Fox confirmed. "Given that there ARE things like identical twins, who aren't truly identical at the genetic level, not to mention shapeshifters and other sorts of doppelgangers, it was thought that a basic read on the genetic structure of an individual—which is done during the entrance physical exam for every agent—would provide a foolproof identification system, enabling sure and certain recognition of every agent in the Division One Earth-based facilities. And you're right, that should be the case. Obviously Slug found a way to take advantage of such a system, meaning it is no longer foolproof." He shrugged, discouraged. "And never was, I suppose."

"Dammit," Echo grumbled.

"But we only jus' got th' upgrade t' this," Romeo pointed out. "An' Slug tinkered with Meg an' Wright, like, a couple decades ago."

"True, but it was the logical next step, Romeo," Fox countered. "Remember, this upgrade has been in work for a couple of years, almost a decade now, and it was planned-for well before that. It just got the timetable accelerated after the incidents last Christmas. Snails plan way the hell ahead. It's a reasonable and expected progression in the security system, and Slug was likely gambling on us doing exactly what we did—assuming the genetic scans would be a sufficient condition."

"Chances are, Slug worked something out to game the security system regardless of how it was set up," Echo said, shaking his head. "That's just how gastropoids think."

"Yes, it is. That is a distinct possibility, alter khaver."

"We'll work it out, Echo," India soothed, laying a light hand on his shoulder. "I promise you. We'll figure it out."

"It better be quick, then, before he finds a way to get to Meg."

"Lemme take care o' that, guys," Romeo volunteered. "Leastways for tonight. We'll come up with somethin' more long-term t'morrow."

"Offer accepted," Fox said at once.

* * *

"Don' worry, guys," Romeo told Echo and Fox shortly thereafter, "I'll keep an eye on this bastard, personally. He won't get loose. Not again. Not on my watch." He led their prisoner out.

"You need to keep an eye on Meg, Echo," India urged from the front doorway as she followed. "I dressed her in another pajama top and sedated her so she'd sleep comfortably, but still, she might have nightmares or something. And sedated, she can't handle things if something else DOES happen. Meanwhile, I'm going to split my time between helping Bet and helping Romeo."

"Wilco." Echo watched silently as the door closed behind them.

"Take it easy, Echo," Fox said as he, too, prepared to depart. "In the morning, I'm sending Alpha One away until we can figure out how to deprogram Wright."

"That sounds like a plan, Fox. I'm on things tonight."

"Echo...are YOU handling this all right?"

"Why shouldn't I?" Echo responded, maintaining an expressionless face.

"Remember who you're talking to, old friend," Fox replied quietly, glancing past Echo's shoulder at Omega's bedroom door, which India had closed behind her upon exiting, and Echo knew he was ensuring Omega couldn't overhear. "Your oldest friend, who already knows how you feel about her. I saw the way you were beating on Wright, as if you had lost all control and were ready to kill him with your bare hands. And I've never seen you like that before."

"I'm fine, Fox." Echo carefully kept his face noncommittal.

"Good," Fox said, a hint of skepticism emerging only in his eyes. "Then I want you to think about two things."

"What?"

"First: Mark Wright is as much a victim as your partner. I don't know what you heard when Omega took you with her into Wright's mind, but chances are, a great deal of it was NOT Wright, but the programming. Don't mistake the one for the other."

Echo paused and blinked, as the statement fully hit home. "You're... right, Fox."

"I'm just reminding you, Echo. You're worried about Omega—and with good reason. But Wright isn't the enemy. The real enemy is long dead. This is just a booby trap he left behind."

Echo nodded. "And the second thing?"

"There are other ways to lose someone than through death or the Agency's 'nonexistence,' zun. Taking them for granted is just as certain. You see...they tend to simply walk away when you're not looking." A knowing Fox met Echo's gaze. "I get that you're waiting for things to develop, meyn khaver. And I understand why; Dihl and Zebra and I have talked about what your mother advised you to do, and it makes a great deal of sense. Just...be careful you don't wait too long." Fox cocked his head. "I heard about Mu."

Echo stared at the Director for a long moment. His eyes closed for an instant, then he glanced down.

"Good night, Fox." His voice was unusually quiet.

"Good night, Echo."

* * *

The tall Agent stood for a time after Fox left, lost in thought. Then Echo disappeared into his apartment for a few minutes, where he stripped his bed, tossing the used linens in a pile in the corner beside the door, and remade it. Then he came back and knocked on Omega's bedroom door.

"Meg?"

"Mmn...Echo?" The voice was a sleepy murmur.

"Yeah, it's me, baby. Just me. The others have left." Echo came into the room and over to the bed; India had left the bedside dimmer lamp on a low setting, presumably so Omega could see if she awoke frightened. "C'mon, partner, it's time for a change of venue," he said, picking up the sedated woman and carrying her out. "If Wright gets loose again, he'll only come right back here."

Echo headed through the back door and into his own bedroom, where he laid Omega in his own bed and very gently tucked her in.

"Sleep tight, Meg," he told her in a soft voice.

His response was a contented sigh as she snuggled in and drifted off to sleep.

He turned off the lamp beside the bed, leaving only the soft orange glow of the nightlight. Then he closed and locked the bedroom door, spread out the pile of discarded sheets on the floor, unfolded a spare blanket obtained from a dresser drawer, and stretched out on the floor in front of the door, wrapping up in the bed linens.

"A.T.L.A.S.S. housekeeping computer, engage special maximum-security program Alpha-One-Echo-Red-Priority," he spoke into the air. "Current occupants: Alpha-One-Echo, companion Alpha-One-Omega. No additional bodies allowed across perimeter until further notice. No duplicate Omegas. Weapons armed. Voice authority: Echo, and only Echo. NO other override authorization. Confirm."

"Alpha. One. Echo. Red. Priority. Security. Program. Engaged. Voice. Command. Echo. Only. No. Override. Confirmed."

A series of clicks sounded for several seconds, then ceased. A soft beep announced confirmation. Echo nodded, satisfied.

The dark room fell silent except for the sounds of soft breathing.

* * *

When a groggy Omega woke the next morning to see a powerful male

75

form bending over her, she assumed Wright had gotten back in and responded appropriately. Lashing out with a backhanded right fist, she heard a satisfying grunt as she connected, and followed up with a roundhouse left to the chin and a karate snap kick at the groin, both of which her adversary only narrowly managed to avoid.

"Damn! Meg, it's okay! It's me! It's Echo!"

A confused, still-woozy Omega continued to fight for several more minutes, unable to determine where her partner was in the mêlée, and Echo's voice said, "Meg, you've gotta...calm...down! I don't want to hurt you."

* * *

Finally Echo simply wrapped his arms around his struggling partner in a bear hug, clamping her flailing arms against her sides as best he could, pinning her against his chest, and accepting the powerful blows while murmuring soothingly.

"Calm down. You're safe. It's Echo. I'm right here. It's me. Ssh; hush, baby. It's just us two. Calm down. We're fine. YOU'RE fine. It's okay. Everything is okay."

With a dry sob, Omega slumped against him, then raised her head; her eyes were disoriented, slightly unfocused, and depicted extreme confusion to his knowledgeable gaze. *Likely left over from the sedative,* he decided.

"Echo? It's...it's you?" Her voice sounded slightly slurred.

"Yeah, baby. I'm right here. I gotcha."

"Thank God. I thought Mark had gotten back in." She sighed, and relaxed into his embrace, just before he saw realization strike, and she sat up straight. "Oh geez, did I hit you?"

"Once or twice. I'm okay. It's nothing that a swipe of Rejuvic won't fix." He paused, then added in all sincerity, "I AM glad I managed to dodge that kick to the groin, though. THAT...woulda hurt. Like hell."

"Where...where am I?"

"My bedroom."

Omega's eyes widened in shock, and she stiffened again. Echo immediately realized what was going on in her still-groggy mind after the previous night's events.

"Meg, stop and think about who you're talking to."

She studied his face for a moment, then closed her eyes, took a long, deep, shuddering breath, and relaxed against him. He realized that she was finally allowing her guard to drop completely as she grasped that he had things under control. Echo nodded in satisfaction.

"There we go. That's better. I brought you in here last night after everybody else left. I thought you were still awake enough to realize what I was doing, 'cause you recognized me, but India said she gave you a mild sedative, so I guess you were too out of it to know. Anyway, I brought you here and I set up a max-secure perimeter in the household computer, answerable only to me, then slept in front of the door, just in case Wright got loose again. I figured I'd make it as damn difficult as I could for him to get to you. He'd literally have to walk over my dead body to do it." He studied the shaken woman in his arms for a moment. "I didn't mean to scare you when I woke you just now. I thought the personal touch would be better than a blaring alarm clock. I...guess I was wrong."

"No, it's all right. I was just...just dreaming. Thank you," she whispered, looking down, "for everything."

"It's cool, baby. I'm just glad I...arrived in time last night," Echo replied quietly. He tightened his hold momentarily, attempting to comfort her as well as let her know he was relieved she was unhurt, and was surprised when Omega began trying to squirm out of his grip. "Meg? What's... wrong?"

"I'm sorry, Echo," she said, pushing him away gently. "It's not...I...I just need a little more...personal space than usual...right now."

"I...don't get it." Echo released her, equally gently. Omega averted her face.

"Do you know what pheromones are?"

"No."

"Ask Bet."

* * *

Mu met them as they entered the Core together. "Hi, Meg, Echo," he called. "Meg, got an answer for me yet? I sure hope it's yes, pretty lady."

Omega glanced up at Echo, and he saw the pain she was trying hard to hide.

"Echo?" she asked, eyes pleading *give me a minute to talk to him,* and he understood the request. Echo hesitated only a moment.

"Sure, Meg. I need to run by the medlab for a bit anyway." Echo turned

77

to Mu. "But Mu? Until I get back, DON'T LEAVE HER ALONE. Got it?"

"Whatever you say, Echo," the other man said, startled at Echo's sudden vehemence. Mu and Omega watched Echo exit the Core, then Omega drew Mu over to a vacant corner.

"Mu, we...need to talk. There's some things you need to know about me...and it's gonna be...hard for me to...to talk about. And maybe...for you to hear. Never mind accept."

* * *

Echo entered the medlab, heading straight back to the research facility. When he found the friendly female medic, he launched into his errand without preamble.

"Bet, what's a pheromone?"

The plump, pretty redhead looked up from the microscope eyepiece. "Oh, hi, Echo. What's a what?"

"A pheromone."

"A means of olfactory communication," Bet responded promptly.

"What?"

"Most humans and animals—quite a few extraterrestrial species, too—emit a number of special scents. These scents are unique to the individual, often tailored to a given situation, and our responses to them, for the most part, are subconscious. You know how animals can sense if you're afraid of them?" Bet explained.

"Not personally, but yes, I'm familiar with the concept."

"They smell your fear pheromone, among other things. And when two people just seem to click, and we say they have good chemistry? They do. Their pheromones are compatible, acceptable to each other. It's especially true in...well, shall we say romantic-type relationships? That's where a lot of the research has gone on—sexual attraction and bonding. There are other factors, of course, but pheromones are involved. It works the other way 'round, too. Like if you can't stand somebody for no good reason. Initially, they weren't believed to exist. Then, for a long time, it wasn't believed that humans produced them—just animals. Now we know they're real, and we all make 'em. Why did you want to know?"

"Why would Meg be interested in pheromones?" Echo asked.

"Ah. Now it makes sense," Bet remarked, knowing. "Echo, have you ever had the experience of suddenly becoming aware someone was near, whether you consciously knew they were there or not?"

Echo nodded immediately.

"Sometimes it happens on patrol," he declared. "And I almost always know when Meg's around."

"Uh-huh. Chances are, you had just caught a whiff of her pheromones. For most humans, it's completely subconscious; we don't know when we smell 'em, we just react to 'em. Now, imagine that sensation raised an order of magnitude. With Omega's artificially-heightened senses, that's what she experiences every day. On a daily basis, she's probably semiconsciously aware of what, to the rest of us, is purely subconscious," Bet explained.

"Okay. Go on."

"Right now, with the hormonal storm that Wright induced in her, and the way the contact has ramped up her systems, I'd guess we need to raise that sensitivity by yet another factor of ten. At least. Maybe more."

"Shit. You mean—"

"Your partner is now consciously aware of the pheromones. It's probably driving her crazy. Especially you guys."

"What?!"

"Think about it, Echo," Bet said firmly. "Slug set up her biochemistry and psychological programming to drive her into Wright's arms at this point. The programming has been 'deleted.' The biochemical triggers... haven't. And right now...we—her doctors—don't know how to do it for her."

Echo stared at her, dumbfounded, as the ramifications hit. The medic watched Echo in silence as the implications of her statement sank in.

"Damn," Echo finally murmured in a low tone.

"Echo," the voice came from behind, "there's something else I think you should know." Echo spun to see India in the doorway.

* * *

"So...that's the situation, Mu," a humiliated Omega finished in a soft voice, staring at the floor. "I thought you had the right to know some stuff up front, though I'd appreciate it if you...kept it to yourself. I'll understand if you want to...forget the whole thing."

"Well...it's a...kind of a surprise, Meg," Mu murmured, struggling to grasp it all. "I'm still trying to take it all in. But...my first impression is... wow."

79

"Wow?"

"Yeah, like in 'exotic-wow'. We've been friends since Dallas, and I always thought you were interesting. But this puts a whole new twist on you."

"You like it?!" Omega was bewildered.

"Well, yeah, it's...kind of a turn-on, to be honest. Like I said, I'm still trying to take it in and understand. But I know you don't need the complication of a new relationship right now, with this brainwashed guy after you. Now I understand what happened the other night. I heard Echo had to carry you out of Fox's office, but word had it Wright...attacked you, or something. Well, I guess in a way, he kinda did, but...not like everybody's thinking. Which it's probably better that they don't know. Don't sweat it; I'll keep this to myself. It's nobody else's business, anyway. Look, don't worry about, about us. Get this situation taken care of—call me in to help if you need to—then we'll talk again. Maybe over coffee."

"O-okay," Omega said uncertainly, caught off guard by the man's complete acceptance.

"Tell Echo he better take real good care of you," Mu told her, mock-stern, then softened the statement with a smile. "Not that you can't take care of yourself. You're Alpha Line! The assistant chief, no less! But this is a really bad sitch. You'll need backup, and I at least want the chance to have that cup of coffee with you when it's over. Take it easy, honey; I'll see you later." The Division One agent headed across the Core and disappeared.

A thunderstruck Omega was left standing alone in the crowded, bustling Core, mouth agape.

* * *

"...So she's REALLY old-fashioned, huh?" Echo nodded as India finished. "I'm not too awfully surprised, to tell the truth. I'd already kinda figured as much, from some offhand comments Meg's made on occasion."

"These days, that's kind of rare." India grinned slightly. "Especially at Meg's age."

"My partner's kind of a rare lady, India." Echo shrugged. "But it means we've gotta be that much more considerate right now. Especially if she's... not experienced, shall we say." He shook his head. "This shit is doin' a number on her, in twelve zillion kinds of ways."

"Exactly. That's why I thought you should know. I figured you'd want to take some, I dunno, extra steps, kinda, to avoid giving her any further embarrassment by accident. I've already given Romeo a heads-up to back way the hell off on the innuendoes, and he...well, let's just say, he WAS surprised. And sorry for the ones he'd already made. He said you'd told him to shut up, but he didn't understand why you were so vehement about it... until I explained. And we figured, well, maybe you'd already kinda picked up on her, uh, lack of experience."

"Yeah. Okay, good," Echo said, somewhat gruff. "Now...we need to figure out where to go from here."

"Actually," Bet volunteered, "I've been giving that some consideration. But I need to ask something personal, Echo, that you're likely the only person who might know. I'm not trying to pry, I just need to know, so I'll know whether my idea even makes sense or not."

"Okay. Shoot."

"What are Omega's, uh, 'preferences'? I mean, does she prefer guys, girls, both...?"

"Oh. She likes guys. We had that discussion early on in our partnership; I wanted to make sure I didn't make any wrong assumptions..."

"Right. All right, that's kinda what I'd picked up on. This'll work, then. So I think, under the circumstances, it might not be a bad idea for the two of you to trade partners temporarily. Echo, I gathered you and Romeo used to be partners, right?"

"Yeah. So...? Oh, wait..."

"Right," Bet confirmed. "If you and Romeo pair back up for a while, then India and Omega can team up, and that way, she's got another woman to work with, who's also one of her physicians..."

"Hm," India considered, as Echo blinked in surprise, "it's an idea. We should run it by Romeo, Meg, and Fox. Come on, Echo. Let's go. Everybody else should be waiting in Fox's office by now."

"No, Meg was gonna wait with Mu for me in the Core before we went."

"Okay, we'll grab her on the way, then."

* * *

India and Echo approached Omega in the Core, and Omega saw Echo glance around with a sharp gaze.

"Meg? Where the hell is Mu?" an exceedingly annoyed Echo fired off as soon as he reached his partner. "He was supposed to be here! Where'd he go?!"

81

"I...don't know. He was...kinda surprised...by what I told him," Omega murmured thoughtfully. "He...left."

"Dammit, I told him not to leave you alone!" Echo grumbled.

"Echo, I'm in the middle of the Core. There's dozens of agents and aliens coming through all the time. I'm hardly alone."

"'Alone' is relative," Echo responded, enigmatic as ever.

"There's Romeo, getting a cup of coffee in the Alpha Line Room," India remarked, waving. "C'mon."

* * *

As the four entered Fox's office, the Director looked up. "Good. There you are. I've got a spacecraft ready at Penn Station. We're getting you and Echo off-planet until this is resolved, Omega."

"Wait a minute, Fox," India interjected. "Bet had an idea, and it's a good one. Under the circumstances, Meg might feel more comfortable with another woman along. Bet thought Echo and I could swap partners temporarily."

"Huh." Fox considered for a moment. "Seems reasonable. How about it, Romeo?"

"As long as it's temporary, it sounds okay t' me," Romeo responded. "I jus' want my lady back when it's over, but if Meg needs her now, 's fine with me."

"Of course," Fox agreed. "Echo?"

"Whatever's best for Meg," Echo answered immediately. Fox turned to Omega.

"Then it's your decision, tekhter."

* * *

Omega studied the room's occupants thoughtfully, mulling her choice.

"India," she finally decided, "I appreciate the offer, but it seems to me like that would just add to the stress right now, dealing with a partner I'm not used to. Even though we get along fine, we're each used to working with somebody else, you know? So there's gonna be subtleties that I'll be constantly tagging and trying to remember and adapt to. No offense, but I think I'd just like to stick with my regular playmate. If he can put up with me, that is. I know I'm not exactly...mentally and emotionally stable right now. Let alone good company."

"It'll be fine, Meg." Echo nodded. "Don't worry about me. Just try to relax, baby."

"I got it!" Romeo exclaimed then, and all eyes turned to look at him. "I know what this reminds me of!"

"What?" India asked.

"That *Trek* episode where th' dude has to go back to 'is homeworld to get married."

The others rolled their eyes heavenward, but Omega said, "Yeah. I noticed that, too. I only wish this was so easy to resolve..."

* * *

"*Otello* launch checklist complete. Ready for departure," Echo spoke into his headset from the helm of their spacecraft as Omega finished final prep.

"*Otello*, you are go for launch at your discretion," Fox's voice replied over the speaker.

"Copy that. Launching...now." Echo initiated the launch sequence, and the ship lifted off smoothly and began a rapid ascent, fairly shooting out of the atmosphere and into space. Beside him, in the copilot seat, the attractive blonde with the haunted expression finally relaxed and dropped her hands from the console controls as the ship went exo and headed out, toward Luna.

"Thank God," Omega whispered, fervent.

"We're off to Aleancë, Meg," Echo said, turning to her as the Moon loomed ahead, rapidly growing in apparent size as they approached it to port. "You're out of harm's—"

"Nngh," Omega groaned, as her fingers sought her temples.

"Meg?"

"Mmmh..."

"What's happening?"

"Mark...nng...head...nnf...link..." Omega hyperventilated for a few seconds, then cried, "Let GO!!"

"Ground Control to *Otello*! Come in!" The speaker emitted India's urgent voice, and Echo slapped the microphone switch as he watched Omega struggle, helpless to do anything to assist her.

"This is *Otello*. Go ahead, Ground Control."

"Is Meg okay?"

"Hell, no." Echo saw Omega strain against the harness straps.

"Wright says he CAN'T let go. Over and over. It's the only thing he says. Whatever it means." India paused. "Well, just once, he said, 'I don't know how.' Still not sure what it means."

"I think I d—"

"NnnghaaAAA..." Omega emitted the gasping cry.

"Echo?! Was that Meg??" India asked.

"Yes."

"Echo, come back! Um, uh, 'return to launch site!' Wright just collapsed! His blood pressure is spiking at alarming levels! Oh shit, there goes a nosebleed! It's killing them!"

"NO!" Omega cried. "Nnn...no, Echo! Please, don't! Mnph...It's better this way! Ahh...AAAGH!"

Echo made a swift decision: He grabbed the helm controls.

"*Otello* returning to Penn Station."

"Ground Control copies that," Fox said.

The ship swung around, executing a wide arc to bleed off velocity and reverse direction. The only thing holding Omega upright by this point was the seat's five-point harness, and now she slumped forward, limp and barely conscious, as the pain eased.

A few minutes later, Echo landed the *Otello* amid the sounds of soft sobs.

* * *

"Well...what if we don't leave the planet?" Echo asked in Fox's office. "We can see how far away we can get before it starts to hurt Meg."

"And Mark," Omega added.

"...and Wright," Echo agreed grudgingly. "I mean, we got almost to the Moon before it started bothering either of 'em. We oughta be able to go anywhere on the planet, right?"

"You sound like you have an idea, Echo," Fox observed.

"Well, I do," Echo admitted. "You guys—Alpha Line, an' anybody else you can line up, Fox—you keep Wright confined here, and I'll get Meg outta Headquarters. Out of state, even. That buys Medical time to figure out what to do about the situation. Priority one being finding a way for the security sensors to tell the difference between him and Meg...and priority two being to stop this whole 'link' thing and deprogram him."

"All right. Where do you figure to take her, zun?"

84

"Ipswich," Echo declared. "To the property on the island."

"Oh! I'd forgotten all about that place. Yes, that should work," Fox decided. "Alpha One, get your things and go at once. Alpha Two and I will handle the rest."

"All over it, Boss. C'mon, Meg. We got this," Echo said, turning for the door.

* * *

"Ipswich, Massachusetts?" India wondered, when Alpha One had left Fox's office.

"The same," Fox confirmed.

"What's in Ipswich?" Romeo asked, curious.

"IN Ipswich? Nothing in particular," Fox noted. "But Echo owns some property outside it, near Sandy Point over on Plum Island."

"ECHO owns property?" India parroted, surprised.

"Oh, man," Romeo murmured, suddenly grasping the situation. "Is 'zat th' place he got to live in, back when he was on sabbatical?"

"It is," Fox averred. "I'm not sure about the wisdom of that choice as a safe house for Alpha One, but it's a reasonable option, I suppose. And probably will serve our purposes in this situation, as he pointed out."

"Why not, Fox?" India queried. "I mean, if Echo owns it, you know it's gonna have security coming out your ears."

"Ears, eyes, nose, mouth, ass..." Romeo added.

"And it does," Fox said, stifling a chuckle at Romeo's addendum. "There are...other reasons...why I wonder about his choice, children."

"What?" India asked. "Why?"

"Nothing that either of you would be aware of, I think," Fox decided. "Alpha Two, you are assigned to heading up security on Wright, as best you can, until we can figure out how to separate his signature from Omega's in the sensor suites. As Echo has already stated, you have all of Alpha Line that isn't already assigned to missions, and I'll give you as many Security agents as you require in addition, and if that's not enough, I'll call in some regular field agents."

"All over it, boss-man," Romeo said, jaw firming.

"What Romeo said," India agreed.

"Is there anything you need to get started?"

"Yeah," Romeo noted. "I ain't normally got access t' Echo's records, an' I didn't think t' ask 'im f'r the current password before he an' Meg left..."

"You need rosters and current assignments."

"Right."

"Consider it done. Get with Lima and Bravo and I'll instruct them to provide you with whatever information you need. And we'll get the password temporarily reset to something you can work with."

"We got this, then."

"Excellent. Alpha Two is dismissed for now."

The determined pair headed out.

* * *

Echo and Omega stopped by their quarters, where Echo gave his partner specific instructions on what clothing and gear to bring.

"...So think casual," he told her. "Grab your sunscreen, and if you can find your bikini and some surf shoes, throw those in there, too, though the water might be colder than you'd prefer to swim in. There's a hot tub, though, so we can maybe soak in that. This is a resort area, so we want to blend in, if we see any tourists or locals."

"Right," Omega agreed, throwing items into her travel kit.

Five minutes later, they were headed for the vehicle hangars.

Ten minutes after that, the Corvette was passive-cloaked, morphed and airborne, headed northeast, out of the Big Apple.

* * *

Upon receipt of the Alpha Line Alert, signaling an all-hands meeting, Yankee pulled his cell phone and swiped off a text message to his partner.

Hey T—mandatory all hands mtg for A-L.
Where are you?

He waited several minutes, then when no answer was forthcoming, he added,

Meet ya in the A-L Room, buddy. CU there.

He waited a little longer, then headed for the Alpha Line Room to attend the all-hands meeting.

* * *

Tare's cell phone went off in the 'incoming message' alert, and he saw the Alpha Line Alert on the High Priority app, as he sat in the observing room of the Treehouse.

"Mm," he hummed to himself, pondering what to do. "I hope everything is okay. Well, if they need me, Echo promised he'd call me directly, and bring me back in."

Then the notification went off again, and Yankee's text message popped up.

"Aw, damn," Tare murmured, perturbed. "Either Fox hasn't had a chance to talk to him yet, or he's ignoring what Fox told him. And I know that Fox and Echo will take care of things, as far as THAT'S concerned. I...I gotta have this time, some private time, away from Yank. And judging by how Zebra all but reamed me a new one...in a nice kinda way," he gave a shaky laugh, even as he stepped out onto the side deck of the Treehouse, "if I come back now, she'll...I dunno, have me committed or something. I don't even know what the Agency does for their people that go 'round the bend, but I'm headed there if I don't get myself straightened out. Never mind getting Yankee straight. If I can. If...WE can," he added, mildly relieved that it was no longer all on his shoulders.

He sighed, and stared out at the rugged, multiply-peaked, cratered top of Mount Rainier in the distance to the southeast of the Treehouse, absently admiring the glorious view; to the northeast could be seen the double peak of Mount Baker; Glacier Peak, yet a third volcano, was nearly due east; to the south-southeast, in the far distance, the snowy peak of volcanic Mount Hood could just be made out, floating, ghostlike, over the horizon. To its left, a lone plume of what appeared to be smoke denoted the location of Mount Saint Helens, which had recently vented significant quantities of ash and steam in a large and ongoing phreatic eruption.

"Maybe, just maybe, my being away like this'll be the wake-up call that Yank needs, just like Fox and I talked about," he decided, staring at the ash plume and thinking it a metaphor for his partner...or rather, the direction his partner seemed to be headed. "And that'd be...really good."

He turned his gaze to his cell phone again. Then, very deliberately, he placed Yankee's cell phone number on the 'temporary block' list. Opening the contact list, he then proceeded to place all other contacts on the same list, except for Fox, Echo, and Omega—his supervisors.

Then he shoved the communications device back into his jeans pocket and sat down in a nearby chair, gazing outward at the splendid view. This time he gave it his full attention, and did his utmost to blank out all other thoughts and worries...for the moment.

* * *

"All right, guys, lissen up," Romeo said to the assembled Agents in the Alpha Line Room. It was not a full-up staff meeting, due to the absence of some third of the teams, already on various assignments; everyone who was available, however, had been called in to be briefed. "We got us a situation."

"That's nothing new," Quebec, one of the recent recruits to the department noted, grinning, and everyone chuckled. "'Situations' are what Alpha Line is all about, right?"

"Pretty much, but this one's a little diff'rent, all th' same," Romeo informed them.

"Um," Yankee offered, "I'm, uh, sorry Tare isn't here, guys. Today is our usual day off, an' he's off someplace, an' when I got the summons, I couldn't raise him to get him back here. I swear I'll make sure I brief him when he gets back."

"Where's Alpha One?" Monkey wondered before Romeo could respond, looking around the room. "If we got a sitch, shouldn't they be part of it, too?"

"They're at the core of the sitch," India explained, as Romeo nodded acknowledgement to Yankee. "It's...complicated. And part of it is...classified. Suffice it to say that an old backup plan of Slug's has cropped up."

"Y'all know 'bout that, right?" Romeo asked. "Echo's old enemy? Th' one that...tinkered...with Meg?"

Heads nodded all around the room.

"Well, there's this dude in a holdin' tank down in th' medical section o' Confinement, an' it turns out, th' new facility security sensors can't tell 'im apart from Meg," Romeo continued the explanation. "Which, th' way I figger it, was deliberate on Slug's part, though I ain't got a clue how 'e did it."

"And neither does Medical, as yet," India interjected.

"I'm, uh, well," Romeo continued, "let's just say that, one way an' another, th' dude is after both Echo AND Meg."

88

"Oh shit," Golf muttered. "An' they're not here. You don't mean they hadda clear out, to get away from the guy? 'Cause the security system couldn't stop him?"

"That's exactly what happened," India confirmed. "Like Romeo just said, the new security system can't tell the difference between him and Omega. The problem is, it seems that Slug created some sort of mental link there, that not even Meg can completely block. Us medical types haven't quite figured it yet, but to extrapolate a software analogy to wetware, we think it's some sort of 'back door' equivalent. So if he can determine where she is through that link, he can walk right through our security—which thinks he's Omega—and go wherever they are. And short of putting Omega in Confinement too, or at least under house arrest, we haven't figured out a way to get around that. But if that were to fail too, it would leave her a sitting duck for our perp. Keep in mind, though, he's not really a perp—he's been telepathically programmed, so he's as innocent as Omega was—they're both victims of Slug."

Soft, sympathetic mumbling ran around the room. Yankee scowled and dropped his gaze to the floor.

"Th' Arcturan embassy is on it," Romeo added, eyeing Yankee, "but they say it's too dangerous t' try t' deprogram him while th' programming's fully operative, especially given the telepathic link t' Meg."

"So vhat are ve doing about it?" Kako, Monkey's partner, a transfer from the Moscow Office, asked in his soft voice.

"Several things," Romeo noted. "Medical is bustin' ass tryin' ta figure out how to undo what Slug did to Wright..."

"That what the poor bastard's name is?" Monkey wondered. "Wright?"

"Yes. Mark Wright," India confirmed. "Go ahead, Romeo."

"An' they're also workin' with Software an' Security, tryin' to figure out how to reprogram th' security sensors t' tell him an' Meg apart," Romeo added. "An' the last thing is why we're all here. We're gonna provide eyes-on-target security over Wright, f'r as long as it takes f'r Medical to fix the other two things. An' before anybody asks, no, only Fox actually knows where Alpha One is right now. An' we need ta keep it that way, for their safety."

"Vhat do you vant us to do?" Kako asked.

"We're gonna set up a shift schedule f'r guard duty," Romeo said, picking up his cell phone and triggering an app. "Two Agents on at a time. India an' me 've already worked that out, an' got Fox's approval on it. So I'm sendin' your shift assignments t' your phones..."

* * *

"It's gonna take us around two and a half hours to get there in the 'Vette at standard cruising speed, Meg," Echo told his companion, as she sat quietly in the passenger seat. Below the morphed vehicle, the dark waters of the Long Island Sound slipped by; off to the right lay Long Island itself. Past that, in the distance, the Atlantic Ocean glimmered in the late summer sunshine. Ahead lay the Connecticut shoreline.

"That's fine, Echo," Omega murmured, folding her hands in her lap to hide their light trembling. "As long as we're up here, Mark can't get to me. To us."

"Well, that's true," Echo decided. "It's a pity we don't have a craft with sufficient fuel and consumables storage to just keep us air- or spaceborne for a buncha days. Low Earth orbit didn't seem to bother you OR Wright, so maybe we shoulda just stayed in the *Otello* and orbited a while."

"No, it didn't bother us too bad, at least. But that gets...complicated, for an Agency that's not supposed to exist," Omega pointed out. "The cloaking system gets persnickety if it's left on too long—you know that. Never mind the power it churns through. We don't need the spacecraft seen, from ground OR orbit. And there's a full crew complement in the space station, and a replacement crew inbound."

"True."

"I gather, if you wanted me to grab my swimsuit, there's probably water where we're headed."

"Yup." Echo waved a hand at the distant waters of the Atlantic, past Long Island. "Alla that blue stuff over there."

"Aha. So we're headed for a coastal resort town of some sort?"

"You got it. And the place where we'll be staying has security out our asses, including some special codes that I've personally programmed in— though I may see about generating some, specific to the situation—so it'll be safe, baby. Wright shouldn't be able to get to you there."

"That...sounds good."

"Yeah. It'll be peaceful and safe, and I figured you could use both of those commodities, about now." He directed a pointed glance at her hands folded in her lap, and she knew she hadn't hidden the trembling from him.

"Good observation," she offered.

* * *

"Kinda figured. Things have been pretty tense since Wright showed up, and that's putting it mildly, especially for you. Just try to relax, if you can, as much as you can." Echo checked his instruments to make sure he wasn't encroaching on another aircraft's airspace; he had engaged the passive cloaking when they left Headquarters, and other aircraft generally couldn't see them unless they got a glimpse at an unusual angle, so it behooved him to stay alert. Then he glanced at the dash chronometer. "Oh yeah, that reminds me. We'll need to stop by a grocery store when we get a little closer."

"Why? Won't Supplies have the place stocked already?"

"No, because this isn't an Agency facility we're headed to. It's a private residence. Only it hasn't been used in a while; probably close on two an' a half years, I think," Echo noted, "at least a solid two; and it got emptied out at the end of the last trip. So we'll need to stock up on food an' toilet paper an' shit like that."

"Oh, okay."

"You good with that? It doesn't make you, I dunno, uncomfortable, does it? I mean, having to shop. I can always lock you in the 'Vette, activate the vehicle security system, and go in by myself, if it does."

"No. As long as Mark stays in Headquarters, I'll be okay, I think. A little frazzled, but okay."

"Frazzled? Why? You worried?"

"Well, a little," Omega confessed. "But remember what kind of biochemical pea soup I got, churning around inside, blenderizing everything. It's not...fun."

"Oh..."

* * *

They decloaked, de-morphed, and landed on a small back road outside Ipswich, before heading to the main highway through town. A quick supply run at a big-chain grocery store—where they would be virtually guaranteed anonymity—in an Ipswich suburb along the highway took care of the essentials, and ensured that the pair had everything they would need to get by for a couple of days. This included paper products, nonperishable food, and a few fresher food items; Echo had notions of a New England clam chowder with salad for the evening meal, and the local clams were known for their delectability.

"And if we have to stay longer, we'll just run out and get more stuff," Echo noted. "Or, if you're not comfortable doing that, we'll turn the place into a fortress, and I'll run out and grab stuff, solo."

"That works," Omega decided. "Either way. We'll see when we get to that point."

"Okay. So once we get there, we'll get settled in, I'll throw together the chowder, cover it, and put it on the back burner on the low setting to do its thing, and then we can go for a walk on the beach," Echo told Omega. "The chowder will be ready in time for dinner. And knowing you like I do, I think you'll like it. I learned this recipe from the locals, when I lived here."

"That sounds really good, Ace," Omega said, uncertain, "but will it be safe for us to walk on the beach? We'd be kinda out of pocket if anything happened..."

"The place where we're going has a private beach," Echo explained. "It's not very big, but it's inside the security zone. It's as safe as the house."

"That...sounds great, then."

"Good. Let's hit the check-out and go. We're not far."

Chapter 4

A quick morph-hop took them over to Plum Island without the need to follow the roads onto the island at its north end, when their destination was closer to the south end of what was essentially a barrier island, long and narrow. Echo checked to ensure there were no inadvertent onlookers or local traffic, then landed on the main road and headed north.

As they approached the wildlife refuge, Echo turned onto a drive leading to one of the elevated, forested portions of the island. The Corvette climbed steadily for a few moments, then leveled out at the top of a short bluff overlooking the Atlantic.

"Look, over there," he told Omega, pointing. "That's where we're going."

* * *

"Oh, it's a beach house!" Omega noted, as they drove up to the front door of the well-maintained, gray and white, wood-frame structure. "It looks nice. Ooo, pretty view. No other houses around, either. But I thought most of this whole island was a nature reserve or something. A park. Several parks, if memory serves."

"It is. Except for this one piece of land, here, and maybe a couple others, farther north," Echo noted. "This sorta thing isn't that uncommon; the original owner just refuses to sell, or offers to be the groundskeeper in exchange for continuing to live there, or something like that. Then the owner dies, or has to move, and someone else snaps up the property. In this case, it was me." He shrugged. "It's a little remote, and in winter it can be a bear to get in and out of by normal means, especially if a nor'easter comes through. Hell, if there's a nor'easter hitting, even the 'Vette can have trouble getting here! Down at Sandy Point at the south end, there's a long history of fatal shipwrecks thanks to nor'easters. But with the kind of tech we've got access to, it really isn't too bad; I've weathered a couple here. There's a nice fireplace that can run on gas or wood or whatever fuel is handy, usually enough driftwood that I don't have to cut wood, and the house is heated and powered by a miniature version of the same system that heats and runs Headquarters. So even in the wintertime, with the snow coming down, it's pretty cozy. The force fields keep the wind and waves to a minimum, so I don't even have to worry about that."

"It sounds nice."

"I always thought so. And it makes a great weekend getaway, if I need a day or two to de-stress. Up until I met you and found more fun things to do with the time, I used this place as a day-off getaway. I dunno about you, but sometimes, remote is good."

"Yeah, I agree."

"I thought you would."

"So this is your place? It belongs to you?"

"Yep."

They got out of the 'Vette and headed for the front door, mounting a short series of steps to the porch. A soft beep coming from the front of the house as they approached told them they were recognized. This was immediately followed by quiet clicking, as the door unlocked.

"But...why?" Omega wondered, as Echo opened the door and ushered her inside.

"Why what?"

"Why did you buy it?"

"Remember how I told you about taking that sabbatical, a few years back?"

"Yeah, back when you were trying to work out a relationship with Chase...oh..."

"Yep, you just caught on. This was where I lived."

"So...I'm not the first lady friend you've brought up here," she tried to tease. *Shit dammit to hell and back, twelve times over,* she cursed mentally. *Great; not only do I have to live with Mark trying to get to me, and the tendrils of the telepathic link like a whole damn fleet of moths flitting around the outskirts of my head despite my best efforts to block it, now I gotta live with Chase's ghost in Echo's old love nest.*

* * *

Echo noted the sudden pallor in his partner's complexion, and wondered at it...until she teased him about 'lady friends.'

Whoa, he thought, surprised. *That looks like...she's trying to hide pain. She's not...JEALOUS, is she? Wow. That would be...great. Well, not great. It doesn't feel good to be jealous, especially if you can't do anything about the*

94

situation; damn, am I in a position to know about that, right now. Between Mu and Wright, I wanna put Meg in a locked room with no windows and stand guard, beating those damn rivals off with a stick. Make that a base-ball bat. Not that she knows I consider 'em rivals, I guess.

But it means that she isn't happy about the notion I was intimate with another woman, I think. I hope. Which is probably good for me. Oh shit, Echo broke off the thought, as the ramifications hit. *This was maybe a bad idea, after all. I better make sure she knows nothing like that ever happened.*

* * *

"Well, she visited some—coming over for dinner an' stuff like that. And she did come up and spend the weekend once," Echo began. "And there IS only the one bedroom..."

I knew it I knew it I knew it, Omega thought, desperately trying to hide the pain. *Dammit dammit dammit. It's gonna bring back all the memories for him, and then he'll hurt, the whole time we're here. Never mind what it'll do to me.*

"...But it was summertime...around about the same time of year as we're in now, come to think of it. And so I gave her the bedroom, and I slept in the hammock on the deck, in back. It sleeps pretty good out there, actually. And the sound of the surf is just awesome, really relaxing. It was so comfortable, I started doing that every once in a while, whether anybody else was here or not." He shrugged. "Anyway, the only thing we ever did here was make out on the deck, once or twice. You know, kissing."

"Oh," Omega said, settling down. "That's...good. Don't get me wrong, Ace. I know you miss her; I'm just glad you're not gonna be tripping over painful memories with every step."

"Nah." Echo waved off the notion. "I'm sorry she and her husband are dead, especially given their murders were an attempt to get back at me, but that was over a long time ago, baby. I'm past it all, now."

"Are you sure?"

"I'm sure." He met her gaze, his own calm and serene. "I'm ready to move on. In fact, when you get down to it, I already have." He turned. "Now, lemme show you around the house before we unload the car. Not that there's a whole lot to it, but it's nice and comfortable. We can use the same sleeping arrangements Chase and I used, or I can drag the sofa up against the bedroom door and sleep on it, or even sleep on the floor inside the room, like I did the other night in our quarters. Personally, I'm voting for me taking the floor in the bedroom, to be honest. It's the safest, in my considered opinion..."

* * *

Echo spent a few minutes familiarizing Omega with his beach house, and she found it a more than acceptable getaway hideout. In fact, she liked it a lot.

The property's layout was simple; the house was a single-story, modified Cape Cod cottage overlooking the beach, perched on structural steel 'stilts'—Echo informed her he had had the original wooden supports replaced—to ensure it was slightly elevated above the surrounding land, bluff-top site notwithstanding; no place on the island was higher than twenty to twenty-five feet above sea level, and a strong enough storm could effectively send waves across most of the island. But, as Echo pointed out, he had installed advantages that the other island dwellers didn't have; it would be next to impossible for the beach house to flood any more—though, he noted, if something happened to the land underneath, there could be problems, hence the support columns, which went rather deep into the bedrock—and which were also equipped with emergency antigrav devices, in the event of bluff collapse in a storm. There was also a separate, reinforced two-car garage, intended for the Corvette, and any visitor's vehicle; it was likewise supported, though the supports were hidden.

It had sophisticated galactic-tech, polymer-composite siding made to look like wood siding, shaded a light gray. The trim was of a similar material, but in white. A small porch kept the front door dry in wet weather, and the windows flanking it had dark-gray storm shutters.

The front door opened onto a kind of den or great-room, with the aforementioned fireplace, an entertainment center and wide-screen television, several pieces of comfy, overstuffed furniture—to include a long sofa, two armchairs, a recliner, several occasional tables, and a broad coffee table. A well-furnished, open-concept kitchen with professional-quality appliances and a cozy breakfast nook opened off to the right, with little more than an intervening counter/cabinet combination; past it, on the far side, was a small mud-room/laundry-room combo. The door to the bedroom, with an en suite bath, was on the left. A powder room and coat closet flanked the kitchen, both opening off the great-room.

The back wall had been modified; here, the traditional multi-paned windows that still stood in the front had been replaced with floor-to-ceiling single-paned windows, to maximize light, and the gorgeous view of the Atlantic Ocean...though they, too, had been outfitted with storm shutters, all of which were automated, according to Echo.

A broad deck, running the entire length of the house, stood there, over-looking the beach; the back door opened onto it, and in its center was a staircase leading down, over the dunes, to a landing on the beach proper. A covered hot tub sat on the north end of the deck, with a retractable roof extension installed under the eave; the south end had a spacious hammock suspended from an extended eave, which had then been cut away to provide for sky viewing. In addition, several deck chairs sat here and there, and a multi-shelved occasional table with small cabinets stood in the corner next to the hammock, holding blankets and pillows; its mate sat next to the hot tub and held bath sheets.

The bedroom contained a California queen bed—Echo's height made the additional length something of a necessity, even in his own apartment at Headquarters—a dresser, chest of drawers, two nightstands, and a closet. An extra door onto the very north end of the deck opened from the back wall of the bedroom, which was likewise made up of floor-to-ceiling windows, though privacy/blackout curtains draped these—and, according to Echo, the windows could be adjusted to one-way or even opaqued, just like the bay window in Fox's office. The sumptuous, spa-like master bath contained a shower AND a separate whirlpool tub, as well as a large vanity with twin sinks, and plenty of cabinets for storage.

The floors throughout were pale hardwood, except the kitchen and bath, which were paved in slate-colored ceramic tiles; the den and bedroom sported ceiling fans. Here and there, rustic hand-braided rugs dotted the floors. The whole house was decorated in soft, peaceful, seaside shades of aqua, tan, gray, and seafoam white. A seashell wind chime hung in one corner, and a few framed photos of sea views decorated the walls.

* * *

"Echo, I got a question," Omega said, when the tour had completed. "If it isn't too personal."

"Sure, baby, go ahead," he said, "though I got a pretty good idea what it's gonna be."

"Probably, yeah. This is a beach house in a resort area, so the property wasn't cheap to begin with," Omega pointed out. "And I'm betting you re-did the bathroom to make it more luxe, and added the hot tub on the deck... because you'd hoped to share 'em with somebody, eventually."

"Well, yeah, a little. And here you are," Echo said, offering her a slight smile.

Omega bit her lip, then offered him a weak smile in return, knowing that those features had originally been intended for Chase. *It's just convenient for me to be here, now,* she thought.

"...Plus, you've done a helluva lot of retrofitting to add security and automation and power and junk," she added. "Where's the power, by the way?"

"Under the foundation, down inside the bluff, sitting on the antigrav platform," Echo informed her. "The conduits come up through the support columns. You're wondering how I could afford all this."

"Um, yeah."

"It was actually a lot easier than you'd think, Meg," Echo explained. "Remember how long I've been working for the Agency. I got serious seniority now, and the Agency hasn't skimped on promotions and raises for me, over the years. I get a really handsome salary, which went up when I was named Director Successor, and up again when I became the Alpha Line chief, like yours did when you became the assistant chief. As the rightful owner, I also get a small percentage of the profits from using Meteor Mountain Ranch as a guest ranch—they should be doing something similar for you with your family farm, though offhand I dunno what they're doing with it yet, other than maintaining it. Still, there should be at least a small rental-type fee coming in to you, since it's effectively an Agency safehouse."

"Oh. So THAT was what that monthly deposit was for..." Omega raised her eyebrows in surprise. "I'd been trying to figure that out, all this time, and didn't know who to ask..."

"Yeah. So taken all combined, that's a fairly hefty income I got, right there. Plus, like all field agents, I get hazard pay. Like all Division One agents, I get my medical taken care of; I get my living quarters and furnishings provided; I get a travel stipend when needed; and I get an allowance for part of my food. I get my basic Suits and accessories provided as a kind of uniform, and a discount on the rest of my clothing, because of the restrictions and specifications in wardrobe. You already know I'm a guy of minimalist tastes, so other than my music and entertainment junk, or occasionally going to a big game or maybe a movie with you, or out to eat after work an' shit...what else do I have to spend that rather lavish salary on, baby?"

"Well, you make a good point," Omega decided. "I had noticed my Agency credit union account was kinda starting to make some nice numbers, there."

"Exactly. Now multiply that by as many years as I've been working for 'em. I'm...pretty well off. And I've done a bit of investing, on-and off-world. If the day ever comes that I truly retire and leave the Agency, I sure won't be hurting financially." He waved a hand at the room. "This was a big chunk of change, yes, but it didn't come close to depleting my bank account. And we can make quite a few mods to it, and it still won't poke a big hole in my savings. So. Do you like it?"

"Yeah, I do. This is really nice, Echo," Omega averred. "I like it a lot. I can see why you'd like using this for a weekend getaway. Did you do the decorating, or did Chase?"

"Neither. Most of the furnishings came with the place when I bought it—and that included most of the bathroom setup, by the way; that was one of the selling points, as far as I was concerned. I did add the hot tub on the deck, though. It's all minimalist enough that I kinda liked it. And the color scheme sorta blends the indoors and the outdoors."

"Good point. I'm loving the wind chime, and the shoreline photographs. I'm gonna have to watch myself that I don't walk into a wall, thinking it's a window or door! Never mind forgetting the floor-to-ceiling windows ARE windows."

"Heh. You'll be fine. If I started doing it again—coming here on our days off—would you like to join me?" he asked, offering her a hesitant smile. "I guess we'd need to do some modifications to allow for additional sleeping space on a regular basis—maybe put in a space warp, to add another bedroom without construction being too obvious from the outside, though that means what neighbors we've got will probably think we're living together, maybe even married, so whenever we went out, we'd have to play to that—but I think we could have fun here. It would get you out of the city more often. And it would give us some real down time."

"I think I'd like that a whole lot," she told him, returning his smile with a shy one of her own.

"Consider it done, then," he decided, smile growing wider. "As soon as the current situation resolves itself, we'll look at making some mods to this place, and start coming up here on our days off. Let's go unload the car."

* * *

They brought in the bags of groceries together, and Omega commenced putting away the perishable stuff, while Echo brought in their new travel kits...which, of course, were equipped with warp modules, for when they headed out on extended missions.

"Meg? I'm putting both kits in the bedroom," he called. "We'll have to share the bathroom anyway. We can go in there together and unpack later, and work out how to share the storage space."

"That's fine," she responded. "We'll work out the sleeping arrangements, too. I'm not worried."

"Hey, listen," Echo said, coming into the kitchen and helping her put away the non-perishable supplies—paper towels, canned and dried food-stuffs, and the like. "I know you said you didn't have a whole lotta resort-type clothes..."

"Yeah, I got next to no shorts any more," Omega verified, getting out the utensils Echo would need to make his clam chowder. "I just haven't needed 'em, except to work out—only those are too ratty now for anything but the gym! And the weather is pretty hot at the moment, even for New England. I'll have to requisition some, I suppose, especially if we start coming here regularly. For now, I could roll up my jeans, I guess..."

"Well, I kept a separate wardrobe up here," he told her. "And that in-cluded probably a dozen pairs of shorts, plus a buncha t-shirts. Now, be-cause I was on sabbatical, they're not all black and white," he warned. "I needed to blend in with the resort crowd. There's some blue denim and navy, khaki, even a red pair, I think. I know I've got a bigger frame than you do, but some of those shorts had drawstrings." He cocked his head to one side, thinking. "There were a couple pairs of nicer ones that I wore with a belt, too. You're welcome to see if you can cinch any of 'em up tight enough to keep 'em on you."

"Oh! I bet I can make a pair of the drawstring shorts work," Omega decided. "It might look a little sloppy on me, though."

* * *

"Meh. Leave your shirt out and pull it down over the waist, if it bothers you." He shrugged, nonchalant. "I doubt anybody but me is gonna see, anyhow...unless we go back to the grocery store or something. And I don't care if it's more casual, that way; you'll look fine to me." He paused, then added, "Actually, come to think on it, I've never seen you look bad in anything."

"Okay." Omega turned slightly pink, and offered him a shy grin; he knew she had caught and appreciated the compliment. "I'll go check it out in a few."

"All right. They should be in the middle right drawer of the dresser." Echo turned his attention to preparing the clam chowder that would comprise their dinner. Abruptly he started banging through cabinets, searching. "Stock pot, stock pot...where the hell did I put the damn stock pot, last time I was here? As big a thing as it is, it oughta be hard to lose! Oh, there it is." He dragged the large cookpot from the under-counter cabinet with a clatter. "Uh, where was I...? Shorts—yeah. Middle right drawer, but I got other clothes that could work for you, too; go ahead and fish around and see what you can find of my stuff to enlarge on your own wardrobe—I don't mind at all. And go ahead and change into whatever you can find that works, otherwise you're gonna get too hot, awful fast—the house is designed for cooling by the trade winds in summer."

"No air conditioning?" Omega wondered.

"Nah. I kept meaning to install one, but never had the need. It stays pretty nice, up here. We're probably, lessee...thirty, thirty-five feet above the actual shoreline, so there's always a good breeze, onshore or off. Open a few windows, an' it's good."

"Oh, okay."

"So go ahead and find something that fits, and change clothes. Once you do that, what say we slap together some sandwiches for lunch, then go for a walk on the beach?"

"Sounds good."

"You found your old surf shoes, right? The beach here is somewhere between rocky and sandy, so you probably don't wanna go barefoot. Never mind the occasional piece of shipwreck that washes up."

"Oh, okay, I get it. An' yeah, I brought 'em."

* * *

101

Omega tried on Echo's shorts until she found three pairs that would work, and donned one of them, a black pair, with one of her own t-shirts untucked over the drawstring waist. Then she slipped on a pair of flip-flops and carried the surf shoes to the back door onto the deck; that way, she concluded, she could don them on her way out, and leave them upon return, thereby avoiding tracking sand into the house. She found Echo's already there, and placed the shoes next to his with a faint smile.

"Hey, Meg?" he called from the kitchen, where he was sorting through the last of their groceries and putting things away, all while throwing together the makings of his clam chowder on the back burner of the stove.

"Yeah, Echo?"

"I was wondering—given we're just kinda here, and it IS a beach, so tides and stuff, and the exterior isn't lit at all unless the moon is up...well, the deck has some lighting, but I rarely ever used it...maybe we want to convert to 24-hour operations? Keep regular Earth hours?"

"We can do that, I guess," Omega decided. "It makes a certain sense, all in all. If there's no outside lighting, I doubt I'm gonna feel comfortable going outside and wandering around at night, and there's only so much we can do INside..."

"Exactly. Okay, I vote we do that."

"So do I."

"Unanimous vote. Motion carries." Echo grinned, put the lid on the stock pot, and adjusted the heat of the burner. "We keep 24-hour days instead of 48, while we're here. All right, the chowder prep is all done. Now we just gotta let it cook. Let's go unpack and work out who's where with what."

"Okay. Then we do lunch?"

"Yup, then we do lunch."

* * *

After they unpacked, they slapped together sandwiches and ate lunch. Then Echo checked in at Headquarters, to verify that all was well.

"No, Wright is still in his detention cell, and I see nothing else in the activity reports that you or Omega would need to be concerned about," Fox told him. "You two try to relax, at least as best you're able, and we'll stay on top of things here. I had Alpha Two set up a shift schedule for all the Alpha Line Agents that aren't currently already assigned to missions, and as a group, your department is going to stand guard over Wright. I'll fill in with agents from Security as needed. We'll make sure he stays put."

"Okay. Thanks, Fox. In that case, I think I'm gonna continue my process of familiarizing Meg with this place, and walk the property lines with her, so she knows where they are. But I wanted to make sure we weren't gonna encounter any nasty surprises along the perimeter, first."

"Understood. Ah, zun?"

"Yeah, Fox?"

"You don't have your phone in speaker mode, do you?"

"No..."

"All right. How did she take it?"

"Huh?"

"Did you tell her how and why you came to own that house? Be careful how you phrase your answer; she doesn't need to know I asked about that. She could take offense...at both of us. But I'm only wanting to make sure all goes well."

"Oh, that. I getcha. Lemme see, here. Yeah, I did, and...well, initially I'd swear that almost went south on me. But then I filled in a few pertinent details in the big picture—I mean, nothing like, like THAT, ever happened here—and everything was, um, okay."

"Do you think she might have been jealous?"

"It looked like it to me. I'd sure like to think so."

"Ooo. Az iz a shtik fun gut nayes."

"A piece of good news? Yeah, I think it was."

"Excellent. This is a bad state of affairs overall for the two of you, I know, especially for her. But if you handle this just so, zun, and we can manage to work things out with Wright, this gants pilke fun vax could come out with things exactly where you want them, alter khaver."

"I hear you, Fox, and I hope so," Echo decided. "But frankly, I'm not gonna worry about that right now. I'm more concerned about the former part than the latter part."

"Understood. And that is as it should be. Anything else?"

"No, and I know you need to get back to it."

"Well, I do."

"Okay. Thanks, Fox. Echo out."

"You're very welcome, old friend. Fox out."

* * *

Back at Headquarters, Fox sat looking at his cell phone, worried for his old friend and his newer friend. *Because this is a damn bad situation,* he realized, *and given Omega's general mindset, it...*

Suddenly he broke off the thought, as another consideration hit him with the force of a sledgehammer.

"No," Fox murmured, eyes widening, as the ramifications hit home. "Surely not. That...but it would make sense. Oh, by the Name..." The Director bit one lip and stared at the office wall in deep thought for long moments. "Oh, but it surely could be. Gronk. I need to think about this a bit...

* * *

"C'mon, Meg, the coast is clear," Echo told her. "Let's slap on some sunscreen, then head out. But the first thing I want to do is to show you the property lines and the extent of the force field, so you'll have a good feel for the place, and better situational awareness. Oh, and in the off chance we see anybody, go into 'girlfriend' mode, all right? That's probably our easiest cover, as usual."

"That works," Omega agreed, swapping her flip-flops for her surf shoes. "And I already put on sunscreen."

"Good," Echo said, following her lead. "So have I. Okay, let's go."

* * *

They headed out the front door first, and explored the area up on top of the cliff face, which was some of the highest land on the island, before heading for the beach proper.

Their walk was relatively uneventful. Echo made sure Omega knew where his property ended in all directions, as well as the general lay of the land, and where he had cached supplies and hidden weapons.

"But I don't really think we'll need any of that," he told her, as they made their way down the rock steps that had been carved into the bluff on the southern end of the property, stepping onto the beach proper at last. "Fox and Alpha Line are all over the situation back at Headquarters, and Wright is locked down, so you an' me, we'll just hang tight here, give you a chance to unwind after...everything, and plan how we're gonna upgrade the beach house for Alpha One." He smiled, and she returned it.

"That sounds good, Ace," she murmured. "I'm looking forward to it." Then she subtly pointed to the south. "There comes a couple, headed this way, up the beach."

"Oh, right. Glad you spotted 'em," Echo replied, pulling out a small remote and checking its setting. "Great. It's already on the 'soft' setting..."

"What is?"

"The force field," Echo explained, steering her to the left. "Let's head north, and walk kinda quick, but casual. We need to put some distance between us and the south property line. We don't really want to be close enough to call when they reach the field."

"But it'll hurt 'em!"

"No, it won't. That's why I have—and tend to maintain—the field here on a special 'soft' setting. That's the 'keep out' sign, rather than the 'terminate with extreme prejudice' setting. They'll...bounce, kinda. Give me your hand."

"Huh?" Omega responded, surprised, as Echo took her hand and held it.

"We're in sight, so we go into 'significant other' mode, remember? Oh, wait. Are you not okay with that, given everything else that's going on?"

"No, I...I think I'm okay with it, for now, anyhow. Things are quiet, and kind of, of distant, so I'm not so stressed. I mean, I can sorta feel Mark banging around on the periphery, I guess you could say," Omega said, and tapped her temple with her other hand. Echo nodded his understanding, and she continued. "But it's not too bad right now, so...yeah. I can deal."

"Good. Pretend you didn't see 'em, and let's head north, away from our would-be visitors. I don't want ANYONE getting into our perimeter right now. I mean, I'd admit Fox if he showed up, and Alpha Two. Ma, if she were on this end of the country. But not much of anybody else."

"Zebra?"

"Yeah, we could let in Zebra. So...family. You know."

"Right. That sounds...good. Maybe one of these days we can have a family beach party up here. You know, like a barbecue or clambake or something. What do you think?"

"Ooo. I like the idea..."

They strolled north along the rocky beach, choosing the sandy sections and walking through the edge of the surf, chatting occasionally and pretending not to hear the faint "Halloo!" calls in the distance behind them. After a few minutes, there was a low-pitched, resonating *POOMP!* from the same direction. A startled exclamation drifted to them on the wind, followed by sounds of increasing puzzlement and confusion, then a string of curses in a decided male voice was followed by female shushing sounds. Alpha One cut amused glances at each other, and Omega bit her lip to prevent inappropriate laughter.

"Told ya," Echo muttered, and Omega couldn't stifle the snort in response. "No, don't you dare laugh. They'll be close enough to hear, given the wind is so gusty it can't make up its mind."

"I won't," Omega mumbled, putting her free hand over her mouth and coughing to cover the quiet snorts and snickers.

"Give it a few minutes," Echo suggested. "Once they give up and turn around and head back, we can unlax a little."

Sure enough, about five minutes later, the sounds of scuffling and repeated *POOMP*s stopped, then grumbling voices receded into the distance. Omega allowed herself a chuckle then, and even Echo snorted his amusement.

Alpha One kept walking, hand in hand, headed north, up the beach.

* * *

Abruptly Omega pulled away with an excited cry, running over to a cleft in the rocks and stooping down. Echo meandered along behind.

"What is it, baby?" he wondered. "Did you find something?"

"Look!" Omega said, turning around and extending her hand. A large, whorled spiral shell, over eight inches long, lay in it.

"Wow!" Echo exclaimed. "That's a gorgeous big ol' knobbed whelk shell, Meg! And it's left-handed!"

"Those are sorta uncommon in this species, right?" Omega asked.

"Yeah, it is. That'll make a nice little trophy paperweight for your desk in the Alpha Line Room! Here; give it to me and I'll stash it in my pocket."

"Don't tell me you actually put a warp pocket in those shorts." Omega gave him a cock-eyed stare as she handed over the large shell.

"Of course I did," Echo said, as the huge shell vanished into his pocket without a trace. "I thought you wanted to beachcomb. Didn't you?"

"Well, yeah, I did."

"And you don't wanna lose this, do you?"

"No, I just never once thought about trying to fit a warp pocket in a pair of shorts!"

They laughed.

"Let's look around some more," Echo decided, "and see what else we can find. This beach usually makes for some good shell hunting, and it's close to low tide."

The pair scavenged the area around the rocky outcroppings, and Echo found the next discovery.

"Hey, Meg, have you ever heard of moon shells?" he wondered, bent over a large rock outcropping.

"No, but I like the name," she said, glancing at him with a grin. "Why?"

"Because I found a little clutch of the shells here. Come look."

Omega trotted over to his side. He held out his palm, on which rested three of the shells, around four or five inches in diameter.

"Ooo. Those are pretty," she declared.

"These are medium-sized; some of the species can get almost as large as that whelk shell you found."

"This one's kinda rosy-pink," Omega decided, nudging one of the shells with a fingertip. "And I like that one, with the stripes. Oh, look down here!" She bent and picked up another, which had a blue-gray tone. "My grandmother would be jealous."

"Why?"

"When I was little, I used to go out with her, early in the morning, and go beachcombing for shells, whenever my family went down to the Gulf of Mexico," Omega told him. "We both loved finding pretty shells. But I don't think she and I ever did as well as you and I have done in the last five minutes."

Echo grinned.

"You having some fun, baby?"

"Yeah, I am, Ace." Omega offered him a grateful smile. "I needed it, too. Let's see what else we can find. I'm thinking a nice cut-glass bowl full of shells on that end table by the couch in the beach house would be pretty, and fit right in with the decor."

"You know what? I think you're right. But your left-handed whelk comes back to Headquarters with us. That thing is seriously worth showing off. I hunted for a left-hander every time I came up here, but I never could find one. They're rare."

"No, they're not, really. I used to find 'em all the time with Grandmomma, beachcombing down on the Gulf o' Mexico."

"Different species, baby. Those are...lessee...lightning whelks. State shell o' Texas. They naturally grow sinistral; knobbed whelks don't. A left-handed KNOBBED whelk is awfully rare."

"OooOOOooo."

"Exactly."

They grinned.

* * *

Yankee prepared to go on duty for guarding Mark Wright, but there was still no sign of Tare, and he found this concerning in the extreme. He popped off another text message to his partner, anxiety rising; to his knowledge, Tare had not been back to his quarters in a couple of days.

Not that I really know for sure, Yankee realized. *It isn't like we keep the back door open all the time...like SOME people I could name. But you never know about Tare. I got a birthday coming up in a few weeks, and he's been wanting us to take a vacay, so it wouldn't surprise me to discover he's off working that up, probably with Alpha One's blessing—I may not like her, but it's something Omega would do. And Echo...he's as tough as his reputation makes him, but I think having Omega for a partner has...I dunno, opened him up a little. He's not quite as inscrutable as he used to be, maybe. Not that that's saying much! He's still pretty damn close-mouthed about everything except missions. Hell, monitoring his transponder implant when he infiltrated that assassin team a couple months ago, I heard him talk more in a few days than I think I've ever heard him speak, the whole time I've been in Alpha Line!*

Anyway, Tare is still not answering. I hope nothing's wrong with his phone. I guess I'll meet up with him as soon as we go on duty for this guard thing, he decided. *I'll just get ready and go, and see him there. We can check his phone then.*

* * *

In the Pacific Northwest, Agent Tare, finally starting to relax, hiked among the trees and mountains of the Olympic peninsula, at peace and content...

...For the moment.

His cell phone never showed any incoming communiques.

* * *

Alpha One stayed on the beach until it was dinnertime; a side effort of collecting driftwood for the fireplace resulted in a goodly-sized pile of wood near the stairs up to the deck, several sticks of which Echo carried up to the deck and deposited next to the back door. Arriving back inside the beach house, they swapped surf shoes for flip-flops; Omega spread paper toweling on the coffee table and they unloaded their haul of seashells, then Echo went out on the deck to shake the sand out of his pockets and clean out the warp pocket while Omega headed for the kitchen.

By the time Echo was relatively sand-free, his partner had rinsed the shells and laid them to one side to dry; a spare glass salad bowl sat nearby, awaiting the dry, clean shells. In addition, a lovely cranberry-walnut salad, with mixed greens and a home-made cranberry vinaigrette dressing, had been tossed and plated. Echo checked the chowder and pronounced it ready, then ladled out heaping bowls next to the plates of salad.

"And I grabbed a whole, deep-dish apple pie from the store deli, for dessert," he noted. "We can nuke it to warm it up a little, and—did we remember the vanilla bean ice cream?"

"We did," Omega averred with a smile. "I got it myself, when I saw you looking at the pies."

"This looks like a great dinner, baby," Echo decided, as they sat down at the table. "Not too heavy in the heat, but not so light that it won't be filling."

"An' delicious as homemade sin, as mah grandmother used to say!" Omega grinned.

"Ah reckon!" Echo drawled, and they both laughed.

* * *

"So how is guard duty going, children?" Fox wondered, as Alpha Two sat in his office.

"Pretty well so far, Fox," Romeo decided. "We got a full two-guard shift system set up, with whatever Alpha Line Agents aren't already on assignment, an' it's up an' running. Security is really helping us fill in any gaps, too; make sure t' thank 'em for us, wouldja?"

"Of course, zun."

"We do have a bit of a concern, though," India admitted.

"Oh? What would that be?"

"Alpha Seven—Yankee an' Tare," Romeo noted.

109

ing.Osborn*

"Oh. Damnation. Yes, I'm afraid I hadn't thought about that," Fox realized. "Can you send Yankee to me before he goes on duty?"

"Too late, I'm afraid," India noted, glancing at her wrist chronometer. "He went on shift ten minutes ago. We didn't realize it until we looked closer at the modifications Lima made to the shift schedule, based on what he knew of the most current duty roster. Lima plugged the hole with a guard out of Security, but we only saw it a few minutes ago ourselves, and we're both worried how Yankee is going to take it."

"Yeah, we kinda gathered that Tare didn't tell him b'fore 'e left," Romeo added. "I'm not even sure Yankee knows he's gone. Just that 'e hasn't been showin' up."

"Mm. That is a difficulty," Fox decided. "And I did promise Tare I'd handle it. Unfortunately, in all of this drek with Wright, it slipped my mind. Well, perhaps I can manage a bit of retro-active patching, then. Send him to me as soon as he gets off duty, and I'll see if I can't explain matters to him."

"What exactly happened, there?" Romeo wondered. "They splittin' up? Is Tare retiring?"

"No; the matter is a private personnel matter, and Echo and Omega both knew about it and approved the various requests," Fox explained, "but since you're heading up Alpha Line for the moment, I suppose you're due a bit of explanation..."

* * *

"Hey, Romeo," Yankee said, as he arrived at the area outside Wright's confinement cell that had been designated as the guard station, "I can't find Tare anywh..."

He broke off, staring at the strange woman standing there, in full Agency body armor, where he had expected to find the temporary department leader, if not his partner.

"Who the hell are you?" he asked, blunt. "Where's Alpha Two? Where's TARE?!"

"Hi, there," the woman said with a friendly smile, holding out a hand. "My code name's Oscar. I'm out of Security. You're Yankee, from Alpha Line, right? You and I will be on guard duty together for this shift."

"Where's my partner?!" Yankee ignored the proffered hand.

"I'm not sure," Oscar said, uncertain, the smile disappearing as she dropped her hand. "Nobody told me much, just that I needed to fill in for an

110

Alpha Line Agent who was on extended medical leave."

"Tare's SICK?!" Yankee exclaimed, horrified. "Extended medical? Did they say why? Is it cancer, or something bad? He's not...not dying, is he?"

"No, my supervisors didn't say anything else, just the extended leave thing," Oscar murmured. "I'm...I'm so sorry, Yankee. I...thought you knew already."

"No," Yankee replied, worried and upset. "Nobody told me...anything. Not even Tare, himself."

* * *

"Oh, man," Romeo muttered. "That ain't good."

"No, not especially," Fox agreed. "But if Yankee insists on an attitude problem where Omega is concerned, that is for them to resolve, as long as it does NOT interfere with their work. It obviously doesn't interfere with Omega's work, at least not negatively, though I suspect it may be affecting her in a more personal fashion, and Echo corroborates that suspicion. I have not seen signs of it interfering with Yankee's work so far, though Echo and I both have given him a few lectures on the matter; he's come very close to insubordination on several occasions, most notably the situation in Dallas earlier this year. Had Omega chosen to press a complaint against him last Christmas, I might have been able to do more. But whenever Echo or I ask her if she wants anything done...about ANY of it...she always turns us down."

"She thinks he has a right to his opinion," India murmured. "I've talked with her about it once or twice. To be honest, though, I think part of it is simply that, somewhere inside, there's a part of her that thinks his opinion might not be wrong."

Fox and Romeo both sighed.

* * *

"Hey, guys, I've had an idea," Zebra said, coming into the consultation room where Zarnix and Bet sat, discussing Mark Wright's case.

"Then let us hear it, by all means," Zarnix declared.

"I'm thinking our security sensor conundrum may be as simple as inserting a homing chip implant into Wright," Zebra declared. "What do you think?"

"Wow," Bet said, eyes going wide.

"What she said," Zarnix agreed. "It is simple, elegant, and should have

111

been the first thing any of us thought of."

"Which makes me think it won't work," Zebra grumbled immediately. "But if it does, it sure solves the problem of telling 'em apart in the security computers."

"It sure does," Bet agreed.

"Let me go get a selection of homing beacon and transponder chips, and we will go to the holding cell and see what we can do," Zarnix decided.

* * *

"Um, hey, Zarnix," Yankee said, approaching the chief of Medical, as the physicians came to see Wright in the containment cell. "Uh, can I, maybe, talk to you for a few minutes?"

"Perhaps in a bit, Yankee," Zarnix replied, preoccupied with the armful of equipment he carried. "We are somewhat engrossed in a possible solution to our quixotic identification problem."

"Um, okay," Yankee agreed. "Yeah, I understand that. In a little while, then."

"Hey, Yankee," Zebra called, trundling a cart in front of her, "can you guys open the force fields so we can get in with our equipment cart?"

"Sure. I'll get that; Oscar, you stand guard, in case he tries to make a run for it."

"I'm there," Oscar said, hefting her weapon, as Yankee moved to the control panel in the wall.

* * *

"Where you guys wanna put the thing?" Zebra wondered, pushing the instrument cart to the corner of the medical containment cell. Outside, Oscar and Yankee re-established the fields and stood guard; all of the physicians were too absorbed with trying to tag Wright to notice the distraught expression Yankee wore.

"I think in his shoulder should do fine, don't you?" Zarnix considered.

"That sounds pretty good to me," Bet noted. "You want it near the body core, but not too awfully near the head, because it could, I dunno, maybe do something wonky when we start getting the Deltiri to deprogram him."

"Which we cannot do until the connection to Omega can be shut down," Zarnix added. "So yes, let us try the right shoulder."

"Okay," Zebra said, game. "You guys grab him and strip the shirt off him. Fox said we should ask the guards for help if he fights us."

"I don't think he will," Bet noted, as the unexpectedly powerful Zarnix—Chesharilzi were far stronger than their appearance indicated—gripped Wright's upper arms in a secure hold, and she began unbuttoning his shirt. "I've come in here and taken blood and tissue samples and all kinds of things like that, and he never resisted. The only time he seems to react is either when Omega is in close proximity, or when there's some sort of telepathic interaction going on between them." She grimaced. "I'd have put him in a medical jumpsuit by now, but since he doesn't react to anything I say or do, I can't order him, and it's a bit much for one person to do on her own."

"We'll take care of that shortly," Zarnix told her, as he helped her ease off Wright's shirt. "All right, Zebra, let us do this thing and solve one of our problems."

A gloved and scrubbed Zebra carefully cleaned the deltoid area of Wright's shoulder, then used a traditional Earth radio-frequency identification, or RFID, chip about the size of a grain of rice, with its fat needle syringe, to 'tag' Wright: She pinched up a fold of skin, injected the chip into the fold, then used a piece of gauze to wipe away the small drop of blood that welled up from the injection. She wiped a swab soaked in Rejuvic over the tiny wound, and seconds later, it was sealed.

"Excellent," Zarnix noted.

"Amen," Bet murmured. She waved a medscanner at the shoulder. "I'm reading the chip."

"Great!" Zebra said, beaming.

"...Wait," Bet continued, a confused expression appearing on her face. "Something's...wrong."

"Let me see," Zarnix said, putting one hand on the device and looking over her shoulder.

Meanwhile, as Zebra watched, the skin around the chip turned pink, then red. Wright, who had been stationary, simply standing in the middle of the room, began to shift his shoulders as if in discomfort, then to moan softly. The flesh around the implant swelled until a large red lump or nodule, nearly an inch high, had raised itself. The skin began to roughen, then to dry, peeling up.

"Uh-oh," Zebra murmured, continuing to observe. "Guys, come here and look at this."

Just as the other two medics reached her side, the flesh of Wright's shoulder split open. He gave a cry of pain as blood and white pus oozed from the wound...

...And carried the chip implant with it.

* * *

"Uhn," Omega grunted, laying down her spoon and slapping at her right shoulder. "Ow! That hurt!"

"What? What's the matter, baby?" Echo wondered, looking up from his bowl of chowder.

"I dunno. Felt like a damn big horsefly bit me," Omega noted, pulling up her short sleeve to check her shoulder. "But I never saw anything flying around, and there's nothing there now."

"Huh," Echo muttered, puzzled. "Maybe you carried something in with you from our walk."

"Maybe. But I didn't see anything near big enough for what that felt like."

"Well, keep an eye on it. If you get some sort of a welt, we'll know something bit you, and I'll hit it with some Rejuvic for you."

"Okay."

* * *

"Well...SHIT," Zebra said, with feeling. She stared at the oozing split in Wright's flesh in dismay.

"What she said," Bet decided.

"Indeed," Zarnix agreed.

"Now what?" Bet wondered, as Zebra cleaned the pus from the wound, removed and discarded the chip, then went to the sink, discarded her gloves, scrubbed up, and donned fresh, sterile gloves. Meanwhile, Zarnix got a new, sterile swab, dipped it in Rejuvic, and applied it to Wright's shoulder, tsking softly as he went.

"He may simply be allergic, though given that extreme level of response, I doubt it," Zarnix decided. "That looked like something the gastropoid may have engineered to prevent us doing precisely what we are trying to do."

"That's what I was thinking," Zebra agreed.

"That does not give us the excuse to be lazy instead of thorough," Zarnix decided. "We have at least three or four other options, made of far more

advanced materials. It may be that one of them will remain undetected...
or at least, unmolested...by Wright's system. However, given the amount
of pain it caused him, I think we shall use a local anesthetic before we try
again."

"I think that's an excellent notion," Zebra agreed. "If I'd known it was
gonna cause that big a reaction, I'd have done it to begin with. And maybe, just maybe, by using a local, it'll keep his body from recognizing that
there's even anything in there."

"Which gives me another idea," Zarnix said, raising an eyebrow. "If
we inject a long-term local anesthesia pellet—such as we sometimes use
for certain wounds that are slow to heal—along with the transmitter chip, it
may keep his body from recognizing it at all."

"Ooo," Zebra said, impressed. "That's a great idea."

"Lemme know how I can help, guys," Bet said.

"By doing just what you did, Bet," Zarnix told her. "You gave us ad-
vance notice that some sort of unusual reaction was in process of occurring.
Keep the medscanner going while we try this, and let us see what we can
get. If nothing else, perhaps the data will help us ascertain what has been
done to him, and what may be done about it."

"I figure we'll have plenty of data to work from, if we just throw him
in a regen pod, when this is all over," Zebra noted.

"Indeed."

* * *

Later that evening after a lengthy gab session with Echo, Omega sat,
alone in the bedroom on the edge of the bed, as the room grew darker with
impending sunset. The room felt colder, somehow, than it had earlier, when
Echo had been there, helping her get settled in.

Foreboding, she decided. *The room feels foreboding. Like it's waiting
for someone...and that someone isn't me OR Echo. And since the room is in-
sensate and doesn't care, it's ME that has the foreboding.* She sighed. *This
is...this is not good. I feel...almost, almost broken in some way. It's getting
to be too much for me to deal with, and I don't know what to do any more.*

Her instinct was to turn to Echo for help and encouragement. *The problem is,* she considered, *that I'm already having enough trouble reining in
my emotions where he's concerned, given this damn hormonal hurricane
I've got going on. And if I goof, and let on how I really feel, I dunno WHAT*

115

he'll do. But damn, she thought, wrapping her arms around herself and rubbing her hands up and down her upper arms, *I could sure use a reassuring hug right now. I know it's stupid, and probably thirteen kinds of juvenile, but I can't help it.*

She stared at the walls around her. *No. I can't stay in here alone. I...I just can't deal. Not any more. Not without some help. I gotta risk it, I think, or go crazy.*

Omega stood and headed for the door. *Pheromones and hormones or not,* she decided, *I gotta find Echo.*

* * *

Echo stretched out in the hammock on the back deck, overlooking the beach, as the last of the light slowly faded from the sky and the eastern horizon darkened. He sighed in contentment and settled into the canvas, just watching the surf, as seagulls called and zoomed about; this had been the kind of day he had originally envisioned for the house, though not with the woman he'd anticipated being there.

But I'm with the right one, he thought, confident. *I'm crazy about Meg, and that's not ever gonna go away. I was trying to settle for Chase, even if I didn't realize it at the time. I was lonely after losing X-ray, and I wanted somebody all to myself, someone I could come home to...and Chase was convenient. I loved her, but I know now, not like I should have, for it to have worked. Then Meg came along, and everything changed. I've got my ultimate partner, in every sense of the word, and she's all I could ever wish for. The only times I'm ever lonely now are when she's not beside me, and I know those times are only temporary. And I DO come home to her, even if we're not lovers yet. And it's great.*

Now, if we can get Meg through this nasty little sitch, then develop a relationship of our own, I can even manage to fulfill the entire dream I had for this place. A romantic little getaway spot for me and my mate. Kind of like what Fox and Zebra started working on, back in June.

Just then, Omega came out the back door and onto the deck. She threw him a slight smile—though he thought something looked odd about it, almost tight—and moved to the railing, gazing out, over the ocean surf.

"This is so pretty," she declared. "I...always liked the beach. Any beach. There's something about the sights and sounds and smells of the surf that..." She broke off, apparently looking for words.

"Yeah, I know what you mean," Echo agreed, able to finish her thought for her, even though he couldn't put it into words either. "There's just something about it. The appeal is almost primal, somehow."

"Yeah. Exactly."

"Based on your comments this afternoon, I gather that your family used to vacation at the beach?"

"Sometimes," Omega confirmed. "Given that it was only about an afternoon's drive away, at the other end of the state, we'd go down to someplace along the Gulf of Mexico at least once a year—even if it was just for a long weekend. That's when Grandmomma and I would beachcomb for shells. We'd vacation other places, too," she added. "But I think we vacationed there the most." She paused. "Where did your family usually go on vacation?"

"Eh," Echo murmured, thinking. "We didn't actually go on vacay that much, really. When you have a spread as big as Meteor Mountain Ranch is, it can get kinda difficult to get away. There's always something that needs doing, never mind taking care of the cattle. Especially since it's basically a legacy ranch, and it's been around a good long while."

"Oh. Yeah, I guess so. We never had more than around a dozen or so horses on our farm at any given time, and we could usually get one o' the neighbors or somebody to come by and drop feed for us an' junk. I guess, with some—what, hundreds? thousands?—of head of cattle, it's more complicated."

"Yeah. Oh, and the Ranch currently has the biggest head count for cattle it's ever had, to my knowledge; it's averaging right around a thousand head, give or take. But when I was a boy, we might run five hundred, seven-hundred-fifty head, depending on weather an' junk. A ranch like that, you could have your good years and your bad years. If we had a couple good years, an' had a capable set of ranch hands hired on, with a reliable boss to run the operation, Dad could usually set aside enough time and money for us to go do something. That generally happened, oh, maybe every three or four years, though we were struggling there after Dad died, Ma and me. Anyway, about half the time, it was a matter of 'got the cash, don't got the time,' you know? It was someplace different every time we went, though. I don't remember ever going to a beach and just spending time there."

"Oh? Well, west Texas; yeah, you'd be a ways away from any really

117

big body of water, I guess," she noted.

"Exactly. We visited Ma's family on the rez a few times. I got to know my way around the Four Corners area pretty well. Headed north into Colorado for some skiing. That sorta thing."

"Sounds like fun."

"It was."

As they talked, Omega took a couple of steps to the side, until she reached the stairs going down to the beach, then eased into a sitting position on the top step. She folded her arms, resting her forearms on her knees and leaning forward. But Echo noted over successive moments how that posture contracted, until, within minutes, she was huddled in a tight little ball. He pushed up on one elbow, watching her.

"Baby?" he began, worried.

"Echo, can I ask you a, a favor?" she said at the same time.

"Of course you can, Meg. Something's wrong; I can see that. You're all crumpled up in a ball. What do you need? What's up?"

"I..." she began, then rose and turned toward him. "I...need some help. I-I'm sorry; I don't mean to be a lotta trouble, I just..."

Echo looked her up and down, studying her posture as well as her troubled countenance. Her arms were still wrapped tightly around herself; her stance was uncharacteristically unsure, somewhat hunched toward him. Her knees were slightly bent, almost as if she were ready to spin and run. *Fight or flight,* the words flittered through his mind. *With nothing to fight, and nowhere to run. And Tt'l'k already pushed her past her limits, by revealing her whole situation—not to mention, condition—to the rest of us, without her consent.* Suddenly he understood.

"Aw, damn," he murmured, sitting up fully. "C'mere, baby. I get it. You need help handling it. You've dealt with this shit for a long time now, all by yourself, showing consideration for the rest of us—especially me, most of all, I think—by not laying that burden on anybody else. Only it's all kinda too much now, isn't it?"

"Yeah, 'cause Mark has brought it all back, and as long as he's...connected, I can't shove it back in the box!" She tapped her temple. "He keeps pulling it out again, see. And I...well, now you know what happened, at least most of it, and I..." Omega tried. "I just...I mean, I need to...it would be nice if..."

118

"C'mere," Echo reiterated, waving her over, and Omega moved to stand beside the hammock. "Climb up in here with me, and kick off your sandals. Let's relax together. I'll help, I swear." He aided her as she clambered into the hammock beside him, and settled down next to him. Then, moving slowly so as not to upset or spook her, he wrapped his arms around her and eased them both into a reclined position. "There. Listen, you were saying a while back that you were having, uh, trouble with, um, 'personal space,' so if this is..."

"No," she sighed, laying one hand on his chest and resting her head on his shoulder. "Not...not right now. I...I...need..." A shudder ran through her entire body.

"Hush, then," he murmured, tucking her into his side, and noting she didn't protest. "You've been strong for a long time, all by yourself, Meg. Nobody can do that indefinitely. Listen, I...never did properly thank you for, for sticking by me when I thought Ma was dying, a couple months ago. I dunno if you realize how much I was leaning on you through all of that, or how much I appreciated it. But I was, and I did."

"Aw."

"Yeah. So, see, Mr. Badass Alpha Line Chief can't always do it, either. And now I know about the whole big ball of shit with Slug, and I can be here for you in a way I never quite could, before."

"I...I guess so, yeah. It's...it feels good. To know I can lean on you for a little while, I mean."

"Good. Will you let me do this, let me kinda repay the debt?"

"Y-yeah, Ace. I...think I'd appreciate that, about now."

"All right. Then what I want you to do now is to just try to relax. I know it's hard, but just do the best you can. Let the defenses drop—if you need to; if you can—and vent some of that stress and pain and grief. When is the last time you did that, I wonder?"

"Um...last Christmas? Like, Christmas Eve eve, after the party, with you? I think so..." Omega decided.

"Damn, baby," Echo murmured. Briefly, he tightened his hold on her, offering a kind of gentle, reassuring hug. "It's the end of summer! That was months ago. And that was mostly about your family, and not about you, or what was done to you. Have you ever cried about all that, since Zz'r'p uncovered it? About what was done to you?"

"N-no...I never...never dared." She shrugged. "I was afraid I'd...lose it...at the wrong time, or, or something."

"Then let it out. I'm here. I'll keep you safe, with everything I've got. Drop your guard, and let ME be your guard."

"You...are you sure, Ace?" she whispered, voice growing wobbly. "It... it won't be...pretty."

"I understand that. And you need to understand that my instinct is gonna be to try to help, somehow; to try to make you feel better, to ease the pain. But I also know you need to get this out, before it messes you up in here," he freed one hand long enough to tap her temple, then wrapped both arms around her again, holding her securely. "Let alone the rest of you. If that means crying, screaming, yelling, cussing the alien bastard out, cussing ME out, or anything else, you DO that, all right? Any of it, and all of it."

"I'm not gonna ever cuss you out for this, Ace," Omega grumbled. "S-slug is another matter, but this isn't your f-fault."

"It sorta kinda is, baby. If not for me, Slug wouldn't have done what he did."

"I don't care," she protested. "Don't you d-dare blame yourself for what that sonuvab-bitch did!"

"Okay, honey, all right. Forget I said that," Echo murmured, seeing anger in her eyes. "That's not where I wanted this to go. I want you to vent, not us get in an argument over whose fault goes where about what."

"O-okay. Yeah, I...I'm sorry."

"Stop that, now. There's no need for you to apologize for anything, baby. Concentrate on letting go and getting all that pain out. Whatever you need to do to get it out, do it. It isn't gonna hurt a thing. There's nobody else within a couple o' miles in every direction; nobody to hear if you need to scream and beat on my chest, or something like that. But like I said, instinct is gonna make me try to soothe you. So if I say some nonsense like 'hush, hush,' or whatever, just nod and don't pay any attention, okay?"

"Heh! O-okay," she said, giving him a shaky smile. The chuckle was likewise uncertain, but sincere, and he smiled back, then slid his hand up to cup the back of her head and hold it in position as he briefly kissed her forehead.

"There. All right," he murmured. "Don't jump too bad, now. This is what the standard voice sounded like when I had the household systems installed; it's kinda...intense."

"Huh?"

"Don't get startled, baby. A.T.L.A.S.S. Junior?"

"WORKING," came the somewhat-stentorian artificial voice, not un-like a certain classic science-fiction-film robot, and Omega blinked, even as Echo felt her body flinch a bit, but she didn't startle as badly as he had feared. "ORDERS?"

"Property force field to maximum; maintain 'soft' configuration until otherwise ordered. NO outside entry permitted. If Division One agents approach, admit only on Echo's authority, voice pattern confirmation. NO duplicate Omegas permitted inside the perimeter."

"CONFIRMED. SOFT FIELD AT MAXIMUM STRENGTH. NO ADMITTANCE TO NON-AGENCY PERSONNEL. AGENCY PERSON-NEL MUST OBTAIN ECHO'S AUTHORITY BEFORE ADMITTANCE. VOICE PATTERN ACTIVATED. NO DUPLICATES OF COMPANION. OPAQUE FORCE FIELD?"

"Affirmative; use active cloaking."

"ACTIVE CLOAKING ACTIVATED. HOUSE HAS NOW DISAP-PEARED FROM EXTERNAL SENSORY CAPABILITIES."

"Household security to maximum. Arm weaponry. Fire only on Echo's authority. Voice command."

"HOUSE SECURITY MAXIMUM. WEAPONS ARMED. FIRE CONTROL ON ECHO'S AUTHORIZATION. VOICE COMMAND AC-TIVATED."

"No land-line calls accepted. Shunt to voice mail."

"VOICE MAIL CONFIRMED. MESSAGE?"

"Use the standard automated computer message: 'This line has been disconnected.'"

"STANDARD AUTOMATED MESSAGE FOR VOICE MAIL CON-FIRMED."

"Initiate."

"INITIATING NOW."

"That takes care of the house," Echo noted to his partner. "And I've got my Winchester & Tesla on me, and you can't imagine all the places I have weapons stashed in this house. But I really need to upgrade the voice on the computer system. It's gonna wake us up in the night with some little update-thing, one of these days, and scare us half to death."

Omega let out a single laugh, then asked, "A.T.L.A.S.S. Junior?"

"Oh. Yeah, have you ever had to use the household computer system back at Headquarters?"

"Not really, but I remember reading the memo about...oh. The Autonomous Technology Lifestyle And Security System. A.T.L.A.S.S. So that means that the system here..."

"Right. It's a pared-down version, so its name is A.T.L.A.S.S. Junior. Remember a few weeks back, when Fox came down to talk to us about it?"

"Oh. I do now. Duh." Omega chuckled again, but this time it broke, ending on a dry sob, as she began to tremble.

Here it comes, he thought, grim. *She's gonna lose it. But damn, she NEEDS to lose it, for once, just to get it all out in the open. She's bottled it all up for so long, it can't be healthy. And now this whole pile o' shit, with Wright an' all, lands on top of it...and drags it ALL out.* He stifled a sigh, even as the first tears spilled over and rolled down her cheeks, dripping, hot, onto his chest.

* * *

Omega cried, her body trembling lightly, for a long time, while Echo held her close, murmuring soothing remarks into her ear and occasionally rubbing her back or shoulders, hoping to get her to relax further. From time to time, he tightened his hold, hugging her when her emotions became too powerful and her body began to shake more violently. This usually had the desired effect of easing her response and relaxing her body, though she continued to cry.

After well more than forty-five minutes of incoherent sobs, she finally offered commentary.

"I...I'm so...so s-sorry," she whispered through convulsive spasms of her diaphragm. "Ah'm actin' l-like a b-blubberin' ba-baby. An' now your t-shirt's all s-soggy."

"Shush that. Don't be sorry," Echo murmured. "You've needed to do this for months, now. You've had it bottled up way too long. You're not a superwoman, Meg. I mean, I know that you..." He broke off, trying to find a gentler way to phrase what he had been about to tell her.

"What?"

"Aw, I just wanted to soften what I was gonna say, baby," Echo sighed,

122

"but I can't figure out a way to do it."

"S-say it anyw-way."

"You sure? It might not help how you're feeling right now."

"Y-yeah. Do it."

"Okay. Look, I understand that...that Slug probably engineered your emotional and intellectual ability to respond to all the crap he did, to ensure that you could handle it mentally. But you still have to let it out once in a while! You might 'handle it' mentally, emotionally—but it's still gonna be generating forty-seven gajillion kinds of biochemical reactions to all that anger, the hate, the pain—cortisol, and epinephrine, and all that junk. If you didn't still have that kind of response, you couldn't function as an Agent at the level you do. So the longer that goes on without getting expressed, the more damage that'll cause in your body. And don't try to tell me you don't feel all that," he declared, as she opened her mouth to protest. "I was in there with you, in your head, experiencing it with you, remember? Yeah, you blocked a lot of the memories of physical pain response, but you didn't think to hide your responses AT THE TIME. I mean the ones you were feeling right then, while you were remembering it. I felt your horror, your anger, your humiliation, your shame, baby," Echo said, dropping his voice. "Now I know how it makes you feel, at least to some extent. A pretty large extent, I think. Don't try to pretend to me that it doesn't, because it's too late to do that."

Omega was silent for a long moment, her head tilted back, staring up at him in something that looked to Echo like shock. Abruptly she burst into fresh tears, turning her face into his chest, and clutching at him with her free hand.

"I'm sorry," Echo whispered, guilt-ridden. "I knew it was gonna upset you, to be reminded of it."

"N-no," she gasped through her tears. "Not...not that. I'm...I can't... just, just hang o-on a sec."

Echo did, literally as well as metaphorically, tightening his hold on the body of the woman he loved, as several powerful spasms of sobbing wracked her form. This went on for another quarter of an hour before easing enough to enable her to speak again.

"Don't...don't be...s-sorry, Ace," she murmured then, talking into his chest. "I was-wasn't crying about, about what Slug did, not that time. I...

this is gonna sound really stupid."

"No, it won't. Tell me."

"It's just..." She threw him a tear-filled glance, eyes red-rimmed, nose pink. Then she blushed and tucked her face back into his chest. "I KNOW this is selfish of me. I shouldn't have LET you do that, see all that horrible stuff. Let you see what it does to me. And I'm sorry for that. But...I'm so GLAD...to finally have, have somebody to, to share this with! And I'm glad," she added, "that the somebody is you. 'Cause I know you understand. You always understand, sooner or later."

"I try, anyway."

"Echo, you've never failed me," she declared. "Oh, we may talk past each other for a while, misunderstand, even argue initially. But sooner or later, you ALWAYS get where I'm coming from. ALWAYS. An' I try...to give back, the same way."

"Well...good. And you do fine. We got each other's backs, baby. We always have, and we always will. And since I finally know, I can watch your six on this, too." Echo used the side of his fist to nudge her chin up, until he could look into her tear-stained face. "Now, will you do something for me?"

"What?"

"Snuggle into me, try your damnedest to unwind as much as you can, and trust me to take care of you tonight."

* * *

Omega was silent for a long time, gazing up at Echo, studying her partner's face as he looked down at her. The dark-chocolate eyes were sincere, his gaze open; his own face was relaxed, yet the chiseled features still managed to evoke concern, determination, and confidence, while he waited for her answer.

He's gonna stay with me tonight, she realized. *Maybe even, us sleep right here in the hammock, right like this. But he'll never take advantage of the situation. He just intends to make sure that, like he said the other night, Mark will have to go through him to get to me. To make sure that he takes care of me, exactly as he promised. And I think...that's exactly what I need, right now. I need to just...be here. And not worry about anything else. Not the past, not the present mess, not the future. Just...be in the moment. If I can still do that. I dunno if I can. I dunno anything, any more, really. All I truly know is, I can't shove all the worries and anxieties and fears away, so*

I can be a tough, strong Agent—not any longer. I...need to let an Agent take care of me for a change. I need to let my favorite Agent take care of me. Because he's the only one who knows, who understands, right now. And he can. And will, with everything he's got.

"Here?" she asked then.

"If you want to," he agreed. "It's kinda nice here. We got the stars in the sky, and the sound of the surf, and the ocean breeze. All that stuff you said earlier that you like. Well, you didn't mention the stars earlier. But I know you better than to leave 'em out." He grinned.

"Okay," she acquiesced, and gave him a shaky smile in return.

Then she did as he had asked: She snuggled into his side, slid her hand across his chest, sighed, and closed her eyes.

* * *

Echo watched his partner, the woman he loved with every fiber of his being, with the benefit of intimate knowledge borne of having spent almost all his waking moments in her presence for well over a year and a half. So he saw when she made her decision, and knew, as soon as she asked, "Here?" that it was a tacit acceptance and implicit trust in him. Warmth filled him.

He felt her nestle against his body, her own body calming, and he smiled to himself. Scant minutes after her poor bloodshot, red-rimmed eyes slid closed, her body went limp, and he blinked, surprised.

"Meg?" he murmured. "Baby? You awake?"

No answer.

Wow, he thought, surprised. *That's a mix of serious trust...and utter exhaustion. She'd never admit it, but...she's been scared. And almost as much about how her 'family' was gonna react to all of it, as to the possibility of rape, I think. Maybe more. I thought sure she'd lie here and stargaze with me for a little bit, at least, but I don't think she had the energy left to do it, after crying her eyes out so hard for so long. She cried almost continuously for way over an hour, and it wasn't simple little sniffles. Those were downright gut-wrenching sobs; I thought it was gonna wrench MY gut out, at times. But she really needed that. And now she needs to just rest. And I need to just take care of her, while she does.*

He slid one hand lightly over her bare arm, feeling the coldness of the skin.

125

That won't do, he decided. *I can't let her get cold, not after venting like that. She'll end up sick or something.*

He glanced at the nearby table, and reached over with his free arm, flipping open a cabinet door and grabbing a folded blanket from the stack he'd placed there earlier, on the protected shelf underneath the tabletop. A quick wrist flick served to unfold it, and he pulled it across both of them, ensuring Omega was well-covered; the sea breeze could turn chill at night, as it swept in across the north Atlantic.

"There, baby," he told the sleeping form. "You lay right there an' rest, honey. I'll take care of things for you."

Then he pressed another kiss into the platinum hair, offering a gentle hug into the bargain, before tucking his free hand behind his head and staring up at the stars.

Chapter 5

The medical trio spent the next several hours working on Wright, trying to find some sort of implant that his body would accept, that would enable them to keep track of him. Outside the cell, a concerned Oscar watched an anxious Yankee pace and try to stay patient.

"We've tried eight different kinds of chip," Zebra noted, cleaning the latest wound, "including that new biomimetic transponder from Edeptis. And they all did the same thing."

"Yes," Zarnix agreed, preparing another swab of Rejuvic. "And, while the anesthesia is keeping Wright fairly free of pain, it seems to be doing nothing for disguising any of the chips. Worse, if we keep this up, even with the Rejuvic, we could end up causing permanent damage. At the very least, he could develop some nasty scar tissue. And in this location, it could limit range of mobility in his shoulder."

"Yeah," Bet murmured. "We don't wanna do that."

"Maybe we should invert it," Zebra brainstormed. "Maybe we put the chip in Omega instead. I haven't seen any indication that she's ever reacted like that, and I've run shit-tons of tests on her, injecting her with all kinds of stuff—dyes, markers, tracers, all that."

"It might work," Zarnix pondered. "Provided this response is something that Slug bio-engineered into Wright only, it could provide our temporary tracking solution. As long as they can be separated from each other, I think it does not matter who we 'tag' with a chip. I just hope she doesn't end up as reactive."

"I can't think she would—we used some chip technology to help kick-start her, right after she and Echo killed Slug and Slug nearly fried her noggin. And she didn't do this."

"Then by all means, let us try it."

"But she's not at Headquarters," Bet pointed out.

"Perhaps Fox can suggest trying out one of the field transponders, the next time Alpha One checks in," Zarnix decided. "It will serve the same purpose. Perhaps even better, as we can more easily keep track of where she is, and what is happening to her."

"Yeah, but we gotta make sure Echo doses the area up really good with a local anesthetic first," Zebra reminded them. "I'd hate to think we layered THAT," she nodded at Wright's shoulder, slowly knitting closed, "on top of all of Omega's other troubles."

"Indeed," Zarnix agreed.

"Lotsa that," Bet concurred.

* * *

"There you are, Yankee," Fox said as the Alpha Line Agent entered his office shortly after a bemused medical team departed Containment... without telling the worried Agent anything, or even stopping to think about it. Fox waved at a visitor chair. "Sit down, please. I'm afraid I've been a bit remiss in having a chat with you. I was supposed to talk to you a day or two ago, but this Mark Wright fellow showed up, and...well. Things got hectic, as I'm sure you know by now."

"Are you talking about why Tare is gone?" Yankee asked, his anxiety obvious as he took the indicated seat. "What's wrong with him? Is he...the guard from Security that I was on duty with said he was on medical leave. The medics were in Wright's cell half the night, it seemed like, but they were too busy working on him to answer my questions, and I didn't wanna bother 'em. Seemed like what they were doing was important, but damn, it was unpleasant as hell. Listen, um...Is...Tare doesn't have cancer or something, does he? Is he gonna be all right?"

"No, no, Yankee, nothing like that," Fox soothed. "Tare is—physically—completely healthy. He simply had some...issues...he needed to work through for his own mental and emotional health."

"Huh? Issues? Why didn't he tell me?" Yankee wondered, patently hurt. "I don't get it. We're, like, the best pals that ever were."

"He couldn't, Yankee. He didn't know how. You see, it's you he's worried about."

"What the hell?!"

"He seems to believe that your attitude toward Agent Omega is deteriorating, and he is worried for the possible consequences," Fox elaborated. "To you."

"To ME? I'm not the one that's getting her ass chased!" Yankee came close to snarling. "So he's elevated our arguments to you, huh? Or did he go to Echo, and Echo bumped it to you?"

"He said nothing about any arguments between you," Fox said, maintaining a calm demeanor, while noting the other man's recalcitrant mindset and instant defensiveness...as well as the disrespectful comment regarding Omega. "He did, however, mention discussing the matter with you, several times. As far as Echo's involvement, I have it to understand that he stopped by Echo's office, and asked to meet with BOTH of us in MY office. Which was what occurred. I do not believe Echo knew anything about the subject matter until Tare broached his concerns to both of us, here."

"That damn lying sack of...!"

"Stop right there," Fox ordered, holding up one hand. "Don't say another word. Before I hear you slander your own partner—I presume you ARE referring to Tare, not Echo—let me ask you something."

"What?" Yankee wondered, his curtness bordering on insolence. Fox narrowed his eyes in response, almost, but not quite, scowling.

"Have you ever seen your partner break down?" he asked the other man.

"Huh?" Yankee stared in surprise.

"Have you ever seen your partner break down?"

"I...don't..." Yankee blinked and gazed at Fox, seeming suddenly uncertain.

"Has Tare ever broken down and cried in front of you? Over anything?"

"No! Never."

"Would it shock you to hear that he broke down and cried in front of Echo and myself?"

"Hell yeah, it would," Yankee said, gaping in bewilderment. "You mean to say...he was so upset..."

"That is exactly what I mean to say," Fox declared. "So concerned... about YOU...that he broke down in front of his department supervisor and his director. And that is why I determined that an extended medical leave of some sort would be best for him—and verified it with Medical. Frankly, while I urged him to do so and he agreed, I didn't intend to give him a great deal of choice. He was far too distraught, and it was plain to me that it was going to end up affecting his ability to function as a field agent, let alone an Alpha Line Agent. I didn't want him, or anyone around him—including you—getting hurt or worse, because he got upset in the middle of a bad situation. He NEEDED the time to go off and think, Yankee. For his own sake, as well as the sake of the people around him. So I want YOU to sit there and think about that."

"Shit," Yankee murmured, becoming subdued. "I knew it bothered him, how I felt, but I didn't know he was that worried. He's been pushing harder and harder in recent weeks, wanting me to...I honestly don't know what he wants me to do, Fox. Yeah, I know he dislikes my opinions of Omega. But there's a difference between not wanting to be buddy-buddy with somebody and not being able to work with 'em. I can work with her; I just don't happen to like her very much."

"And you don't mind letting it show," Fox pointed out. "Whether in front of her, or other agents, or not."

Yankee shrugged, but said nothing.

"Has it occurred to you that your attitude can affect morale in the department?"

"What?"

"Have you realized that you could be undermining morale and discipline within Alpha Line?"

"No, Fox, because it isn't. It can't be," Yankee claimed. "Everybody else there thinks she can do no wrong—she's, like, Saint Omega—so there's no chance that my opinion is gonna sway anybody."

"Except someone new to the department, just transferring in, who doesn't yet know Echo or Omega," Fox pointed out. "Yankee, just out of curiosity, what is your opinion of Echo?"

"Oh, he's a good guy," Yankee decided. "I think he's a little too close to his partner for his own good, some days, but he knows his stuff, and he runs the department fairly and efficiently. He's a good leader."

"And how much do you think Omega helps him run that department?"

"Eh. She does a lotta the paperwork, I think. And he's taught her well, so she knows her stuff, too. I gotta admit, the coordination she pulled off, both for the Cortian sitch and the Dallas mission, were pretty sweet. I don't have any objection to her as an assistant department chief, Fox. I just don't happen to care for her as a person, much."

"Mm. You do understand the consequences, if your opinion ends up affecting her authority, or her ability to do her job in the field? Or YOUR ability to do your job in the field?"

"Meh, as Echo says," Yankee brushed off the warning.

"Tare thought it behooved you to consider the possibility, so much so that your refusal to do it has pushed him to the brink," Fox pointed out. "I see the same possible problem."

"All right, all right, Fox," Yankee said, mildly exasperated and showing it. "I get that you're concerned for Tare, and that Tare's worried for me. And I'm sorry I started to get mad at him earlier. I've been...upset... wondering what happened to him, so I was on edge. I'm glad it was nothing serious."

"I suppose that depends upon your point of view."

"Look, if you'll tell me where he is, I'll go have a long heart to heart with him, and get him to come home."

"No."

"No?"

"No. That will not be happening, Yankee. Tare needs time to settle; to consider the situation, and decide how HE wants to respond to it, apart from your refusal to do so."

"You're seriously not going to let me even talk to my partner?"

"You have a cell phone."

"He isn't answering it!"

"That has nothing to do with me. Though it should tell you something."

"Sonuvabitch! This can't be happening!" Yankee leaped to his feet and stormed toward the door.

"I don't believe I dismissed you, Yankee."

* * *

Yankee heard the tone Fox used, which brooked no countermanding, and immediately spun to face the Director.

Sonuvabitch, he thought, irked. *He's seriously pulling rank on me. Now. Of all times. Dammit. All right; we'll play this his way.*

"Permission to return to duty, sir," he noted, standing at attention.

* * *

Fox was silent for a long moment, studying the other man. Finally he replied.

"Permission granted, Yankee."

Without another word, Yankee turned and left the office.

Fox sighed, and moved to the bay window overlooking the Core to watch him walk across that large area.

"Tare is right," he decided. "We're going to have trouble out of him... sooner or later."

* * *

Echo woke the next morning when the pre-dawn light became too bright for him to continue sleeping—which really didn't take much; while he had rested well, his subconscious had remained alert all night. And that was as he had intended it, many years of practice having honed the skill and made it relatively easy to do. *It means that I stay rested enough to be of use protecting Meg, WHILE protecting Meg,* he thought. *So I keep my promise to her, goin' an' comin'.*

Unsurprisingly, therefore, he found himself still in the hammock, Omega curled against his side. Both were still fully dressed in t-shirts and shorts, though they had kicked off their flip-flops the evening before, when they climbed into the hammock.

Somewhat to his surprise, he had drawn up the knee nearest to her, just high enough to admit a leg underneath it, and she had subsequently wrapped both her legs about his leg in her sleep, her upper arm stretching across his chest to tuck her hand under his body on the opposite side. The arm she kept underneath her stretched downward, pressed alongside his torso, the wrist cocked, hand tucked under his near side; she lay twisted slightly at the waist, which enabled her upper body to rest partly atop his. Her cheek remained pillowed on his shoulder and upper chest.

She's clinging to me in her sleep, he realized then. *Even in our sleep, she's been drawing comfort and strength from my being right here.* He looked into her face, checking for signs of tension or indications that she was not sleeping well, but it was peaceful, the full lips almost smiling. *Good. It helped, then. I kinda expected nightmares, all things considered, but apparently I was wrong...thank God. She looks like she's slept really well. If I don't move around a whole lot, she can probably keep sleeping a while longer. Damn, my baby really needed this, I guess. And now I can be there for her, just like this, from now on.*

He sighed in contentment, gathering her close, as his body instinctively responded to her. However, he was careful to keep her tucked into his side, so she couldn't inadvertently discover the fact; he was thankful that the leg nearest her was raised, effectively blocking her from being able to find out much about it.

I can't help the response, especially given the way I feel about her, he realized, *but I'm sure not gonna take advantage of the situation, or even give her reason for it to cross her mind that I might, if I can help it. Especially not now, when she's in a...sensitive...state. Damn, I hate to think how close she came to getting raped! I can't get that image out of my mind, Wright on top of her like that. But what actually happened was trauma enough, to her. No, she doesn't need to deal with my responses right now. The 'guy bits,' as she calls 'em, oughta settle down by the time she wakes up. If I have to, I can ease outta the hammock and let her sleep. Assuming she'll let go of me, I suppose.*

Just then, a slight sound from Omega drew his attention, and he stared at his partner quizzically, trying to ascertain what he had heard. He heard it again, just before it dawned on him what was causing it: The sinus congestion caused by her crying the night before was now resulting in soft snores from his partner, and he grinned.

Aw. That's cute, he decided. *And she's still sound asleep, and evidently nothing happened last night; that security setting I applied would have sent off thirty-seven kinds of alarms and given us both coronaries, if anybody had managed to show up on the doorstep. Or, well, on the force field perimeter.*

But she's gonna be all stuffed up today, I bet, just like she was on Christmas Eve. And I don't have any of India's special mint unstuffing strips. I better dig around in the pantry and see if I have any dried mint or basil or...anything in the mint family, I guess, based on what Ma used to give me as a kid, whenever I caught a cold. I can steep it as a tea, put a little honey in it, and it should at least help clear some of the congestion.

He studied her face again, which was still relaxed and now held a more-obvious slight smile. *Oh, that's good. She's probably having a nice dream.*

Echo pressed his lips against her forehead, right at the hairline, and she sighed in her sleep, then mumbled something.

"Iss hokay, Ace," she murmured, sleep slurring her words. "We goddit, you an' me."

Jubilation filled the male Agent.

She's dreaming about ME! he realized. *It doesn't sound like it's especially romantic, necessarily, but I'm...*

"Nuh-uh," she continued. "We don' need Mu. Nuh, you stay here, Mu.

133

Look af'er Mark. He doesn' know 'bout all 'is stuff. A'pha One goddit tak'n care ob."

Huh, Echo thought, perturbed. *I'm...not sure what to make of THAT. Looks like, not only is she dreaming about me, she's dreaming about the two men I consider my competition for her attention. Not that one of 'em is actually in the running, but the whole reason we're here is 'cause SHE'S running—from him.*

"I...sai'...NUH!" Omega muttered just then, sounding annoyed. She scowled in her sleep for a moment. "A'pha One goddit unner c'ntrol! We DUN NEED HE'P!"

That's interesting, he decided, feeling vaguely amused. *Somebody's pushing, evidently declaring that Meg an' me can't handle...whatever it is she's dreaming about...and she's not having it! She's not just standing firm, she's pushing back. I wonder if Fox is in her dream too, or if Mu...or maybe even Wright, since she's halfway sympathetic to him, given he's been programmed, same as she was...is the one doing the pushing. And the way she's slurring her words is damned adorable.*

After a moment to consider, he leaned forward to murmur in her ear.

"That's right, baby," he told her. "We've got this. We've always got this, you and me, together." Then he paused, debating about the rightness of what he wanted to say next. Finally he shrugged, concluding, as determined as his partner tended to be about making up her own mind, it wasn't likely to make much difference if he said it or not. *But at least,* he decided, *it might clue in her subconscious about how I feel.* So he continued. "You know I'm always going to be beside you, honey. We don't need anybody else, you an' me. Friends and family are always good, but we can get along, just you and me, if we need to. I'll do whatever you want, however you want it, as long as you let me stay beside you...forever."

With that, Omega sighed and relaxed again.

"See dere?" she told someone in her dream. "Tolju. Me 'n Echo, we go' dis unner c'ntrol. Go siddown."

Echo stifled a laugh.

* * *

Echo drifted back into a light doze while he waited for Omega to awaken. When she began to stir, it brought him back to full wakefulness. He was relieved to find the 'guy bits' had settled down; that was one matter he wouldn't have to try to gloss over to ensure his partner's comfort.

Though, if this becomes a thing, for the duration of the situation, I probably want to discuss it with her, make sure she KNOWS, without doubt, she can trust me, he thought. *That's not a conversation I'm looking forward to, just on account of it's gonna be embarrassing as hell for both of us. But it'll need to be done, and I'll man up and do it, dammit.*

"Mmmh," Omega sighed just then. "Where...oh yeah. Um...Ace?"

"Right here, Sleeping Beauty." Abruptly Echo flashed back to Omega finally waking after Alpha One had killed Slug. *And I called her the same thing. I knew, even then, how beautiful she was,* he realized. *Even though I hadn't fallen for her yet. Well, at least, I wasn't in love with her yet. Or... maybe I was, and just didn't know it. I had to get almost hit in the face with a two by four to sit up and pay attention. Damn, I can be thick. Well,* he rationalized, *it wasn't like we weren't busy at the time, I guess. Maybe I'll ask Fox when he started noticing; that'll tell me a few things, and satisfy my curiosity. And probably embarrass the hell outta me, but he's the closest thing I have any more to a father figure, so...*

"I didn't...uh...wow," Omega said then, apparently still trying to get her wits about her. "Were you able, um, to get any sleep?"

"Yeah, I slept fine," Echo noted. "No problem. I pretty much went into mission mode, and was able to unwind and rest, while my subconscious stayed alert, guarding you. I'm good. What about you, though? I know you were dreaming at one point, 'cause you were talking in your sleep."

* * *

"Oh, geez," she murmured, rubbing one fist in her eye as she tried to wake up more fully. At the same time, she tried hard to recall her dreams, wondering if she had revealed anything she wasn't ready to reveal. "I, um, didn' say anything, like, embarrassing, did I...?"

"Nah. Matter of fact, it sounded complimentary of you an' me as a team. Nearest I could make out from what little you were saying, somebody in your dream kept insisting that Alpha One needed help on a mission, and it was royally pissing you off. You stood firm on the notion that we had a handle on it, you an' me. JUST you an' me." He smiled, and she returned it, realizing it was weak, but too groggy to help it.

"Huh." She sniffed once, trying to open up her nose, then coughed for a moment, and sniffled a bit more. "I think I remember that, kinda sorta,"

135

Omega decided, then shifted position...and rather abruptly became aware of being wrapped around Echo's body.

Horror and embarrassment seized her. Immediately she flushed, pushed away from him, and began trying to untangle their limbs.

"Oh geez oh geez oh geez! I, I'm so sorry, Ace!" she babbled, frantic. "Oh man, I can't believe I did this! I swear, Echo, I didn't know I—"

* * *

"Hey, whoa, hush, baby," he told her, grabbing her and holding on, trying to calm her frenzied flailing. "Settle down, here. Everything is fine. I've been awake, off and on, for over an hour now; I knew you were hangin' on for dear life, and I knew why, and I knew you were sound asleep. I'm not offended or anything. Matter of fact, I'm honored. Not only that you trust me this much, but that you feel safe and secure enough with me to sleep as well as it looked like you did. DID you sleep that good?"

"Yeah, I did," she agreed. She was still gradually untangling herself from him, he noticed, except she was doing so more calmly now, without the dismayed frenzy. "That was the best I've slept in...I dunno when."

"Great! I'm glad I could do that for you, baby," he told her, hiding his regret as she moved away and sat up. "The fresh salt air probably helped, too. Are you hungry?"

"A little," she admitted. "I'm still tryin' to wake up good. And I'm really stuffed up." She wiped both hands over her face, erasing the salty residue of her tears, then sniffled again. "Ugh."

"I figured you would be, and I've got some ideas for fixing that. Your eyes are a little puffy, too, but that's to be expected. If the puffiness doesn't go down in the next couple hours, we'll see about a cool compress or something. For now, why don't we head for the kitchen and fix some coffee?"

"I think you've got a plan there, Ace. On all of it."

* * *

"That's better," Omega considered, sitting next to Echo at the dining table as they sipped mugs of coffee. He had dug in the cabinets until he had located where he'd stashed the culinary herbs and spices the last time he had been at the beach house, then brewed a mug of strong mint tea, added a big spoonful of honey, and insisted she drink that before he would fix coffee. The hot, aromatic tisane helped open her congested sinus passages, and only then did he prepare their morning coffee.

"Good. Then why don't you go shower and get dressed while I rustle up some breakfast? Then we can decide what to do today," Echo suggested, pushing back from the table and going to the refrigerator, as Omega stood.

"But I can help fix breakfast," Omega offered. "This is my mess, after all. You just got dragged into it 'cause you're my partner."

"No," Echo demurred. "I'm part of this because MY old enemy did this to you to get revenge on ME. It's as much my mess as yours, baby. More, in a lotta ways." He came over to stand before her. "Listen to me a minute, Meg," he told her. "And...bear with me. This is gonna be one of those kinda rare 'Echo opens up' moments, so it'll probably be a little hard for me to get it out. Be patient."

"Okay..." She cocked her head to one side and looked up at him, puzzled.

"All right, to start—I know you're independent, and you're capable. You're...brilliant, in every sense of the word, and...you're one hell of an Agent," he murmured, taking her shoulders in a gentle hold. "And I respect all of those things, and I respect the hell outta you. I want you to know that, up front."

"Aw. Thanks." She blushed, and smiled.

"But...but what you, um, may not have stopped to, to think about is that, well, not only do I bear a certain responsibility for this situation due to my merely existing, there's...another factor...to consider, I guess you could call it."

"Which is?" Omega wondered.

Echo cupped both hands around her face to hold her head still, so he could look into her sapphire eyes unimpeded. *This is gonna get tricky,* he thought. *I gotta say enough that she understands, and get her thinking in that general direction, without, I dunno, spooking her...in the middle of all this...crap. Never mind explaining my motivations now.*

"This is the hard part for me to say. It, um, you probably haven't realized it, but...but you're...somebody special to me," Echo confessed, plunging ahead. "And, well, I'm like you, a little bit old-fashioned. You already know that, but you might not understand how it can come into play in our current circumstances. See, guys like me, when a, a special lady...OUR special lady...finds herself in trouble—in danger, even...well, we wanna help. *I* wanna help. Only..." He broke off, looking for words.

"Only what?" Omega said, looking up at him with wide eyes, a kind of guileless confusion written on her face, and Echo knew she was trying to take it all in, and determine how to interpret it...and what, exactly, he meant by all of it.

"Only...we haven't figured out how to solve the situation yet, so there's not a lot I CAN do. Of substance, anyway," he added, then shrugged. "Sure, I can stand guard, as it were. But that's...kinda passive, and you know I'm a man of action..."

"Oh..."

"Oh?"

"Well..." Omega considered, her azure gaze going distant for a brief moment. "I guess that means I need to go shower and get dressed, while you make breakfast."

"That...is a good idea," he said, and they both smiled. Then he bent his head and deposited another light kiss to her forehead, taking a few scant seconds longer this time, before dropping his hands and turning back to the fridge, to inventory what was available for breakfast and develop a rudimentary menu.

Omega stared at his back for a long moment, wide-eyed, before betaking herself to the master—and so far, only—suite, there to prepare for the day.

* * *

"Well, I was gonna suggest another walk on the beach," Omega said over a breakfast of bacon, scrambled eggs, and canned biscuits, as they discussed their options for the day. "But it's gone and clouded up while we've been inside, and the weather app on my phone says it's gonna rain."

"Meh," Echo responded, waving his fork dismissively. "It's August. Even if it rains, it'll be a warm drizzle, at least initially. We can still go for a walk, if you don't mind getting a little wet. If you don't wanna get wet, I can, I dunno, maybe adjust the force field to storm-conditions mode or something. That would block out most of the wind, rain, and high surf."

"That would work," Omega decided. "And as long as it isn't an outright downpour, I don't mind a little rain."

"It's not supposed to storm, is it?" Echo wondered. "I haven't had a chance to check the forecast, but we probably don't wanna be on the beach in a storm, even with the force field locked out. Lightning strikes can move through wet ground, and the field truncates a couple feet below ground level."

"No, just some rain, I think. It's a cool front moving through." She pulled her phone and double-checked the weather app. "According to this, the main body of rain won't get here until the afternoon, anyway. Light showers this morning, and rain this afternoon."

"Okay; that'll actually be kinda nice. It'll help break up that heat wave we've been having. Let's go for a walk this morning, then, and we can kick back this afternoon in the house. Hell, we can even get in the hot tub for a while, after lunch, if you want to. Maybe light the fireplace later tonight, if it gets cool enough...which it might, if the clouds keep us socked in."

"Aha! Now I know why you grabbed that huge bag of marshmallows at the store!" Omega laughed. "And those long skewers!"

"Fireplace, beach bonfire—one way or another, I figured we'd use 'em," Echo chuckled. "Why do you think I brought up that shitload of driftwood, and dumped it by the deck stairs, yesterday?"

"All right! Let's do it!"

* * *

After they finished breakfast, Echo got out his cell phone and checked in with Headquarters, just to get the latest information before they headed out for their walk.

"Oh, Echo, I'm glad you called," Fox told him. "I have a message for you from the medlab. First, do you have a proper medikit with you?"

"Yeah, Boss. We brought that."

"What about that portable field command center you and Omega took on your vacation?"

"Yeah, I grabbed that, too, just in case. In fact, half the time, it lives in the 'Vette's trunk, these days."

"Excellent. Then here's what Medical wants you to do. We need you to get out a good local anesthetic, and one of those subcutaneous transponders like you used in Dallas. Then I want you and Omega to decide where she wants the transponder inserted, and dose that place up heavily with the local anesthetic, then inject the transponder into her."

"But Fox, injecting the transponder doesn't hurt. It's just a little pinprick."

"Trust me on this, zun. Something strange has been going on here;

Zebra has shown me the security video of their testing. If Omega reacts the way Wright has—and believe me, we really hope she doesn't, for many reasons—she's going to need that anesthetic."

"Ooookay..."

"Then I want you to call me back and let me know what happens. But have the Rejuvic, and some swabs, and lots of gauze ready, just in case."

Echo raised an eyebrow, concerned.

"This...doesn't sound good, Fox."

"The video I saw wasn't, Echo. It may be that Omega handles this fine, and it will function as advertised, and you two can come back at your leisure while we lock down Wright and the medlab works on returning him to normal. But Wright reacted...VERY badly. And I don't want Omega having to...mm. Just be ready for anything, zun."

"All right, Fox," Echo murmured, as Omega came to stand beside him, having overheard the latter part of Echo's side of the conversation. "Let me get off the horn and take care of that, then I'll call you back with a report. I don't have a whole lot else to tell you at the moment, anyway. I was only checking in to see if you had anything for us."

"How is Omega doing?"

Echo, who had put the phone in speaker mode when she came to his side, held it out to her.

"Fox, it's Omega," she responded. "I'm right here; I heard Echo talking to you, so I came over to see what was up, and he just now put you on speaker. I'm...doing okay, I guess, in the circumstances. I had a little...um, I guess you could say everything kinda got to me last night, but Echo, bless him, has stuck it out with me."

"Is that why you sound a bit congested, tekhter?"

"Yeah, Fox, it is. I'm kind of ashamed of myself—"

"Don't be," Echo interjected. "I already told you, you can't bottle up big shit like that forever. It's not good for you, in any way."

"Precisely," Fox added.

"...But Echo's been treating that, too. I'm already better than I was."

"Vunderlekh. Keep up the good work, zun."

"I'm doing my best, Fox."

"I know. And Omega?"

"Yes sir?"

"Echo is dead right, meyn teyere. And Zebra, in her capacity as physician, would be the first to tell you. I spent part of my childhood in a concentration camp, and saw my family wiped out, as well as quite a few other atrocities; I can speak to this, first hand, if it helps."

"...Oh," Omega murmured. "Um, Fox?"

"Yes, tekhter?"

"Would you object to, to sitting down with me and, and talking about that, sometime? I...sorta think it MIGHT help, if it isn't more than you want to do. I'll understand if it is. Damn, if anybody would understand, it'd be me."

"No, after all this time, I think I could manage it," Fox decided. "But you have plenty on your plate, for the time being, and you don't need my memories overlaid on that until we get the current matter resolved. Now the two of you run do this thing the medlab wants, and report back to me what happens."

* * *

Once Echo had all of the required equipment gathered, he laid it out on the dining table and looked at his partner.

"Meg, where do you want this thing injected? From the sound of what Fox said, you might have a bit of an allergic reaction, so take that into consideration before you decide."

Omega thought for a moment, then frowned.

"What is it?" Echo wondered.

"I'm just wondering," she thought out loud. "Remember how something 'bit me' at dinner last night, only we never found anything? No bug, no bug bite, no nothing?"

"What, you think you picked up on the medics trying to tag Wright with a chip?"

"It's a possibility," she decided. "That was my right shoulder. Let's try my left shoulder."

"Okay. Push your sleeve up as high as it'll go, and gimme."

Omega rolled the short sleeve of her t-shirt all the way to the shoulder seam, and Echo swabbed the deltoid area well with alcohol to sterilize it, then used an osmosive micropore syringe to inject a hefty dose of pratordicaine into her shoulder.

"Whoa," Omega murmured, as it kicked in. "Ace, that was a whoppin'

141

big dose, hon. I can't even feel my fingers now!"

"Well, Fox gave me express instructions to make it 'honkin' big,' as you like to call it. So I did," Echo said with a shrug. Then he reached for the pre-loaded transponder syringe. Holding it to her shoulder at a low angle, he looked up at Omega. "Here goes, baby," he told her. "I dunno what to expect. It didn't sound nice, but maybe that's just 'cause Slug tweaked Wright. You've never had a problem, have you?"

"No," Omega said, confident. "I think I'll be good. And this will solve some major problems."

"All right then. Bombs away."

He injected the transponder chip in the deltoid area, then set aside the syringe and grabbed the medscanner, running it over her shoulder.

"Great! That looks good, Meg," he told her. "Oh, wait a minute. The localized skin temp is going up. Huh. Why is it turning all red and swelling like that?"

"I don't—uhn," Omega grunted, then winced. "Echo...something's not right. This...HURTS! A lot!"

"But I shot you up with a HUGE dose—DAMN!!" Echo exclaimed, as Omega's now-massively-swollen shoulder suddenly burst open, spewing pus and blood, which ran down her arm even as she screamed in pain.

Echo grabbed for the roll of paper towels, mopping up blood and pus, as Omega cringed and gasped, trying to control the pain, or at least her response to it. Abruptly the chip was ejected like a tiny cork from a miniature champagne bottle, tumbling down to the tabletop. Omega let out one more gasp, then began to pant, even as Echo used a fist-sized wad of gauze to mop the three-inch-long, deep gash in her shoulder.

"Damn, baby!" he exclaimed, horrified. "Shit! Your shoulder almost looks filleted! No, you don't," he said, grabbing for her as she swayed. "I shoulda made you sit down. Here," he said, shoving a chair under her, then pushing her head between her knees. He gingerly picked up her arm and rested it on the tabletop beside her. "Now stay there and don't look, and try to ignore it as much as you can, while I get this patched up as fast as I can go."

"If that was...what it felt like...with a big dose of anesthetic in there, I hate to think...what it woulda felt like...without it," Omega murmured, still panting.

Meanwhile, Echo finished mopping away the blood and the pus, then he applied a topical anti-pathogen with a swab, disposing of everything in the kitchen waste can since they had no medical disposal container. Then he picked up the bottle of Rejuvic and a fresh swab, and stood staring at the bottle for a few seconds, considering.

"Nah, that ain't gonna cut it," he said, putting the wrapped, sterile swab back in the medikit and opening the dropper top of the Rejuvic bottle. He filled the little dropper full, and dribbled it directly into the open wound on Omega's shoulder. Then he refilled it and added more, keeping up the process until Omega's gaping shoulder wound had knit closed.

By that time, the pain had eased, and Omega sat up slowly.

"I...don't think this is gonna work," she said, wry.

* * *

"It did WHAT?!" Zebra, in Fox's office, exclaimed, when Alpha One debriefed their attempt to tag Omega. "Why didn't you use a local??"

"We DID," Echo noted, crisp. "I dosed her with so damn much pratordicaine, she was complaining that she couldn't feel her fingers, Zebra."

"And I'm pretty sure I felt it, when you tried it on Mark," Omega added.

"YOU felt it?!"

"Yup. Right shoulder, medial deltoid, about two inches down, around 17:00 D1 last night?"

"Damn," Zebra replied, sounding dumbfounded. "Bang-on, in every detail."

"Told ya, Ace," Omega murmured, as she exchanged glances with Echo.

"Yeah, you did, baby," Echo agreed. "Looks like you nailed it."

"Shit, Fox," Zebra murmured through the cell phone. "It should have worked."

"Why do you think it did not, bubeleh?"

"If I had to guess, I think that this is a bio-engineered response triggered by the telepathic contact between Wright and Omega, to prevent us doing exactly what we were trying to do," Zebra decided. "In BOTH of 'em. I know for a fact that Meg never reacted like this before, on the several occasions when I've used implants to, say, gather data. Obviously I can't say Wright never did, but even if some civilian doctor tried implanting

143

something, a reaction like this would just be considered a very unusually-powerful allergic reaction. But like I said, I've used temporary implants on Omega before, in order to get some specialized data, especially after her skull fracture last spring, and it never fazed her. Let alone generated a dreadful reaction like what Alpha One is describing." The two Agents heard the physician's sigh. "But that sounds exactly like how Wright responded. It might even have been more severe. It sounds like Meg's shoulder almost... exploded, kinda."

"It did, sort of," Echo agreed. "I had to clean pus and blood off the dining table."

"Ugh," Fox grunted.

"Yeah," Omega agreed. "I splattered it but good. And it hurt like hell."

"It looks like Slug has out-thought us at every turn," Fox muttered.

"Dammit," Echo grumbled.

"Well, I'll return to Bet and Zarnix in the medlab and tell 'em we're back to square one," Zebra decided, sounding discouraged. "I'm sorry, guys. We're trying, I swear."

"Are y'all getting any help out of the Deltiri Embassy?" Echo wondered.

"Some, yes," Fox noted. "But right now, they're in a bit of a stir, after you filed the complaint report on Tt'l'k, and I initialed my approval on it. It's been...not unlike a hornet's nest."

"Mm. Maybe I shoulda waited until after we got this mess worked out before I submitted it," Echo sighed.

"It's okay, Ace," Omega murmured. "I didn't even know you did that. But thank you."

"Tt'l'k went far beyond what I asked for, Omega, and kept going, even with me telling—ordering—him to stop," Fox noted. "Why in hell he thought he needed to bring all that out, I've no idea. Let alone why anyone would think that my hand-picked, duly designated successor and his partner might try to force a coup against me; it's meshuginah!"

"I know," Omega replied, shaking her head. "Echo's gonna have your office one day; all he has to do is wait for it to happen. It would be easier—and way more in character, though that's relative, 'cause I don't even see him doing it at all—to urge you to retire, take Zebra with you, and go back to work for Pulgey."

"Which is exactly what I plan to do, one day," Fox agreed. "And you're right. It's utter drek to think otherwise. But it needed reporting to Tt'l'k's superiors."

"Have the Arcturans given any explanation for Tt'l'k's behavior?" Echo wondered.

"Not so much, no, though they are testing him medically," Fox answered. "There seems to be some concern that he may...well, it seems there's a condition that's similar to a Deltiri form of Asperger's, or the more general autism spectrum. Except in Deltiri, it seems it's more of an acquired condition that develops later in life, rather than something that tends to show up in genetically-predisposed infants and toddlers, like it seems to do in humans. And unlike the human version, under certain circumstances, their version can also cause a kind of mild dementia, a sort of disconnect with the rest of the world."

"Hm," Echo hummed. "That sounds a lot like what we saw in your office, all right."

"Is Zz'r'p back?" Omega asked.

"Not yet, but he will be back soon," Fox told her. "Within the next day or so; maybe within the next few hours—he's rushing his work to completion, and coming as fast as he can. Given his levels of experience, I have high hopes that, as soon as he's here, we can get this situation resolved once and for all."

"Well, Fox, I'm gonna take Meg for a walk on the beach," Echo said, "and there's wet weather moving in, so we better do it while we can. And I got nothing else to report. Meg?"

"No, I'm done," she murmured.

"A walk on the beach sounds quite nice, zun. Very...serene. I expect you both could use that, after...recent events. I gather you two are keeping normal Earth time?"

"Yeah," Echo said. "We discussed it, and it seemed logical, given the location an' stuff. The house isn't big; the outside isn't lit. It just made more sense."

"All right; I'll keep that in mind if I should need to reach you. Omega, I know this is stressing you. Are you coping all right? Is the more tranquil setting helping? Most important, do you feel safe?"

"Yeah, Fox, it is, and I do," she told him in a soft voice. "We went for a long walk yesterday, all around the property, and it helped. Especially the whole beach, surf, water thing. I dunno; I don't quite understand it, but it's definitely...calming."

"Good. Then go do that. I'll let you know when I hear anything, and I want Alpha One to keep checking in at least once a day. And yes, once per Earth day is fine."

"Consider it done, Fox," Echo said. "Alpha One out."

"Fox out."

* * *

"After that nasty little episode with the chip, are you even gonna feel like going for a walk now, baby? Or are you gonna wanna, maybe, lie down?" Echo asked, watching her in concern for several moments before glancing out the nearest window. "Oh. It started to sprinkle while we were doing all that..."

"Yeah, I wanna go anyway. I know this sounds...maybe not so good, Ace, but yeah, I really wanna do it," Omega said, meeting his eyes, frank. "The weather...matches my mood, today."

He shot her a sharp glance, concerned, and she shrugged. *She's doing that more and more, shrugging,* he thought. *Like...it's not important. Like... NOTHING is important, if it's to do with her. And that...is not good.*

"All right," he said. "Shove on your surf shoes and let's go."

* * *

They wandered down to the beach and headed south this time, to enable Omega to see that corner of the property a little better, given that there were no outsiders around and they could take their time. Omega was much quieter than she had been the day before, and her stride correspondingly slower. Her attitude seemed, as she had said, somewhat bleak, not unlike the weather...which soon had them both quite damp, though not drenched.

"Gray skies, gray sea, gray surf, gray mood," she said, when Echo said something about it. "It all goes together, somehow. And when the rain showers move through, it's...like the sky is crying for me, 'cause I'm all cried out."

Echo sighed. Omega replicated it, then shrugged again. They meandered along the edge of the surf, allowing the odd larger wave to splash over their feet.

"C'mere," Echo murmured, after they had progressed a little farther,

146

largely in silence, with no indication that her mood would improve. He reached for her, lightly hugging her very briefly, then taking her hand in his. "There."

"What's up with this, Ace?" Omega wondered, holding up their joined hands. "Nobody else is out here in the wet, so we don't need to pretend, or go into one of our covers."

"I'm not pretending anything," Echo retorted, but gently. "I know what it's like to get lost in your own thoughts. You can spiral straight down the drain that way. I decided you needed a reminder that you're not alone. I'm here, and I'm gonna stay right beside you." He squeezed her hand. "And I'm not letting go."

Omega offered him a shy smile by way of thanks, then laced her fingers through his.

They kept on walking.

* * *

When the western sky started to grow leaden with approaching thick rain clouds, they headed back to the beach house for a lunch of cold-cut sandwiches and leftover chowder. Shortly after the meal, the rain became steady and heavier.

"It's not storming, and there's no indication of lightning anywhere in the system within a couple hundred miles of here," Echo decided, checking the weather app on his special Agency cell phone. "Even with the most sophisticated instrumentation the Agency has for weather detection."

"Okay. You have something in mind," Omega noted.

"Yeah. Wanna put on swimsuits and hop in the hot tub?"

"That...actually sounds kinda nice," Omega decided. "With glasses of wine or something?"

"We can do that," Echo agreed. "I've got a stocked wet bar in one corner of the kitchen. But I expect we need to take some DeTox tabs first. The heat of the tub tends to make the alcohol go into your system a little faster, I've found, and we don't need to be tipsy if something unexpected goes down with Wright. Or anything else."

"Okay. You pour the drinks and get the hot tub ready while I go climb into my bikini, then I'll put out the roof extension and get out the bottle of DeTox while you get into your trunks."

"Roger that."

147

* * *

Fifteen minutes later, both members of Alpha One were cozily ensconced in the hot tub, slouching comfortably and gazing out over a wide, gray ocean. Curtains of rain fell over the beach, creating a hazy, misty effect, even as a light fog began to roll inland.

"The surf is up a little," Echo noted. "And we've got a fog moving in. This rain system, and the cool front behind it, must be interacting with that low out over the north Atlantic. Damn, but I'd hate to be on a ship in the middle of that."

"Yeah," Omega agreed, settling in and sipping her glass of shiraz. "Talk about motion sickness! The air is definitely starting to feel cooler already. I can deal with this, though. I think the comfy hot tub makes for a nice contrast with the weather and the ocean. Especially with the light from the windows spilling over the deck."

"Yup, it makes it even cozier. You'd almost think we were on vacation again, instead of hiding out."

"...Almost." Omega sighed. "I could really wish we were."

"I'm sorry," Echo apologized, shamefaced. "You'd managed to stuff it down into your subconscious, and I brought it up again."

"No, it's okay. It wasn't very far down, to tell the truth," Omega admitted. "There's...I dunno how to explain it. Mark's attempts to communicate with me mentally...they're always there, always just on the edge of my thoughts, never quite breaking through my telepathic block, but never quite going away, either. Like...moths fluttering around a garden light."

"So you can't really forget."

"No."

Echo drew a deep breath. "Which means we need to discuss sleeping arrangements for tonight," he decided. "What with the rain, we can't sleep in the hammock again, which is what I'd intended to suggest..."

"Hey, you slept pretty good last night, right?"

"Yeah, I actually did. I mean, I did the mission mode thing, so there was a part of me that was on alert the whole time, looking out for you, but I feel great. Really well-rested."

"But you were wearing shorts and a t-shirt."

"Okay. So?"

"Mr. 'I Can't Wear Pajamas' slept in SHORTS and a T-SHIRT," Omega emphasized. "And slept great, per his own testimony."

"Oh," Echo realized, sitting up straight. "Oh! And it was a knit shirt and knit, drawstring shorts—nice and soft, but not that much different from undershorts and -shirt. Maybe that's the ticket."

"Yeah. You've been trying to sleep with bottoms, but no shirt, right?"

"Uh-huh. You think maybe I need both, to subtly cue my subconscious in on...something?"

"Maybe. I dunno. Maybe wearing both tells your subconscious that you're dressed. And you've learned how to 'sleep' on a mission while fully dressed, so..."

"This...might work," Echo decided. "I'll try it again tonight and see what happens."

"Okay."

"So...with the rain, no hammock," Echo continued. "You sleep in the bedroom."

"I can sleep on the couch, Ace."

"No. This isn't about comfort as such, or who 'owns' the bedroom. This is about ensuring you're safe, and that you FEEL safe, baby. And frankly, when I retrofitted this place, I designed the bedroom to be the saferoom. Or rather, the safest room in a safehouse." Echo paused, considering. "Therefore, to that end..."

"You're thinking about joining me in the bed. Which, as you'd be dressed, and I could be dressed, wouldn't be that much different from some of the stuff we've had to do on missions. Never mind last night."

"Yeah."

Omega pondered for a moment.

"I...I don't know," she finally admitted.

"You don't trust me?"

"If I didn't, I wouldn't have done it last night in the hammock," Omega pointed out. "The problem is those pheromones an' junk. I was sufficiently... upset...last night to override my responses to those. But combine your innate pheromones with my current...hormonal nor'easter of a storm, I guess you could say...well, it isn't YOU I don't trust, Ace; lemme put it like that."

"You can't tell me that one hour of venting is all you needed to get it all out, baby."

"No. But you helped me get past the acute phase, at least for now, Ace."

"Well, whether I'm in the bed with you or not, I intend to be in the bedroom with you, Meg."

"Okay. I can handle that, I think. I, um...you're not upset, or, or offended, are you?"

"No. I don't fully understand what's happening to you, but male biochemistry doesn't operate the way female does, so I probably never will, even under normal conditions. I can still respect that you're struggling."

"Thank you for that, and I'm glad I didn't hurt your feelings."

"No. We're good. How about this?" Echo proposed. "Let's not worry about the details of exactly where I bed down, for now. It's only just past lunch. Let's see how you're doing when we decide to crash, and let that determine what I do."

"That'll work, I think. And thanks for providing options."

"No problem. But," Echo said, his face heating, "I promised myself I'd man up and do something, and I think now is maybe the time to do it."

"Huh?"

"Well, it's gonna be a little bit embarrassing, baby, so try to bear with me."

"Okay..." Omega cocked her head, and took another sip of her wine; Echo, who had an old-fashioned glass containing a couple of shots of his preferred whisky on the rocks, sipped his as well.

"All right. The first thing I need to do is to 'fess up that, well, that when I woke up this morning—you were still asleep—the, uh, the 'guy bits' as you like to call 'em, were...active."

"Oh, I see," Omega said. She sounded unflustered to him, but her cheeks turned slightly pink, and she chose to hide her face in her wine glass as she took another sip.

"I was really careful to position us so it wouldn't be...well, you know," Echo told her. "I didn't want it to upset you, or worse, bring back memories of...of Wright in your bedroom at home. And I'll do my damnedest to keep on doing that, as best I'm able, if you decide you want me...closer than the floor, tonight...and any nights in the future, for as long as this mess persists. I'm trying hard to live up to your trust in me, Meg. I can't help certain physiological reactions, but I can damn straight do all I can to avoid them making your mental state worse."

"I...got a question," Omega said, looking quizzical.

"All right. Shoot."

Omega was silent for long moments, while Echo waited patiently. Finally he tried again.

"Meg?"

"Hang on a sec," she told him, staring out, over the ocean. "I'm working on wording."

"Oh, okay."

After several more moments, she turned back to him.

"I was..." she began, then broke off, shook her head, and tried again. "Look. I think you realize that...that the whole thing with what Slug did to me, did a number on my self-confidence and self-esteem, certain aspects of 'em, at least, once I found out about it all...and I never really have recovered from that, at least not yet."

"I know."

"And you seem to try really hard to ensure that I feel good about myself, even when I...don't. Even when someone else has made comments that effectively stomp all over any self-esteem I've managed to build back up about...about who, and more importantly, what, I am."

Echo sighed.

"I notice. I see and hear it when they do that," he told her. "I know exactly the specific people you're talking about. Some days I wanna slam heads together. They'd never think about saying and doing those things to Romeo or India, because of their skin, or to one of the ambassadors, who are legitimately of other species. But they think it's okay to do it to you! No, Meg, it isn't right, and yes, I've been doing my best to try to..." He shrugged, then continued, "...build up what they tear down. Let alone buffer their remarks and behavior, when I can." He sipped his whisky, then looked back at her. "You still haven't asked a question."

"I know. I'm sorta building up to it, so you can see my train of thought," Omega explained. "'Cause, what I want to know is, are you really, um, isolating the 'guy bits' for my sake, or are you telling me that to keep from hurting me, because you don't truly wanna even risk going there with me, the being...the creature...created to be your killer?"

Echo gaped at her, shocked. *Of all the questions I thought she might ask, that wasn't even in the list,* he thought absently. *But at least she's asking me directly for a change, and neither assuming nor dancing around it.*

Now I gotta figure out how to answer her without chancing spooking her, or lying to her, or making her suspicious of what I DO mean. 'Cause if I do any of that, I'll mess things up with the relationship...which I think might be starting to finally head in the right direction. So I wanna keep the progress we've made, and not screw it up.

"Well, that's a Blue Screen of Death expression, if ever I saw one," Omega chuckled, as Echo tried to gather his scattered wits. "Evidently that wasn't even in the realm of what you considered I might ask, huh, Ace?"

Echo snorted.

"Sometimes you read me like a book, baby," he told her. "Yeah, you caught me totally off-guard with that question. I've been debating the best way to answer, 'cause I don't want to say anything to upset you, so I think the best thing to do is to be straight-out."

"You're not comfortable risking going there with me."

"And then other times, you project onto me," Echo corrected. "No. I'm not afraid of you, Meg. Not at all. There are really only two things in the universe that truly scare me, though, and both of 'em have to do with you. Okay, well, maybe three, and the third one has to do with Ma."

"You're afraid of losing her, now that you got her back."

"Bingo. But the other two things are: one—I'm honestly afraid of you getting yourself killed, and two—I don't want to do anything, or have anything happen, that would send, or drive, you away from me...from being beside me."

"Aw," she murmured, and retreated to her wineglass again. Echo recognized the response as *pleased, but embarrassed*. He pressed on.

"So I really am trying to avoid upsetting you by the physiological responses I can't control, baby," he added. "Because I know what happened the other night was traumatic for you, and I want to give you plenty of time and space to deal with it. As far as whether or not I'd wanna go there with you, have you looked in the mirror lately? You're a beautiful, intelligent, talented woman, honey. And damn strong, damn tough, and damn resourceful. Granted, certain persons to whom we alluded earlier are too closed-minded to see it, but otherwise, I think there aren't too many straight, unattached males who wouldn't be interested, Meg, given half a chance and maybe some encouragement."

There, he thought. *I think I said that pretty good. That's as direct as I*

*can be without coming out and saying, 'Meg, I'm crazy about you.' Here's
hoping it's enough to nudge her into providing some of that encouragement.*

Omega stared at him, blinking.

"Okay, baby," he chuckled. "Talking about a Blue Screen of Death expression, it's looking at me, right now. With big blue eyes."

Omega physically shook herself, then they both laughed.

"Reboot! Sorry, Ace," she told him. "I just...wasn't expecting...I think that's maybe one of, if not THE, nicest things you've ever said to me. That...anybody...has ever said to me."

"I meant every word."

"I know. I could see it in your face, in your eyes. That's what makes it so very special."

"Let it sink in, then. When certain people sound off their big fat damn mouths, remember that your partner thinks you're hot stuff." He grinned. "And he's the one that counts, anyway, right?"

"Right!"

They laughed.

But Echo noticed that she inched a little closer to him in the hot tub. Then she sank down in the water, leaning her head on the pillowed rest and looking out over the ocean, with a singularly calm, contented expression in the sapphire gaze.

Chapter 6

As the temperatures dropped and the rain became heavier, the pair decided to go inside. Echo grabbed some of the dry driftwood he'd stacked by the back door and carried it in, depositing it in the wrought-iron firewood rack beside the fireplace. Then he waved a towel-wrapped Omega at the bedroom door, while snugging the towel tied about his own waist.

"Go get stripped, dried off, and dressed," he told her. "Hang your wet suit on the cord over the tub. I'm gonna lay and set a fire in the fireplace, then we can trade places, and you can get out the marshmallows and skewers."

"Ooo, that sounds good!" Omega said with a grin.

* * *

Twenty minutes later, Alpha One was dry, dressed, and sitting cross-legged on the hearth roasting marshmallows in the fireplace, which flickered with multicolored flame as the salt-impregnated driftwood burned. The sky outside was very dark despite the time of day, and the pair had decided to leave most of the lights off in the house for the time, allowing for the cozy ambiance of the flickering firelight.

"Did we grab that package of hot dogs at the store?" Echo wondered.

"Yeah, it's in the meat drawer in the fridge."

"Fire-roasted hot dogs for dinner?"

"Sounds great!"

They were quiet for a few minutes, staring into the fire.

"It isn't quite a campfire, so I don't suppose we can get away with telling ghost stories," Echo remarked with a chuckle.

"Meh. No. I...don't think I'm really in the mood for ghost stories right now anyway," Omega decided. "Whenever any of Slug's machinations crop up, I always feel like I'm surrounded by ghosts, somehow."

"I'll bet," Echo agreed, sobering. "Sorry if that hit a nerve."

"Nah. I'm just up for something more cheerful. If I let myself introspect too much right now, I'll start to disappear in the dark and drear." Omega gestured to the windows, and the dark clouds pouring rain beyond.

"What about general adventures?" Echo wondered.

"What do you mean?"

"I've been in the Agency for around a couple decades, Meg. Shipwrecked together on a protoplanet notwithstanding, you haven't begun to hear all of my tales. Let alone those of my friends, that I know about."

"Oh, now THAT all sounds good!" Omega decreed, and settled back with a marshmallow and her glass of wine, which Echo had refilled along with his whisky. "Let's hear some!"

"Okay, lessee. Oh, there was the first time Fox took me an' X-ray off-planet, to provide security to the diplomatic team Fox was headin' up, back when he only headed the Diplomacy department..."

* * *

That morning before setting out on their damp beach stroll, Echo had brought all of the driftwood they'd previously collected to the back door on the deck, and stacked and covered it to ensure it stayed dry. As the afternoon progressed into evening, he brought it all in and stacked it in the rack beside the fireplace, then turned on the television, flipping it over to the weather station.

"Uh-oh," Omega decided, watching the forecast. "It looks like we might have a mess developing."

"Yeah. I'm betting that this cool front moving through now winds up hooking up with that low-pressure system out in the Atlantic, wrapping up, and making a doozy of a storm," Echo agreed.

"You think we need to batten down for a nor'easter?" Omega wondered. "I've never actually been through one of those, so you'll have to tell me what to do, and what to expect."

"No, not here; it's forming too far off the coast," Echo concluded, studying the map the television weatherman was presenting. "Northern New England might be in for a blow, but once the front finally makes it through here—which might take longer than I thought; it's wrapping up pretty tight around the low and might go stationary, at least through this area—the sky should clear out and go back to sunshine and fair weather. We might have some high surf for a few days, though."

"So...what? Another day or two of wet weather, then it clears off, but the wave action stays up?"

"Exactly. Taking an afternoon swim is gonna be out for a while. It'll be too dangerous. There'll be rip currents and undertow and all kinds of shit."

155

"But we can still go for walks on the beach, right?"

"Sure, but I'd recommend staying a little farther back from the surf than usual. These kinds of conditions can generate those rogue waves we talked about. Never mind just bigger than usual ones."

"Okay. That makes sense. I've seen some video of unwary tourists getting slammed by those things in various places around the world."

"Yeah. And some of 'em get washed away and don't come back to tell about it."

"...Let's be careful, then."

"Bingo."

* * *

"Thank you both for coming here," Fox said, as his two visitors sat in chairs across the desk from him. "I know, in the circumstances, you are both very busy, trying to work out this whole farkakte piece of drek with Wright—especially given Ambassador Zz'r'p has only just returned from his negotiating mission—but I think there is an aspect of this situation that we may need to address that is at least as important as the more obvious problem."

"So this isn't a social visit," Zebra noted.

"No, I suspect it is not, Zebra," Zz'r'p agreed. "More, since I am here, I suspect it has to do with the...PSYCHOLOGY...of our very special Agent, who needs our help."

"And you'd be right," Fox averred. "Now, this is going to get a little tricky, and I will need both of you to assist me in keeping this aboveboard, and limited to the people in this room, at least for now..."

"Why?" Zebra wondered, confused.

"Because, bubeleh, there is only one person in this room who is actually authorized to know what is in Omega's medical records—YOU," Fox explained. "And never mind the farshtinkener rules, that is as it should be, and I have done my best, all this time, to maintain Omega's privacy—as has Echo, I might add. However, by dint of deprogramming her, Zz'r'p already has a great deal of knowledge of what was done to her. And since we initiated the ongoing efforts to close various cold cases generated by Slug when he modified Omega, I have been able to...deduce...quite a bit, myself. And I think that is going to factor into this discussion of Omega's current mental state...which, I have gathered from, ah, certain surreptitious communiqués from both Echo and India, is deteriorating, or at least beginning to."

"It's deteriorating, all right, but..." Zebra confirmed. "I'm sorry, Fox; I've had my head into the whole biochemistry problem, and I guess I need to come up for air and shift gears, if you don't mind my mixing metaphors..." She shook her head. "I'm afraid I'm not gettin' it, hon. What is it you're worried about?"

"No, let me, Fox," Zz'r'p suggested, as Fox pursed his lips in thought, then opened them to speak. Fox nodded and waved at the Deltiri, who turned to Zebra. "Omega's mental state is deteriorating, Zebra, as you say, and this is perfectly understandable given what is happening to her. Stalking, attempted rape, the hormonal 'storm' she is likely only beginning to experience, the telepathic bombardment from Wright, all will be combining to create a negative frame of mind in her. But I believe Fox thinks there may be other factors involved, factors that date back to her...'creation,' if you will...as a sleeper agent, and to her sudden realization last year of what had been done to her. Things that we have yet to take into account, in the current situation. Things that it is possible we should have foreseen, should have taken steps to counter before now."

"Exactly," Fox confirmed. "But I have only just come to recognize it in the time since Wright arrived, unfortunately. You see, bubeleh, I think there is a kind of PTSD layering over, or maybe under, this whole thing. And I think it is tied up in her understanding of what Slug was attempting to do to her." He paused, and looked at them both. "I think this is why she has had trouble accepting herself as human, pretty much ever since she realized the magnitude of what was done to her."

"Keep going, honey," Zebra said, forehead creasing as her brows drew together. "I'm thinking you may be about to hit on what I've been trying to put my finger on for months."

"It is not going to be a pleasant discussion, meyn teyere," Fox warned.

"I know. But it needs to happen, just the same. Keep going."

"All right, the first thing you need to realize—Zebra, keep your mouth shut, my dear, and Zz'r'p, whatever you do, do NOT attempt to read her in these moments—is that, based on those cold cases, I now suspect that there was quite a good bit of genetic material that was inserted into Omega that was...not sentient," Fox said. "In fact, it was likely derived from various animals, though probably not from Earth."

157

Zebra clamped her lips firmly shut, and Zz'r'p drew a deep breath. Fox watched both of them in silence, until they gestured for him to continue.

"I have no idea what the ratio of sentient to non-sentient material was, and I'm not sure it matters," he went on. "What I do know was important was that each was there for a purpose, and each was forced to express in Omega's body...or mind, as the case might be. Our first collective thought, when all of this came to light, was that he was attempting to create the perfect Agent candidate, in order to ensure her successful insertion into our ranks. But I'm no longer certain that was true, and I suspect that Omega has come to a very different conclusion about what he was attempting...and I'm not sure but that she's not right."

"Go on, my friend," Zz'r'p murmured.

"We look at Omega, who is a wonderful, truly outstanding individual, with so many capabilities, and think that Slug picked the best candidate and worked to make her better," Fox noted. "But what if what he REALLY wanted was to DEVOLVE her, while maintaining her intellect?"

A perturbed Zz'r'p immediately sat back in his chair, eyes wide. Zebra glanced from one male to the other.

"Devolve?" she echoed. "What— I don't..."

"You don't want to face it, meyn gelibte, because it is painful, because she is a dear friend, even family," Fox said, voice very soft. "Open your eyes and look. Slug didn't want a superhuman. He wanted a beast with above-average human intellect. Something he could control, that was smart enough to pass as an Agent."

Zebra gaped at him, paling.

"Oh, dear God," she whispered. "Meg was right. All along, she was right. He wanted her to be...an animal."

"A bestial, corrupted remnant of a human," Zz'r'p murmured, seeming to suddenly understand. "With Omega's intellect."

"Something he could control," Fox reiterated. "A killing machine, astute and canny enough to fool the rest of us, to fool Echo while standing right beside him, to seem like the perfect partner to him...all while preparing to kill him."

"Oh, damn," Zebra breathed. "Damn, damn, damn. Yeah. That's what she thinks she is. I've heard her say so. And you think that's what he actually did?"

"Does it not make sense, bubeleh? Based on what you know?"

Zebra stared at him for a long time, then slowly nodded.

"Zz'r'p?" Fox wondered.

"It...makes amazing sense," the ambassador admitted. "More, it makes...when I deprogrammed Omega and freed her memories of the abduction and modification, I perforce shared most of it with her. And...I did not understand certain of the procedures, at that time. I knew what they DID, but not WHY he did them. Or at least, why he did them the WAY he did them. This...causes all of the puzzle pieces to fall into place." He looked up and met the Director's eyes. "That was almost certainly the way of it, Fox," the Deltiri declared. "He tried to create an intelligent brute, a kind of fiend in human skin. His own distorted, demented hand in action against Echo and the Agency."

Fox winced.

"You're confirming it, then?" he asked.

"I am," Zz'r'p said, voice low. "I wish to Maker I could disprove it."

"But you can't," Zebra whispered.

"No. I cannot. Because it is the only thing that makes sense of what I 'saw' in her mind, in her memories."

"And...Fox, you think Meg...realizes this?" Zebra wondered, horrified.

"I think she does, Zebra," Fox said, somber. "Doesn't it cause her responses to things to make more sense? How she has lost so much of her self-confidence, her sense of self, why she has been willing to risk her very life in missions, especially if it means Echo survives?"

"Well, that could partly be because she's trying to atone," Zebra pointed out. "Never mind how she— uhm, never mind."

"How she feels about him," Zz'r'p finished for the physician. "It seems I am not the only one to know of her feelings, then."

"No," Zebra admitted. "Though she hasn't exactly come out and SAID so. So I'm not bound by my oath to keep THAT secret."

"And I know her well enough at this point that I suspected, too," Fox averred. "But no. Omega's...willingness to give all...goes far beyond any of that. She is so willing to die—I think—because she isn't sure she's worthy to live. And because," Fox added, "it may be easier to face death than to face life with that kind of understanding of oneself."

* * *

159

"But she's NOT a beast! She's not a thing!" Zebra cried. "She's one of the kindest, most thoughtful people I know!"

"No she is not, and yes, she is; and in that regard, Slug failed miserably," Zz'r'p agreed. "Because no matter what he did to her, what he could NOT do was to expunge the great heart, the glowing soul, and the indomitable spirit, that dwells in that poor mutilated, dissected-and-reassembled body."

"But even her body is beautiful," Zebra pointed out. "She could be a supermodel, with that body and face."

"And a gurfdin is beautiful on the outside," Fox observed, "but I wouldn't want to face one without a force field wall between me and it. I like my internal organs to STAY on the inside."

"Well, point..."

"But you're right, gelibte," Fox agreed. "Our Omega—and I use the possessive pronoun deliberately, for she is our family now—is neither monster, beast, nor animal. She is human—an augmented human, without doubt—but still, HUMAN. A brilliant, loving, caring sentient, fierce to any who threaten those she loves, tender with those same loved ones. Have either of you ever seen her with a child?"

Zebra and Zz'r'p shook their heads.

"I have," Fox confessed. "We don't often get many children through Headquarters, and some agents don't quite know what to do with 'em. Echo used to be one of those...until he worked with Omega. Then he saw how she handled them, and...learned. It was that same Dendroid child that got lost in Central Park last year, early in her career as an Agent, and she and Echo found it; the family came back for a visit a few months later. When Preeg came running to Omega, she crouched down, then sat on the floor, and took the child into her lap...she held it and talked to it for nearly twenty minutes. There was no impatience, no discomfort, in Omega OR Preeg. In moments, the little one was giggling and laughing and hugging her...and she hugged back, a huge smile on her face, those blue eyes of hers fairly glowing..." Fox's hazel eyes were distant, a soft smile on his face, his expression that of a proud father for his daughter.

"That is not the act of a degenerate monstrosity, such as she believes herself to be," Zz'r'p noted. "And yes, I have 'heard' those words, and others like them, in her mind."

"So she does believe it," Fox breathed.

"She does."

"No wonder her mental state is so bad," Zebra realized. "And now this whole ball of shit with Wright is just playing into that mental self-image. Because it's trying to force her to turn into nothing more than...well, than an animal in heat."

"Exactly, gelibte." Fox shrugged. "We—those of us who love her— know it is not true, of course; we know that Slug failed in his efforts, as you pointed out earlier, Zz'r'p. The question I have is...what do we do about it?"

"We tell her she's wrong, that he failed," Zebra declared, staunch. "Because he did."

"That may be easier said than done," Zz'r'p pointed out. "And I, for one, am not even certain where to start, given her mindset. But yes, we must try."

"We have to do better than try," Zebra averred. "We gotta succeed. Or we're not gonna be able to keep her from going out with a bang, sooner or later."

"And that, we will prevent at all costs," Fox added.

* * *

Dinner was a quiet affair that night, hot dogs cooked over the fire along with mugs of the last of the clam chowder, eaten on the sofa in front of the fireplace. Echo turned on a couple of lamps and set the windows to one-way so the pair would not be visible from outside. But he kept the interior light levels low in favor of the coziness of the firelight, and they leaned against each other and chatted, mostly of inconsequential things, for several hours.

The rain eased, and the cloud cover became somewhat broken, as patches of rain moved through and then cleared. Far out over the ocean, an occasional flash could be seen, as the developing storm system released a lightning bolt, but it was much too distant to hear any thunder.

Finally they both began to yawn.

"Welp," Echo murmured around a prodigious yawn, "I guess that means it's time for bed. How are you feeling, baby?"

"Meaning, where do I want you to sleep?" Omega confirmed.

"Yup. I'll do whatever you need me to do. I figured on sleeping in this," he waved a hand at his t-shirt and drawstring shorts, "so if you need me to hold you so you feel safe, I can do that, and all the proprieties will

161

still get observed. But I also brought along an air mattress I can put on the floor against the door. Throw on the spare set of sheets and add a couple extra pillows, and I'll be fine...if you prefer a little more elbow room, in the circumstances."

Omega sat for a moment, thinking.

"I've been...the weather is affecting my mood, a little bit," she admitted. "And that's making me notice Mark more, so I'm...feeling sensitive..."

"Does that mean you need me close, or you don't think you can handle me that close?"

"I, well...I don't think I can handle it tonight, Ace," she confessed. "Part of me would really like to, I'll admit. I felt..." she shook her head. "I don't think I've felt...as safe...as I felt last night, since I was a little girl, taking a nap in Momma's arms while she rocked me to sleep."

"Aw." Echo flushed. "I'm glad it helped that much, Meg."

"Me too. And I really wish I dared do it tonight. But I'm...I've noticed the, um, sensations...MY sensations...seem to be a little, uh, hyped-up today. Which means if we try to do that again tonight, I'm gonna be too aware of you being there to actually SLEEP."

"Which kinda defeats the purpose," Echo realized. "Okay. Let me bank the fire and close the fire screens, and we'll head to bed. Once we're both in the bedroom suite, I'll close an' lock the doors and inflate the air mattress, then you can help me put sheets on it. Once THAT'S done, I'll hit the bathroom to brush my teeth an' shit while you put on your jams, then you can have the bathroom and I'll go ahead and climb into bed, after I've checked the security on the master suite with A.T.L.A.S.S. Junior. How does that work for you?"

"That'll work."

"Let's go, then."

* * *

Once they were both in bed, Omega turned out the bedside lamp, only to discover that the bedroom had the same little orange nightlight that Echo had ensured their bedrooms had at Headquarters.

"Oh, good," she murmured.

"What?" Echo's voice came from the shadows near the door.

"The nightlight. Just a familiar comfort, is all. That, and even if it's cloudy tonight, I'm not gonna run into something if I have to get up and go to the bathroom in the middle of the night."

"Well, that was kinda the point, yeah. You know me—if I do have to get up in the night, my eyes are barely open. I need all the advantages I can get to avoid giving myself a black eye or busting my nose. Never mind smashing my foot into the nightstand and breaking a few toes, or tripping over something."

"Let alone running into the wall, because you're drugged to the gills on accounta being shot, an' haven't got a clue where you are," Omega reminded him of a certain minor incident the previous holiday season, and they both snorted in amusement.

"That, too," he agreed.

"Are you comfortable over there on that thing?" she wondered then.

"Yeah, it's gonna sleep great. Just the right amount of support."

"But the floor..."

"This air mattress is one of the Agency specials," Echo said, and Omega could hear the grin in his voice. "Let's just say it's not ON the floor."

"Oh..."

"Yup. G'night, Meg. Sleep well, baby."

"Good night, Echo. An' back atcha."

* * *

Judging by his breathing, Echo fell asleep relatively quickly, but sleep took considerably longer for Omega. Wright had seemed to increase his efforts to break through her telepathic block as the day progressed, with the result that she was left with a feeling of being watched constantly. This was particularly disconcerting for the Agent, who was used to disappearing into a crowd if need be.

It also meant that, no matter how much she might want Echo closer, she felt as if their private time was being spied-upon. And given his remarks in the hot tub after lunch, Omega was no longer entirely sure that matters would remain platonic if Echo shared the bed, especially given the increasing hormonal turmoil within her.

I suppose it was designed to keep escalating until I had no choice but to mate, Omega considered with a disconsolate sigh, staring up at the dim, blurred silhouette of the rotating ceiling fan. *I mean, that's pretty much how estrus works in most animals; why should it be any different for me? I sure hope we can manage to end this before it gets much worse, though.*

163

It's already like PMS raised to the twelfth power or something. Whatever it is, it ain't fun.

Omega shifted position, then rolled over, trying to find a posture that enabled her to settle and go to sleep, but had little luck. Finally she threw back the covers and rose, glanced at Echo to make sure she hadn't awakened him, then tiptoed around him and across to the big floor-to-ceiling window overlooking the deck. The effort was not an easy one, as the door onto the deck was close enough to the main bedroom door that Echo had simply positioned his air mattress against both. Omega smiled slightly at that realization; nobody was coming after her unless Echo knew about it. And he would have a say in the matter.

It was misting heavily outside, with gusty winds thoroughly soaking everything, or she might have tried to slip out the door onto the deck so she could listen to the surf. As it was, she eased under the privacy curtains to ensure any outside light did not disturb Echo, and stood there for long minutes, watching the waves by the faint light of the crescent Moon, shining out between the broken clouds.

The levels of estrogens have gotta be going crazy, if I go by the way I feel, she decided, wishing she could hear the sounds of the surf. *And that, in turn, is slowly DRIVING me crazy. Not in the truly insane way, just in the 'how much of this can I take' way. Damn. I'm restless, and if there isn't some kinda breakthrough soon, I'm gonna be hopping around here. Thank the good Lord that Echo is being so understan—*

Just then, a male hand came to rest on her back, fingers splayed.

"YEEP!" a badly-startled Omega squealed, jumping and spinning into a horse stance, fists up. The privacy curtains flew about.

"Hey!" Echo exclaimed, taking a step back and holding out his hands. "It's just me, baby! Settle down! Wow, you ARE restless tonight."

"Oh geez! I'm sorry, Ace," Omega apologized, relaxing and sagging just a little. She ran one hand over her face, then up into her hair, which spilled loose around her shoulders; she raked it back, out of her eyes, with that same hand. "I thought you were still asleep. I didn't mean to wake you. Yeah, I'm restless. What with the telepathic link that I can't quite block, it feels...it feels like I have an invisible peeping Tom or something, watching me all the time."

"Ugh."

"Bingo."

"And I bet that's another reason you weren't comfortable with having me closer, tonight."

"Yeah, a little bit. Even just talking to you, it feels like we're being spied on, somehow." She sighed. "I wanted to sit out on the deck for a while and let the sound of the waves kinda lull me enough to maybe get some sleep, but it's raining again. Not a lot, just enough to get me dripping wet in about five minutes."

"Yeah, I see that," Echo said, pulling the curtain aside to peer out. "I dunno what to tell you. Is there anything I can do? Maybe get something outta the medikit to help you sleep? Or, well, Ma used to make me an herbal tea blend when I was little and had nightmares or something; I could maybe try to put it together outta what we got here. Or something similar, maybe. I can even call her and get her to recommend something, if I need to."

"Uhm," Omega considered. "Is the medikit in the bedroom? I don't really wanna undo all the security stuff you put on the bedroom. I wasn't gonna go past the eaves, 'cause you said that's how far it extended, right?"

"Yeah. But the wind is gusting out there a little, and you'd get soaked anyway."

"I know. Which is why I didn't. But..." Omega sighed. "I feel as safe as I'm gonna get, in here, so..."

"Got it," Echo said, turning and heading for the bathroom. "Medikit coming right up."

* * *

Echo fished out a mild soporific for his partner, administered it via a small pill, and Omega knocked back a glass of water to wash it down.

"Now," he said, patting the mattress, "let's get you back in bed and resting before that kicks in. Otherwise, you may fall over on me."

He held the covers for Omega to crawl back in bed, then very gently and affectionately tucked her back in. *I can get away with this here,* he thought, *because there's nobody to see, and because she needs me close and we both know it. And because we're comfortable with each other...and I hope that's getting even MORE so. I can tell, just by looking at her, that she appreciates it. But Romeo would carry me high over it, if he were here and saw that. I'd just tell him to shut up and go to hell, but it would probably embarrass Meg. Especially in the last couple of days, with...everything.*

165

But Romeo wasn't there, and Omega definitely did appreciate the consideration and affection; she offered him a small smile as a reward, and he returned it.

"Everything's gonna be okay, baby," he murmured. "I gather Wright's been knocking on the metaphorical door of your head again?"

"You nailed it, Ace," Omega replied in kind, then she sighed. "All day long, dammit. Harder an' harder as the day went on. Aaand the ol' hormones are makin' like the waves out there." She nodded at the windows, just as the Moon emerged from the clouds to illuminate a roiling, foamy surf. "It sorta leaves me...all churned up inside."

"Gotcha. Anything I can do?"

"Nothing but what you're doing now, what you've been doing," Omega noted. "Which is being incredibly considerate and understanding, for Mr. Badass Tough Guy Original Agent."

"You know me better than to think my reputation is all I am."

"I know. I was just tryin' to tease you a little. My humor may be a little...off...for a while, Echo. Please bear with me, as much as you can. With the way things are right now, sometimes I need to just find something to laugh at, otherwise I'm gonna scream instead."

"Oh. Okay." He sat down on the edge of the bed. "Can I ask a question?"

"Sure. I dunno if I'll know the answer, but I'll give it a shot."

"When Wright is...doing what he's doing now to make you restless," Echo tried to express it, "what is he doing? What's he telling you?"

"He's not really saying anything, to speak of," Omega explained. "He tries to, to watch, like I said, but he doesn't actually say much. It's more like some obnoxious salesman who won't stop knocking on the door, or...OH! Do you remember that video-compilation show we watched last week, with the wee little kid who just kept going, 'Mom! Mom! Mom! Mom! Mom!' over and over again, until it was about to drive everybody up the wall?"

"Yeah?"

"Exactly like that! It's like he's saying, 'Meg! Meg! Meg! Meg! Meg!' and just won't quit."

"Yeeargh."

"EGG-zackly!"

They laughed.

166

* * *

Echo sat on the bedside and chatted quietly with his partner. Eventually the medication enabled Omega to simmer down, get sleepy, and fall into a quiet repose. Moments after that, she was asleep.

Echo gently tucked the covers around her shoulders and returned to his own bed, and in minutes the room was dark and quiet, as two tired Agents got some well-earned rest.

* * *

The next morning, Omega was still sleeping when Echo woke up. He tiptoed over to the bed and checked on her, to find her soundly asleep, apparently calm, and though not smiling, her expression was relatively peaceful. So he slipped back over to his own bed on the floor against the door, crawled between the sheets, and curled up, falling back asleep within minutes.

They slept in for more than two hours past that point, before Omega began to stir. Her movements woke Echo, who was still in 'mission mode,' so they rose at the same time. They took turns relieving themselves in the bathroom, then shared it while they brushed their teeth and splashed water on their faces.

"Feel like breakfast?" Echo wondered.

"Yeah, I'm hungry," Omega admitted. "But this morning, you gotta let me help."

"I still kinda need to do something for you, baby."

"I know. But I'm...jumpy...you saw that, last night...so letting me help make breakfast will be the something you're doing, Ace. I...need to have something to keep my mind occupied."

"Oh, I get it. Okay, let's go see what we got, and make some breakfast."

Echo brought down the topmost-level security he'd set around the bedroom, and they headed for the kitchen together.

* * *

After a basic breakfast of scrambled eggs, bacon, and pancakes with butter and maple syrup, Alpha One checked in with Headquarters, but there was no news: Medical was still working to figure out how to undo what had been done to Wright; Security, Software, and Medical were working to ascertain how to make A.T.L.A.S.S. tell the difference between Wright and Omega, without having to fall back to an outdated version that would cause security problems for the others inside Headquarters; and the Arcturan Deltiri embassage was working on a way to end Wright's programming and thereafter deprogram him.

"Well, shit," Echo grumbled when they ended the call.

"That right there," Omega decreed, and sighed. "So...now what? It's still raining and yucky. And the surf's kinda rough."

"Yeah. Probably better we don't go beachcombing again until the weather settles down a little bit."

"I suppose." Omega sounded—and looked—morose.

"Aw, baby," Echo murmured. "Everything's gonna be okay. We just gotta work with the weather for another day or so, and then we can get back out and about. Even so, if you wanna get out of the house, we have a couple of options."

"Lay out all our options, then, please sir." She offered him a slight smile, and he returned it, with interest.

"All right. If we stay inside, we can watch tv, or we can throw in a movie—I got duplicates of some of my favorites up here—or we can light a fresh fire in the fireplace and talk, or roast marshmallows, or read, or all of the above. If you really need to get outside, we CAN do it. Because, remember, the house has a deck, and is itself up on pylons. And there is a little stairway that'll take us down under the house, opening off the mud room. I even have a fire pit down there, for weather like this, and there's stone benches around it. So I can grab some of the driftwood and take it down there, you can grab the bag of marshmallows, the chocolate bars, and the graham crackers, and we can go down there and feel the wind on our faces and hear the surf, but stay dry. Then we can light a fire in the pit and make s'mores, yak our heads off, or just sit and kinda let be, for a while. Whatever you wanna do. Or, if you're up for it, we can drive into town and go to a movie."

"I...don't think I feel comfortable going into town. Not right now."

"Does any of the rest of it appeal, then?"

Omega thought for a few minutes.

"Let's go down and light a fire in the pit."

"Consider it done, baby."

* * *

The breeze off the water was cool and damp, but refreshing, and they

168

did indeed stay dry under the house proper, especially after Echo got a fire going in the pit. He was careful not to use too much wood; they didn't need it to stay warm, and there was only a limited amount of it. Plus, as he told Omega, they weren't likely to stay out there all day, and he didn't want to go off and leave a fire burning UNDER the house.

"So I'd prefer keeping it small enough that it'll burn out pretty quick, unless we keep feeding it," he pointed out.

"That works," she agreed, and they sat and made s'mores and watched the wind and waves. Omega seemed disinclined to talk, and Echo refused to push her on the matter. She was, after all, somewhat preoccupied with a kind of mental battle, or at least a sort of telepathic duel, and if she needed to focus on that, it was not something with which he could help, and it would be best if he remained silent and let her concentrate.

But it was not an unpleasant silence; the two were used to each other's company and enjoyed it even when they were feeling subdued. So it was a companionable time despite the lack of conversation.

Eventually, by mutual consent, they decided to extinguish the fire and go back inside for a late lunch.

"Then we can see what we wanna do this afternoon," Echo said.

"Okay," Omega agreed. "You want salads, sandwiches, or something hot for lunch...?"

"How 'bout a combo? I got a panini iron in the cabinets someplace..."

"Ooo, that sounds good!"

* * *

On their second shift together, Oscar turned to Yankee.

"I hate to do this, but I really need a break, Yankee," she murmured, wincing. "I'm in some pain."

"Huh? What's wrong?" Yankee wondered, concerned. "You were fine the last time we were on duty."

"Yeah, well...I did something stupid last night," she admitted. "The LED in my nightlight finally went bad and I haven't gotten around to re-placing it yet. Last night, I got up in the dark, and I ran into the END of the bathroom door. Hard. I think I broke some toes on the door, and maybe a rib on the doorknob. And wearing this body armor isn't helping anything. It's supposed to be adaptive, so it conforms to my body, but it's also supposed to fit snug, so..."

169

"Ow! Damn, woman! Why the hell didn't you go to the medlab?!" Yankee wanted to know. "Here, lemme help you get off some of that armor, then I want you to go straight to the medlab and get seen to."

"But I'm supposed to be..."

"I'm Alpha Line," Yankee noted. "That puts me in charge at the moment. If something happens—big if, I know, but hey—it isn't gonna help me any if you're in too much pain to back me up. Not that anything is gonna happen; this guy, Mr. Statue there," he jerked a thumb over his shoulder at the immobile Wright, now clad in a medical jumpsuit, "doesn't do shit. He just stands there and stares into space. I dunno what the hell the problem was with him, or why Alpha One couldn't handle him." He moved to Oscar's side. "Now, lemme help you get off some of this armor, then you can head for the medlab..."

* * *

Chairs had long since been provided for the guards on duty, so they didn't have to stand for many hours on end, and Yankee piled Oscar's body armor in one, then sat down in the other, facing the force field 'window' by himself, to wait until she returned. He sighed, and addressed the man inside.

"Dude, you are about the most boring duty assignment I think I've ever gotten," Yankee noted. "At least blink or something."

Mark Wright simply stood, staring into nothingness.

Yankee sighed again.

* * *

The branch of Security responsible for the brig had been instructed to ensure that all guards on Wright were well supplied with food and drink and anything else they might need, so periodically a carafe of coffee, with disposable cups, showed up on the small table provided with the chairs... though meals were a bit farther between than some of the Alpha Line Agents could have wished, and tended to be lighter on fare than their usual activity levels required. So Yankee consumed his share of the coffee, AND Oscar's, while waiting for her to come back from the medlab.

Meanwhile, he popped off a few text messages. Most were to Tare, as he continued to attempt to raise his partner, though he now suspected that Tare had him blocked—which hurt Yankee deeply, though he would never admit to it; he considered his partner his best friend, almost a brother, and felt betrayed.

But he also notified Romeo that Oscar was in the medlab after an overnight accident. Some few minutes later, Romeo replied.

She gonna b ok?

Dunno. Havent heard back frm her yet.

Do I need 2 grab somebody & send 2 back U up?

Not yet. Perp quiet as usual.
Just sitting here staring @ each other.
If O gets put on sick leave will notify U 4 new shift partner.

Roger. Keep us posted.

Wilco.

Yankee sighed, grabbed his coffee and sipped from it, and tried texting Tare again.

* * *

When a couple of hours had passed with no sign of Oscar returning from the medlab, Yankee began to realize that he'd consumed a bit too much coffee, with all of the physiological responses that entailed. Unfortunately the nearest men's room was down the hall and around the corner, and no one was responding to his summons at the 'front desk' of the detention area. He stood and stared at the prisoner in the cell facing him.

There's nothing to this guy, he thought. *This Wright dude has barely moved, except when the medics were working on 'im the other day, and that was mostly to squirm whenever his shoulder popped open. Damn, that was disgusting! An' it hadda hurt. I can't say I'd want that done to ME,* Yankee considered. *But he's no big wup. I heard he attacked Omega, but it can't have been any big deal. Then again, 'Saint Omega' probably made a fuss or something. And when she says jump, everybody else is supposed to say, 'How high?'* He shook his head.

Anyway, he's inside a double force field; he's not goin' anywhere. And

171

I'll only be gone a couple minutes, just long enough to take a quick leak before my bladder blows. I shouldn't have had so much coffee, but I'm worried about Tare and I guess I wasn't payin' attention. He moved to the corner and glanced around it. *Damn. Not a soul in sight. An' I gotta GO.*

He glanced between the men's room door, just visible at the end of the corridor, and Wright, in his cell. As usual, Wright stood in the center of the high-tech enclosure, unmoving and unblinking. Yankee made his decision.

He headed down the hall toward the restroom.

* * *

Once Yankee was well out of sight, Wright seemed to wake up. Though his gaze remained unfocused, he moved to the force field wall, stood before it, and waved one hand. Then he stepped forward...

...And walked into the corridor, as the force field dropped in obedience to the fact that Agent Omega, assistant chief of the Alpha Line department, was not on the logged roster of prisoners.

But Wright was still clad in a medical jumpsuit, and as such, tended to stand out.

Wright moved to the chair containing Agent Oscar's discarded body armor, and reached for the vest.

* * *

Yankee came back to Wright's cell only a few minutes later, and sat down in his chair. But when he glanced up, he was horrified to see an empty cell. He leaped up and ran to the control panel on the wall adjacent to the force field, checking its status: the force field wall was completely down.

He spun and surveyed the area, looking for any place Wright could be hiding; there was nothing sufficient for a grown man to hide under or behind.

Then Yankee did a double-take, and paled.

All of Oscar's body armor was missing.

"Oh, shit," Yankee whispered.

* * *

"...He did WHAT?!" Fox roared at his cell phone.

"Ow! Ease up, Fox," Romeo's voice said over that instrument. "You preachin' at th' choir, here. Yeah, you heard right. 'Stead o' notifyin' me that Oscar never came back—which, by the way, was an oversight on the medlab's part, too, bein' as Zarnix an' Zebra are both workin' on Wright's case an' turned over the emergency room shit t' a new guy..."

"Where is Oscar? Is she all right?"

"She's been admitted t' th' medlab, boss-man. Got a couple o' busted toes, a busted rib, possible busted cheekbone..."

"From WHAT?"

"'Cordin' to Yankee, th' nightlight in her quarters went out, an' she ran into a door end-ways when she got up in the night, last night."

"Ouch," Fox said, wincing. "That would do it."

"No shit. An' Oscar confirms it; India done checked out that end o' things. So Yankee can't raise anybody in Security 'cause they got something else goin' down an' everybody's over in Manhattan helpin' th' field agents chase it. An' rather than contactin' me or India, Yankee decided t' bebop down th' hall t' take a leak."

"Leaving the prisoner alone."

"Yup. He swears up an' down he was only gone a couple minutes, which is prob'ly true. A preliminary look-see on th' security video seems t' back 'im up on that. He also swears that Wright ain't moved a muscle the whole time he's been down here. But evidently it ain't registered on 'im that the sensors can't tell Wright from Meg, even though I briefed that in th' departmental all-hands. Or else he don't care; I haven't decided which. Maybe both."

"So Wright is roaming Headquarters somewhere. I'll put out an alert to look for a man of his description in a medical jumpsuit."

"No, Fox; that won't help. It gets worse."

"How MUCH worse?"

"Well, it turns out, Oscar's body armor was hurtin' her on account 'a all those busted bones, so Yankee helped her take it off before she went to the medlab, 'cause she could hardly move, it hurt so bad..."

"Uh-oh."

"Yeah, you got it. The armor is missing. All of it. Every single piece. An' since it's body-adaptive, all he hadda do was put it on, and it adjusted to fit 'im. So Wright is decked out in a complete suit of Agency body armor, not in a medical jumpsuit. An' that includes a helmet, so you prob'ly can't even see his head or face. An' he'll have th' headset alertin' 'im to anything we broadcast."

"Abdab."

"Pretty much, yeah. The way India an' me figure it, he's gonna be lookin' for a way to head to Ipswich an' find Meg. Which means we need to do two things: lock down Headquarters, and…"

"Notify Alpha One," Fox finished for him.

"Right."

"I'd rather wait to notify Alpha One until we know there is reason to do so," Fox considered. "Omega…has been struggling a bit with the stress."

"Aw, shit."

"Yes. So I don't want to add to that stress unless it becomes absolutely necessary. Once we know if he's already left Headquarters, I'll notify them immediately, but I suspect we have a goodly probability that he has not, at least as yet. So I'll get on the facility lockdown right away."

"Okay. I got Yankee confined to quarters for th' time being," Romeo noted. "Once you talk t' Echo about it, lemme know what he wants done."

"Will do, zun. Fox out."

"Romeo out."

* * *

No sooner had the link broken with Romeo than Fox hit the intercom to his assistants.

"Lima here, Fox."

"Good. Lima, I need some fast work, here."

"Name it, boss."

"I need a facility lockdown, sufficient to stop a disguised Mark Wright from escaping Headquarters, and I need it done five minutes ago, if not sooner."

"Perfect timing; Bravo just walked up. We'll get on it right now, Fox. Question—"

"Ask."

"Can we issue a Maximum General Emergency?"

"Do it. In fact, I'm considering a Level 3 Facility Alert. We don't need this man possibly accessing everything Omega is cleared to access." Fox paused, thinking. "Yes, do it. Level 3."

"On it, then. We'll have it done inside sixty seconds, which is about as fast as it CAN be done."

"Good man. Thank you, zun."

"You're welcome. I hope Agent Omega stays safe."

"So do I, Lima. So do I."

* * *

"...So that's the whole story, boss-man," Romeo said, as Alpha Two stood in Fox's office a bit later. Outside the bay window, the Core fairly swarmed with scurrying agents sweeping the locked-down facility, looking for their missing prisoner.

"Yeah," India tag-teamed. "He was so worried about where Tare was, and why he didn't show for the all-hands departmental meeting—'cause he thought Tare would be in trouble—that he evidently missed the part where Wright is Omega's identical twin to the sensors. And the same anxiety caused him to down...like, nearly two-thirds of that whole big carafe of coffee, without paying attention to how much he was consuming...until nature called."

"So...he was distracted by the very thing that I was supposed to prevent," Fox sighed. "Maybe I need to just retire and let Echo have this job."

"No, man," Romeo noted in protest. "You done fine, Fox. You can't help it if things get crazy now an' then. Sometimes shit just comes atcha from all directions, an' all you can do is try ta dodge it. 'Sides, me 'n India have had a couple private, friend-to-friend talks with Meg 'n Echo..."

"Uh-huh, and they're not nearly ready for those promotions yet," India agreed. "Oh, Echo is probably plenty ready to do the Directorship, though he'd argue with you on the point. I think that's more a psychological resistance to the idea than any actual lack of knowledge or skill, though. But Meg...Fox, we need to give her more time to deal with her own body, with what was done to her, before dumping her into the full leadership of Alpha Line. Especially given this whole big problem with Alpha Seven."

"Uhn. Good point," Fox acknowledged. "I just can't help feeling...and this doesn't go any farther than this room, for now...but I can't help feeling I have skrud aroyf, kinder."

"Huh?" Romeo said, blank. "Uh, Fox, I'm not too good with th' Yiddish..."

"Oh, I'm sorry, zun; I wasn't thinking. It's just...I can't help feeling I've screwed up, children."

"Nah, Fox, you're good, man," Romeo demurred. "You done talked to Yankee, right?"

"Yes, though not quite as soon as I'd hoped to do..."

175

"How did he react?" India wondered.

"Not...well," Fox admitted. "He got hostile and defensive very quickly. Are you sure about your decision, Romeo? I won't countervene it, but make very sure."

"No, I'm not a hundred percent sure, Fox," Romeo confessed. "But there's mitigating circumstances there. He honestly didn't know about Wright's an' Meg's genetic mess, an' he's been distracted real bad by th' whole shit goin' down with Tare. I'm not takin' 'im off report, but I'm not throwin' 'im in the brig yet, either."

"I'm just doubtful you should be putting him back on duty, honey," India pointed out. "Remember how he came to be in Alpha Line, after all— he, his partner, and Monkey, all three, due to being suckered into what amounts to a small insurrection. If he's that distracted, he doesn't need to be doing an Alpha Line job. Let alone standing guard over a perp that's after Alpha One...assuming we can recapture said perp."

"There's a lockdown on Headquarters," Fox declared. "The visitors aren't happy, but the new arrivals are being rerouted to other Offices, and we're trying to process the departing aliens as fast as we can...without letting Wright out with 'em."

"Good," India said. She turned to her partner.

"Right. I'm not too sure 'bout lettin' Yankee back on duty, either," Romeo admitted. "An' I ain't forgot how he got inta Alpha Line. But Tare an' Monkey turned out okay, once they realized th' truth. So th' way I see it, we've filled him in, an' he just got a hard lesson on payin' attention. He was...pretty embarrassed an' upset that Wright got away on his watch, literally. So now he needs a chance t' redeem himself an' shit."

"Which puts Meg in danger of being raped, if he screws up again and we're not on top of it enough," India pointed out.

"I know," Romeo said, voice low, and sighed, then shook his head. "B'lieve me, honey, I know. This is one o' those hard leadership choices."

"And do I know about those, zun," Fox noted, sober. "How is Oscar? What's the latest?"

"Still in the medlab," India informed him, "and likely to be there for a few days, while they get her patched up. It turns out that one of the broken ribs caused a small puncture in her lung, and there are torn tendons in the foot. Never mind the fact that a cheekbone break is essentially a skull fracture. She really did a number on herself."

"Ow. Gronk and merde."

"Pretty much, yeah. We're looking into dependable, alternative personnel to fill in with Yankee. And keep an eye on him, to make sure he does it right, next time."

"Yeah," Romeo vouched. "Way we figure is, if we're gonna give 'im that chance t' redeem 'imself, we need t' stack th' deck in favor of."

"Good. Keep me posted."

"We will, Fox," Romeo averred.

"Very good. Unless there's anything else, Alpha Two is dismissed; I figure you two need to get back to it."

"Got that right," Romeo said, and he and India headed for the Alpha Line Room.

* * *

"Echo?" Omega said, coming up to her partner as he sat on the couch and sketched on a large notepad. "Whatcha doin'?"

"Mm?" he said, looking up. "Oh, I was trying to sketch out what I think the modification to the house should look like. I'm figuring, if we use a small internal space warp and rotate the current bedroom/bathroom suite ninety degrees, then we can leave the current suite like it is, add a short hallway, open the old bedroom door into it, add a bedroom an' bathroom combo across the hall, and maybe even a home office for two—well, with two desks and laptop ports, at any rate—at the end of the hall. The new bedroom wouldn't have deck access...unless we extended the deck...but if we work it right, the whole wing becomes a safe space." He held up the pad. "What do you think?"

Omega studied the rough-penciled floor plan for several moments, then decided, "I like it. I think that'll work." She smiled at him.

* * *

"Terrific," he said, returning her smile. "Did you need something, baby?" He blinked, and studied her for several moments. "You look...bothered."

"Yeah," she sighed. "I think I need to kinda...move. I'm gettin' antsy. I'm considering going for a walk on the beach."

"You want me to go with?"

"Um, no offense, Ace, but I expect I sorta need to be alone with my thoughts for a while," Omega tried. "I need to think over some stuff. But see, if you come along, in the state I'm in with the hormones an' pheromones an'... everything...I'll be paying more attention to you than to thinking. Then I'll get all self-conscious and start babbling, and we'll get into some sort of conversation, and then I'll be thinking about that instead of...stuff."

"What sort of stuff?" Echo wondered, eyeing her, concerned. Omega sighed.

"You aren't gonna like it."

"Try me."

"I need to figure out where I'm going with the rest of my life, Echo," Omega said, meeting his eyes, earnest. "I...look. Your comments—your compliments—yesterday in the hot tub got me thinking. There's a reason I sometimes joke about being a lab rat, you know—that's how Slug treated me, and apparently Mark, too—and this whole mess with Mark has only reinforced that for me."

"Come on, Meg," Echo offered, keeping his voice and manner as gentle as he could. "Anybody that really cares about you—like me, for example—doesn't give a shit about all that."

"I know. But I also know that...well, in spite of my sharing the memories with you, hon, you still don't...don't know everything about...that. I've tried and tried, but I just don't have the nerve to tell you EVERYthing! I'm sorry," she murmured, looking away. "It has nothing to do with trust, and everything to do with...with...being ashamed of it."

Her voice dropped to a whisper, then cracked and went away entirely. Echo watched as she swallowed several times, then tried to speak again, but nothing would come out. He stood and took her shoulders in a light grip.

"You know you don't have to be ashamed of anything, as far as I'm concerned, right?" Echo breathed.

"You say that now, Ace, but..." Omega shook her head, still refusing to look at him. "If you knew every last detail, you...might not."

"Then again, I just might. *I* think I would."

"I can't take that risk!" Omega cried, pulling away and turning her back on him, wrapping her arms about herself and covering the places he had just held with her own hands, as if trying to keep the sensation of his hands on her body without actually allowing the contact. "Ace, if you... turned away from me...because of it, I...I couldn't...you're the core of what-

178

ever 'family' I have left, hon. I..."

"Is that what you need to think about? What to do about it?"

"Yeah," she confessed. "If I can...can get up the nerve to...to actually tell you. That's part of it, anyway."

"What's the rest?"

"Whether anybody deserves to get saddled with it, with...me," she sighed.

"I'd say I already am," he teased, trying to lighten her mood.

"Not like I'm talking about. You said you weren't afraid of me, but...I mean..."

"Mu isn't afraid of you."

"He knows less than you do, when you get right down to it," Omega pointed out. "A helluva lot less. You know...almost all of it, now."

"And it's whatever that last little bit is that's bugging you, isn't it, baby?"

"Boy, is it. Anyway," she glanced over her shoulder and offered him a weak smile, "you know so much, and, and you've been so...UNDER-STANDING...about all of it...I'm trying to decide if I should..." Omega drew a deep breath. "I'm...scared, Echo."

"Of Wright?"

"No, not so much, not at the moment, anyway. I'm scared of losing the wonderful relationships I've got. With you, with your mom, with Romeo and India, with Zebra and Fox..."

"Your family."

"Yeah."

"How is telling me gonna lose the whole family, baby? Besides, I'd think Zebra and India already know, surely. And probably Fox."

"No." Omega shook her head. "Well, Zebra knows. She kinda has to."

"So it's medical. And? What was her reaction?"

"She...didn't seem to think it was a big deal, though she admitted she could understand why it might upset me. I'm...not really sure she...compre-hends the big picture, but...she accepted it, at least to the point she under-stood it."

"And why should I be any different?"

"I don't know!" Omega cried. "I...that's why I need to think. I'm won-dering now if maybe you wouldn't even blink, but I'm scared, and I'm all messed up with Wright banging around outside my head and mucking up my insides with the biochem run wild, and..."

"Ohhh," Echo said, starting to understand. "You need to get by yourself for a bit and try to get settled, so you can sort through it."

"Yeah. And I can't seem to manage to do that inside the house. I need to MOVE."

"It's still kinda rough out there, baby. That cool front did merge with the low out in the Atlantic, and the sucker is forming a nasty storm offshore. It isn't likely to come back and hit us, but we're still catching the ass end real good." Echo waved his hand at the back wall of windows. "It's still overcast and prone to rain, not to mention the banks of fog that keep rolling in. And the surf's up pretty high."

"That's actually kinda why I want to go," Omega murmured. "The weather...appeals."

"But you're gonna walk along the beach?"

"Yeah."

"You do know what a rogue wave is, right? We talked about those a couple times before..."

"Yeah. I'll be careful, and stay far enough away that the surf won't get me. And I'll even take my phone, and turn on the beacon app, if that helps."

"Yeah, okay; that makes me feel a little better, baby," Echo murmured. "The force field is on, there's been nothing new out of Headquarters, and I haven't reset the security from our first night here, so everything will be okay. Just be REALLY careful."

"Always."

* * *

Echo watched from the windows for several minutes as Omega descended the stairs from the deck and wandered down toward the water.

She's trying, he thought, pleased. *She's really trying. She wants us closer. And she as much as confessed that she'd be devastated to lose me in some way, assuming I'd actually turn my back on her because of what Slug did—which I wouldn't. And she referenced the conversation in the hot tub, which was about whether or not I'd be interested in an amorous relationship with her. So she caught on to that. She's just...scared. Which may mean that the few things that truly scare her are an awful lot like the ones that truly scare me, only reciprocal. Which...is good.*

Echo glanced at the sketch notebook, which he'd discarded on the end table when Omega had approved of it.

Hm. We might not end up needing that wing addition after all.

He grinned, and headed for the kitchen, planning on preparing a nice hot meal for a certain very special companion, who would likely return to his side cold and wet.

* * *

Aimless, Omega wandered the beach alone. It was desolate, cool, and sprayed by wind-blown spume, but the churning waters and gray skies, peppered by intermittent rain showers, suited her mood and somehow assuaged her roiling mental and emotional state.

"I think part of it is the rhythm of the surf," she told herself. "There's something soothing about that whole 'Bloosh-shushhhhh' sound, over and over." She chuckled, then sighed. "Okay, girl. What do you do now? I thought I'd never hear anything out of Echo that would indicate he was actually...interested. Not given I'm Ms. Engineered Echo-Assassin Creature, anyway. Then, lo and behold, he comes out with that beautiful compliment yesterday...that sure sounded like he WAS actually interested. And NOT only as a friend...or even a best friend." She ran a hand over her platinum braid, already starting to grow damp in the blustery weather. "I sure hope I was right. Well, then again, though...should I do this to him? Given...what I am? Do I have that right? IS it right? Should I do it to ANYbody? After all, Mu is waiting to know if we're going on a date when this is all over, too. Damn! I sound like a blasted soap opera," she declared, and snorted in grim amusement.

She glanced up at the lighted windows on the bluff. *Now he's gonna be expecting the last details when I get back,* she realized, spotting a silhouetted male figure watching her through the windows, just before it turned and went deeper into the house. *I know him too well to think he won't. He knows now that I haven't told him everything, and he'll want to know those details too. And be disappointed—in me, in the situation, in general—if I don't. And I probably owe them to him. I just don't know how. Or even if I can.* She turned to gaze out into the deep. *How do you tell the man you love, the man who might be interested in you, that not only were you treated like an animal, not only do you have the biochemistry of an animal, you have the genetics of one, too? Hell, I got the alien equivalent of Rover spliced in*

181

here. Several versions thereof, several times over. Then forced to express.
She stared at her hands. *That's why I can smell better, and hear better, and run fast, and ALL that shit. Because I'm Slug's little bloodhound bitch. Or... or worse, really. I'm a THING. And now he wants to breed me. At least the bastard is dead and can't watch.*

Omega kicked at a pebble and headed farther down the beach.

* * *

The vehicle hangar master was preparing to hand over to her shift relief, so she was busy conducting the standard end-of-shift inventory of Agency vehicles, comparing the security video to her logs of craft. Said inventory included vehicles checked out as well as vehicles brought in to the hangar. Just as her shift opposite came into the office, she frowned.

"What's wrong, Union?" Chocolate asked.

"I got a discrepancy," she noted.

"How so?"

"I got a car missing, and no record it was checked out."

"Lessee."

Chocolate bent over the electronic log and studied the entries under Union's index finger, then looked up at the security video that viewed every parking space in the hangar.

"Huh. I see what you mean. The Beemer in space Charlie Sierra Foxtrot two-one-one is missing..."

"Exactly. And it shouldn't be." Union pulled over her keyboard and began typing commands.

"Whatcha doin'? Checking the video to see who took it?"

"Yeah. It's probably just somebody who forgot to log it, but with this Level 3 going down, we need to make sure."

* * *

A couple of minutes later, both hangar masters watched as an armored male Security agent with an average build moved to the vehicle and picked up the key fob hooked over the driver's-side rear-view mirror. A couple of quick button taps, and the BMW was unlocked, the driver's-side door open. The agent removed his helmet...

...To reveal a rather handsome, tow-headed man whose image had gone out on the Level 3 Facility Alert: Mark Wright.

* * *

"Oh shit," Union whispered.

"That's the guy they're looking for!" Chocolate exclaimed. "How the hell did he get by you?"

"Lookit the time stamp on the video," Union said, tapping the screen. "I had a whole slew of Erikians from the embassy in here, demanding to know why they weren't allowed to check out any vehicles and leave Headquarters! Have you ever heard a pissed-off Erikian yelling? With those special suits of theirs? Damn! I couldn't even hear myself think! Besides, why didn't the new security system flag him?!"

"Uh-oh," Chocolate murmured. "I think maybe we just found a bug in the new security system. In which case, it's a security risk to publicize the fact."

"Ooo. Good point. Well," Union murmured, reaching for the comm, "time to report the breach. Dammit."

"Yeah. I'll see about filing the paperwork while you report it."

"Thanks, buddy."

"No prob, hon. Hey, we still on for drinks tomorrow?"

"Sure. Assuming I'm not in the brig or something."

"Aw. What about the hangar guards? They coulda spotted him too, but apparently didn't."

"Yeah. It's almost like...the guy has some sort of ability to, I dunno, make people not notice him, or something."

* * *

"Yeah, I've got it," Lima said into the comm. "No, don't sweat it, Union. It's not good news, but I don't think you're in trouble, especially given you were busy and nobody else on your team saw it, either. Yes, there's a glitch in the new security system, and you and Chocolate need to be aware of it. Yes, you should have been notified. No, I'll chase that oversight down the rabbit hole; it went down quickly, and there have been a few slip-ups like that, so don't worry about it. We'll handle it. Thanks for the info." He broke the comm connection.

"That didn't sound good," Bravo noted, sitting at the adjacent desk.

"It's not. Wright stole an Agency car and left Headquarters."

"Damn."

"Yeah. Listen, I'm gonna pop you the specs on the car, and we need to get out word to all field agents in the area to watch for it. Can you do that?

I need to notify Fox...and I guess, Alpha Two...about this."

"Okay, dude," Bravo agreed. "But Fox isn't gonna like it."

"I'm not too thrilled either, but it's gotta be done. They're gonna want to put together a team to go find him and bring him back, before he gets to Alpha One."

"Yeah. Pop me the specs, then call Fox asap."

"Right."

* * *

Fox drew a deep breath and raked a hand across his face, up into his salt-and-pepper hair, but did not curse...in any language, Earth-based or not. In point of fact, he was not only tired, he was deeply disappointed and concerned that the Agency—an organization he viewed as his 'kids'—was underperforming so grossly.

We—I—have done something very wrong in setting up this organization, I suppose, he decided. *Or perhaps we are simply too systematic, too predictable, and Slug was able to develop a kind of fault tree, the places where he determined he could most readily break down our system. After all, he had secured access to Headquarters itself for at least two years, prior to the attack on Omega. Two years to watch. Never mind whatever he managed to do when the organization was still in its relative infancy, in the years immediately after his original confrontation with Echo. Nearly two decades...to watch for holes. And damnation, did he find them.*

"Fox, man, you okay?" Romeo asked, his concern obvious. "I ain't never seen you look like that."

"I'm wondering where we went wrong, zun," Fox murmured, not trying to hide his emotions...not from these two. "And how far back it was. And if there was anything we might have done to plug the holes. Then... or now."

"You look...very tired," India tried.

"Say it, India," Fox sighed. "You need not be concerned for my feelings. I already know it."

"Say...what, Fox?" India wondered, puzzled.

"That, for the first time since you've known me, I look my true, chronological age," Fox told her, giving her a rueful half-smile that even he knew did not reach his eyes. "I look tired, and I look old."

"But you don't," India said, soothing. "Not old, certainly. You look tired, yes. But more, you look...really, really...worried."

"I am. Our system is breaking down. We are failing to protect our own. And I...don't know how to stop it."

"I'm not sure you can stop it, not the way you think," India decided. "Did you hear what Lima reported from the hangar master?"

"Which part? That Wright walked right past everyone and drove away? That no one was paying attention?"

"Yes, but no," India said, thoughtful. "The part where the hangar master said that nobody seemed ABLE to notice Wright."

"What?" Fox looked up, hazel eyes suddenly alert and sharp. "Wait. You're right. He DID report that."

"Exactly. And we already know there's some sort of loose telepathic link to Omega," India pointed out. "And likely another link formed when her programming triggered, in order to start his 'countdown clock,' to use one of Meg's terms."

"Are you saying, India...?" Fox began.

"I am, Fox," India declared. "What if Slug hard-wired in some sort of, I dunno, loose ability to influence the minds around Wright? Nothing fancy, not like a true telepath could do. Just enough to where we all get a kind of subliminal suggestion, 'This isn't the man you're looking for. Go about your business,' or whatever. Like that classic space opera movie Echo gets such a kick out of."

Fox stared at India for a long moment.

"Get down to the medlab and tell Zebra, Zarnix, and Bet your idea," he ordered. "Right now. Have them look at their tissue samples and medical data and ascertain if it might be possible. Especially look at any genetic data they might have gotten; I know they won't have a full genetic analysis run, because that takes too long to be complete yet. But they might have something. Maybe something they can compare to Omega's, or the like, and determine if there is enough 'tinkering' to make that possible."

"On it, Fox," India said, heading for the door. "Romeo? You coming?"

"Romeo stays here for the moment, India," Fox commanded. "Run on, and come back here when the medlab is done with you. Romeo," he added, as India nodded and headed out, "I need you to help me round up a team of volunteers to search for Wright. I'll get Bravo and Lima to get me the time Wright departed, because I'll also have to call Alpha One and warn them, in case we don't catch Wright before he gets in their vicinity."

"Then you take care o' that, boss-man," Romeo declared. "I'll take care o' roundin' up a posse to go after Wright."

"Good man," Fox agreed. "Run with it. I'll call Echo."

Romeo headed out as Fox reached for his cell phone.

* * *

"Yeah, man," Mu told Romeo as he sat at Echo's desk, trying to coordinate a team to track down Wright. "As former Secret Service, I've got some experience at this. I've chased down dudes that were after the President; I can do this. I know I'm not Alpha Line...at least, not yet; I was planning to drop in an application once I finish my shakedown period with the Agency...but the way I figure it is, if I'm out there helping catch this dude, your special forces people can run interference for Meg. Besides, I don't want anything to happen to her."

"You're volunteerin', then?" Romeo confirmed.

"Absolutely. I've already checked it with my supervisor, and he's good with it. Hell, I'll head up the team, if you want me to."

"All right. That actually does help me out, then. I got half my people workin' on figurin' out how to block off the medical confinement area, an' half settin' up various perimeter levels between here an' Alpha One, an' a general mess with one of my Agents confined to quarters." Romeo leaned back with a sigh and shook his head. "DAMN. I do NOT want this job on a permanent basis. Not any time soon."

"Hey, pal," Mu said, laying a hand on Romeo's shoulder and squeezing lightly. "It's gonna be okay. You, your partner, Echo, and me, we're gonna keep Omega safe."

"We're tryin', dammit." Romeo sat up straight. "Okay, Mu. Given your background, I'm gonna put you in charge of Team 1, searching for Wright. I'll pop you th' information in a file to your cell phone, here in a minute. Then I'll call in the rest o' th' team and brief y'all, an' you c'n go."

"All over it."

* * *

Echo was just starting to prepare a nice hot meal—it was his special Texas red chili, with various toppings, and a salad on the side, a basic meal he knew Omega adored, and which would warm her chilled, wet body when she returned from her walk—when his cell phone rang. He yanked it from his hip pocket and stared at it for a moment before answering, then activated it.

"Echo. That you, Fox?"

"It is, zun. What does your security system show?"

"Huh? Uh-oh. Something's wrong, isn't it?" Echo said, immediately pulling out his force field remote and double-checking it, before hurrying to the bedroom and opening the wall panel that revealed the hidden control monitor setup.

"You could certainly say so. Wright is gone again; Security agent Oscar is in the medlab emergency room with quite a few broken bones, thanks to a rather nasty little accident in her quarters last night, and Yankee is currently confined to his quarters, because he left his post when he should have been on duty—that's a long story in itself. The video shows Wright just... walking out...of the cell, donning Oscar's body armor, and heading out."

"Oh, shit," Echo whispered. "Did he hurt her bad? No, wait—she got hurt while she was off-duty, you said?"

"Yes, she did; Wright didn't do it. Nor did Yankee. But Echo, that's not all." Fox's sigh was audible. "One of the spare automobiles is missing, with security video showing him taking it. He shouldn't know how to morph it, but he has a driver's license—they kept his wallet in the cell with him for easy identification purposes, as well as ready access to personal details, and it's gone now—so he's got a way to get to you."

"Damn, damn, damn. How long have we got?"

"You don't. The hangar video indicates he got out of Headquarters about four and a half hours ago. Security told me they were sure they had it programmed to register Wright this time! Dammit, shit, merde, gronk, and abdab. The only way to fix the security at this point is to drop back to an older, visual-sensor-based form, but that leaves us wide open to spoofing, which is why we left that technique to begin with. Eventually we'll have to go to a two-to-three-part ID verification, I guess. But that slows down the system..."

"Wait. How long did you say?"

"About four and a half hours ago."

"Four and a half...Fox! He could BE here by now! Or at least in Ipswich, proper."

"I know. I called as soon as it was elevated to me, which was pretty quick after it was discovered, only a couple minutes. It seems that Yankee drank too much coffee and had no one to stand guard while he ducked into the men's room, given Oscar was in the medlab at that point—and they're at fault, too, for not notifying anybody they'd admitted her. When he got back from the restroom, Wright was gone, along with all of Oscar's body armor, which she'd left there to increase mobility enough to get to the med-lab. The woman has multiple fractures in her foot, a couple of cracked ribs, and a possible cracked cheekbone!"

"Damn!"

"Exactly. At least Wright isn't responsible for her injuries, though Omega wouldn't be so lucky, if he gets to her. What do you see on your security monitors?"

"Nothing," Echo noted, then snarled, "Put Yankee on report, and throw him in a cell in Confinement. I'll deal with him when this is over."

"He's already on report. And confined to quarters."

"Put him in Confinement!"

"You think he did it deliberately."

"I don't know, but I damn well intend to find out."

"Echo, let Alpha Two and me handle this," Fox said. "We've already discussed it, and they believe there may be mitigating circumstances, and that it was NOT deliberate."

"I don't care. I—"

Just then, a loud klaxon went off in the house.

"INTRUDER DETECTED. INTRUDER DETECTED," the house-hold computer blared. This was immediately followed by a loud, resonating *POOMP* from somewhere outside. "DUPLICATE OMEGAS DETECTED. EXTRANEOUS OMEGA EXCLUDED."

"Aaand there he is on the monitor, right on time," Echo noted. "Wait... what...? He's on the INSIDE of the force field! How the hell...? Then where is...? Uh-oh..."

* * *

On the beach outside, as Omega strolled, she suddenly saw the force field dome flare a dim yellow, about fifty feet out, over the ocean. Abruptly it flickered and died, then flashed back into being—BETWEEN Omega and the beach house. Before she could react, it suddenly re-established its original perimeter...

...And with a resonating *POOMP*, Omega found herself knocked fully thirty yards through the air, soaring over the beach and into the heavy surf some sixty feet from shore...

...As a monster wave crashed over her head.

* * *

"A.T.L.A.S.S. Junior!" Echo cried, "locate Omega!"

"OMEGA LOCATED NEAR DRIVEWAY PERIMETER."

"What the hell is she doing there...? She went for a walk on the beach! On display!"

The video monitor shifted to depict a human form walking up the driveway. But it was male—in fact, it was the image Echo had just been observing, except from a different angle.

"Oh shit! That's Wright!" Echo realized. "A.T.L.A.S.S. Junior! Locate the other Omega!"

"THE DUPLICATE IS NOW OUTSIDE THE FORCE FIELD PE-RIMETER."

"Show me!"

This time the video monitor depicted high storm surf...just as a plati-num-blonde head, streaming water, bobbed to the surface in the near dis-tance.

"Damn, damn, damn, with an abdab and gronk thrown in!" Echo cursed.

"Zun, I'm still on the line. What's happened?" Fox's voice came from the cell phone.

"I gave the computer an order not to allow any duplicate companions," Echo explained, "but since Meg wasn't actually here beside me, and she and Wright were about equidistant from me, one at the front and one at the back, evidently the household computer flipped a coin and got it dead wrong, Fox. Wright is inside the force field dome, and Meg got punted out-side it—straight into the heavy surf this storm is producing! And it looks like she's in a rip tide, to boot!"

"Damnation! GO, zun!"

"Later, Fox!"

* * *

Echo ended the call, then brought up the locator app on his phone, ty-ing it into the beacon app. *I only hope she remembered to actually set it,* he thought as he waited to see if the app picked up anything. *Not to mention hoping that these phones are way the hell more waterproof than their standard terrestrial analogs.*

The locator app abruptly pinged and depicted a bright red, moving dot.

"THERE she is!" Echo exclaimed. "Shit, that rip is moving fast! At least I know she's a good swimmer from our training, but that's some hella rough surf out there. Okay, take care of Wright first, or get Meg?" He spent precious seconds bringing up a split-screen, so he could see Wright on the left and Omega on the right. "Wright's cut across in front of the house. Now why...oh. He's gotta be headed for the rock stairs on the south end of the property, which he'd know about because MEG knows," Echo realized. "That means his programming has enough sense not to want to confront me if he doesn't have to. But if I don't move fast, he might out-flank me. Maybe it's good that I didn't show Meg exactly where all my weapons caches are..."

At that very moment, Omega got another ducking beneath a huge wave. She emerged on the surface seconds later, gasping and panting, struggling to tread water, even as the powerful rip current carried her farther out.

"And that just answered my question," Echo decided.

Echo ran to the corner and grabbed the high-tech air mattress he had used the night before, hitting the instant-deflate button and rolling it into a loose cylinder, then stuffing it into a warp pocket. He headed into the den and scrabbled in an old chest in the corner, bringing out what looked like a lifeguard float...with several buttons that lifeguard floats shouldn't have. He kicked off his flip-flops; one soared across the room and landed on the couch, but he paid it no attention. He ran to the back door and shoved his feet into his surf shoes, yanking them up and over his heels, then he was on the deck, overlooking the ocean.

"Damn," he muttered, staring out. "No sign of her in all that wave action."

So he lunged for the stairs to the beach, vaulting over the railing...and grabbing what he thought of as his fireman's pole, a special emergency route down the twenty-five feet to the beach proper which was disguised as one of the support columns, that he'd installed for just such situations as this. *Though I gotta admit, I didn't think I would be racing anybody to get to the distressed swimmer,* he thought, as he grabbed it with legs and arms and slid down it.

Within seconds, Echo was sprinting across the sand toward the surf.

* * *

As he neared the water's edge, he pulled the force field remote, shut the field down entirely, then set a one-hour timer to re-establish it. The remote went into another warp pocket. Then he dragged the air mattress from the first warp pocket, hitting the auto-inflate button; a second later, it was inflated and in the water. Echo lunged forward, pushing it into the surf and past the breakers, then he clambered up onto it and dug in the pillow pocket, fishing out a control.

"All right," he muttered, "adjust settings to...stiff base, hover mode, and...there." Suddenly the entire thing was suspended several inches above the water. "That takes care of that. Now for the other." He shoved the 'lifeguard float' into the pillow pocket along with the mattress control panel, hitting a hidden button on the 'float.'

The 'float' turned into an antigrav propulsion system, and the air mattress hovered roughly a foot above the waves, sailing out, toward where he estimated his partner to be.

Behind him, Wright was already halfway down the stairs cut into the side of the bluff.

* * *

A stunned Omega watched, startled and bemused, as the water closed over her head with a huge splash.

What the hell just happened? she wondered, as dark gray-green water swirled above her. She kicked, and popped to the surface, gasping and choking before taking a deep breath. Then she began to tread water, and looked around to orient herself and figure out the quickest route back to land.

Uh-oh, she thought. *I didn't think I was THIS far out. Wait a minute...* She paused and focused on a specific rock on the beach, watching as it grew farther away by the moment. *Oh shit. I'm caught in a rip tide!* she realized...just as another huge wave smacked her in the back of the head. She sputtered and coughed, then turned and tried to swim parallel to shore in an effort to get out of the rip current. Each time another massive wave approached—which was entirely too frequently—she dived under it, emerging on the back side.

191

I don't expect Echo even knows anything is wrong, dammit to hell and back. I should have brought him with me after all, I guess. But then it might just be both of us that's in this pickle. What I'll do when I reach the force field dome, I have no idea, she considered. *I really hope I don't have to swim all the way to the edge of Echo's property. Not in this sea. I'm not sure I have the endurance for that, Alpha Line training or no; this water's turned COLD. And it's way the hell too rough to try to float; I'd get slapped from here to Long Island and back.*

Just then, she saw the force field glow a pale, washed-out yellow again, in the murky fog that had swept in with the higher waves...then it disappeared altogether.

Ooo! she thought. *That might just mean Echo brought down the field! In which case he DOES know I'm in trouble. Thank You, God.*

Omega tried to keep her head as far above water as she could, and surveyed the area, looking for Echo somewhere—on the beach, in the water, it didn't matter; he would have help of some sort with him.

* * *

From time to time, water washed over the top of the air mattress as a wave crest managed to reach it. Echo held his cell phone in one hand, watching the locator app, and steered his makeshift craft with the other. Within moments, his position drew close to the red beacon location. But there was no sign of Omega.

"Oh shit," he breathed. "She oughta be around her somewhere. Unless she's already gone under, in which case I get to go pearl diving. Damn this fog! Meg?! MEG! ANSWER ME! It's Echo! WHERE ARE YOU?"

Then he kept silent for long moments, straining his ears, listening over the crash of the surf.

"ACE!" came the cry at last. "Ackggl! Ptui! ACE! OVER HERE, ACE! OVER HERE!"

Echo dared to rise to a kneeling position on the hovering air mattress, risking a wave crest hitting him broadside, scanning in the direction of the cries, until he saw arms waving desperately between the swells. Relieved, he turned the mattress and drove it to her location, then pressed the <stabilize> control to ensure that the mattress would stay put and rigid while he grabbed Omega's arms and dragged her onto the mattress.

"Baby?!" Echo said, as she lay on the mattress and coughed up water.

"Are you okay?"

"I will be," she murmured. "I don't think I've ever been this water-logged, though."

"Any in the lungs?"

"No, not really. I'll take something for it, just in case, when—"

"When we get back to Headquarters."

"Oh-kaaay. What the hell happened?!"

"Wright is here. I'll tell you more about that later. Evidently the two of you were about equidistant from me, so the damn household security computer flipped a coin and picked slap dead wrong."

"That 'soft' setting on the force field is the biggest damn trampoline I ever saw," Omega noted, as Echo turned their makeshift hovercraft and headed north, up the beach, away from Wright, who was now on the beach proper, and moving toward the water at speed. "I went from several yards away from the edge of the surf, to getting ducked way the hell out in the drink before I could blink."

"Damn. It didn't hurt you, did it?"

"Other than nearly getting me drowned, no. Surprised as hell, but un-hurt."

"All right, baby, hang on. I'm about to head back inland, and I'll be taking us up."

"I had no idea you could rig something like this with what you had—is this the air mattress you were SLEEPING on, last night?!"

"Yup. Keep your center of mass low, baby. Here we go."

A few adjustments of the 'float' and the mattress, and the odd hover-craft lifted a couple of feet into the air, headed for the sand and rocks of the beach proper, and gradually continuing to gain altitude.

But as they crossed the surf onto land, Echo glanced to the left and spotted Wright, sprinting up the beach toward them.

"SHIT!" he exclaimed. "I didn't know the dude could run like THAT! Hang on, Meg!"

Swiftly Echo adjusted the altitude controls, but the lifeguard 'float' was overloaded and Wright was running too fast; the improvised hovercraft was only about seven feet in the air when Wright reached it and grabbed for it as it shot past him. He caught the rear corner for a few seconds, and the stabi-lization mode overcompensated; the entire platform flipped, flinging Echo and Omega onto the beach. Echo hit a boulder sidelong and lay, stunned, as Omega picked herself up off the sand a few feet away.

* * *

As Omega turned to look, she saw Wright advancing, and Echo lying slumped against the boulder. Her partner's eyes were open and he was stirring slightly, but he had obviously had the wind knocked out of him, and was not going to be in any condition to move—or do much of anything else, for that matter—for a few more moments. *Oh shit,* she thought. *Well, at least I'm awake this time.*

But to Omega's surprise, Wright was not advancing on her, but on Echo. *Oh boy. I wonder if he's decided that Echo is competition...or generally a threat,* Omega wondered. *Which raises a whole 'nother kettle of fish, but I don't got time to think about it now!*

Omega leaped between her partner and the man their old enemy had slated to be her mate, and dropped into a horse stance, fists coming up.

"Oh, no you don't," she growled. "Nobody gets Echo without a fight! Even if he's out of it, I'm not!"

Wright reached out to try to shove her aside, but Omega blocked his arm, then threw a hard punch to his jaw. It connected, and they both grunted with the force of the blow.

Wright threw a somewhat awkward roundhouse, and the fight was on.

* * *

Omega successfully blocked the roundhouse, choosing to use a hybrid of several martial arts in her repertoire, while rapidly analyzing Wright's fighting skills.

He's not that great a fighter, she decided. *Heh. I guess the old saw about 'I'm a lover, not a fighter,' is true for him! But he's still bigger and stronger than I am, just as hyped by what's happening between us, and he's not holding back much, if at all. He seems to realize—on some level—who I am, and that he shouldn't damage me too badly. But—*

She paused long enough to throw a flurry of palm heel strikes and jabs to Wright's midsection, blocking a couple of powerhouse blows that he threw.

Oof. Damn, hitting him hurts ME, she grumbled. *In order to take him out, I gotta basically beat myself up. At least it doesn't seem like his injuries actually create bruising an' shit in me. Well, let's see if I can take him down in such a way that it doesn't bash me up too bad. Never mind that it's in my ability to permanently maim or even kill him; I'm not gonna do that. I can sense some part of him trying to ask me to make him stop. Which sounds awful damn familiar.* She hid a wince, then pushed a thought through her block at him: *I wish I could, hon. You don't seem to have a trigger we can work with, like I did. So I don't know how to stop it.*

Just then, Wright grabbed her wrist in what felt like an iron grip. Quicker than thought, his other hand joined the first, holding her right wrist imprisoned. Before he could pull her in, however, Omega stepped back, relaxed her right arm, then wove her left arm through both of his until she could grab the wrist of his arm nearest her hand. Then she pulled up and toward herself, while twisting her imprisoned wrist and jerking away; in fractions of a second, she was free. Startled, Wright stepped back for a moment, before raising his fists and advancing once more.

Wright kept swinging, in an almost rhythmic fashion, and she knew that he must have little experience in hand-to-hand fighting from which to draw, so the programming was falling into a rote pattern. It was, therefore, relatively easy for her to counter most of the blows; she allowed a few to land in order to get inside his reach and deliver some powerful blows of her own, mostly to his shoulder and ribcage. But she watched closely, working out the full pattern of his attack.

Then, when she had the pattern down, she threw in a low roundhouse kick, intended to take Wright's near leg from beneath him. He staggered, but did not fall; his instinctive stance too evenly distributed his weight.

Okay, so I gotta get him off balance first, she decided, *then try again.*

* * *

Echo never truly lost consciousness, but his vision went away temporarily, and there was a roaring in his ears that was not the surf. As sensation began to return and he realized he was going to have a few bruises and sore spots for a couple of days, he pushed into a semi-seated position, and looked up at the sound of a loud grunt from his partner.

Omega was locked in a fierce, hand-to-hand combat with Wright. But it looked more like something from a science fiction film than a real fight—both combatants were enhanced humans, hormonally accelerated, and their moves were almost blurred with the speed of the fight.

Shit, he thought, startled. *It's almost like the guys in that old film trilogy*

195

where everybody was in a virtual world and didn't know it. Wow. And Meg is getting in about two or three hits for every one that Wright manages. And I'd swear she's letting him get those in, to gain an advantage in positioning. Whoa.

Echo gaped, blinked and shoved himself fully upright, then rubbed a fist in his eyes, uncertain he could trust what he was seeing—just as Omega, who was a far more skilled fighter than Wright thanks to her Agency training, delivered a one-two-three combo: a left cross, hard to Wright's solar plexus, followed almost immediately by an uppercut to his chin, then a low snap kick to his back leg. The combination was especially effective, since the gut punch caused Wright to double up somewhat, increasing the closing speed between fist and chin. His upper body snapped backward at the force of the chin impact, and he staggered to the rear...just as Omega kicked his leg out from under him. Momentum carried the day, and he fell hard onto his back with a loud, grunting exhalation, and lay still. Omega spun toward her partner.

"Oh, thank God! You're okay! C'mon," she said, running to Echo's side and helping him stand. "He won't be down long. I just knocked the wind out of him. We've gotta get out of here before he comes to."

* * *

Echo regained his feet and together they righted their rudimentary craft and climbed aboard. He re-initiated the hover function, turning the height setting to MAX, and this time it shot straight up for fully twenty feet. Fortunately, the bluff was lower on the north end, only about fifteen feet above beach level, but set back some twenty-five or thirty yards from the shoreline, a good fifteen yards farther than the rest of the bluff in that area. So he activated the propulsion in the 'float,' likewise setting it to maximum, and suddenly they were skimming high over the rocky beach, as they soared over a couple of dunes and approached the bluff.

"That was...some fight," he murmured then.

"Eh. Mark isn't that good a fighter. He's just more muscular, and as amped-up as I am."

"You didn't see it from my perspective. Y'all were goin' at each other at, like, super-speed or something."

"What?! It was? We were?"

"Yeah." Echo shrugged. "Maybe we can access the house security video later—once you're safe—and I'll show you."

"O-okay."

Moments later, they had topped the bluff and headed for the garage. Echo set down next to that structure, then tossed his partner the keys to the Corvette.

"Here," he told her. "Get in, start it, morph, and get it airborne."

"I'm not gonna go off and leave you!"

"I'm not asking you to. Circle the house; I'm gonna stow stuff inside, then grab up our personal shit, throw it in our kits, and come back out. You watch the front porch for me. Since the house is on stilts, you can bring the 'Vette down and hover next to the porch and pick me up. Unless Wright comes in from the rear, he won't be able to reach us. And he won't."

"But Mark—"

"Is after you. Short of a telepathic link, he won't bother me—he's already demonstrated that—and he won't bother the house, or anything in it," Echo explained, deflating the air mattress and stowing it and the lifeguard 'float' in the Corvette's warp trunk.

"I'm not so sure of that any more," Omega declared. "Down on the beach just now, when you were out of it, he didn't come directly after me. He came after YOU. Evidently some part of his programming decided to designate you as a threat to his 'mission success,' I guess. The odd part is, if he'd succeeded in killing you, it would have ended the mission altogether, and maybe even shut down his programming. 'Cause there wouldn't be any need for another generation of assassins, if you're d-dead."

"Huh," Echo said, surprised—though he caught her stutter when she referenced him as dead. "You're kidding. He really came after me?"

"Yup. That's why I positioned myself where I did, to get between him and you. I wasn't gonna let anything happen to ya while you were down, Ace. Otherwise, I'd have waited for him to come after me, instead of running at my assailant."

"Okay, I can see that, I guess. And...thanks, baby. But I still don't want to leave anything behind that his programming might recognize as a tool to use against us."

"Okay, it makes sense," Omega admitted. "Wilco."

"Good girl. Now go."

"I'm gone. Just be careful."

"You know that answer."

"Yeah—'always.'"

"Right."

Seconds later, the morphed 'Vette was in the air, circling the roof of the beach house in a loose kind of orbit, as Echo ducked through the front door.

* * *

Inside the house, Echo made sure all nonessential equipment and appliances were shut off. Trash—including what had been intended as their next meal—was quickly shucked into the appropriate chutes; it would be broken down and the non-organics sent for recycling, while the organics would be incinerated and the sterilized ash used to help fertilize what little landscaping existed around the house.

A quick glance at his wrist chronometer told him he only had twenty minutes before the force field re-established itself, so he ran around the house, grabbing his and Omega's clothing, hygiene products, and other personal items, throwing them into the small kit bags, thankful that, in the most recent version of the agents' travel bags, the main compartment of each held a small space warp—because he wasn't bothering to fold or compress anything to minimize volume.

On his way out the front door, he commanded, "A.T.L.A.S.S. Junior, please turn off all lights, lock all doors behind me, close and lock all storm shutters, re-set for non-occupancy."

"ORDERS RECEIVED AND IN PROCESS."

He stepped onto the front porch, letting the door swing closed behind him. He heard the series of clicks as it locked, and several loud knocks as the storm shutters slammed closed and latched all around the house, then a soft whirr descended from high above.

* * *

Omega circled the house over and over, careful to keep the vehicle low and inside the perimeter formed by Echo's property line, since she was no longer sure if the force field was in place or not; she had not thought to ask Echo. With each pass by the front of the house, she watched for Echo. With each pass over the beach, she could see the lone figure of Mark Wright, standing still, head tilted back, gazing up at the flying car.

"Shit," she murmured, disturbed by the solo observer on several levels. Just then, Echo came out the front door.

198

"Oh, thank the good Lord," she said, fervent, and headed down.

* * *

Omega brought the passenger door of the Corvette close to the edge of the porch, and one part of Echo's mind registered the fact that she had maneuvered skillfully to within inches of the structure without any difficulty, barely even slowing down until she came to a sudden dead stop, level with the tiny porch.

He grabbed the door handle and opened it, flinging both kit bags into the back seat, then plopping into the passenger seat himself. He slammed the car door shut, grabbed the seat belt, and said, "GO."

Omega went.

Chapter 7

"Crank the heat up a bit, baby," Echo decided, as they crossed over to the mainland. "I'm soaked and getting cold, and you're probably downright soggy."

"No shit," Omega noted, adjusting the thermostat. "I'm still dripping. I...you're right. I'm cold enough to shiver. I thought it was...reaction to the adrenaline."

"Aw. I wish we had a blanket for you; I didn't think to grab one. Hey, you got the passive cloaking on? I dunno that anybody is gonna be looking in this pea soup, but this is the sorta atmospheric shit guaranteed to ensure we're noticeable if they are."

"Yeah, I hit that as soon as you closed the car door. Ooo. Is that...? Yeah. Look down there." She pointed to the roadside below. "That looks like an Agency vehicle. But there's nobody in or around it."

"It's probably what Wright came in, then. Oh yeah; look at the front bumper. It's all crunched. I bet he tried to drive it into the force field and got bounced off. That's why he walked up to the house—as the 'alternative you,' he could get in, where the car couldn't." Echo pulled his cell phone. "Fox? Echo. Yeah, we're headed your way—BOTH of us. No, we're kinda sopping. I thought for a couple minutes I was gonna lose Meg to the surf. Yeah, I went out to get her, and I managed a kluged sorta thing...only between the waves, the spray, and the rain, I'm still pretty wet. Yeah, some towels and a change of clothes waiting for us in the vehicle hangar would be real good. And maybe somebody to clean the sand an' salt water outta the upholstery in the 'Vette. Look, Fox, we can see the car Wright commandeered, parked along the roadside. I don't really wanna stop and try to disable it, and I don't know if he knows how to set the security...yeah, if you can. I put a timer on the force field and it oughta be re-establishing itself in the next couple minutes or so. If he doesn't cross the property line before then, he's probably there for at least a few minutes, or I hope so, at least. How fast can you get somebody up here to take him back into custody?" Echo paused to listen, and Omega kept one eye on him as she flew. "Really? That would be good. Yeah, even if he manages to get out, they oughta get him before he gets too far. Okay. Yeah, we should be there in..."

"About an hour and a half," Omega declared. "I'm flooring it."

"Did you hear that, Fox? Yeah, about an hour and a half. No, I don't blame her either. Damn, this is turning into a mess. No, that's fine. Echo out." He deactivated the phone and put it in his pocket. "Oh, that makes me think. How well did your phone survive?"

"Okay, I guess. I haven't had a chance to look, but after you hauled me onto your, uh, dinghy-thingie," she paused and grinned while Echo snorted at the deliberate rhyme, "I saw you deactivating the beacon locator app you used to track me down, and the beacon was still flashing, so I expect it survived okay. I can always have somebody look at it when we get home."

* * *

A complete change of clothing, plus plenty of toweling, was waiting for them when Omega pulled into the Corvette's slot in the vehicle hangar, along with a male and female agent from Supplies to serve as squires. The four ducked into the hangar manager's office—Chocolate was on duty—and used a back room to change and dry off. By the time they were halfway dry—Omega's braid was still damp, despite taking it down, towel-drying it, and re-braiding—India had arrived, to run a medscanner over them both and ensure they were all right.

"Here, Meg," India said, offering a capsule. "I'm not that keen on your left lung; it looks like you did get a little water in there. This will help that situation, clear out some of the crud, and ensure you don't develop an infection."

Omega nodded and popped the capsule with the paper cup of water that the hangar manager proffered.

"Now what?" she asked then.

"I think we're expected in Fox's office," India said.

"Let's go," Echo declared.

* * *

Agent Mu led a small contingent of field agents up to the perimeter of Echo's beach house; Fox had relayed express instructions from the Alpha Line chief on where to 'handshake' with A.T.L.A.S.S. Junior, and how to inquire who was home.

"It sure looks like the place is empty," one of the other agents, Como by code name, observed.

"The mailbox?" Quintal queried, puzzled.

"Yeah," Mu said. "Hang on a minute, here. Fox sent a file with the instructions to my cell phone."

Mu pulled up the file, then crouched in front of the brick mailbox post. He tapped the street number in a certain sequence, then raised and lowered the flag on the side. A brick façade promptly popped out of the front, and he pulled open the little door it formed, revealing a small control panel. Mu pressed his palm to the pad, then spoke.

"A.T.L.A.S.S. Junior, this is Agent Mu, Echo's colleague. Code Alpha-One-Echo-Purple-Two."

"THIS IS A.T.L.A.S.S. JUNIOR. CODE RECOGNIZED AND AC-CEPTED. WELCOME, COLLEAGUE OF ECHO. WHAT IS YOUR RE-QUEST?"

"Is anyone on the premises?"

"NEGATIVE. NO SENTIENT LIFE FORMS INSIDE HOUSE. NO SENTIENT LIFE FORMS WITHIN GROUNDS PERIMETER."

"Shit," Quintal grumbled. "I was afraid of that, when we didn't find the car where Echo said it would be."

"A.T.L.A.S.S. Junior, additional inquiry," Mu added.

"READY FOR ADDITIONAL INQUIRY."

"Who was the last to leave?"

"Agent Omega."

"But she left with Echo," Como noted.

"Shush," Mu muttered. "The security systems can't tell the difference between her and Wright, remember?"

"Oh yeah..."

"A.T.L.A.S.S. Junior, when did this Omega leave?" Mu asked.

"ECHO AND OMEGA LEFT ONE HOUR AND TWENTY MIN-UTES AGO. OMEGA LEFT AGAIN FORTY MINUTES AGO."

"Right," Quintal realized. "He's got a forty-minute head start on us."

"But where is he...oh, duh," Como said, hitting his forehead with his palm. "Back to Headquarters."

"Right, because that's where Omega is now, or will be, real soon quick," Mu said. "A.T.L.A.S.S. Junior, increment password code by one."

"PASSWORD CODE INCREMENTED. MAY I BE OF FURTHER ASSISTANCE?"

"No, thank you, A.T.L.A.S.S. Junior," Mu told the polite computer.

"YOU ARE WELCOME. RETURNING TO POWER-SAVING HI-BERNATION MODE. GOODBYE."

"Come on," Mu said, closing the brick façade panel and turning to head back to their waiting vehicles. "We need to report in to Fox, and then track this dude down, before he gets to Meg."

* * *

"Yes, Mu?" Fox murmured into his cell phone. "No, they've arrived at Headquarters; I got word about fifteen minutes ago. I expect them here any moment, but they needed a change of clothing and to dry out a bit; there was a bit of an ocean adventure. No, India has already sent the code that they're both all right."

Fox paused and listened for long moments.

"He did, eh? Well, gronk, but I cannot say I am surprised. No, that's good. Yes, stay on his trail as best you can. If you can get his ass, we can try to put him in a cell that only I have the code for accessing, maybe. But that does cause problems whenever Medical wants access. No, let me worry about that, Mu. You worry about finding that ass, and I'll figure out what to do with it when you get it."

Fox listened to the other man for another moment or two.

"Really? No, I quite understand. No, it's my understanding she's fine. India did say she inhaled a bit of water, but Omega has already been treated for that. No, she'll be okay. Yes, Echo is taking VERY good care of her. No worries there." Fox bit his lip. "Yes, zun, go find his ass. Fox out."

Fox ended the call, then frowned.

He sat and stared at the top of his desk for a long time.

* * *

"He's already headed back this way?!" Omega exclaimed, once they arrived in Fox's office and he briefed them on the latest information. "Aw... SHIT."

"Well, I guess we need to get away from Headquarters...again," Echo sighed.

"Yes. And this time, you're not going alone," Fox said firmly. "I want India along for Omega's medical care. And Romeo, you can provide extra muscle if it should be needed, and moral support."

"But what about Alpha Line leadership?" India wondered. "I mean, it was fine when the department was still small, but now..."

"We can handle that remotely, as necessary," Fox declared. "You've already got everything set up that I can foresee needing set up, so if we can maintain the status quo while Alpha One and -Two are away from Headquarters, we should be fine. And I can handle any housekeeping duties that might come up, with the help of Bravo and Lima. Will that do?"

Omega and Echo both nodded; Omega bit her lip and offered an apologetic shrug, which Fox waved away.

"Yeah. You got it, Fox," Romeo responded. "An' glad t' hand it over."

"Done," added India. "I'll keep in touch with Bet via cell phone. If she—when she—" India glanced contritely at Omega, "comes up with anything, I can start Meg's treatment."

"Good," Echo said. "Next question: Anybody got any ideas where to go?"

"Yeah. I do," Omega said quietly. "Home."

"But, Meg, he's already broke inta your quarters once," Romeo protested.

"I don't think that's what she means, junior," Echo said thoughtfully. "'Home to Tara,' Scarlett?"

Omega offered a weak grin, and unleashed her full Southern dialect.

"Why, of course, Rhett. Seriously, Ah think my old family farm might be neutral territory—don't ask me why."

"Maybe it's something you're picking up through the link," India surmised.

"Could be."

"I'm not so sure about that. But it's a start," Echo remarked, cautious. "How about it, Fox?"

"It's doable," Fox replied. "I'll get in touch with the caretakers. It'll take a little while, and the best thing to do in the meantime is likely to be letting the search party find Wright and take him back into custody. But it'll be ready for you when you get there tomorrow."

"I'll get on addin' t' that search party, Fox," Romeo said. "The more heads we got on it, the faster it'll happen."

"Lemme help you," Echo decided. "Fox, is it okay if Meg uses your office as a safe zone for a little bit?"

"Of course, zun."

"India, if you would, stay here in Fox's office with Meg?"

"Sure, Echo," the physician agreed.

Echo and Romeo headed for the Alpha Line Room, and Omega sighed and settled down in Fox's office with India, as Fox commenced arranging matters for her next escape attempt.

* * *

"I guess we need to leave immediately?" Omega wondered, when they all reconvened back in Fox's office. "Do we have time to go back to our quarters and re-pack clothes?"

"I think you have time," Fox decided. "Wright seems to be limited to normal road driving, and while he may or may not know that our vehicles are...'special,' he doesn't seem to know how to operate one in the morphed, airborne mode."

"Unlike Meg, who has it down to an art," Echo murmured, just loud enough for his partner and his director to hear. "Damn, Fox, you should have seen her fly the 'Vette tonight." A sheepish Omega turned pink and grinned, while Fox hid a smile.

"Just so, alter khaver," he replied. "So according to the report I had, it will be several more hours before he reaches Headquarters again. And that is assuming he isn't caught first. But as all Agency vehicles have emergency transponders, and Bravo remembered to obtain the specifics on the stolen vehicle and 'ping' it, we are now getting data on where he is...which is now being forwarded to our hunt team. I anticipate notification that he has been taken back into custody at any moment."

"Good," Echo said. "Then I'll escort Meg back to our quarters to swap out clothes in our kits, and Alpha Two can swing by and pick up their own kits, then we'll meet at the 'Vette in the vehicle hangar. It's a lead-pipe cinch Wright won't be waltzing back in there."

"I can also see to it that a suitable wardrobe is left at the Farmhouse," Fox noted, "if you'll tell me what is reasonable attire, Omega. That way, you don't have to pack anything except essentials."

"Well, it's late summer, so think hot and humid," Omega pointed out. "This is northern Alabama, so the temps are gonna be in the 90s—"

"Fahrenheit," Echo appended with a slight grin, teasing. Omega responded in kind, though her grin was a little weaker.

"Fahrenheit," she confirmed, "and the humidity won't be much behind.

205

It ain't tropical, but it ain't far off, either."

"Got it," Fox averred, entering some orders on his virtual desktop keyboard. "There. The four of you gather the essentials, and head out. Never mind waiting until tomorrow. If we can get you out of Headquarters before we get Wright back in it, I'll feel better. Oh, one more thing. India?"

"Yes, sir?"

"Any word on that 'mental ninja' concept that you proposed earlier?"

"Huh?" Echo said, puzzled. "The who-what, now?"

"Uh-oh," Omega murmured, eyes widening. "You don't mean..."

"I'm afraid we do, tekhter," Fox explained. "India has a theory that perhaps Slug gave Wright some sort of low-level psionic ability to..." Fox broke off, and shrugged, looking for words. "To make himself, well, not quite invisible, but to ensure he's not noticed if he doesn't want to be. Or rather, if the programming doesn't want him to be."

"Sorta like that line from th' movie you enjoy, Echo," Romeo offered. "You know, where th' knight dude tells the guard, 'these ain't the guys you're lookin' for,'" he added.

"Ooo, shit. Mind games," Echo grumbled, understanding.

"Precisely, zun. India? Any news on that front?"

"No, Fox, not yet," India informed him. "Zarnix told me to tell you—I just haven't slowed down long enough—that he can't say Wright can, but he can't say Wright can't, either. Not yet, anyway. He's going off with the preliminary genetic analysis, while Zebra does what she can to help Bet. And I throw my weight in wherever I can, whenever they need me."

"All right," Fox sighed. "The answer is, 'We don't know.' Right now, I want you with Omega, helping her where you can. If you haven't already, I'll notify Zebra that's where you'll be, so we have a medic with Omega that she can relay any instructions to. The lot of you, get your things and get out of Headquarters as soon as you can."

"We're gone, Boss," Echo said, herding the others out of the Director's office.

* * *

Inside half an hour, the four had rendezvoused at Alpha One's special Corvette in the vehicle hangar, which was now clean and dry, inside and out. They threw their kits in the warp trunk alongside Alpha One's specialized equipment cases, then Alpha Two clambered into the warp seat in the back. Omega headed for the passenger seat, but Echo held up a hand and stopped her.

"What?" she wondered.

"I don't know where we're going, baby," he reminded her. "I've never been to your family farm. You drive."

"Oh. Okay."

And Echo eased his tall form back into the passenger seat, while Omega strapped into the driver's seat.

Moments later, they were off.

Minutes after that, they were cloaked, morphed, and airborne, headed south, out of New York.

* * *

The small flight of morphed vehicles took off from Plum Island, cloaked, and initiated a search pattern. Mu was flying his own car, with Orange, a fellow field agent out of Headquarters, in the passenger seat; given his experience as a Secret Service agent assigned to the President of the United States before Omega recruited him to the Agency, Romeo had given him the lead on the search...and his team had not questioned his authority, nor had reason to question his skills.

"You think we'll find 'im before he manages to do something bad?" Orange wondered.

"I dunno," Mu said, then scowled, "but I'll take him apart if he hurts Omega."

"You and she got a thing? I thought she was with Echo."

"She and Echo are partnered together, but they aren't an item," Mu explained. "I made sure of that before I asked her out. I didn't wanna poach on Echo's territory, ya know? No disrespect to Meg; she's not property. I'm just sayin', if they got something going, I don't wanna interfere."

"Yeah, I hear ya. So she's a free agent?"

"Yup. I'm gonna see what I can do about that, though, once this mess is over."

"Roger tha—"

Just then, Mu's cell phone went off with an incoming ring. A few quick dashboard commands, and his vehicle had been placed in an automated search mode. "Keep an eye out while I get this," he told Orange, pulling his cell.

* * *

"Mu here."

"Mu, this is Bravo."

"Hey, Bravo. You got anything for us?"

"Yeah, I do, as a matter of fact. It turns out that the car Wright took was outfitted with the new tracking/location systems, intended for emergency location of an agent in distress, stuff like that," Bravo told him. "And I've got the ID for the vehicle, and I've hacked it and triggered the locator beacon. Hang on, and I'll send the feed to the tracker in your car."

"Mu standing by."

The field agent waited several moments, as typing could be heard in the background on Bravo's end of the line. Occasionally Lima could be heard murmuring identification codes, with Bravo acknowledging. Finally he came back on the line.

"There you go," he told Mu. "Go into your GPS system and find the <special> menu, then go down and select <locate>. That should bring up the map in the correct mode, and lead you right to Wright's vehicle."

"All over it, Bravo," Mu said, punching up the correct menu selections on his dash control panel. "And there we go. Thanks, man!"

"No prob," Bravo said, a grin audible in his voice. "We lucked out on you and him both having vehicles with the latest model of the positioning equipment."

"We did, that," Mu agreed. "I'm gonna get off here now, and go find this bastard."

"Roger that. Bravo out."

"Mu out."

* * *

Mu turned to Orange as he pulled back the vehicle control from the onboard computer. "Orange, get the rest of the search team on the horn and tell 'em to follow me. I'm pinging Wright's car, and it's gonna take us straight to him."

"On it," Orange said, getting out his own cell phone.

* * *

Seventeen minutes later, they had homed in on Wright in his stolen Agency vehicle, driving down Interstate 95 south of Providence, Rhode Island. Mu reached over and toggled the short-range comm in his vehicle, making sure it was quantum-ciphered so that Wright's helmet comm couldn't read it.

"Okay, fellas, that's him down there. Get ready to blockade the road in front of him, and be glad the weather has people mostly indoors today; there'll be fewer drivers and passengers to brain-bleach, that way."

Numerous variants on, "Got that right," "Copy," "Affirmative," and similar came back to him from half a dozen vehicles.

"On my mark, guys. Take your positions...annnd...GO."

* * *

Mere moments after that, Wright was in force cuffs in the back seat of Mu's car. Berta, another field agent out of Headquarters, had commandeered the car Wright had been driving; the others were busy brain-bleaching the onlookers in three nearby automobiles.

The fleet of Agency cars convoyed down the interstate to the next exit. Taking the exit, they turned right, drove about a half-mile away from the interstate, then turned on a back road.

Seconds later, they had vanished, as all seven vehicles cloaked, morphed, and went airborne, en route back to Headquarters.

* * *

It ended up being the following morning when Alpha One and -Two arrived, by the time all was said and done; it was well over 800 miles to Huntsville, Alabama from Headquarters, and took most of the night to fly the distance in the Corvette at standard cruising speeds. And it had been quite late the previous evening by the time they'd departed Headquarters.

Omega drove the black Corvette up to the front of the farmhouse on a hilltop in north Alabama and switched off the ignition. The other three Division One Agents released seat belt latches and prepared to disembark. But when Echo, in the front passenger seat, realized that Omega hadn't moved, he slipped his hand over the seat back and gestured subtly to Alpha Two in the warp seat in the rear, and the activity ceased.

The three watched their friend sitting, looking silently at the old farmhouse, a succession of emotions playing across her unusually-expressive face.

"Meg?" Echo said quietly, careful not to break her train of thought. "What are you thinking, baby?"

"Remembering." Her voice was soft, distant.

"Remembering what?"

"Little stuff, mostly." She pointed. "That's the tree I had a rope swing on when I was little. That big rock over there? I crashed my bike on it when I was just learning to ride. The porch swing, a tall glass of iced tea, and a good book made for a perfect summer afternoon..." The other Agents listened quietly as Omega opened a small window on her past for them. Then she shook herself out of her reverie. "Sorry, y'all. Didn't mean to bore you to death. Let's go."

As they climbed out of the car, an agent emerged from the farmhouse.

"Agent Omega?"

"Here." Omega stepped forward.

"Everything is ready for you and your colleagues. Here are the keys." The agent dropped the electronic devices in Omega's palm. "Call Fox when you're ready for us to resume caretaking. Perimeter sensors are active, by the way. Per Fox's orders."

"Thank you," Omega said, succinct and simple. The caretaker headed for the barn, and departed moments later in another Agency vehicle. "Well, y'all," she said after a pause, "shall we go in?"

Omega led the way into the comfortable, open, cheerful old farmhouse. "Everything's exactly like I left it..." she murmured to herself. "Make yourselves at home, guys. 'Mi casa es su casa,' an' all that. Dining room an' kitchen to the left, den to the right, study behind that. Downstairs bath straight back, bedrooms and more bathrooms upstairs. Pick a bedroom and settle in. Just don't pick mine."

"How will we know which one is yours?" India asked, heading upstairs with Romeo, both carrying their field kits.

"You'll know."

* * *

"Damn straight," Romeo's voice floated downstairs a few minutes later, mirth in it. "Nobody else's it could be." India's laughter rang out in the background.

Omega chuckled. Echo, surveying the foyer in his typically thorough way, shot her a curious glance at the sound; her eyes twinkled for the first time in a couple of days, and she jerked her head up the stairs in invitation, as she looked at him.

Echo accepted the invitation and headed for the staircase; he took them two at a time, and Omega froze for a split-second, staring up after him for long moments. A few minutes later he came down grinning, then saw Omega's face and stopped halfway down.

"Meg? What's up?"

"Oh." She shook herself. "Nothing."

"Not with that face." Echo jogged down the last few steps.

"Ghosts, Echo." Omega made light of the incident, waving a dismissive hand. "When you took the stairs two at a time, it...suddenly reminded me of Dad. That's the way he used to go up 'em when I was a kid. I'd... forgotten." She sighed. "This whole place is like that for me now. Maybe this wasn't such a good idea after all." Another sigh. "Are Romeo and India getting settled in good?"

"Yeah."

"How 'bout you?" she asked.

"I thought I'd grab the bedroom next to yours—which IS pretty obvious, by the way. You'd never tell its occupant was an astronomer."

"What, you mean the books, posters, and telescopic equipment didn't give it away?" Omega teased.

"Nah," Echo deadpanned. "Not to mention the glow-in-the-dark starfield on the ceiling. Now I see why you love the galactic map hologram on the ceiling in Headquarters. Anyway, I figured if I took the next room, I'd be close by if...something came up."

"So to speak," Omega muttered. Echo raised an eyebrow at the suggestiveness of the remark, and she shook her head. "Never mind. Listen, it looks like we'll be here a few days, and there's nobody else around to see us. If y'all wanna get out of the Suits and get relaxed and comfortable in all this humidity, go for it. Jeans and t-shirts or something. Fox probably had appropriate stuff left for us."

"He did. We've already found it."

"Good," Omega replied. "While y'all change, then, I'm gonna go... check on something."

"All right," Echo said, heading back upstairs. "See you in a bit."

* * *

The three Agents, now dressed in black jeans and shirts, came in search of their missing fourth member together. As they walked up behind Omega—still in her Suit—in a far corner of the yard, she crouched in front of

211

a tombstone and laid down a bouquet fresh-picked from the flower garden at the side of the farmhouse. Nearby was another, smaller tombstone; a fresh bouquet already rested on it. The other Agents glanced at each other in some surprise and mild trepidation, then stopped at a respectful distance.

"Hi, Mom and Dad. It's been a long time. Sorry. I've been...really busy. It's great, though. Believe it or not, I'm part of the Pan-Galactic Division One Agency. Yeah, that's right—it's part of a galactic government! We police aliens and patrol the galaxy. Cool, huh? I love the work. It's even better than NASA. I know that's hard to believe," Omega's smile was audible, and the listening Agents grinned, "but it's true. You'd really like my buddies. Especially my partner. I wish you could meet 'em. Romeo says they're the cream of the crop, and he's right. But..." the voice began to tremble, "but I...I think I'm glad...that you...that you can't see what I've become..." Her voice finally broke. Omega buried her face in her hands. "Momma...Daddy...God, please help me..." the gut-wrenching plea was nearly inaudible.

Three pairs of eyes glanced at each other, worry and pain written in all. Then a determined Echo started forward, and Romeo and India followed close behind.

All Echo did, when he reached his partner's side, was to crouch down behind her and put his right hand lightly on the center of Omega's back. But it was as if Echo had given a tranquilizer to Omega. Her body relaxed, and the turmoil of emotions calmed.

"Damn, Echo," Romeo muttered. "Whatchu do?"

Omega raised her head and looked over her shoulder at Echo, a weak, crooked grin on her face, and together they responded, "Pheromones."

* * *

"Nicely done, Echo," India remarked, when they were assembled in the kitchen. A now-content—or at least, calm—Omega rummaged in the fridge and pantry, checking to see what the Agency's caretakers had left for them to eat; the kitchen was where her family had always assembled, and to her delight, her current 'family' had instinctively gathered in the same place. In moments tall glasses of iced tea and a plateful of snacks—cookies, fresh fruit, sliced cheese, crackers, sliced deli meats—sat on the table, in lieu of the breakfast they hadn't had; first lunch was only a couple of hours away. "How did you control it?" India continued, as they all dug in to the snack.

212

"Well, I figured if it was a subconscious thing, this pheromone shit, all I really had to do was stay calm and think about settling Meg down, and my body would do the rest," Echo said. "I guess it worked all right." He felt a hand on his shoulder, and glanced up into his partner's face, as she stood close behind him.

"Yes," was all Omega said. But her eyes told him volumes.

* * *

"Hey, Meg, I got a question," Romeo said.

"Sure, hot shot, what is it?" she responded.

"If you c'n smell these whatchacallems, whadda they smell like?"

Omega looked blank.

"Huh. That's...a good question. I'm not sure how to answer." She sat down at the empty place at the table, beside Echo, and sipped her iced tea thoughtfully. "Most of the time, it's kind of a low-level thing, and I don't pay a lot of attention, see. It's just, it's all ramped-up now, and so I notice it more. Besides, each of you is a little different, and it changes, depending on your mood."

"Like how?" India's medical curiosity kicked in.

"Good grief, guys! You're askin' me to describe how emotions smell!" Omega exclaimed, a whimsical grin on her face. Three faces grinned back at her in expectation.

"Well, Meg, you're the only one we know who can," Echo pointed out in reply.

"Okay, lemme think. Mm...fear smells kinda...sour. Sour like...like something's gone 'off,' like it's spoiled. It doesn't happen often in this bunch, I can tell you. Anger is...tart. Biting. Almost bitter. Irritation is similar, but more...subtle. Hate is even more bitter; the um, farther into the 'negative spectrum' it goes, the more bitter it smells to me...I can almost taste it sometimes, if it's strong enough. Happiness is...um...like smelling a flower garden, is how I think of it. Romantic love is kind of...musky, I guess you'd call it. Like a sexy perfume." She grinned suggestively at Romeo and India, who returned the grin sheepishly. "Keep in mind, these are just my impressions. So the descriptions are very subjective."

"When Echo calmed you down, what did that smell like?" Romeo queried.

"Oooh." Omega's eyes glazed as she thought back. "Calm smells like...

213

like..." She paused, and her brows knit in puzzlement. "I dunno, Romeo. It's the nearest to just being that person's own scent, I think. Especially in Echo's case." Omega smiled at her partner.

"Yeah," a mischievous Romeo agreed, "Webster's has Echo's picture beside the words 'calm' and 'cool.'"

Echo's expression never changed at the remark, but Omega thought she detected a satisfied smile hidden in the dark eyes.

* * *

"So what does Echo smell like? What do each of us smell like?" India pressed.

Omega blinked, rested her chin on her hand and turned to Echo with a *help me out, here, partner; get me outta this* expression.

"Don't look at me, Meg," Echo said, raising an eyebrow. "I was kinda curious myself."

"How individual is it?" India queried.

"What do you mean?" Omega asked.

"Can you, say, identify us by our pheromones?" India clarified, pointing around the table.

"...Yes. At least, I think so." Omega began showing signs of discomfort. Echo spotted the fact and blinked in dismay, then turned to Romeo and India, intending to cut off the discussion, but he was too late.

"Fascinating," India murmured. "Let's find out. Meg, have you got anything around here we can use as a blindfold?"

* * *

Omega's body language abruptly closed tight; the pain that appeared in the blue eyes stopped them all dead. Echo hid a sympathetic wince.

"Am I a bloodhound now?" Omega asked in a low voice. She shot a single glance at Echo before pushing away from the table and getting herself blindly out of the room.

"Oh, damn!" India exclaimed. "I didn't mean it like that! Meg! I'm sorry!"

But Omega was gone, out of the house, disappearing into the stand of old oaks and maples behind it.

* * *

Oh, dear God, how that hurt, Omega thought, in deep pain as she ran across the back yard and into the woods. *Bad enough that I already know that's exactly what Slug intended. Then my friends, the only family I have left, reach the same conclusion through different, independent means. If that's really what Echo thinks, if he knows what Slug really intended for me to be, I guess I can throw that whole dream of settling down with him right out the window. Talk about defenestration. From orbit, no less.*

When, half-blind from the tears filling her eyes, she nearly ran into a tree, she decided to slow down. Omega dropped into a walk, then looked around her to determine exactly where she was.

Oh, over here, she realized, with a sad smile. *If I head this way a few hundred yards, I should find my old playhouse. I wonder if it's even still standing.*

Omega pressed on, deeper into the woods, and soon came on a tiny clearing, in which stood the dilapidated remains of an old wooden play-house. She moved to stand beside it with a smile, fondly remembering better days, when she was very young and the world was far more forgiving.

She sighed.

Daddy built this for me the day after I fell down the stairs, trying to play house with too many dolls on the landing, she remembered. *Momma was convinced I'd broken my neck there, for a few moments. Wow. I'd almost forgotten. Maybe...in another reality, maybe I did. Maybe I didn't survive. Maybe I shouldn't have survived. Who knew I'd end up like this?*

Then again, she considered, *if I hadn't, who knows what things would be like now? Echo could be dead at Slug's... 'hands.' Or, if Slug had failed, the Cortians might have got him. He could have died a slave on some horrible planet, half-starved and beaten. Romeo and India wouldn't be together, and Romeo might be dead, too, beside Echo... 'cause they'd still have been partners. And no telling WHAT might have happened to Fox. Which would leave Zebra all alone.*

Maybe...maybe, in the big picture, it's good I am what I am, I suppose. But damn. Why can't it ever just be easy? Why can't I be happy? Why can't I ever be...me? Not a thing, not an animal. Not breeding stock. Just...me. Meg. The girl that loves Echo to pieces, around the world, across the galaxy and back. Happy...beside him. Fighting...with him. Fighting...FOR him.

A weary Omega sighed, then sat down on a nearby stump and stared at the crumbling remains of the play house, as the tears spilled over despite her best efforts to hold them in.

* * *

Some time later, Romeo came out of the study, a large book in hand. Echo and India still sat silently around the kitchen table. "She been gone all afternoon, guys. It's way past first lunch. Second lunch ain't even that far off, now. She back yet?" Romeo asked.

"No," Echo replied, typically short and succinct.

"Damn. Don'tcha think maybe we oughta go after her?"

"No," Echo said again, this time with a sigh. "It wouldn't do any good, hot shot. Meg knows this place a damn sight better than the rest of us could hope to. If she needs to get away, she can avoid us for hours, maybe days. Besides, she's okay. India's remark hit a sore spot, yeah, I guess on account of what's going on inside her right now." India glanced down, ashamed, as Echo spoke. Then he added, "But I know Meg well enough to know she just needs some time to herself."

"How do you know that, Echo?" India asked softly.

"I saw it," Echo replied with a shrug. "She looked me in the eye before she left the table."

"Oh. Well...good, I guess. I...never meant to hurt her."

"I wouldn't 'a thought that woulda hurt her, though," Romeo observed, puzzled, taking a seat beside India.

"India didn't hurt her; the situation did. And...what she thinks it implies...about her. She's...really sensitive right now, guys," Echo tried to explain for his partner. "Think about...think about what Tt'l'k told us was going on. Think about HOW Tt'l'k told us what was going on—his wording. It turns out, per her own admission, he was pretty much..." Echo broke off and sighed. Then he tried again. "She's already told me a couple times, she's got this whole kinda hormonal storm going on inside, and it's doing a number on her emotions."

The others were silent for long moments, considering. Abruptly both members of Alpha Two sat up straighter, eyes widening, eyebrows rising as they suddenly understood.

"Aw, shit," Romeo muttered. "She feels like a' animal?"

"Something like, yeah, near as I can tell," Echo sighed. "The smartest agent in the whole organization...and she feels less than human. Because of this...shit." *My poor baby,* he added mentally, hurting for his partner, but helpless to change the situation.

"That kinda makes sense, I suppose," India decided. "I had a cousin who used to get, like, super-PMS, and it was 'cause her hormones were messed up really bad, thanks to a growth on one ovary. I guess Meg's situation is sort of like that, only maybe raised an order of magnitude."

"Or two, or three," Echo added. The group fell silent.

* * *

"Look what I found, guys," Romeo said then.

"What is it, Romeo?" India asked.

"I think it's an old family album of Meg's." Romeo grinned. "Look at this." He opened the album on the kitchen table for them all to peruse. "Meg looks almost just like her mom did at her age. See?" Romeo pointed to the pictures.

"You're right, Romeo. Her mother was a beautiful woman, too. And does her father maybe make you think—just a little bit—of anybody we know?" India grinned at Echo, who shifted in his seat, uncomfortable with the comparison and wondering just how much they knew or suspected.

"Oh, look!" India exclaimed, looking back at the album. "Here's pictures of Meg as a little girl. Oh, she's adorable! Those little white braids and those huge blue eyes! Look, Echo! Would you ever guess this cute little girl would grow up and become the tough, cool, capable lady she is now?"

* * *

Echo studied the faded pictures on the pages of the album with warm, dark eyes in which there was more than a hint of affection. *She looks exactly like I thought she would at that age,* he decided. *And India's right...she IS adorable. But that's no surprise. Not to me.*

Suddenly he had a mental image of Omega working happily in the farmhouse kitchen, preparing a meal, while a small duplicate of her ran and played outside, shrill, high-pitched, childish laughter floating in through the window on a summer breeze. A contented Echo smiled to himself at the picture.

As the vision continued to unfold, a smiling Omega walked to the window to look out at her daughter playing with its father. The sandy-haired man picked up the little girl and swung her high in the air.

Echo inhaled sharply.

* * *

"Echo?" Romeo's voice broke in on his thoughts. The mental image

217

crashed and vanished. "Something wrong?"

"I don't know, Romeo," Echo responded, thoughtful. "I...don't know..."

* * *

Yankee was escorted to Confinement from his quarters by two field agents—neither of whom was in Alpha Line—and taken straight to Wright's cell; Wright was back inside it. There, another agent stood waiting, in full body armor save for the helmet, which was under his left arm. He introduced himself as Easy, an agent from the Security department, and a friend of Oscar's.

"Hey, dude," Easy murmured, shaking hands with the Agent as the two strange field agents departed. "Relax. I got your back on this. I talked to Oscar, and I got the whole scoop on what's going down. Have you heard from your partner yet?"

"Not a word," Yankee sighed, unwinding slightly. "Thanks, man. I... things are not going at all right lately, and I can't seem to dig out from under."

"Understood," Easy replied. "Listen, Oscar and I are good buddies, and she told me how much you helped her, getting her out of the armor where it was pressing on the busted bones an' shit, then ordering her off to the medlab using your Alpha Line authority, so nobody could fuss at her about it. Our department lead can be kinda drill-sergeant, an' she has a good record with him and didn't wanna mess it up. She appreciates what you did, and so do I. I did a little, um, discreet questioning, and I gathered the medlab didn't tell you they'd admitted her, but then you didn't report in that you hadn't heard back, either..."

"Yeah," Yankee said, hanging his head. "That was stupid on my part. But I kept thinking surely I'd hear something any minute. And I know how the medlab can get backed up, so..."

"Right. No, I get it. All I was tryin' to say was that I'm here to help you out of a bind. After I talked to Oscar, I volunteered to work shifts with you, to try to help clear you. But because of what went down, we're gonna play this by the book as much as we can, all right?"

"All right," Yankee agreed. "Have you been briefed on the perp's, uh, unusual abilities?"

"Yeah," Easy said, nodding. "Damn, that gastropoid musta really had it in for Agent Echo."

"Evidently," Yankee decided. "Which...really makes me think about some shit, you know?"

"Echo's partner? Yeah. You think this dude," Easy jerked a thumb at the man behind the force-field wall, "is here to take her out as punishment for being strong enough to deliberately fail at her 'mission'? You know, to kill Echo?"

"Dunno. It...could be," Yankee said, finding himself unwilling to reveal the true reason for Wright's programmed obsession with Omega, even to this friendly fellow agent. *Because that's some pretty private shit right there,* he considered. *And I only just found out about it myself when Romeo told me more about what was going down. I still don't have all the details, but I grasp what 'mate to create next-gen assassin' means, for sure. I also understand that Omega, bein' anything but stupid, doesn't want within a parsec of the guy. And no matter how much I may dislike her personally, I don't wish rape on anybody. Never mind it's probably classified to high heaven. Besides which, now I'm startin' to wonder about the reasons I don't like her. How much is really HER, and how much is what Slug did?* So he kept his mouth shut about what he did know. *Because, after all, she's my assistant department chief,* he rationalized, not consciously realizing that he was mentally defending her for the first time. Instead, he allowed, "All I can say is, this guy ain't gettin' out again on MY watch. We'll do whatever we have to do."

"Good man, then. We got this, Yankee."

"Thanks, Easy."

"No prob. Thanks for helping Oscar." Easy flushed a bit, then admitted, "I, uh, she's...kinda special, ya know?"

"Aha. That explains a lot," Yankee said, offering a grin of male camaraderie. "Yeah, I know what you're trying to say. Does she know? I mean, that you kinda...?"

"Um, sorta," Easy said, as they turned to watch their designated prisoner. "Thing is, she used to be a field agent, and she and her partner had a thing goin'. They were gonna take it spousal, had already filed the life partnership forms an' everything. She's here because he got killed about a year ago in an accident; he had their car morphed and moving at speed—but not airborne yet—when somebody pulled out in front of him. Nobody walked away from it, and there wasn't much left of their vehicle—let alone the other one—afterward. She had been following their perp undercover, so she wasn't in the car when it happened."

"Aw, damn," Yankee murmured, wincing. "She didn't tell me anything about that. I sure hope I didn't accidentally say something that hurt her."

"Nah. She said you were a good guy. Blunt, but understanding. Anyhow, she transferred out of field work because of it—said the memories were too much for her. I met her when she transferred into Security, an' kinda fell hard. Only she's not quite ready for a new relationship yet, so I told her I was willing to wait."

"That means at least you have an understanding," Yankee realized. "Right?"

"Right. We're kinda goin' together, you know, more or less exclusive dating an' shit. Keeping each other company, an' all that. Just holding off on doing much with it until she's ready. I mean, I've kissed her a time or two, but..." he shrugged.

"Well, that's good," Yankee decided. "Hang in there; it sounds like it'll get where you want it."

"Yeah. I just gotta be patient. So what's up with your partner? Tare, right?"

"Aw. That's a long story," Yankee sighed.

"We got all shift, man," Easy pointed out. "But if you don't wanna discuss it, I can understand. We can talk about something else. I was just tryin' to get to know ya. And they got the sound system worked so we can hear Wright, but he can't hear us, so..."

"No, I get it, an' I guess it's okay," Yankee said, letting out another sigh. "If you'd kinda not discuss it with anybody, I'd appreciate it, though. But I think I need to talk it out with somebody that I don't feel..."

"Somebody you don't have to worry about being judgmental, or anybody in a position of authority over you," Easy finished for him. "Somebody where there's no pressure, can maybe brainstorm with ya."

"Exactly."

"Have at it, then."

"So, we've been partners, Tare an' me, pretty much ever since I was brought into the Agency..."

* * *

Yankee and Easy got along quite well, and soon each was considering the other a new, trusted friend. Wright, as usual, stayed quiet in his cell, unmoving, staring into space with empty eyes, and the pair kept a close watch on him, but had concluded that the only real danger was leaving him alone, unguarded. So the pair chatted, gradually consumed the coffee that had been placed nearby for their use in helping to stay alert, and took turns in heading to the men's room to void said coffee, in order to ensure that there was always someone there, keeping an eye on their prisoner.

Unfortunately, the Headquarters lockdown, coupled with the search for Wright, had meant that quite a few agents had worked long past their usual shifts, and many were now off duty, resting after the intense workload— most of the embassies, as well as the offworld visitors, had been unhappy about the situation, creating a stressful environment as the entire facility was searched, top to bottom, for Wright.

"...So it's not surprising that there's nobody handy to see about bringing us food," Easy noted. "Any chance you can hail somebody from Alpha Line to bring us a meal?"

"I can try," Yankee said, pulling his cell phone and swiping off a message to Romeo.

But moments later a response came back from Director Fox's executive assistant, Bravo, and he looked at it and frowned.

"Looks like we're on our own," Yankee said. "Bravo says—"

"That's one of Director Fox's assistants, right?"

"Yeah. Evidently Fox sent Alpha Two off with Alpha One this time, so they'd have extra muscle and medical, so Romeo handed me off to Bravo. And BRAVO said that all of the on-duty agents...from pretty much all departments...are being assigned to processing the backlog of offworlders coming through Headquarters. The perils of being a hub, I guess," Yankee said with a wry grin. "Anyway, he said we're gonna have to see to our own meals. Since there's two of us, he recommended one of us run out and grab something, while the other stands guard."

"I'm not keen on that," Easy said. "That's pretty much what happened to you last time."

"Yeah, but there was just me, and Oscar was gone for hours," Yankee pointed out. "Maybe this time, we can make it work."

"I'd still rather wait until somebody can bring something to us," Easy said. "They really need to put some sort of break room down here, with a microwave an' shit. But Uncle—he's the head of Security I was tellin' you about—says it's a security risk."

"Well, I can see that," Yankee agreed. "Maybe if we wait long enough, somebody can shake loose. Hope you had a big breakfast, though, 'cause it might be a while."

"I did."

* * *

The shadows lengthened, and Omega glanced at her wrist chronometer, then sighed.

"I better get back," she murmured. "It's way late. Romeo an' India will be worried, and even Echo is gonna get antsy here pretty soon."

She stood and turned for the house.

* * *

The soft sound of voices floated through the kitchen window when Omega drew near the old farmhouse. *I'm not quite ready to face 'em yet, though,* she decided. *I need to see if I can figure out how they feel about me, after the whole 'bloodhound' thing.*

So instead of going in, Omega used all her Alpha-Line-honed skills to slip up onto the back porch, unnoticed, even remembering which step squeaked and avoiding it. She aimed for the porch swing, a classic Amish-style wooden bench seat, stained a pale mountain ash shade and suspended from the rafters of the porch roof on galvanized steel chain.

Omega eased into the seat and leaned back, ensuring nothing creaked, then watched the sun sink ever lower toward the distant horizon, as her companions worried about her.

* * *

Echo, Romeo, and India still sat around the kitchen table as the sun rode low, nearing the horizon. The photo album lay to one side. Second lunch had gone by, unnoticed by the trio except for some growling stomachs, which were absent-mindedly sated with the remains of the snack tray.

"Maybe we shoulda gone after her," Romeo said quietly. "I'm way past worried 'bout our pretty lady."

"She'll be back—when she's ready," Echo said, confident. "She's not far away, I'd swear to it."

"Echo, I don't want to worry you, but this isn't quite the Meg we're used to," India pointed out. "With that biochemical storm raging, she's on

edge—a knife edge. And I don't blame her in the least. It's probably like...
like..."

"It's like having an IV pumping a pepper-spray an' itching powder
solution into your bloodstream," a low, familiar voice floated in the open
window. "An' getting worse."

* * *

Echo followed the voice out onto the porch. Omega sat in the porch
swing, watching the sunset from the excellent vantage of the west-facing
porch, high on the hilltop, and bathed in the soft golden light. Romeo and
India ventured out, hesitant, as Echo sat down beside his partner in the
swing.

"Come on out, y'all. It's okay. I'm not upset with you," Omega said
without looking.

"How'd you know—?" Romeo began.

"I'm downwind."

"Huh?" Romeo wondered.

"Pheromones," Echo noted.

"Oh."

India claimed a porch chair, and Romeo sat in the rocking chair nearby;
a tap of his foot set it in motion, and it provided gentle creaking counterpoint to the quiet conversation that ensued.

"Nice place," Echo remarked. "As many stories as you've told me that
happened here, baby, I've been curious about how it looked. I like it. It's
really homey and comfortable."

"Thanks. I'll take y'all around the place tomorrow, if you want me to,"
Omega said, giving him a pleased, grateful glance. "There's not a whole lot
more to it, just the stable and barn, an' a bunch of fields and pastures—oh,
and a small orchard—but it's pretty. And it's home." She shrugged.

"Sounds good," Romeo said. "I'd like t' look around some more. An' I
guess we oughta, just t' get the lay o' the land."

"Meg, I'm sorry," India offered softly.

"Forget it, India. It's okay. I'm a scientist, too. I know now that you
didn't mean it that way. I'm only...I keep expecting the only family I got
left to, to fall apart on me because of this. To...reject me. When y'all already
told me you wouldn't, every last one of you. It isn't you, hon; I'm just
not dealing with things too good lately. Y'all just please overlook me right

223

now. I'm...really, really hypersensitive, given everything that's going on." Omega waved a dismissing hand. "We'll try your experiment later. I've got to admit, the more I thought about it, the more interesting it became as a scientific question. Now it has my curiosity going, too. Ooo...pretty sunset tonight."

"Yep," Echo agreed. "I bet you've seen a lot of 'em from this porch."

"Yeah. Yeah, I have." Omega smiled, a faraway, dreamy, reminiscent look on her face. "Many's the evening I've spent out here, shelling peas, or snapping beans, shuckin' corn an' the like, while talking with my family. Sometimes JUST talking. Like I'm doin' now."

"Bet that ol' porch swing could tell some tales on ya, too, huh, Meg?" Romeo teased.

"You mean old boyfriends?" Omega glanced at Romeo.

"Yeah."

"Not as many as you might think, Romeo." Omega grinned, but the expression was rueful. "You're kind of exceptional, as India could probably tell you. A lot of guys don't care for intellectual women, even if they're as gorgeous as India."

"That's the truth, girlfriend," India agreed, giving her friend and colleague a smile in repayment for the sincere compliment.

The two men stared at their partners, disbelieving.

"You're kidding," Echo said, stunned.

"Yeah! As beautiful as you two pretty ladies are?!" Romeo agreed, equally shocked.

"Romeo, I'll tell you a tale on myself," Omega said. Echo started the swing in gentle motion, and they all leaned forward to listen. "It'll show you what I mean. Y'all know how I don't look my age?"

They all nodded, and Echo remarked, "Yeah, you look almost ten years younger."

"Well, I never have looked my age," she continued. "When I was in grad school, I was the teaching assistant, so I came in at the end of another professor's lecture to start setting up the Astronomy 101 class that I was about to teach. The class that was ending was physics for med and pre-med students, 500-level, seniors and first-year grad students or medical school students."

"Okay," India murmured. "Bright people all."

"Exactly," Omega continued. "Anyway, one of the guys comes up to me after the 500 class ends, an' starts puttin' a move on me. You know, the Big Man On Campus routine? 'Astronomy? Tough course. Let me know if you need help. Want somebody to show you around campus?' That sort of thing."

"He thought you were a freshman?" Echo chuckled.

"Yep. So I said, 'Oh, no, I've been here a few years. I'll handle the class just fine.' And he says, 'Well, whatcha majoring in?' Then I kinda toss off, like it's no big deal, 'cause I never have thought it was a big deal, 'I'm in the doctoral program in astrophysics. I'm teaching the 101 class in ten minutes.' The poor guy literally leaped backwards, and knocked over three desks trying to get away from me."

India howled, laughing until she clutched her aching sides and she had to wipe tears off her cheeks. The two men practically gaped.

"That is so typical!" India exclaimed.

"That is so stupid!" Romeo added, disgusted.

"His loss," Echo remarked, offended on Omega's behalf, and nodded firm agreement with Romeo. Omega shrugged.

"Oh, I dunno," she said. "An awful lot of guys have agreed with him over the years. When I got absorbed into Division One, I didn't leave much of anybody behind to miss me, that's for sure."

* * *

Romeo shot a concerned look at Echo, worried that the other man would feel guilty at that remark, and was surprised to see him watching Omega, unperturbed, with no indication that her comment had found a chink in his armor. The brown eyes of the department chief remained calm and interested.

"Well, there's always Mu now," Romeo said, returning his attention to Omega.

"Oh? Does Meg have a 'significant other' now?" India said, intrigued.

* * *

"That—" Omega began. Abruptly, she shot a startled glance at Echo. He gazed down at her calmly, silently noting her slightly-flared nostrils. "... remains to be seen," she finished, glancing at her partner again, seeming uncertain.

"Why? I thought he was gonna ask you out," Romeo puzzled. "He expressly tol' me t' make sure th' coast was clear on that."

"He did," Omega told him. "He asked me out the same day Mark Wright arrived at Headquarters. But...then all that went down, and...and I thought it was only fair to tell him...about me. About what's...happening. That way, it gives him a chance to think it over."

"If he needs to think it over, I wouldn't go out with him," India huffed in outrage, and the men nodded.

"Give him a break, y'all," Omega said, shaking her head. "It's a pretty big shock to find out the woman you've just asked out is not only part-alien, but...but...and then her designated mate shows up, and..." Omega couldn't bring herself to finish. "Put yourself in his shoes. Would any of you still want to take me out?"

"In a heartbeat," Echo responded immediately, as firm as he knew how to be. *And hopefully, she'll remember a certain conversation in the hot tub up in Massachusetts,* he thought.

"No hesitation," Romeo agreed.

"If I were a guy, or leaned that way, sure," India said. "You're a really cool, fascinating person, Meg."

"Funny, that was kinda his initial reaction, too; he said it was 'exotic,'" Omega mused. A heartsick Echo, unnoticed, closed his eyes to hide his discouragement, bowing his head momentarily in the shadows of the twilit porch as Omega continued. "Anyway, we'll see what happens. Thanks, y'all. You guys are...are..."

"The creamiest of the whole damn crop?" Romeo grinned.

"Yeah!" Omega laughed. "You know, I just thought of something."

"What?" Echo asked, looking up, and managing to sound normal with an effort.

"My family is all sitting on my porch with me—well, all except Fox and Zebra—"

"Don't forget Dihl," Echo interjected.

"Ooo, yeah, her too—sorry, Ace; I'm not trying to exclude her. I'm just still getting used to her being in the Agency—so anyhow, we're not ALL here. But I got family joining me on the porch of my family home for the first time in...a very long time."

"Not 'zactly the same family," Romeo observed.

"Maybe not. But family all the same. It feels...good," Omega said, as

Echo laid his arm along the back of the swing behind her and unobtrusively rubbed her far shoulder for a moment with the tip of his thumb. "Really, really...just so awfully good."

They all smiled and sat in companionable silence, watching the light fade from the sky. Finally Omega rose, as the last of the twilight deepened to full darkness. "Hey, y'all. We missed all our meals today, and only got snackie-stuff. Let's go fix something proper to eat."

* * *

Four hours later, Yankee and Easy still had not eaten.

"I'm gonna fall over if I have to wait any longer," Easy noted. "And I still can't raise anybody to bring us anything. You?"

"Nope. The place is a zoo," Yankee noted. "I'm thinking the school break in the Ulyffon Alliance isn't helping matters; we're inundated with tourists. Families with kids on spring break, essentially."

"Yeah. I guess if we want to eat, one of us is gonna have to go get something, like it or not."

"Flip a coin?"

"Nah," Easy said. "If something happens, and you're gone to get food, it could look like you deserted your post again. But if I'm gone to get food, it'll be okay, because you're Alpha Line..."

"Oh, okay. Yeah, that'll work. And I swear I will not move from this spot, even if I shit my pants," Yankee averred. "Wright is not getting away on my watch again."

"That's the spirit! The deli is probably the closest; will that work for you?"

"Yeah, bring me a Reuben with a double order o' kettle chips an' a soda."

"What kinda soda?"

"Whatever lemon-lime thingy they got in there this week."

"Right. Back in a flash."

* * *

And here we go again, Yankee thought, looking at the sandy-blond man with the unblinking gaze. *Round two with the weird guy. Figures he'd be just as weird as Omega. I wonder if he's as nigh-impossible to kill as she is. Huh. If that telepath they killed wanted him to take out her AND Echo, then probably, I guess. Maybe even harder. Of course, that's not primarily*

227

why he's here, but it could be a secondary program. No matter what, he's not gonna get past ME again. I'm not taking my eyes off him! I'm gonna sit right here and watch this dude until Easy comes back. He'll have to kill me to get past me this time. This fella smeared my reputation as an Agent, and I'm damned if I won't get it back.

So Yankee moved his chair to the corridor wall directly across from the force field, sat down, and stared at Mark Wright, determined not to let the man out of his sight.

If anything, he was far more intense in his scrutiny than he had been when Easy was there, since the other man had been keeping an eye on the prisoner, too.

* * *

Yankee had been sitting there some ten to fifteen minutes, and Wright had yet to move or even blink. *Ow,* Yankee considered. *Why the hell aren't his eyeballs dried an' fried? Must be just another one 'a those creepy-as-shit things like Omega's got. Dude probably doesn't even NEED to blink.*

Yankee did need to blink, and did so rather frequently during this little mental monologue, as the psychological effect was causing his eyes to sting and water. But he never stopped watching Wright; he was determined not to let the genetically and physically altered man one-up him again.

So when Wright's entire body seemed to grow pale, Yankee sat up and paid even closer attention, realizing that something was happening. *Not this time, you sonuvabitch,* he thought, decisive. But the effect did not stop with Wright becoming pale.

Yankee fairly stared in shock as Wright grew translucent...

...Then faded away completely. The force field flickered, then switched off. Yankee gaped for long moments, utterly astonished.

"Oh HELL no!" Yankee finally exclaimed, leaping to his feet. "Not again, dammit!"

He ran to the wall console and hit the emergency alert call.

* * *

Wright left the Confinement area and headed down to the sub-basement and Grand Central Station. There, even despite having been put back into a medical jumpsuit upon his return to custody, and still being clad in it, he stepped onto a maglev train...

...Headed to the basement terminal at Marshall Space Flight Center in

228

Huntsville, Alabama.

No one seemed to notice.

* * *

"Hey, Meg," Echo said as they finished dinner, when an idea struck, "this is where the astrophysicist got her start. It's solid dark now. Why don't you show us your favorite stargazing site? You know, from when you were growing up?"

"Cool!" Romeo exclaimed, and India pushed back from the table and stood, ready to go.

"Um—" Omega tried.

"You're still in your Suit," Echo observed. "Run upstairs and change, then you can show us."

"Uh—" she tried again.

"I'll find a couple of blankets," India volunteered.

"Well—" Omega blinked, at a loss.

"Get goin', pretty lady," Romeo remarked. "We c'n talk on th' way."

* * *

"Don't shit me, zun," a pacing, deeply angry Fox declared, sterner than Yankee had ever seen him, as that dumbfounded Agent sat in his office once more. "Wright did NOT become invisible. That ability is not innately possible for any known race in the galaxy. Therefore there is zero chance of Slug having gene-geneered it into Wright. Never mind why he didn't do it in Omega, when it would have been a sure-fire method of ensuring Echo's assassination by her unwilling hands. And there was NO cloaking device on—or in—the man. And that is per the head of Security, as well as both the head and assistant head of Medical."

"Fox, I'm not lying," Yankee told the Director, as earnest as he knew how to be. "I swear to you on my grandfather's grave. I. Am. Not. Lying." He shook his head. "Maybe...look. Didn't somebody say that Omega had Glu'gu'ik genes spliced in?"

"I can neither confirm nor deny that."

"Well, but we know that Glu'gu'ik can teleport, using quantum foam manipulation! Maybe Wright..."

"Then why can't Omega teleport?"

"Huh?"

"Again, that ability would have been a certain way to ensure Echo's

229

death at her hands," Fox explained. "She was intended to be Slug's ultimate weapon; he would have gone to great lengths to give her any abilities he could that he thought would ensure the success of his plan. But she can't."

"Do you KNOW that she can't?"

"One hundred percent? No. But when Alpha One was fighting that rogue Glu'g'ik last fall, it would have come in handy. For that matter, when we went up against that crazy Glu'g'ik nobleman in Texas a couple of months back, it would have made her the more obvious candidate to infiltrate the assassin team, not Echo."

"Well yeah, but she got that snakebite, too..."

"Which ability to survive might have been the whole point to incorporating such a thing into their systems...assuming Slug did so."

Yankee noted that Fox went to some lengths to talk around confirming whether or not Omega had such specific augmentations.

"Huh. You mean...it isn't strong enough to work outside their own bodies, but there's enough there to enable 'em to...sorta repair the damage? If there's any there at all, I mean," Yankee added with a sigh.

"Precisely."

"That...makes a certain bass-ackwards kinda sense, I guess," Yankee decided. "This Slug dude...he was pretty messed up in the head, huh?" He tapped his temple.

"Yes, he was," Fox said with a sigh of his own, and sat down heavily in his chair. "Look, Yankee. Omega cannot teleport. If she could, do you not think she would have used that ability to get herself and Echo out from under the *Trindak*, back in the winter? She was willing to sacrifice herself if it came to it, in the face of saving the man who was at once her partner, her department chief, and the Director's successor. Do you think she would have allowed herself to be killed merely to hide that ability? For, had it not been for Echo and Doron, she would have died, and it is worth noting that she fully expected to do so."

"Well...no..." Yankee did a double-take. "Wait—she did? She went in expecting to die?!"

"Then if she does not have the capability, Wright does not!" Fox said, ignoring the addendum. "Tell me what really happened, and perhaps I can mitigate whatever punishment must be meted out."

"Fox," Yankee protested, "I'm telling you the truth. I swear I am! Get a Deltiri down here if you think I'm lying."

"That can be arranged," Fox said, reaching for his comm. "Meanwhile, you'll be placed into Confinement, while an investigation is performed."

* * *

When he was alone in his office, Fox pondered for long moments, then pulled his cell phone. He pulled up a roster on his virtual desktop, then used an entry from it to dial a number on his phone. He waited several moments while it rang on the other end.

"Tare?" he said, when the other end answered. "This is Fox. Zun, I'm sorry to say, you were entirely right. Yankee has gotten himself into a bad situation, and he's under guard in the brig now." He paused, listening. "I don't know. No, that's up to you. No, we have a situation as a result of his actions, and we have to chase that down and end it, first. No, take your time. He's not going anywhere."

Fox waited for several moments, while Tare spoke.

"Yes, zun, I'm sorry, too. I'll do the best I can, for your sake, but the matter looks pretty cut and dried. Yes, that's probably going to be what happens. No, we'd probably have to convene a tribunal for that, much like what happened after last Christmas. No, I'd rather wait to fill you in on those details until you get here; I'd prefer not to discuss it like this. All right. Don't do anything rash, zun. I'll see you when you arrive. Fox out."

* * *

Omega came downstairs a short while later, attired in black denim and t-shirt like the others, and hesitated on the threshold of the front door.

"Ready?" India asked, waiting with the others on the front porch. "I've got the blankets." She waved the quilts draped over her arm.

"Guys, I—" Omega took a deep breath, and let it out in a defeated sigh. Then she squared her shoulders. "Okay. Let's go." She headed down the porch steps and turned left, past the barn. "This way."

The four traipsed companionably together through several twilit fields, climbing fences, chatting, and looking at Omega's farm through the eyes of her memory as she showed them around. Along the way, she also showed the city-born Alpha Two team how to catch 'lightning bugs,' much to Echo's amusement, as the duo enthusiastically proceeded to chase the elusive little firefly insects through the fields and pastures. Echo stood beside Omega, both wearing wide grins, watching their companions "stalk the dreaded,

231

dangerous Lightnin' Bugs of Sol Three," as Romeo put it.

"Wait'll I introduce 'em to katydids and dry flies," Omega muttered to Echo with a grin.

"Don't," Echo warned. "I'd like to get some sleep tonight. If they bring one of those things in the house, it'll deafen us."

"Okay," Omega chuckled. "Katydidn't." Echo groaned at the kluged pun as she automatically and absently headed up a tall, open hill with a slight capstone, taking a gentler, sloped path cut into its side. "Come on, y'all," she called. They all followed her up to the top, whereupon Omega actually paused to look around, then stopped dead. "We're...here," she offered, suddenly hesitant; the last word came out rather flat.

* * *

Echo, Romeo, and India turned around to survey the site.

"Whoa," Romeo remarked lamely, looking at the diamond-spangled dark sky, bounded by a full, unobstructed, three-hundred-sixty-degree horizon about them. Slightly east of due south, the diffuse, twin glows of Huntsville and Madison could be seen against the dark horizon, and in the distance to the southwest, another glow marked the city of Decatur. Fainter glows to north, south, and east hinted at the presence of other cities in the distance, but otherwise, the star field was impressively unimpeded.

"What he said," India agreed, then started spreading out the quilts on the short, cropped grass. "Here we go. One for Alpha One, and one for Alpha Two."

The appreciative Agents stretched out to enjoy the unmarred view of the heavens—all except a suddenly-uncomfortable Omega. She hovered nervously near the edge of the hilltop, like a moth fluttering around the outside of a lampshade, unable to settle.

"Meg?" Echo called, patting the blanket beside him.

"Honey," India sat up to speak to her friend, "if you're uncomfortable, you can share my blanket, and Romeo and Echo can take the other one."

"N-no, it's...it's not that," Omega stammered, glancing at the sky and wrapping her arms about herself.

* * *

Echo's brows knit as he watched his partner in bemusement, trying to determine the reason for her strange behavior, then he looked around thoughtfully; something about their location was ringing bells in the back of his mind. He glanced upward, into the night sky...and the ghostly memory of a flying saucer flitted into his field of view. Suddenly the picture became disturbingly clear.

"Oh, SHIT!" he exclaimed, sitting up swiftly and turning toward his partner, worried. "Meg, I'm so sorry, baby. I should've thought. I knew this place seemed familiar."

"What's wrong?" Romeo sat up, too.

"This is the place, isn't it?" Echo asked, getting up and going to Omega. "This is where it happened. I recognize it from the memory link."

* * *

"Yes," Omega whispered, nodding, then abruptly turned to Echo and buried her face in his chest. Romeo and India glanced at each other in deep concern—they had never seen Omega react like that—then they looked back at Alpha One.

"Where what happened?" India asked, already suspecting the answer as a gravely-worried Echo gently did the only thing left for him to do— wrap his arms around his distressed partner, offering comfort.

"The abduction," Echo answered. He jabbed an index finger at the ground. "Here. RIGHT here."

"Aw, DAMN," Romeo said with feeling. "Why'd you let us drag you out here, Meg?"

"We didn't give her much choice, Romeo," India answered. "We never thought she might not want to—even though, now that I think about it, she wasn't too thrilled. Remember how she kept trying to tell us something, but we never really let her get a word in edgewise? Damn it, we gotta remember to be more thoughtful and considerate, guys." India studied Echo and Omega, then asked, "Meg—have you been here since...since you remembered the abduction and programming?"

"No," Echo's chest said in Omega's muffled voice.

"So you haven't come to grips with being here, have you?" India continued. "With what this place represents to you psychologically?"

"No."

"Are you scared, Meg?" Romeo asked, sympathetic.

"I...no."

"Meg," Echo remonstrated quietly with the top of the blonde head. "Don't lie to us. Don't lie to ME. Remember, I've been in your head with this memory."

"...Yes." Omega was silent for a moment. "Why do I feel like such a child right now? It's been almost twenty years since it happened..."

"It's your psychological response to it, Meg," India explained. "You're flashing back to what happened when you WERE a child—early teens, anyway, I guess; maybe pre-teens?—and emotionally, you're responding like you did then. The adult hasn't had to deal with it before—not here, at least."

"Oh. That makes sense, I guess. So I'm a highly-trained BABY animal. A bloodhound puppy, maybe. Yap, yap." A somewhat hysterical giggle came from the front of Echo's shirt, and the other three Agents winced, as much from the black humor as at the obvious signs their colleague was nearing some sort of breakdown. Omega continued, "No, that can't be right. Puppies can't...can't mate. I'm precocious, I guess..."

* * *

"Meg," Echo spoke again to the top of the platinum head, attempting to interrupt her morbid train of thought, "do you want to go back to the house?"

"Yeah," Romeo agreed. "Let's all jus' go on back. No sense in makin' Meg go through this."

"No!" Omega pushed away from Echo as suddenly as she had turned to him. "I want to beat this thing," she said fiercely, voice higher-pitched than normal, hanging onto emotional stability with obvious desperation. Omega's jaws clenched; her hands balled into fists. "I won't let a dead psychopath rule my life any longer!!"

"So you're staying here with us?" India asked.

"No. You're all going back to the house. I'm staying here alone."

"Oh. Kinda like walkin' through the graveyard after dark, huh?" Romeo observed, wincing again.

"More than you know, Romeo," Omega said simply.

"Then let's take it in steps," Echo suggested after a pause to consider. "C'mon over here and give us an astronomy lesson, baby. Then Romeo and India can leave, and I'll stay. That way, it gives you a chance to get more comfortable here, and ramp things down gradually, before you have to deal with it all alone."

"...Okay," Omega agreed, moving slowly to the 'Alpha One' blanket and sitting down stiffly. "That makes sense, I suppose. But you start the lesson, Echo."

"Me?!"

"Sure." She smiled; it was still a bit weak, but in Echo's knowledge-able judgement, it was a sincere smile; he decided to encourage it and play along. "I wanna show off my star pupil. Get yourself oriented facing south..."

Obliging, Echo scanned the sky, then turned. "Okay."

"Good. Now stretch out here." Echo obediently laid down close beside her on the blanket, with the soles of his feet facing south. "Romeo, India, follow Echo's lead." Under cover of Alpha Two's movement, Omega murmured to her partner, "Move over a little bit."

"Why?" Echo asked, startled; she had, only moments before, welcomed his nearness as comforting, and his position on the blanket had been especially calculated to continue that effect.

"I...need a little space, Echo. I may be nervous being here...but my senses are still very aware of...of the people around me. And...there's more than just you now, so...it's that much harder." Silently a confused Echo inched away. "Thanks, Ace." She raised her voice to normal. "All right, y'all, listen up. Echo, the sky's all yours. As opposed to the floor, that is."

"Or th' ground," Romeo appended, and they all chuckled.

"Okay, let's see. It's August, so...yeah. See the big cross up there, going right along the Milky Way?" Echo began, putting aside the question of his partner's mercurial responses for the time being, as he waved a hand at a section of sky.

"Yeah..."

"Uh-huh..."

"That's Cygnus, the Swan. The long leg of the cross is its neck, the top is its ass, and the two arms are its wings. See that? Good. Okay, um, oh. Two of the Milky Way's four spiral arms kinda head off thataway. Depending on what astrocartographer you use—'cause it isn't like the arms have hard edges, after all, and some of 'em fork an' all kinds 'a shit—anyway, if you follow it far enough, it turns into the 'Outer Arm.' The far end of that arm, way over on the other side of the galactic core, is where Doron's star system, Edeptis, is."

"Oh."

"Cool."

"If you trace it back, in toward the core, it becomes the Norma Arm, and that's one of the innermost arms of the Milky Way spiral," Echo continued. "So the same arm is at once outside and inside."

"Whoa."

"Interesting."

"There's some debate, though, as to whether the Outer-slash-Norma Arm is also the Cygnus Arm, or whether they're just adjacent," Echo added. "Even in the Galactic Coalition, there's debate, because of course like I said, the arms aren't hard-edged, and there's spurs and splits an' all kinds of things like that. And in any case, while it's one of the four principal galactic arms, it's one of the two SMALLER arms of the four."

"Oh," India said. "Now I get why there's always those territorial disputes. It all depends on which arm you want to assign a given region to..."

"Exactly! Now look kind of southeast of Cygnus. Over there. See the big J turned on its side? That's Scorpius..."

Chapter 8

Roughly an hour and a half after he departed Grand Central Station, Mark Wright arrived—unnoticed—in the terminal in the basement of Building 4300 at NASA's George C. Marshall Space Flight Center. He headed straight for the automobile hangar.

There, he picked up the key fob to an unused vehicle, unlocked it, and got into the driver's seat.

Moments later, he was headed down the tunnel that would emerge inside a nondescript prefabricated building off Patton Road, outside the boundaries of Redstone Arsenal. He drove through the big garage doors and down the drive to the unmarked back road along which the building stood. Then he followed the road north until he hit Reserve Way, jogged east until he hit Patton Road, then headed north, out Jordan Lane.

Some fifteen minutes later, Wright was in the countryside to the northwest of Huntsville.

* * *

As Echo talked his way through their hillside stargazing session on Omega's family farm, Omega slowly relaxed and leaned back until she, too, was lying comfortably on the blanket like the others, absorbed in the night sky. Temporarily, she forgot the evil memories of her abduction from that very hillside, able to lose herself in the heavens with the people she loved.

"Wow," Romeo remarked in enthusiasm, as Echo paused for a moment, "that makes it all kinda...real. Connects it all up."

"Yeah," Echo agreed. "That's why Meg has been working to get a basic observational astronomy class going for Division One University. I've had the benefit of a lotta sessions like this one, one-on-one with her, usually in our off hours, but sometimes when we're on a stakeout or waiting for something to go down. And I can tell you first-hand, it's one thing to study it in books, but it's another entirely to lie out here at night and look up at it, and try to figure out what's going on."

"I'll bet," India agreed. "Does it ever...connect, for you? Like, the big picture?"

"Yeah, it does," Echo averred. "Once in a while, we'll be someplace like this, with good dark skies, and suddenly I can SEE—the Milky Way is a huge spiral galaxy, and we're seein' it edge-on, 'cause we're INSIDE it..." He waved a hand, and Alpha Two looked back at the sky where he indicated. Suddenly India gasped, and Romeo gave an exclamation.

"Hey!" Romeo cried, pointing a hand into the sky. "There it is! Just like what you said, man!"

"Yes!" India agreed, pushing up slightly. "I see it! Like in the pictures in Meg's class textbook!"

"Bingo," Echo murmured, nudging Omega with a gentle elbow. "You just hooked two more."

"Nah," Omega said, offering him a slight smile. "You did that."

"Maybe. But you taught me enough to be ABLE to."

"What 'e said," Romeo agreed. "Don't sell y'rself short, Meg. Echo didn' know half this shit when he an' I were partnered. An' it wadn' f'r lack o' gray matter on his part. That is COOL," he added, looking back heavenward.

"Yeah, Meg," India agreed, "if you teach that class, I expect Romeo and I will be there."

"And a lot of the rest of Alpha Line, too," Echo agreed. "Meg, you wanna take over, baby?"

"I don't have to," Omega said with a smile. "You're doing fine. I'm proud of ya."

"The feeling's mutual, partner." Echo grinned.

"Ooo. Sounds like somebody's trying to get ON the prof's good side, and get OFF the hook," Omega chuckled, and Romeo and India laughed.

"No," Echo responded with a slightly sheepish grin. "But you look pretty calm to me. You're gonna beat this, Meg."

"Yeah. One way or another." Omega was quiet for a moment. "Okay, y'all, we're gonna get a little tougher now."

"Uh-oh. Watch it, guys. Doctor Meg just took over the class," Romeo teased.

"Damn straight," Echo grinned. "Hang on to your gray matter, boys and girls."

"Listen up. There'll be a quiz at the end of class," Omega retorted, and the hillside echoed with the sound of laughter, chasing away dark memories. "Echo's already pointed out Cygnus. Now, the compact x-ray object, Cygnus X-1, was the first suspected black hole ever observationally identified—on Earth, at least—and it's about...there." Omega pointed. Echo crunched his body and sighted along Omega's outstretched arm, then nodded.

"Where?" India wondered. "Romeo and I can't line it up from over here."

"It's near Eta Cygni," Omega explained. "Find the intersection of that cross that Echo was telling you about—Cygnus is sometimes called the Northern Cross..."

"Got it."

"Right."

"Now slide down the long leg of the cross to the next star."

"Oh."

"Okay."

"That's Eta Cygni. You can't see it with the naked eye, but Cygnus X-1 is gonna be above and to the left, by about half the width of your little finger held at arm's length, and over six thousand light years past it..."

* * *

"I cannot say if he is deranged or not," Zz'r'p, the telepathic Deltiri ambassador from Arcturus VII, told Fox a little later in the latter's office, after a telepathic interrogation of Yankee—who was now in a cell around the corner from the one that had held Wright—that was rather more compassionate than the one to which Tt'l'k had subjected Omega. "All I can say is that he is not lying—either it truly happened as he says, or he sincerely believes it to have happened that way."

"Could he have talked himself into a delusion?" Fox wondered.

"Possibly. I have seen humans, and other species, do it before. I do detect severe emotional distress in him."

"Sufficient to either account for this, or result from it?"

"Either one, yes," Zz'r'p averred. "And he definitely neither likes, nor completely trusts, Omega. So it is possible. But," the blue, fish-like alien added, "I was in the medlab earlier, reviewing Wright's files in an effort to help with...everything, now that I am finally back where I should have been all along, and I was informed by Agent India—just before she departed with Alpha One—of a hypothesis she had about Wright, that wanted testing?"

"What? Oh, wait. You mean the notion that Wright has been given the ability to influence others not to notice him?"

"Yes."

"Well, but surely not, in this case. By his own admission, Yankee was staring straight at Wright. It wasn't a case of Wright sneaking along the periphery."

"Have you looked at the security video?"

"That was the first thing I did, after I got the news," Fox noted. "The video shows Yankee sitting there staring directly at Wright, when Wright walked up to the force field, immediately in front of Yankee. The field went down—because, of course, the system believes him to be Omega despite our best efforts, and short of putting one of our top Agents on the 'detainee' roster, we have found no effective way to prevent it, at least as yet. And we cannot do that, because that would ensure that Omega herself would wind up in Confinement in one or another field Office, probably sooner rather than later, and it potentially gives Wright access by limiting her ability to get away..."

"Understood. What happened next?"

"Well, Wright simply...walked out, right in front of Yankee, who sat there and let him go. It was fully ten seconds before Yankee even moved. He LET him walk out, Zz'r'p."

"Apparently," Zz'r'p agreed. "Or just possibly, it all happened as Yankee said...AND as the monitors depicted, because it was Yankee's MIND that could no longer detect Wright."

"What? Explain."

"It is entirely possible that the very act of concentrating solely upon Wright, in such an isolated environment, enabled Wright's...'camouflage ability,' we will call it...to function even more efficiently," Zz'r'p elaborated. "The longer Yankee focused on Wright, the easier it was for Wright to make him 'not notice.' It is a bizarre little quirk of certain sentients' brains, and humans are in that group."

"Did you see any sign of it in Yankee's mind?"

"No, but nor did I see any indication to the contrary," Zz'r'p pointed out.

"Do we even know if the genetics for such a thing exist in Wright?" Fox wondered.

"Not yet, no. I have it to understand that Zarnix is giving it his full, undivided attention."

"Then tell him to take a break," a wry Fox commented. "The last thing we need is our chief medic losing the whole data set on Wright, in plain sight." He chuckled, but it was a grim sound. "So what you're telling me is, Yankee could be lying through his teeth, even to himself...or he could be telling the complete truth. Despite the evidence of the security video."

"That is, unfortunately, exactly what I am telling you, Director."

"And you still can't deprogram Wright."

"Not until the link between him and Omega is broken. It would almost certainly cause mental damage to Wright, if not outrightly kill him, and the neural feedback would injure, perhaps kill, Omega. And it likely would not be very healthy for the Deltiri attempting the deprogramming, either. You could end up with a dead civilian, a dead Agent, and a dead ambassador. And I do not think that would help you overmuch."

"No, it wouldn't, and I would be VERY upset at the loss of two friends."

"Indeed. And thank you."

"You know there is such a link?"

"Without doubt. Not only could I detect it, the information that Omega felt Wright's physiological response to the attempts to implant a tracer chip in him confirmed it. Most likely she can, to some extent, feel any strong impulse that Wright feels."

"Oh, now THAT suddenly made sense of something..."

"What?"

"When Wright broke into Omega's quarters, when I got there, she was alone in the bed, and Echo was literally sitting on a naked Wright, beating him unconscious..."

"Oh my. That seems...somewhat unlike Echo."

"Well, I probably don't have to tell you certain things. Especially after our little talk when you got back to this mess."

"No, probably not. And in light of those things, it is...understandable."

"Yes, it is."

"Go on, then."

"...But one thing I noted," Fox said, thinking back, "was that Omega was thrashing about in the bed, as if she was in pain...and her movements were in perfect counterpoint to the sounds of Echo's fists hitting Wright,

241

behind me."

"Ah, yes. That is more proof, then," Zz'r'p agreed. "She felt the blows that Echo was dealing Wright."

"But she didn't bruise..."

"She would not. Her tissues did not experience the trauma, only her nervous system."

"Mm," Fox hummed, wincing. "So whatever we do to him, she feels."

"Yes."

"If he were knocked unconscious?"

"She might or might not become unconscious; it is hard to say. She is very strong-willed. I suspect it would depend upon several factors, including how severe the trauma to Wright, and whether or not she was in an emergency situation requiring consciousness be maintained. And even then, it might be a near thing."

"If he were inadvertently killed?"

"The neural feedback would almost certainly incapacitate her, and possibly kill her, as well. Even were she to survive it, the long-term prognosis for mental health would be...poor. Remember Slug's condition, after the Shell died."

"Gronk."

"Indeed."

"Do you think she knows it?"

"I suspect so. Or, at least, has deduced it, based on events."

The two beings were silent for long moments.

"I assume Headquarters is back under lockdown?" Zz'r'p asked.

"Of course," Fox sighed. "Again."

"Slug was a wily one. We are fortunate he is dead, and we are only dealing with legacy plots."

"True. Even so, his rab'dr'b ghost is running damn rings around us, Zz'r'p!"

"Patience, my friend," the alien ambassador counseled. "That is only because we are still learning everything that Slug did, whereas Slug was able to prepare and anticipate much, based on many years of studying us. We had no idea he was working on such a long-term vendetta until he initiated his end game. As we learn more, we will be able to counter more."

"But—"

"Fox, I have thought about this a good deal, especially as I work with Omega from time to time, helping her develop her slowly-budding mental abilities. I have also discussed it with her, and she and I are in agreement on something."

"What would that be?"

"That Slug deliberately chose genetic manipulation to insert these abilities into Omega—and now we know, into Wright—for several reasons. One of the main reasons was because he knew that, of all the technology available to the Agency, genetic analysis takes the longest to perform, even with galactic equipment and techniques. It is not something that can be immediately scanned, analyzed, and reacted-to. He chose it DELIBERATELY, Fox, to slow us down. It gives his...'tools'...the ability to act as he wished, WHEN he wished, while keeping us from understanding what is going on, or readily determining any effective countermeasures. And by making one tool a member of our own organization—a dear friend—and the other an otherwise-innocent civilian, the terminal option is taken off the table."

"Merde, shit, and abdab," Fox murmured, as the ramifications hit him. "That...is exactly what he did."

"Precisely. So do not 'beat up' yourself or your agents about the matter. What is happening is exactly what Slug expected to happen, what he wanted to happen, what he planned to happen, and it is why he did it in that fashion. What we must do is find ways around this, somehow. And we, all of us, are working on just that." Zz'r'p watched as Fox relaxed, ever so slightly, then added, "Let me assure you that the Arcturan embassy is doing all we can to help, my old friend; not only are we studying the mental programming, but we are trying to ease tensions over the matter among the other embassies and the visiting offworlders, as well."

"And that's appreciated. Oh, speaking of embassy personnel..."

"Tt'l'k is definitely...ill," Zz'r'p anticipated, surface-reading the Director. "There is almost certainly a developing condition which is being exacerbated by certain...resentments, shall we say...and he requires more medical attention and skill than any of us here can provide. We will be sending him back to the homeworld very soon for proper diagnosis and treatment. He is not happy about it, and does not, himself, believe anything is wrong. But it is obvious now, to the rest of us, and it must be done."

"I see. Are you going to request a new assistant?"

243

"I am, yes. In fact, I have already done so."

"Very good, then. Let me know if there is anything the Agency can do to assist."

"No, but my thanks; we have already arranged transport and an escort for Tt'l'k, of both medical and security personnel."

"All right."

"Is there anything else I can do for you at this time, Fox?"

"No, Zz'r'p. Thank you; you've already done so much. Know that I... and mine...appreciate it sincerely."

"I know," Zz'r'p said simply. "And I welcome the opportunity to assist. You are friends, dear friends. You should know that."

"I do. And the feeling is mutual."

"Very well, then. I will get back to work studying the data on Wright. Keep me apprised when you apprehend him again."

"I will. And likewise on your researches and deprogramming attempts."

"Of course. We will talk later, Fox."

"Later, Zz'r'p."

The Deltiri left, descending the ramp and cutting through the Core, and Fox all but collapsed in his chair with a sigh.

* * *

"Fox, this is not good," Uncle, head of Security, noted in the Director's office. "When I got no reports of Wright anywhere, I started using the security videos to try to trace where he went after he left the confinement cell. I don't know if we need to put a whole slew of agents in the brig or not, but he walked right past a shit-ton of people, still dressed in a medical jumpsuit, all the way from Confinement straight down to Grand Central Station, and hopped a maglev train."

"When? And to where?" Fox demanded. "And no, I have reason to believe that they may have been rendered unable to notice him, so unless I get more substantive evidence, there's no point in putting half of Headquarters in confinement..."

"He left pretty much as soon as he got loose," Uncle said. He glanced at his wrist chronometer. "He's been gone at least an hour. Maybe as long as an hour and a quarter. And he was headed for—"

"No, wait, let me guess," Fox said, putting his fingers to the bridge of his nose as a headache threatened. "He was headed for the Huntsville Local

Station."

"Nailed it in one," Uncle declared. "How'd you know?"

"Shit. Uncle, thank you; you're dismissed. No offense, but I have to get on this immediately."

"I'm gone, Fox," Uncle said, headed out. Fox hit the intercom to his assistants.

"Lima here, Boss," came the instant response.

"Lima, I need you to round up the same team that we sent after Wright in Massachusetts, and get 'em ready to head to Alabama, effective five minutes ago, please."

"Consider it done, sir. Anything else?"

"Be ready to send an emergency alert to Echo."

"Roger that."

* * *

"All right, guys," Mu said, as the group gathered in a corner of the Alpha Line Room, with Fox's express permission. "It's round two. Wright got loose again, same song second verse, only with what sounds like a few additional complications, and this time he's headed to Alabama. Are you all game for going after him again?"

Nods went around the group.

"This is gettin' old, though," Como noted.

"No doubt, but evidently this old foe of Echo's was one helluva wily dude," Mu averred. "According to what I've been told, he spent years, maybe decades, planning this."

"Shit," Orange grumbled, wide-eyed.

"What he said," Quintal agreed. "So that's why this guy keeps slipping out; the perp that set him up knows all our moves."

"Exactly," Mu confirmed. "So we do this as many times as it takes, and hope we at least keep him busy enough escaping that he can't do anything else." *Like hurt Meg,* the agent thought, but chose not to say. "Okeydoke, then. Let's head for Grand Central; Fox has an emergency maglev waiting for us. We'll be there in about half an hour, and we'll have vehicles waiting to perform the search. I'll tell you the rest once we're aboard the maglev."

The detachment of field agents headed for the bank of elevators at speed.

* * *

"How are you making it, Meg?" Echo asked, after Romeo and India had departed for the farmhouse.

"...Okay."

"You sure?"

"Yeah."

"Attagirl." They looked into the heavens companionably, as they had done many times in off-duty hours throughout their partnership, but when Echo rolled onto his side to talk to Omega, pointing into the sky while asking questions, Omega tensed despite herself. Echo noticed her tension, and moved even closer to reassure her. She sat up.

"It's okay, Meg," he murmured, soothing, sitting up as well and putting an arm about her shoulders, pulling her into his side. "Slug's dead—we killed him together—and it's all in the past."

"Not...entirely."

"Well, no; but we'll get through it. We always do. There's nothing to be afraid of, here, not any more."

* * *

"Echo," Omega said then, "it's time for you to go back to the house."

"No."

"Echo, I need to do this alone."

"After everything that's happened, I am not leaving you way out here alone. Damn, Meg, you were nearly raped the other night. I'm sorry, baby, but I can't get that out of my head, on a buncha different levels. Never mind him coming after us both last night."

"Echo, listen to me. I appreciate your protecting me, but A—I'm just as much a capable Agent as you are. B—I'm awake now, not asleep. C—I need to face this place," she gestured at the hillside, "on my own. And D—I...I need you to leave, Ace, before I embarrass you and humiliate me."

She gently removed his arm from her shoulders and eased away. Echo blinked in surprise.

"But..."

"Look, Echo. Like I've said a few times before, I'm in a very...sensitive...state right now," Omega said earnestly. "I know I'm giving you all kinds of mixed signals lately, and I'm awful sorry, but I can't help it. I'm extremely...aware...of the people around me—especially..." she looked down, and Echo was certain she blushed in the dark, "especially the men.

246

When it was just you an' me, I could kinda deal. But it's not just you anymore; India and Romeo are around, too, and with their life partnership and how in love they are, the pheromones are just pouring off 'em. So it's hyping me up even more than just the hormones are doing. And in case you haven't looked in the mirror lately, Ace," she tried to affect a teasing, light tone as she deliberately reminded him of his own words from the hot tub at his beach house, but the strain in her voice belied her desperation, "you're pretty easy on the eyes..."

* * *

Echo sat silently beside her, unresponsive, uncertain what to think, what to feel, let alone what to do. He heard the reference to their previous conversation, and understood, at least partly, what she was trying to invoke, but he was unsure what she expected of him in those moments. Omega looked up then, and her blue eyes caught the starlight.

"Please, Ace," she pleaded softly. "We're the best of friends. We're partners. Of all people, I don't want to offend you. Help me get through this with my dignity and self-respect intact. Give me some breathing room for now."

"You don't trust me?" Echo finally asked in a low voice, letting some of the hurt show in his tone.

"Implicitly. With my life," Omega responded immediately. "The lack of faith is not in you." She paused, and looked away. "We spend so much time together. I enjoy being with you, Echo, being around you, but right now..." her voice died to a whisper, "it's hard...I don't know how to handle it..."

Oh shit, he suddenly realized. *If she really is attracted to me, like Ma and Fox think, and the contact with Wright is hyping up all her responses, AND she can smell the pheromones...and she picked up on my reaction to her in the porch swing, I'd lay a year's salary on it...* He mentally shook his head. *And with the whole hormonal soup she's got in her system right now...wow. It may be all she can do to keep from throwing herself at me and ripping clothes. No wonder she's struggling to maintain her 'dignity and self-respect.' Especially if, like she just mentioned, she can pick up on when Romeo and India get all hot an' bothered.* He drew a deep, considering breath. *But I really don't want to leave her out here alone. Especially if she's in that kind of state. There's no telling what might happen, if a coyote*

or cougar or something showed up. Let alone a less-than-reputable human.
* * *

After a moment to consider, Echo spoke.

"Compromise?" He held out an entreating hand, palm open.

"I'm listening," she murmured, wondering what he intended to offer her.

"How long do you want to be alone up here?"

"Oh...ten, fifteen minutes, maybe? No more than that, I don't think. I don't believe I'd NEED to stay up here any longer. I just need...to prove to myself that I can do it, I think."

"All right." Echo stood. "While you're doing whatever you need to do, I'll wait at the bottom of the hill, out of sight, for exactly ten minutes. Then we go back to the house. Both of us. Together."

Omega's eyebrows shot up in surprise. *It's perfect,* she thought. *He does understand.*

"Done," she accepted the deal.

Echo quickly surveyed the area for anyone or anything that shouldn't be there; then, apparently seeing nothing to set off any alarms, strode down the hillside, disappearing from sight under a copse of trees near the foot of the hill. A fresh, cool breeze wafted over her, and Omega laid back down on the blanket, sighing as multiple levels of tension slowly drained from her body.

"You know," she murmured to herself, "in spite of what happened a couple decades ago, it's still just as beautiful as ever..."
* * *

"No, Fox," Mu's voice came over the Director's personal cell phone, "security video shows he arrived here, swiped a car, and headed out. He's completely out of the facility, including the external hangar." There was a pause. "Don't worry. We're after him."

"Good, zun," Fox replied, concerned. "Stay after him. Get on with it, now; just keep me posted."

"Wilco, sir. Mu out."

"Fox out."

The comm link broke, and Fox deactivated his phone, laying it on his desk and staring at it for long moments. Finally he reached for the internal comm switch.

248

"Lima here. What do you need, Fox?"

"Lima? You and Bravo send that emergency notification to Echo. Now."

"Don't you mean Alpha One, sir?"

"No; Omega is...struggling mentally and emotionally. The emergency alert is going to disturb her badly enough, as is. I think Echo should be the one to handle notifying her. But that's why we need to notify him NOW."

"All over it, Boss," came Bravo's voice, slightly remote, and Fox realized he was leaning over Lima's shoulder. "C'mon, Lima. I got this."

"Thank you both."

"No problem, Fox," Bravo said.

Fox switched off the internal comm and sat staring at it, chewing his lip.

* * *

The ten minutes had almost elapsed when Omega heard a shout from Echo. "MEG! Get down here! NOW!!"

Reacting to the urgency in his tone, Omega leaped to her feet, snatched up the blanket and threw it over her shoulder, then sprinted sure-footedly down the familiar slope toward the recognized, welcome figure emerging from the trees.

"Echo?! What's wrong??"

Echo still held his cell phone.

"Meg—Wright's escaped."

* * *

"Come on, Echo! This way!" Omega exclaimed, leading the retreat back to the house. The blanket, now only a hindrance, hung over a fence rail in a field, far behind. "When did he get loose?"

"Headquarters didn't say," Echo replied, hot on her heels. "I'm not certain, but I don't think they really know for sure. Dammit, I wish SOME-BODY could figure out how Slug engineered you two to look just alike to the sensors. Fox said they thought they had 'em reprogrammed to tell the difference this time, but it obviously didn't work."

"What happened this time?"

"It was Yankee again," Echo snarled. "There was evidently some mitigating circumstance last time, and Romeo and Fox decided to give him a second chance. As far as I'm concerned, he doesn't get a third strike; he's out!"

"You think he let Wright out deliberately?"

"If he didn't, he's little enough concerned about the consequences to you that he couldn't be bothered to pay attention. That's the way I read it, anyway."

"But do you know that, Ace? Did Fox tell you?"

"No. I didn't actually talk to Fox. I got an emergency alert on my phone. It was a variant on an Alpha Line Alert, sent to a limited distribution. Didn't you get it?"

"No."

"Maybe Fox had it sent just to me, then," Echo decided, "to avoid giving you a coronary right off."

"Maybe so. But Ace, I understand that you're upset, but I don't think... that just doesn't sound like Yankee. He may not like me, but he's pretty thorough as an Agent."

"Yeah, well. We'll see. The alert indicated there was an ongoing investigation. I assume they'll keep me posted on what they find, if they find anything."

"Keep me in the loop?"

"As much as I can without upsetting you more than this whole sitch is already doing."

"Okay. When was the last time anybody saw him? Mark, I mean," Omega panted, scrambling over a fence, Echo right behind.

"Lemme check." Echo pulled his cell phone as they ran. "Fox? Echo. When's the last time anybody saw Wright? Oh? And that was?...Aw, shit. Yeah, she's here with me. We will. Later, Fox." Echo deactivated the phone, slipping it in his hip pocket. "Last time anybody actually saw him was when Yankee let him walk right out past him. Nearly two hours ago. Security video has him hopping a maglev a few minutes later."

Horrified, Omega stopped dead, and Echo nearly ran into her before he could stop.

"But that means—"

* * *

Echo nodded.

"Exactly. He could already be in the area." The cell phone beeped, and he extracted and activated it again. "Echo." He listened for a moment. "Romeo, break out the blasters, sweep an area around the house, and watch for us. We're on the way." He replaced the cell phone in his pocket. "The perimeter sensors have triggered, Meg," Echo told her, his voice quiet.

"Oh, no," Omega whispered. "Oh shit, oh shit, oh shit."

"Stay calm, baby. It may just be a neighbor out for a walk," Echo said.

"Hang on a minute, and I'll check," Omega murmured, "but keep an eye out for me while I do..." Echo nodded, and turned to quickly scan the area as Omega's eyes defocused. After a moment or two, she snapped back. "Echo," she breathed, and he moved closer, adopting a ready stance.

"So it's him?" he verified.

"Yes." She paused. "I've just re-erected my telepathic block, as strong as I can make it. That might slow him some. But it also leaves me mind-blind to his location, too."

Echo activated his cell phone again.

"India? Meg says it's Wright. Yeah, no doubt at all in her mind; she made loose contact with him telepathically. You two are in the clear. He'll be trying to come through me to get to Meg. No, I think he'll make straight for her. Get Romeo and rendezvous with us. Yeah, meet us on the far side of the peach orchard, behind the barn. Keep an eye out for Wright."

"Echo—tell them not to kill him," Omega pleaded. Echo turned to her.

"Meg, we'll try. But we're not gonna leave you defenseless, just be-cause—"

"Echo, stop and think about the *Otello*, and the 'horsefly bite,'" she pointed out. "If you take him out, you take me out, too."

"Oh, damn. The link..." His eyes narrowed, and he turned his attention back to the phone. "India? Did you hear that? Don't shoot Wright if you can avoid it at all—and do NOT shoot to kill, under any circumstances. It could hurt Meg, or worse. Got it? Good. We're on our way." The cell phone went into Echo's pocket yet again, and he turned to his partner. "Okay, Meg. We just became conjoined twins. I don't want you out of arm's reach until we get back in the house. Understood?"

"Copy that," she replied. "How do you want to do this?"

"Well, there's no sense hiding. Wright knows where you are, whether he can see you or not. Let's take the shortest distance between two points, but do it slow, cautious, and alert."

* * *

"Okay. Let's go. We're at least halfway home," Omega told Echo, and

251

they set back out through the dark fields. They moved stealthily, warily, keeping watchful eyes out all around them. Echo kept in touch-contact with his partner at all times, determined to ensure that Wright couldn't snatch her without Echo's having a shot at him. Omega tensed more and more, trying to deal with the dual stresses of being stalked, and being in constant contact with Echo. At last, she could take no more.

"Echo...give me some space," she panted.

"What?" He turned to glance at her.

"I'm wired, Echo," Omega whispered. "Between Mark out there somewhere, and you right here, I'm...losin' it."

"What do you want me to do about it?"

"We're almost to the peach orchard. Let me go the rest of the way without being on a leash."

"No."

"Echo, please."

"No."

"Why?!"

"Dammit, Meg, I'm not even gonna answer that." Echo tugged on her hand, still firmly in his grip, and they moved forward.

"Echo...you don't think I'm a good enough Agent, do you?" Omega's voice was low, pained.

"Hell. Don't pull that shit with me. You know better. The only reason I'm sticking to you so tight is because Wright's turning your insides wrong-side-out. If he weren't, you'd never even think of trying to manipulate me like you just did." Echo checked the next field, then climbed the fence. "If it weren't for that, you could take him out alone, unarmed, probably with one hand. Especially the way I saw you fighting back in Ipswich. Now come on." He helped her over the fence, still maintaining contact. "How much farther?"

"Far side of this field, through the gate," Omega replied, mentally shaking herself as she realized how she was behaving. Echo scanned the open field.

"Shall we make a run for it?"

"With you still hangin' onto me? I'll try."

"Dammit. All right, have it your way." Echo released Omega's hand. "But stay close. Go." They set out across the field at a dead run.

252

* * *

Echo was substantially taller than Omega, with a correspondingly longer stride, but Omega's pace was faster, and the two were fairly evenly matched. As they approached the gate into the orchard, neither slowed down. Instead, they vaulted the gate together, nigh-perfect mirror images, and lunged forward under the peach trees, coming to a halt.

"Now," Omega panted, "where are Romeo and India?"

"Over here, Meg," Romeo called softly. "Have you seen 'im?"

"No, no sign," Echo replied, following Romeo's voice to locate Alpha Two. "How 'bout you, Meg? Any sign?" He glanced around; she was gone.

"Ohhh, yeah! Sign, sign!" Omega's voice cried. Shocked, Echo spun and ran in the direction of his partner's cries. Footfalls behind told him Romeo and India were also in pursuit. Ahead, he heard Omega emit a gutteral scream.

"MEG!!" Echo shouted then, putting on a burst of speed, as a cold vise gripped his gut.

Abruptly, an unsteady Omega ran up. Echo caught her by the shoulders.

"Are you okay?!"

"Yeah," she gasped.

"Where's Wright?" India asked, urgent. Omega pointed up and behind her.

"He's in the tree."

"The tree?!" Romeo exclaimed. "What th' hell is he doin up there?!"

"Um, yeah," Omega grinned sheepishly. "It's amazing what a judo throw will do when you get a hormonal pump behind it, especially when it's adrenaline-charged, to boot. Now, before he can climb down—let's get outta here!!"

"Damn straight!" Echo replied, and they headed for the farmhouse as if each was powered by one of Fox's hot-rodded engines.

* * *

"So he knows you're in here?" India asked the platinum-blonde Agent as they held an emergency strategy session in the farmhouse kitchen. All four Agents were back in 'uniform,' Suits complete with weapons and other gear. All of the doors and windows had been locked, and the window blinds closed; the farmhouse appeared under siege. Omega's eyes glazed momentarily, checking.

"Yes. And he's out there. Waiting. But not for long. He'll try to get in, soon."

"An' you know this how, exactly?" Romeo wondered.

"The link?" Echo verified.

"Yeah. I can't block him out completely, despite my best efforts. His mind has been...rewired...too."

"We gotta do somethin'," Romeo said, shaking his head. "He'll be headed here."

"I still think this is neutral territory," Omega replied.

"Maybe, and maybe not," Echo said. "I already told you about the image I had of the two of you—three of you—here at the farm. That isn't something I'd just...imagine. There's no reason for me to see a thing like that if it isn't something I picked up from my telepathic exposure to the programming. And if that's the case, it's really a trap, and you're in big trouble if you stay here, Meg. The Farm isn't intended to be a true safehouse; it was never set up like that, when you signed it into Agency holding. I know for a fact that they've been trying to set it up as a horse training facility, to try to bring in some additional income for you, and keep it viable and ready if you ever decided to come back to it. It's far less secure than our quarters, and Wright walked right into those."

Omega slumped into a kitchen chair.

"What do you want to do?" she asked, discouraged.

"We need to take you somewhere Wright physically can't get to," Echo brainstormed. "But someplace on-planet, so it doesn't threaten the link and hurt you—both. To give Bet a chance to figure out a solution. To give us what we need—time."

"So we're on the run?" Omega asked, downcast. "Again?"

"Looks like it."

"Damn. Talk about bloodhounds on my trail...blast it. Now I'm doing it."

"Any ideas, Echo?" Romeo asked.

"Mmm...could be. I need to check with Fox."

* * *

"India, can I talk to you in private?" Omega requested.

"Sure, Meg," India responded, waving the men out of the kitchen as

Echo pulled his cell phone. "What's up, girlfriend?"

"Am I...um...With me in...uh...If Mark gets to me right now, I'll almost certainly wind up..."

"Pregnant?"

Omega nodded, eyes troubled.

"Maybe. Didn't you get the appropriate treatment when you came into the Agency?"

"To be honest, I have no idea," Omega admitted. "They did so much to me, I don't know what was for which thing. And it isn't like, um, I've ever had the chance to, uh, find out, if you know what I mean."

"Okay. Well, better safe than sorry, I guess. We can fix that, if you're worried, and it won't hurt if they already did it when you came aboard. And I came prepared; Boy Scout motto and all that. I just haven't had a chance to say anything—"

"Do it. Now."

* * *

India pulled her medikit and extracted an osmosive micropore hypodermic. Then she selected a medication and filled the hypo.

"Gimme an arm, Meg. It doesn't matter which one." India pumped the hypo's contents into the proffered arm, then timed off two minutes on her watch. "Done. Infallible."

Omega sat and stared at her arm for long moments as if waiting, somewhat to India's surprise. Finally she looked up, expression wry.

"At least my arm didn't split open this time."

"What?!" India exclaimed. "What are you talking about?"

"Never mind. How long does it last?"

"As long as you want it to. I have to give you a different medication to counter it. The entire reproductive system is now shut down until further notice, basically."

"Will...will that gradually stop this...this hormone storm I got?"

"Uh, well, no," India said, trying to be honest but encouraging. "Like, I still sometimes get PMS an' stuff, so I doubt it'll help that, either, otherwise Zebra would have thought to do it. Which also means it was probably already done, I guess. But it WILL ensure that no eggs develop, and it sets up your system to ensure sperm don't make it far—almost like it's your immune system after a virus or something. It's...complicated, and truthfully,

255

I'm still learning the whole biological process. There aren't any negative side effects, like osteoporosis, though. Ain't alien science wonderful?"

"Sometimes. All right," Omega said with a sigh. "Now take Romeo and Echo and...and go."

"What?!" India reiterated, shocked. "Meg!"

"I'm sick of it, India. I'm miserable. Mark's miserable. Have you checked with Bet?" Omega's jaw clenched; her face was bleak.

"Just a half-hour ago."

"And?"

"...No ideas." India shook her head.

"That's what I thought. So let's...get it over with. Y'all get out of here and I'll...just wait for Mark. As long as there aren't any genetically-programmed assassins forthcoming, I'll...handle it." Her expression was determined, but the blue eyes were empty.

* * *

"Is that what you want?" The quiet, deep-timbred voice came from the kitchen door.

India turned. The familiar man standing there wore his characteristic neutral expression, but India thought there was something strange about the dark eyes.

They're...tight. Narrowed. Almost like Echo's in pain, the physician thought. *Pain that he's trying hard to hide. And he's awfully pale.*

* * *

Omega looked away from her partner.

"No, Echo. Not at all."

"Then why do you refer to Wright so...familiarly?"

"What?"

"Since when are most women on a first-name basis with their attempted rapists?"

Omega looked down, pained.

"He's...not a rapist on the inside, Echo," she explained. "Any more than I was a murderer. I identify with him. Try to understand, Echo. In a bizarre sort of way, when you...attack him, when you label him a criminal, you're doing the same to me."

"All right. Fair enough." Echo crouched in front of Omega's chair. "Look at me, Meg." Omega raised her head and met his somber eyes. "You

256

didn't really answer my question. Do. You. Want. This. Man?"

"NO."

Echo studied Omega's eyes for a long moment, then stood and held out a hand.

"Then come on. I just talked to Fox. Romeo's already throwing our stuff in the 'Vette. We're taking you someplace Wright CAN'T go."

* * *

"All right, ladies." Echo stood at the front door of the farmhouse, proto-cyclotron blaster in hand. "Set your weapons to minimum—level oh-point-five—and shoot to stun, only, if you can. Think...minor flesh wound; a graze. I wish we had some stunner pistols, but we don't, because ramping DOWN is not something we normally have to do in a confrontation, so we'll just have to be careful. Romeo's bringing up the Corvette," he remarked, as they all adjusted blaster settings. "Seat assignments are as follows: Romeo will exit the driver's seat, and move directly behind it to the driver's-side rear. India, you will take passenger-side rear; Omega, passenger-side front. I'll drive."

"Echo, I know the roads better," Omega pointed out.

"Yeah, I know, Meg. And you're good. But I've still got a few years on you when it comes to handling the Corvette. That's why you're up front with me. You're gonna navigate."

"Copy that," she acquiesced.

"Here comes Romeo in the Corvette," India noted.

"Get ready," Echo said. "A.T.L.A.S.S. Minor: Security lock code Fox on voice authorization Alpha-One-Echo immediately upon my departure. Confirm."

"CONFIRMED," a by-now-familiar electronic voice floated through the air inside the farmhouse.

"Boy, would Mom freak at that," Omega muttered. "So you're the last man out, Echo?"

"Yep. India, you're first. We're sandwiching Meg between us."

"Got it," India responded.

"Okay, ladies, on three. One...two...three."

* * *

The Alpha Line Agents exploded from the farmhouse and down the porch steps toward the waiting 'Vette, weapons ready. Simultaneously, Romeo sprang from the driver's seat, covering them with his blaster over the roof of the car. Suddenly he brought up his weapon.

"Meg—LOOK OUT!!"

Out of the corner of her eye, a running Omega saw a blur launch itself from the shrubs by the steps.

"Shit!" Echo exclaimed behind her, automatically bringing his own weapon to bear.

"NO, Echo!" Omega cried, as he and Romeo fired off rounds at the same instant. They both struck Wright, one in the right shoulder, the other in the left leg, and he went down in mid-leap, his forward momentum carrying him to Omega's feet. "AAAHHH!!" Omega cried, falling to the ground beside her assailant, her left leg buckling beneath her as she clutched her right shoulder.

"Dammit!" Echo cursed. "No, stay there, Romeo!" he told the Agent, who was about to leave his post to help. "Get in the car! India, cover me!" Echo holstered his blaster, roughly pushed the stunned Wright away, then scooped up his partner and sprinted for the Corvette. India opened the passenger-side door, then clambered in herself, and Echo deposited Omega in the front seat. He slammed the door, and ran for the driver's seat.

Once inside the vehicle, Echo activated the locks and started the engine, then turned to the dazed blonde woman beside him as Alpha Two strapped in behind them.

"Meg? Are you okay, baby?"

"Y-yeah," she panted. "It hurts, but...I can...can ignore it. He's...it's a couple flesh wounds, like you said. A bit more than a graze, especially on the leg, but...nothing serious."

"Here," he said, reaching across her, "let's get you strapped in so we can get outta here." Omega pulled the seat belt up with her left hand and awkwardly passed it to Echo, who inserted it in the buckle and latched it for her. Then he put the car in gear while strapping in himself, and the Corvette spat loose gravel in the direction of the already-recovering Wright as it departed the farmhouse at speed.

"Hang on, guys," Echo said. "We're about to morph. Meg, care to do the honors?"

"Done," Omega said, her hand slamming down on the Corvette's dashboard emergency-morph switch, and the vehicle transformed, tearing down

258

the country lane in the dark. Echo pulled back delicately on the steering wheel, and the vehicle went airborne, flying down the roads some three to four feet above the pavement.

"An' we're off!" Romeo crowed from the back seat.

"And running," Omega added somberly, pointing over Echo's shoulder to give direction as they headed for the main roads. Some little distance down the road, she spoke again. "It would help me navigate if I knew where we were headed."

"Atlanta Office spaceport," Echo responded.

* * *

As the Corvette rocketed across the Alabama state line into Georgia, high above the busy interstate, Echo's cell phone beeped. Calmly steering the vehicle with one hand, he punched a button on the dash. An earpiece, looking not unlike a bluetooth but far more sophisticated, emerged from a small recess in the dashboard, and he grabbed it and donned it in one smooth, swift motion, before putting both hands back on the wheel. The matter was done in scant seconds. Automatically, the incoming call rerouted to the earpiece; he tapped a tiny button on its side.

"Echo." He listened for a moment. "That so? When...? Uh-huh. Shit. Yeah, I sure did. Yep, it sure sounds like it. Aw, hell, Fox. There's gotta be a better way. Don't ask me to do that." Echo sighed. "Yeah, Fox, I know. Yeah, all right; I'll do it. I guess we don't have much choice." He tapped the earpiece button with a sigh, leaving it in his ear, just in case.

"Echo? What's up?" India asked.

"Wright has been spotted in one of the farm's trucks," Echo answered, "headed in the general direction of...Atlanta."

"Shit!" Romeo exclaimed. "When did he start?"

"Judging from when and where he was seen, and how fast he was going," Echo elaborated, "he started...about the time I told Meg we were headed for Atlanta."

Alpha Two gasped.

Omega put her head in her hands.

* * *

At the Atlanta Office spaceport, Echo de-morphed the Corvette, and the four traded it for Alpha One's T-Bird and Alpha Two's Jet, the black, extensively-modified T-38s the Agents flew, and which Fox had had brought

259

to the spaceport. As a flight-suited Omega climbed into the back seat of the T-Bird and prepared to don her helmet and oxygen mask, Echo climbed up behind her.

"Meg? How's your stomach?"

"Fine, Echo. Why?"

"Is your head okay? No vertigo, or anything like that? Congestion better?"

"Yeah, I'm all right, Ace. What's up?"

"Damn, I hate to do this. Here, then." Echo handed her a blindfold. "It seems it may be better if you don't know where we're going, baby. And give me your wrist chronometer."

Omega stared at the blindfold, then at her partner. "Okay. It makes sense," she sighed, removing her highly specialized timepiece and exchanging it for the blindfold mask. "This telepathy stuff is a pain, huh?"

"Yeah, sometimes. Finish getting your gear on, baby. Checkout's complete. We're ready to go as soon as I get into the cockpit."

"Roger that."

Moments later, two extremely high-performance black jets roared into the sky.

* * *

The flight was an unusually long one, but eventually Omega sensed the T-Bird start its descent.

"Echo, Omega. It feels like we're headed down. Are we getting close?"

"That's an affirmative. You still okay back there?"

"Affirm. Been trying to rest and zone out a little bit."

"Good. Keep the blindfold on until we've landed, Meg."

"Wilco. Is Alpha Two still with us?"

"That's a roger, Meg," Romeo's voice replied.

"Oh, sorry, y'all," Omega apologized. "I didn't realize I was hot."

"Whoa—" Romeo began, the grin audible as he pounced on the inadvertent double-entendre.

* * *

"I set us on broadcast, Meg," Echo interrupted, helmeted visage glaring over his shoulder at his impertinent wingman. "I knew you couldn't find the external talk switch blindfolded. I wanted you enabled, just in case."

"Copy that. I appreciate it, Ace."

"We're coming in," Echo said, as a series of beeps registered in the audio. "There's the electronic handshake. Open approach window Alpha-One-Echo. Division One aircraft designates T-Bird, Jet. Pilots: Echo, Romeo. GIBs: Omega, India." There was another beep as their destination's security system acknowledged the command. "Alpha One T-bird on active approach; Alpha Two Jet standing by."

"Alpha Two standing by for approach," Romeo replied.

The T-Bird touched down smoothly and taxied into a hangar, followed moments later by the Jet.

Chapter 9

"Okay, Meg, we're here, baby. Ditch the blindfold and help me secure the T-Bird," Echo told her, and she peeled off helmet, blindfold, and oxygen mask in one smooth motion. Echo popped the canopy, and warm, humid air rushed into the cockpit.

"Mmm. Feels like I'm gonna enjoy myself, wherever we are," Omega purred throatily, climbing down out of the cockpit. At her tone, Echo cast a puzzled glance at his companion.

"Te.S.S., resume safe mode, authorization Alpha-One-Echo. All authorization modes deactivated except voice-only; approved voice patterns Alpha-One-Echo, Alpha-One-Omega, Alpha-Two-Romeo, Alpha-Two-India. No genetic scan patterns acceptable," Omega's partner murmured into the mike before joining her. Two long beeps in his headset acknowledged the command.

The two aircraft were secured quickly and efficiently, and Echo led the other three Agents out of the hangar. "This is an Agency safehouse-type location," he explained. "It's called The Beach. It's physically isolated and very remote, with a security system—called Te.S.S, which stands for Technology Security System—equivalent to the entire Headquarters building itself. We use it for political asylum, visiting potentates and the like. If Wright can get to you here, Meg, he's not now and never was human—or anything from this universe."

"I take it, he isn't a pilot?" India asked.

"Nope. And believe me, Fox and his assistants have dug into his background like moles in a garden. Here," Echo jabbed his index finger at the ground, "Meg is safe."

"It's...an island, I think," Omega observed, looking around at the tropical foliage. "Where, I don't know...but it's gorgeous."

"Yep. To alla that. I kinda figured nobody would object to a working vacation at the beach." Echo grinned.

"You figured right," Romeo remarked. "Now, if I just had a pair o' Speedos..."

"Have you checked the fresh kits Fox had waiting for us in Atlanta?"

Echo asked, and Romeo and India immediately started scrabbling in their bags. Echo moved to stand closer to Omega.

"And I noticed how a seashore environment had a positive effect on you, baby, so I thought it might be good to try again," he told her in a low tone meant only for her. "This one's just a little more tropical than my place. And way the hell more isolated...not that my place is in the hustle and bustle. It turns out, it was just easier for him to get to."

"I...appreciate that, Ace. Very much. So, um...is there a welcome party?" a grateful Omega asked.

"Nope. Nobody here but us chickens," Echo replied. "No new faces, nobody but...'family.' No one unfamiliar for you to have to deal with in... your condition. I've been thinking about the, the info you've been feeding me about...how all this is affecting you, and...well, I...thought it'd be easier that way."

"Have I ever mentioned what a considerate partner I've got?" Omega murmured, voice husky. She kept her gaze directed downward. "Thanks, Ace."

"Well..." Echo stared intently at the waves splashing on the nearby beach. "I still don't understand everything, but I'm trying my damnedest, baby. I've even looked up a few, um," he felt his face heat, "gynecological studies, just trying to understand better. It's helped, a little, at least. I know now, this is not an easy hand you've been dealt this game, Meg—and I'm only starting to get a grasp on just how much. So, as best I can, I'm trying to help you set up your play—"

"Like a good...bridge...partner."

"Besides, Fox agreed with me."

"Tell Fox thanks, too, then."

"Wilco. Now come on. Let's get settled in. It was a damn long flight— did you know when we had to refuel in flight?—and it's late."

* * *

The house at The Beach was a moderately-sized structure, intended to hold a number of occupants. On one end of the long, low, single-story building were the common areas; on the other was a hallway with bedrooms opening off it, and the Agents made for this to unpack what little they were accustomed to carrying. Omega selected a bedroom as near the middle of the structure as she could get, preferring the feel of walls around

263

her, for obvious reasons. Once again, Echo chose the bedroom next to his partner's, intending to stand guard—from inside her room, should need arise. Romeo and India chose a bedroom farther down the hall, for matters of personal privacy.

In short order, the Agents were out of their flight suits, and into the shorts and t-shirts that Fox had provided for the sultry climate.

"Who's up for dinner?" India asked, and was the immediate recipient of three eager responses.

"Looks like you volunteered to cook tonight, India," Echo deadpanned, then grinned. "There should be stuff in the kitchen ready to go."

"I've got an idea," Omega piped up. "Is there a grill around here somewhere?"

"Oh, mama, jammin'!" Romeo exclaimed, eager about the notion. "I'll scope it out."

"We'll help," Echo added. "Sounds like a winner to me."

With the equivalent of four highly-experienced investigators on the 'case,' the grill turned up quickly, and a half-hour later, the mouth-watering smell of steaks grilling wafted through the house, borne on the night breeze off the water.

* * *

"This is the life!" Romeo remarked, chowing down on a juicy sirloin and roasted, stuffed potato at the patio table on the deck overlooking the beach. India agreed.

"Listening to the sound of the surf, nice cool breeze, big juicy steaks, good company. Not much missing," she noted.

"I can't be-lieve we're gettin' duty time for this!" Romeo grinned.

"I can," Omega murmured, subdued, and Romeo and India quieted. "Listen, y'all, I'm really glad Echo came up with some place everybody can enjoy. I'm...sorry I had to drag y'all into exile with me."

"This ain't exile, Meg. This is livin'!" Romeo said, enthusiastic. "Un-lax an' enjoy it. You're safe, pretty lady."

"What Meg's saying, guys, is 'wait and see how long we have to stay here before you get too excited.' Right, Meg?" Echo verified. Omega nodded.

"Kind of a 'bird in a gilded cage' syndrome," she added. "But Romeo's right. I'm gonna enjoy it," Omega said, determined; she thrust out her jaw and squared her shoulders. "Echo, I got a question for you, Ace."

"Shoot," Echo said.

"Do you think it's safe for me to go out and do some stargazing? Or will I figure out too much about where we are?"

"Hmm..." Echo considered, and Romeo and India perked up, interested in another lesson from Professor Omega—as she was known at Division One University.

"Let me tell you what I already know," Omega suggested, to aid Echo in his decision. "I know I'll be able to see Southern Hemisphere constellations from here, just by the climate. It's tropical, ergo, equatorial or thereabouts, though I have no idea whether it's north or south of the equator..."

"Wouldn't th' drains tell ya?" Romeo wondered. "You know, th' direction the water circulates."

"Only to a point; plumbing can be made to do it either way, or not at all, depending how you construct it," Omega said, then continued. "Y'all took my wrist chronometer away from me, so I have no idea what the time difference is between here and home. And not much way to easily infer it, because I really have no idea how long we were in the air. And even if I did, I can't prove you flew a great circle path; for all I know, we went a certain distance, then started flying in big, broad loops. And, while somebody experienced in the botany of the tropics might be able to tell more, that wasn't my biological specialty, and I CAN'T tell. All of which means, while I could estimate a latitude range, I'm clueless about longitude. So that's a pretty large chunk of planet for Mark—for Wright—to search in...and not a lot of way for him to actually search."

"Yeah. Okay, I think it'll be all right," Echo agreed, and India and Romeo whooped.

"All right! Let's go, Dr. Meg!" India said, and they grabbed a couple of beach blankets and headed out.

* * *

"Okay, y'all," Omega began, "this lecture's mine. Echo doesn't have enough experience with Southern Hemisphere constellations to tackle this one quite yet."

"Good," Echo muttered.

"Don't think that gets you off the hook, Ace," she told him with a mischievous grin...though the blue eyes were still haunted. "I'll be expecting you to learn this stuff, too."

"Shit. Well, no...it's actually been kinda fun. A whole lotta fun, to be honest. So...okay, baby. Lay it on us."

"All right. You've already seen the 'Northern Cross.' Look way over there," she continued, pointing. "There's the Southern Cross. Real easy, basic constellation. Got it?"

There was a general chorus of, "Yeah."

"Good. Now let's look over here. See this grouping? Can you use a lot of imagination and picture a mythological centaur?" Her finger traced out the pattern of stars in the constellation.

"Yeah, Meg."

"We got it."

"Good. You're better than I am, then!" Omega grinned, and they all laughed. "Anyway, that's Centaurus, and the brightest star there is the closest star system to our own, Alpha Centauri. If memory serves, a couple of different inhabited planets are in and around that system."

"Cool," Romeo decided.

"Yeah," Omega smiled. "But it gets even cooler. See, Alpha Centauri is actually a trinary star system: Alpha A and Alpha B, which are a close pair, and Proxima, sometimes called Alpha C, which orbits at a distance."

"Kinda like you, Echo, and Wright," Romeo joked. Echo shot him a hard glance.

"Uh...yeah," Omega replied, disconcerted. "At least that's the idea behind this trip. Proxima, strictly speaking, is currently the closest of the three, by about a tenth of a light year. Earth astronomers have spotted one or two planets around Proxima and Alpha B, but WE know that all THREE stars have planets, which is how there's more than one planet in the system with an independent civilization!"

"Neat," India decided.

"Yeah. Now, one of the weirdest objects astronomers know of, Centaurus A, is right about...there."

"Where?" India tried to correlate Omega's pointed finger with an object in the sky.

"Oh, well, you couldn't see it without a telescope," Omega explained, "though an amateur 'scope is plenty good enough, and a lotta amateurs observe it. See that sorta fuzzy star up there, left of the constellation's middle?"

"Yeah?"

"That's Omega Centauri. It isn't really a star, though it looks like one to the naked eye; it's around ten million stars—a globular cluster. Hold up three fingers, all together. The width of those three fingers—well, about two and a half—above Omega Centauri is about where Centaurus A is, except it's somewhere around eleven to thirteen million light years away, which means it's way the hell outside our galaxy. It's probably a pair of colliding galaxies..."

* * *

Omega, Echo, India, and Romeo stayed out on the beach for several hours, fascinated at just watching the heavens slowly rotate overhead. When Omega got tired of instructing—which took a while—and the others tired of asking her questions—which took longer—they wandered on to other topics, the conversation carefully steered by India and Echo to keep it innocuous.

"Hey, India," Omega volunteered then, "let's try out your bloodhound theory."

The conversation stopped dead. The other Agents shifted uncomfortably.

"...It's all right, Meg," India said after a moment. "You don't have to."

"I know. But we're all curious about it. You know we are." Omega pulled the flight blindfold from the pocket of her shorts.

"Meg, let it go," Echo said quietly. "Put the blindfold away."

Omega sat up on the blanket beside Echo.

"Look, guys," she said softly. "I know I reacted badly about it initially, and...I'm sorry. It's...you'd have to be in my head since this whole mess with Mark started, to understand why I...did that. Maybe since we discovered...what I truly am, even. But we really ought to investigate this. This is something I can do. We might as well find out how good I am at doing it. We may need to know, sometime."

Echo, India, and Romeo exchanged worried glances.

"We just don't want to hurt you," Echo spoke for all of them.

"The whole situation hurts, Echo. If I can make something useful, something constructive, out of it, then at least there'll be something to offset the pain." Omega sighed and put her head in her hands, hiding her face. "Now I've gone and made y'all uncomfortable. Y' ever have a day when

267

you just couldn't do anything right?" she tried to laugh, but it ended in something closer to a sob.

"Hey—it's a game," Romeo said, and the others looked at him. "You know, like hide an' seek. Only Meg's gotta find us with her nose." Omega smiled then, and Romeo and India stood, prepared to find hiding spots.

"Hold the phone," Echo remarked, and the others turned. "Let me get this straight. You want us all to play a children's game..."

Romeo and India froze in their tracks, and Omega turned away, embarrassed.

"Well...yeah...but..." Omega hesitated, "n-never mind..."

"So how are we gonna make sure Meg doesn't run into a tree or something, with that blindfold on?" Echo asked, standing. He offered his hand to Omega and pulled her to her feet.

"Uh—it's dark. Maybe she doesn't need it," India said, shifting gears rapidly. "We can hide while she covers her eyes."

"No. Meg's too sharp-eyed. If we're gonna test her nose, we need to eliminate visual cues," Echo disagreed.

"But th' pretty lady's got ears like a cat, too," Romeo protested. "You gonna make 'er wear ear plugs?"

"Hmm..." Echo considered. "Meg?"

"As quiet as y'all are capable of bein', and with the surf in the background, I'll have a hard time hearing you," Omega responded. "At least, enough to sort out who's who, an' what's what. Like Echo said, I'm more worried about finding a tree trunk the hard way."

"Tell you what," Echo proposed. "Let Romeo and India hide. I'll be your seeing-eye dog, you can find 'em, then I can swap with one of 'em, and you can find me."

"That works," Omega said, putting on the blindfold. Romeo stepped forward and took her by the shoulders.

"Mix ya up!" he exclaimed, spinning her quickly, then darting off.

"Woo," Omega said, staggering to a stop and wobbling for a moment before regaining her equilibrium. "Echo, stay where you are, and be quiet," she anticipated, as Echo started forward to help her. Romeo and India watched from their hiding places in the trees further inland.

* * *

"All right, Ace," Omega murmured, turning in a slow circle. "This is gonna be interesting with the sea breeze...”

From where he stood, Echo could see Omega’s nostrils flare slightly with each inhalation. After a few seconds, she turned in his general direction and moved slowly forward. A couple of steps later, she paused, sniffed, and adjusted her course. Echo stood stock-still and watched in fascination as Omega slowly homed in on him. She stopped with her nose scant inches from his chest.

“Hello, Ace,” she said confidently. Omega raised her right hand, spread her fingers, and laid her palm lightly on Echo’s breastbone. “On general principles, I think I found you.”

“I think so,” Echo agreed with a grin. “Now, can you find India and Romeo as easily?”

“No,” Omega admitted. “I’m around you all the time. I know what you smell like—I can ID you around a corner. But I should be able to tag them, too. It’ll just take longer. Give me your hand, now, and guide me into the trees...”

* * *

A little while later, the Alpha Line Agents were convinced that their colleague could, indeed, not only identify but also locate them by scent. As a last test, they grouped themselves tightly together. Omega moved close, and inhaled slowly. Then she pointed.

“India.”

India stared in surprise at the finger aimed at her chest, and moved aside.

“How on Earth did you know?” the physician-Agent wondered.

“Men tend to smell muskier to me than women,” Omega explained. “Your scent is sweeter—like fruit. Or honey.” She turned back to the men. “Okay. Let’s see.” Seconds later, she pointed in turn with each hand. “Romeo. Echo.”

“Nailed it,” Romeo grinned, and Omega removed the blindfold. “How?”

“You...you’re just different.”

“How, Meg?” Echo pressed. “How are we different?”

Omega walked over to one of the blankets and sat down to think. The others joined her.

“Hm,” she murmured. “Echo, sit right here.” She patted the blanket with her left hand, and Echo obligingly moved into position. "Romeo, you're over here." Omega patted with her right hand.

When the two men were seated close beside her, she closed her eyes and focused on the scents she could detect from them, comparing and contrasting. Occasionally, she tilted her head to one side or the other.

"Okay, Romeo," she tried, "you have that male muskiness I was talking about, but there's also a...you know how some scents are kind of...eye-openers? Like that ozone smell just before a summer storm..."

The others nodded, understanding what she was trying to get across.

"That sounds just like Romeo," India grinned. "And Echo?"

"Very musky..." Omega murmured, concentrating, eyes still closed. "More complex...subtler...that's why it's hard to describe...touches of that ozone-like smell, but...some other stuff, too..."

"Free-associate, Meg," Echo suggested.

"Fresh outdoors...smoky campfires...strong, athletic...confident..." Omega brainstormed. "Tough—not afraid to get dirty...alert...but also...a quieter side...you know, homey, comfortable smells, like apple pie or fresh-baked bread...scents that give you a sense of calm...contentment...affection!" Omega opened her eyes and smiled at her partner. Echo abruptly began staring at his feet as the others grinned fondly at him. "Very sophisticated, multi-dimensional," she added, continuing to associate descriptors with Echo's scent. "Which generally adds up to an intelligent, cultivated, suave 'man of the galaxy,' you might say—basically, someone who can handle any situation that gets thrown at him, I guess. Which is pretty much Echo." Omega sighed. "It's complicated. I mean, really, really complex. And it's hard for me to disassociate your scent from who you are and how I react to it and you. Of all the senses, smell is the most...visceral. Do y'all understand?"

"Yes, Meg," India answered, as Romeo and Echo nodded.

"You've already done way more than we could," Echo added. "Can you do it all the time, or is it hyped up right now, like other stuff?"

"I think it's hyped up a good bit, yeah," Omega decided, "but, like I said, I can still identify you around a blind corner, Echo. I just might not be able to do as well with India and Romeo, is all."

"I got a question," Romeo said.

"Okay—what?" Omega responded amiably.

"What do YOU smell like?" Romeo asked Omega.

"I have no idea."

"What?!" Romeo exclaimed, surprised.

"Why not?" Echo followed up.

"Olfactory fatigue, I suppose," she answered.

"Like when you quit smelling perfume or cologne after you've been exposed to it for several minutes, even if it's your own fragrance," India elaborated. "Meg's own scent is around her all the time, so she doesn't notice it."

"Aha. That makes sense." Echo stretched back out on the blanket. "No offense to ex-partners present or absent, but Meg, you're the most... unique...partner I've ever had."

Romeo sputtered good-humoredly, and Omega made a face.

"Thanks...I think," she replied, lying back on the beach blanket beside Echo as Alpha Two returned to their own blanket.

"It was intended as a compliment, Meg," Echo murmured, gazing up into the black sky.

"I know," Omega returned softly. "That's why I thanked you. It just doesn't...feel like a good thing, you know? At least...not right now."

"Yeah. I understand, baby."

"Hey, Meg, is that a comet over there?" India called from the other blanket.

"You mean, that fuzzy object over there? Yeah, that's Comet 102P/ Shoemaker," Omega answered, pointing. "Look streaming east; you can just see the ion tail, if you use averted vision..."

* * *

The conversation wandered back into the sky, this time meandering into a discussion of alien cultures. Eventually, they declared by mutual consent that it was time to get some sleep. Shaking the sand out of their blankets, Alpha One and Alpha Two made their way back to the beach house.

"You doing okay, partner?" Echo asked quietly, as Romeo and India forged ahead.

"Yeah. Y'all are doing a good job of keeping me too busy to notice what's going on inside me," Omega replied, voice soft. "Thanks. I do have a question, though."

"What?"

"Well, there's no real air conditioning that I can see in the beach house. It doesn't really need it because of the trade winds, I guess. But I don't know if I'm that comfortable sleeping with an open window in my bedroom right now. It's not that I don't trust y'all," Omega added hastily, lest Echo get the wrong impression, "it's just..."

"You don't have to explain, Meg, it makes perfect sense to me," Echo said. "Especially after everything that's happened. No worries, though. There's a security system on each room, as well as the entire building, and around the island. And that includes a couple layers of force field, each one of which is every bit as powerful as the one I had at my beach house, maybe more—and they're NOT on a 'soft' setting. The island system is already active, but I'll activate all of it on voice-only authorization when we go in. You can leave your window wide open, and nothing—not even a mosquito—will come in but the breeze off the ocean."

* * *

Echo woke to muffled sounds in the bedroom next. "Meg?" he called, sitting up. "Baby? Are you awake?"

"You might...say that." The voice came through the window, distantly.

"Hey. Are you okay over there?"

"Y-yes."

"What's up?"

"Noth-nothing."

"Are you crying, honey?"

"...No."

Echo listened closely, then frowned and shook his head.

"Is my best pal lying to me?"

"Through. My. Teeth."

Echo got out of bed, grabbing the nearest item of clothing to hand: The shorts he had had on before going to bed. A few minutes later, he was knocking on his partner's door.

"Meg? Are you decent?"

"That's a helluva thing to ask these days. I'm decorously covered, if that's what you mean," Omega said in a strained tone. "Come on in."

"Voice ID: Echo," he said, and the door unlocked. Omega was standing at the window, wrapped in her favorite black silk robe over a pajama top—though both pajama top and robe were somewhat askew—looking out at the moonlit surf. The state of the bedclothes resembled a war zone. Echo walked up behind his partner. "Nightmares?" he asked quietly, then stopped, shocked. Omega was shaking violently. Her arms were wrapped tightly around herself, and her face was tearstained, although no tears fell from her eyes at that moment.

"Damn. You're a mess, baby. What happened, Meg?" Echo asked softly.

"You had it right, Echo. Nightmares," she answered, staring out the window. "Real beauts. Remember my abduction memories?"

"Yeah." *And not likely to ever forget, either,* he added mentally. *I don't think even the brain-bleacher would wipe those completely. Hell.*

"Now add to that our battle with Slug when we inaugurated the Alpha One team."

"Damn."

"Now add Wright...raping me. Succeeding, this time."

"Shit. All in one dream?"

"All in one dream. All at once."

"Come on, baby." Echo tried to draw her away from the window. "Let's get you back in bed and relaxed. You're pretty shaken up."

"No. Way. In. Hell."

"What?"

"Don't even try to make me go back to sleep after that one." Omega looked at Echo, fiercely determined, and slightly wild-eyed. "Sleep-deprivation psychosis can't be as bad as that dream was. I'll stay up until I drop dead before I go back to sleep."

Well, shit, he thought, deeply concerned. Echo looked at Omega blankly for a moment, then studied her carefully, thinking fast. "Okay, Meg. But at least sit down and try to rest a bit. You know you're not being rational right now. Just sit on the side of the bed and try to calm down. I'll sit over here in the chair and we can talk for a little while." Omega acquiesced, and tentatively sat down on the edge of the bed, while Echo took the cushioned wicker rocking chair in the near corner.

"So whaddaya want to talk about, Ace?" Omega asked in a low tone. "You better get creative on this one. I've got the creepies just sitting here."

"Mmm..." Echo considered for a bit. "Tell me more about your mother and father. You remarked at the Farm how my step on the stairs reminded you of your father. And Romeo found a photo album in one of the rooms downstairs. We all agreed you look a lot like your mom did at your age." He neglected to tell her of the slight resemblance to her father the others had seen in him. "You've already met my mom, and evidently met my grandfather—after a fashion, anyway—and seen my family photo album. Tell me more about your family."

"Okay," Omega said slowly. "On one condition."

"What?"

"You reciprocate when I'm done. Tell me more about your dad."

Echo studied her, eyes narrowed.

"Best buddies, pal," Omega reminded him. "If you can't trust me, you can't trust anybody. Besides, turn about is fair play, and all that stuff."

"...All right," Echo agreed. "Point taken. And you're right." She nodded.

"I'm glad y'all thought I looked like Momma. Mom was a really pretty lady. Your basic Southern belle, well-bred, but not afraid of hard work. Daddy was crazy about her, but I don't remember him ever really coming out and saying anything, although he had one or two pet names for her. He was the tall, dark, silent type. It was mostly the way he looked at her. She just...understood. That's the way he was. The way they were..."

* * *

"An'...an' I kinda...mmh...take after Dad...Daddy...on...that..." Omega's sleepy voice trailed away. At last, the exhausted blue eyes slid closed.

Her partner nodded with satisfaction, stood, and moved to the bedside. Echo eased an arm under her, lifted gently, and slipped the silk robe off the still form, then pulled the sheet up and over her. But as he turned to go, he heard a soft groan and looked back at the bed.

Omega stirred restlessly, moaning, already in the grip of another nightmare.

* * *

"Breakfaaast!" an early-bird, industrious Romeo called from the beach house kitchen the next morning, waking most of the household. "Come an' get it!"

After a few minutes, India entered the kitchen, followed shortly thereafter by a slightly weary Echo.

"Hey, man," Romeo said to Echo, concerned, "are you okay? You look a little out of it."

"Yeah, I'm fine," Echo replied, trying not to sigh.

"Is the pretty lady up yet?"

"No. Let her sleep," Echo told India as she headed for Omega's door. "She...had a bad night last night. A really...bad...night. That's why I'm a little frazzled this morning."

"Oh, damn," India said softly. "Nightmares?"

"Yeah. Slug, Wright, the whole works. Hitchcock visits the *Twilight Zone*."

"Shit," Romeo mumbled, worried. "Anything we can do?"

"Hell, I dunno," Echo replied, and shrugged. "I was up with her for about...oh, around three or four hours all told, I guess, just trying to get her calmed down enough to go back to sleep. Maybe tonight India can give her something to help."

"I'll take care of it, Echo. Can I check on her, though?" India asked.

"Yeah, come on. I'll let you in." He led the two Agents to Omega's door. "Voice authorization Alpha-One-Echo priority one: door unlock." The latch clicked, and India quietly opened the door to look inside.

Omega was asleep, curled on her side, cheek pillowed on her hand like a child. As they watched, she stirred restlessly, then moaned. She rolled over on her back, flung her arms out, then murmured, "No. Please, no. Don't...No!" Omega writhed, whether in pain, pleasure, or a combination, it would have been difficult to say; then she rolled to her other side with a groan and curled into a tight ball. India glanced at Echo.

"She was like this all night?"

"From what I could tell." Echo nodded. "I...didn't exactly spend the whole night in here."

"Damn," Romeo remarked. It was all he could think of to say.

"There's no doubt in my mind she's suffering from PTSD, a pretty bad case, and it's probably aggravated by the link with Wright. I gotta think about the best way to treat this; I may need to call back to Headquarters and discuss it with Bet. Come on." India closed the door. "I'll take care of it by tonight, I swear. Or at least have some idea of how to help her sleep without all...that...going on in her head. Let's go eat breakfast. I'll fix Meg something to eat when she gets up."

* * *

275

"Hi, Echo! Where's Meg?" a bikini-clad India called to the male Agent from the edge of the waves, as he made his way to the beach later that day.

"Hi, guys," the strong, athletic man in the black swim trunks replied. "I think she's showering in sunblock. That pale skin of hers, you know. She'll come on down in a few. She said to tell you thanks for breakfast, by the way."

India nodded acknowledgement, and Echo strode out into the water, dove through a wave, and commenced swimming away from shore with long, powerful strokes. Romeo bobbed up nearby.

"Race?" Romeo called.

"Down to the point and back?" Echo challenged.

"Go!"

India watched the two men rapidly moving away, down the beach, and chuckled.

"Honestly. Testosterone," she remarked aloud in a whimsical fashion, the affection apparent in face and tone.

"Yeah," a throaty voice said from behind. "But it's who they are. And neither of us would have it any other way. Even if it is driving me insane."

India turned, to see Omega in a black bikini, a matching pareo wrapped about her hips, sapphire eyes shaded by her goggle-glasses, watching the swim race. Given her stance—weight on one foot, the toes of the other foot drawn close to the weight-bearing one, with hip thrust out, one hand resting on it—the impression she left was unconsciously provocative.

"Girlfriend," India teased, choosing to ignore Omega's last statement, "I'm gonna have to bury you in the sand before Romeo gets a look at you."

"Yeah, right." Omega grinned ruefully. "Like Romeo would even bother to look at me with you around. The man's crazy about you, India."

"Well, it works well that way, I suppose," India said, turning to watch the men on the return leg of the race. "Because the feeling's mutual."

* * *

"Why don't you two get married, India?" Omega asked softly. "You and I girl-talked about it once, some time back. Hasn't Romeo asked?"

"I thought you knew that." India blinked, an odd look in her eyes. "We...can't, Meg."

"Why not?"

"Division One agents don't exist outside of the Agency, at least not on

276

Earth, so it wouldn't be...possible. Offworld marriages aren't legal here, at least not for Earth natives. And nobody thought to include it in the Agency's charter..."

"Oh. Duh. I'm not thinking. Yeah, Echo told me about that, once or twice."

"Yeah. The life partnership is good, don't get me wrong. It just... doesn't feel quite complete, you know?"

"I'm so sorry, India."

"It's okay. We'll...figure it out. Go get your feet wet."

"You know it!" Omega untied and dropped the pareo, running, uninhibited, down the beach and into the water. In moments, she was yards out. A few minutes later, the men splashed their way up the beach to India.

"Has Meg come down yet?" Echo panted, dripping.

"Yeah. She's out there," India pointed to the distant silver-blonde float bobbing in the waves. "Who won?"

"Echo," Romeo said in disgust, and Echo grinned.

"That'll teach you to ignore swimming laps in the gym next time, huh?" Echo said, shading his eyes and gazing seaward. "Meg's doing pretty well, too."

"Ooo, damn!" Romeo said, shading his eyes and watching as well. "I didn't know the girl could body-surf!"

"No shit, Sherlock!" India exclaimed. "You go, girl!"

"Wooo!" a distant cry came floating in on the ocean breeze. "Romeo! Find me a board!"

Romeo stuck a thumb in the air, and headed for the beach house, India behind him. Echo watched with a small smile and folded arms as Omega glided into the breakers some distance away, stood, and started walking up the beach. As the svelte Agent exited the water, however, the smile on Echo's face faded, his eyes narrowed and darkened as the pupils dilated, and he merely stood silently, watching Omega stride sensually, almost flirtatiously, up the beach toward Romeo, who now held a body board.

"Thanks, bro'!" Omega took the board with a coquettish smile, turned, and sprinted back into the water, lunging forward with the board and paddling out.

* * *

Half an hour later, Omega had unintentionally demonstrated her prowess in the surf to her friends and colleagues, and Romeo waved her into the beach.

"Hey, pretty lady! Where'd you learn how t' do that?!" he asked.

"Romeo! Houston is a Gulf Coast port city, after all." She grinned. "I thought your geography was better than that. Most astronauts do live around Houston, you know. And Galveston is basically a resort town, of sorts. Keep going south from there, you got Galveston Island, Matagorda Island, Padre Island, South Padre...really just one long barrier island all the way down the coast. With a boatload of good beaches!"

"And I'll bet you've hit 'em all," India said with a grin.

"Yup!"

Romeo smacked his forehead. "D'oh!" he said, grinning. "How 'bout a lesson?"

"Uh...okay," Omega responded hesitantly, glancing at India.

"Romeo," India laid a light, restraining hand on his arm, watching Omega, "maybe later. Go on, Meg."

Romeo glanced at India, startled, as Omega ran back into the surf.

"What was that all about?" he muttered.

"Think about Meg's...condition, Romeo," India murmured.

"Okay..."

"Think about what we're all wearing."

"Okay."

"Now think about what you were asking her to do."

"Okay. I don't get it," a confused Romeo admitted.

"Romeo, are you dense?!" India was exasperated. "Haven't you noticed Meg's been staying out in the water, away from the rest of us? There's way too much skin showing for her to be comfortable being around you guys in the state she's in."

"But...she said okay."

"Of course she did! That's because she's trying her damnedest to act normal around us."

"She ain't havin' problems with Echo." Romeo glanced at Echo, seated on the sand a few yards away, watching Omega.

"Then you haven't been paying attention."

"So...is it just me an' Echo?"

"No, honey, it's...well, it's men in general, actually. If she had leanings that way, it'd probably be me, too. You know what's going on inside her, Romeo. You know how having any men around her has to be affecting her right now. But she's closest to the two of you—so she reacts more to you. Haven't you noticed how unconsciously seductive she's become—particularly today?"

"No..."

"Meg was right." India grinned.

"'Bout what?"

"Never mind."

"Well...whadda we do?" Romeo asked, puzzled.

"Be considerate and keep some distance, Romeo. And try to minimize actual, physical contact, too. You might mean well," India warned, "but the worst thing you could possibly do would be to give her a brotherly hug right now."

* * *

Omega returned to the beach a couple of hours later, to find Echo sitting comfortably on the sand a little way above the high-tide mark, gazing out to sea with what Romeo and India would have thought the uncharacteristic expression of a daydreamer; Omega, however, well knew that usually-hidden side of her partner's personality, and merely smiled in understanding.

About twenty yards away, India had engaged Romeo in an attempt to sand-sculpt an Erikian battleship, with indifferent success. Omega grinned as a weapons turret suddenly crumbled and collapsed, then called, "Hey, y'all, did anybody bring anything to drink down to the beach? Preferably something cold?"

"Yeah, Meg," Echo answered, emerging from his reverie. "It's over here." He stood and walked over to the shade of a tree up the beach. He bent and picked up one of several high-tech insulated sport bottles, holding it out to his partner. Omega jammed the end of the board into the sand, and strolled up the gentle slope toward Echo, hips rolling sensually with each stride.

"Thanks, Ace," she murmured, stopping just before she reached him and taking the bottle from him. "Mmm," she sighed, as she turned the bottle up and let the cool water trickle down her throat. "Ahh, that's better. Thanks."

Handing the container back to Echo, Omega turned and made her sultry way back to the water. Echo's only visible response was to raise an eyebrow as his eyes followed her into the water; Romeo completely stopped working on the sand sculpture in order to watch his colleague slink down the beach.

Intent on watching them, India studied the reactions of the two men, then headed casually for the water, herself.

* * *

"Hi, India!" Omega offered cheerfully as the two female Alpha Line Agents met up some distance out in the water. "Did you come out to body-surf with me?"

"No, Meg, I came out to talk," India said, treading water. "Come over here a minute."

"Oh-kay..." Omega paddled her board over to her friend, and India grabbed its edge to anchor herself. "What's up, hon?" Omega asked, folding her arms across the board and resting her chin on them.

"Meg...do you...realize...how you're behaving?"

"What?"

"I thought so." India sighed. "Meg, you're coming on to the guys. Big time."

"I'm what?!"

"You're unconsciously trying to seduce the men around you."

Omega stared at her colleague in shock, then lowered her forehead to her forearms. In a muffled voice, she asked, "What exactly am I doing?"

"Your voice is unusually low-pitched and throaty, your facial expressions are suggestive and flirtatious, and your body language is...arousing, to say the least. Especially the way you walk. You've got what my mama would have called a real back-porch swing going, there."

"Shit. Have Romeo and Echo noticed?" Omega asked, without raising her head.

"Yes," India answered softly.

"Both?"

"Yes."

Omega drew a deep breath, and India thought she heard a muttered, "Damn." This was followed by a more audible, "...I'm sorry, India."

"It's okay. I'm not mad, I swear. I didn't think you realized what you were doing. I was over 99% sure of it."

"What...what do I do?" Omega raised her head and looked into India's eyes, desperate pleading in her gaze. "It's getting harder and harder to... control what's happening to me. I thought I was at least managing to maintain a sense of dignity an' decorum, but..." She looked down, shaking her head, as India listened. "And Echo, bless his heart...he's so determined to stick by me, to help me. I can't seem to get it across to him that he can help me most right now by keeping his distance. I guess I should've swapped partners after all, but..."

"You and Echo are basically what you'd call 'best friends,' aren't you, Meg?" India asked quietly.

"Yeah. He's the best, the closest, the most dependable, buddy I've ever had in my whole life."

"He's just trying to do everything he can for you. We all are."

"I know," Omega said, miserable. "But I don't think he has any idea of what's really going on inside me, India. I mean, he was raised on a ranch, so I'd have thought he might...but I think he's refusing to see me in the same light he sees his horses and cattle. I don't think anybody really gets it—except Mark, 'cause he's going through it, too. But of course I don't dare get close to him, and he can't really talk, anyway. And it's awakened a...a loneliness, a need...a Pandora's box I thought I'd closed off long, long ago. Echo, though...Echo's still trying to treat me as if I'm an ordinary, normal human, like this is something a cold shower can fix!" Omega gave a humorless laugh through her tears. "Believe me, it doesn't help. I've taken three, just since we got here to the Beach!"

"Okay. Then help me to help you. Tell me—how should we be treating you, Meg?" India asked, puzzled.

"Like a...like a bitch in heat." The low voice dripped self-loathing, and India mentally recoiled from the image. Unfortunately, she also let her reaction show on her face; Omega saw the expression. "Oh, come on. Don't look so shocked, India. That's all I am, after all. It's all that Slug made me to be. And...and it's only a matter of time...before I start acting like it." Omega's voice cracked, and she paused, evidently trying to regain control over it. "Go back to the beach, India. Go back to Romeo."

India released the bodyboard, and Omega turned it, paddling powerfully outbound. In moments, she was several tens of yards away.

"Meg? Where are you going?" India called, suddenly worried. A now-distant Omega pointed out to sea.

"Thataway. Maybe if we're lucky, I'll get caught in a rip current again and solve everybody's problem."

* * *

India exited the water as fast as she could and headed straight for Echo at a run. "Echo, keep a close eye on Meg," she urged as she neared him.

"Huh? Why?"

"Because you're the only one who has a chance of catching her if she tries something. She just said it'd solve everybody's problem if she got caught in a riptide again."

"Shit!" Echo exclaimed, scrambling to his feet and searching the waves for signs of the silver-white head. "Oh! Whew. There she is. She looks okay, India."

"Where?" India queried, shading her eyes.

"Right there." Echo pointed.

"Oh, I see her. Good. Keep an eye on her," India reiterated.

"I will," Echo replied. India continued to stand beside him. "Is something else on your mind, India?"

"Yeah, I'm just...trying to figure out how to say it," India answered, pondering how—and where—to start. "Meg is reaching the end of her rope, Echo."

"What do you mean?" Echo looked down at India with knit brows.

"She called herself a 'bitch in heat.' And said that's how we should be treating her. AND how she was starting to act."

"Aw, damn. Meg, get a grip," Echo murmured, staring at his seafaring partner. "It'll be okay."

"No, Echo, it won't be okay," India remonstrated. "She's fighting now, just to maintain a semblance of the Meg we know and love. And she's losing, Echo. It's getting worse. Her sense of humanity is slowly being stripped away. Between the hormones—which seem to still be ramping up, which itself is incredible, and possibly dangerous—and the stuff from Wright that's apparently getting through her telepathic block, she's being bombarded, and her defenses are starting to crumble. Meg can't win this battle. Not on her own. Not like this."

"No. Meg is stronger than that." Echo shook his head. "You didn't experience what Slug put her through. And she deals with it. We've all seen that. She'll deal with this, too. I'll help. We'll help." He was completely confident, certain of his partner's strength, physically and mentally—that much was obvious to the physician-Agent.

"The best thing you could do to help her right now, Echo, is...stay away."

* * *

"What?! Where the hell did you get a damn fool idea like that?" Echo demanded to know.

"From Meg."

"Is that what she told you?" Echo stared at India.

"Yes. She didn't want to. She likes having you around, but...well. You've seen the way she's been acting today."

"Mmm...yeah. Suggestive."

"To put it mildly. Echo, it's completely subconscious. She didn't even realize she was acting differently. And you'll note that it doesn't happen around me," India said, pointed. "Look, just...keep your distance. Give her a chance to catch her breath. She's struggling. Bad."

Echo scanned the Agent beside him, mulling over the information she had presented, then turned his attention back to the attractive figure floating in the surf. "I'll keep a close watch on her, India."

"Echo—"

"I'll do what needs to be done, India."

India studied the tall, enigmatic Agent thoughtfully, then returned to her partner, who still strove to complete the battle cruiser.

* * *

When Omega finally got the nerve to come back in to the beach, Romeo and India had returned to the beach house to prepare lunch. Echo still sat watching Omega play in the surf...effectively standing guard over his partner, even against herself.

"Hi, Echo!" she called as she walked self-consciously up the beach, trying to minimize her hip motions; the effect came off stilted and awkward. "Are Romeo and India handlin' lunch, Ace?"

"Yeah."

"Is it ready yet?" Omega picked up the discarded pareo and brought it up the beach with her board.

"Nope. They'll yell." Echo grinned. "I, uh, got the feeling that maybe lunch wasn't the only thing on their minds."

"Oh. Okay." Omega returned the grin, putting the board down nearby and lying down on her belly on it. "I'm gonna catch my breath a minute."

Echo studied the shapely female form near him.

"Where'd you stash your sunscreen?"

"Under the tree." Omega gestured with a thumb. She closed her eyes and relaxed in the hot sun, finding herself drowsy after the previous night's restlessness, and the morning's physical activity. Abruptly she stiffened, as she felt gentle male fingers slide lightly down her spine. "Echo?! What the hell do you think you're doing??"

"Ease up and hold still, Meg," Echo responded, "or you really will embarrass yourself—I've got your top undone. You're starting to turn pink. I'm just gonna slap some more sunscreen on you." He rubbed the cool lotion into her back.

"Echo—please stop."

"You'd rather make like steamed lobster than...have me touch you?" Could she have seen, there was a pained expression in the brown eyes as they gazed down at Omega's back.

"You have no idea, do you, Ace?" she murmured, enigmatic.

"Meg, what if Bet and Zebra and Zarnix can't come up with anything?" Echo asked, continuing to spread sunblock on his partner's pale skin.

"Wh-what?" Omega stammered, completely ignoring Echo's nearness for a moment, in her horror at the notion that there would be no way out.

* * *

"What if there's nothing they can do for you? You need to try to start dealing with it, Meg. You're tough; you're an incredibly strong woman. You've proved that to me time and time again. Don't let this incapacitate you." Echo finished applying sunscreen and fastened her bikini top, sitting down in the sand beside her board. "There. You forgot all about what I was doing, didn't you?"

"K-kinda..."

"So you can do it."

"Echo, you don't really think..."

"Hell, I don't know, Meg. But I do know you can't keep on like this. And neither can I." Echo sat back, drew up his knees, and folded his forearms across them.

"What do you mean?" Omega rolled over to look at him. Echo's face was bleak as he replied.

* * *

"Aside from the fact that I've essentially lost my best friend, I can't function as an Alpha Line Agent with a partner who can't handle having me inside six feet away." *Damn,* he thought, discouraged. *Of all the ways I've feared losing her, this wasn't one of 'em. But it's the one that seems to be happening. Just when I thought we might actually be starting to go there, too. It feels like my guts are being ripped out. Not that she can help it.*

"Echo..." Omega's face was even paler than usual, "are you really considering...getting a new partner?? I mean, we had the defined...Alpha One is...you and me."

Echo sighed, deeply pained, and looked out across the waves with troubled eyes. *I've been thinking about that very thing,* he wanted to tell her, *but all of the answers I've come up with...suck.*

"If you don't want me around, Meg, what choice have I got?" he said then, morose. "I guess we can dissolve the special 'defined' partnership if that's what you want to do, or...maybe I can take a desk job..."

A spray of sand hit Echo in the side, and he turned.

Omega was already halfway to the point, sprinting as if she were trying to evade a gurfdin on her heels.

Echo sighed again.

* * *

"Yeah, I think we're gonna be fortunate that the Agency had already installed the tracking system in the farm vehicles," Mu decided, as the recovery team's cloaked vehicles flew low toward the Atlanta-Hartsfield International Airport. "And I'm gonna recommend that, unless there are security reasons for NOT doing it, the Agency do that on ALL its vehicles, dammit."

"Don't worry," Bravo told him on the comm, "we're already working on that as fast as we can. There was a lot of resistance among some of the various departments initially, for various reasons, but Fox already ordered that done across the board. Because of this sitch."

"Good."

"Do you see him yet on the tracker?"

"Yeah, we got him," Mu noted, studying the dashboard display. "It looks like he's just pinging around the periphery of the Atlanta airport."

"What, the airport loop road?"

"Exactly. Back and forth. Back and forth."

"Perfect. I'll get the Atlanta Office on it, and arrange a pincer maneuver like we talked about."

"Great. Listen, Bravo, I'm gonna let you go for now, and see if we can't get this guy back into custody...and KEEP him there, this time. I'll call you once we've got him, so you can notify Fox for us."

"Perfect. I'll wait to hear. Bravo out."

"Mu out."

Mu ended the call, then immediately set the comm to address the other Agency vehicles near him.

"Mu to recovery team. Okay, boys and girls, we're coming up on the airport. The air traffic is damn heavy here, so keep a watchful eye out; we don't need to get in a close call with the local aircraft. Everybody got Wright on the tracker?"

Varied responses on, "Yeah," came back to him.

"All right. We're gonna try the same maneuver on him that we used up in Massachusetts, okay?"

"Mu," York, a field agent in one of the other vehicles, queried. "Do we have the Atlanta Office involved in this? After all, we're practically on top of 'em."

"Yup," Mu said, calm. "Headquarters is all over that, and has a squad of Atlanta agents on the ground to assist. They're gonna block off the loop road and try to limit his movement from the ground, while we come in from above."

"Heads up! This is Harry," a female voice announced. "I have visual. Repeat, I have visual. And there goes the Atlanta Office personnel..."

"Okay then. All units, assume formation," Mu ordered. "Prepare to execute encirclement on my mark. In three...two...one..."

* * *

Five minutes later, Mu was calling Headquarters.

"Bravo here."

"Bravo, this is Mu. We've got him...again."

"Good. Is he in force cuffs?"

"Yep."

"Okay. Fox says to put force leg cuffs on him, too. And this time, we wanna leave those on him, even after he gets put in Confinement. We may actually manually restrain him, with physical locks, so there's no way for the security system to inadvertently let him go."

"What, handcuff him to the table, like cops do to violent perps being interrogated?"

"Exactly. It's just that we're having to actually GET some, because it's been so long since we've needed 'em."

"Oh, damn," Mu murmured, not sure whether to laugh or be annoyed. "Well, okay. I guess, Omega told me about the Glu'g'ik that Alpha One chased last fall, and how she could even phase out of the force cuffs, so I guess it makes sense that you'd go to ever more sophisticated restraint techniques."

"Yeah. This is the first time anybody has ever been able to circumvent 'em. Fox has even been pondering how to put Omega on the restraint list in Security, without actually having her wind up in Confinement in one of the other Offices."

"Ugh."

"Yeah."

"Okay, well, we're inbound to Headquarters with Wright," Mu reiterated.

"Fox wants to know if it was difficult."

"No, not particularly; not at this point," Mu decided. "He was just sort of wandering around. He didn't seem to know where Omega had gone, so he didn't have any direction..."

"Perfect," Fox's voice could be heard in the background. "It worked. Tell 'em to bring it on in."

"Roger that, Fox," Bravo said. "Mu, did you hear that?"

"I sure did," Mu averred. "Tell Fox we're on the way."

* * *

A few hours later, a handcuffed and leg-cuffed Wright—using old-fashioned metal cuffs—was put back in the same cell in the Confinement area in Headquarters.

Two cells down, and around the corner, from Yankee.

* * *

"Hey, Echo," Romeo greeted the older Agent as he entered the beach house. "Where's Meg?"

"She...decided to go for a run on the beach," Echo replied, evasive.

287

"She'll be along later."

"So you're alone?"

"Yeah."

"Good," India said, coming into the room. "Perfect timing. We've got news."

"What?" Echo's attention was immediately engaged.

"Fox's search teams found Wright," India said. "When we took off from Atlanta, apparently he lost track of Meg and kind of went around in circles, in a daze."

"Hmm..." Echo murmured. "Interesting. As soon as Meg lost track of where she was, so did Wright. Despite her telepathic block."

"Exactly. So Bet and I had an idea," India continued. "Something Romeo said..."

"Go ahead," Echo ordered. "I'm listening..."

* * *

"So what do you think?" India asked when she finished.

Romeo and Echo both looked thoughtful.

"I think it just might," Echo muttered. "In fact, I'm pretty sure of it."

"Why?"

"Because of something Meg told me up in Massachusetts, when Wright showed up there," Echo said.

"Tell me," India demanded.

* * *

"Shit. It sure ain't gonna be fun, Echo," Romeo pointed out, some time later, after Echo had finished narrating certain events, and the three Agents joined in additional brainstorming. "F'r any of us. But especially f'r her."

Echo walked out onto the deck. Far down the beach, he could see Omega wandering dejectedly, aimless and alone.

"Damn," he whispered.

* * *

Omega wandered the beach for several hours—not that there was THAT much of it; it was on the scant side of half a mile to the point at the far end of the island—her heart seeming to rip itself to shreds every time she mentally replayed that last conversation with Echo.

I'm gonna lose everything because of this, she thought. *And I don't know if I can stand that. He wants me there, right beside him, and I CAN'T.*

288

Not without...without embarrassing the hell out of myself, sooner or later, when I slip up and let him know how I feel. Which is amped up clear to the Andromeda Galaxy about now, with what Mark is doing to my insides.

She stepped into the trees to get in the shade and cool off, and stood looking out at the surf, trying to use the soft susurration to soothe her inner turmoil, even as she'd done at Echo's beach house in Massachusetts. But somehow it didn't seem to work this time.

Either I'm too upset, or I'm deteriorating...or both, she decided. *Probably both, by the feel. But I just can't settle.* She came out of her covert, and looked up the beach toward the beach house, only to find that no one was in sight. She sighed. *They must have all gone inside, I guess. Probably Romeo and India got lunch ready and called Echo. Well, called both of us, but I was too far away to hear. And it may be significant that Echo didn't come looking for me, either. Then again, I guess I made it plain I didn't want to be bothered.*

Damn, every time Echo gets anywhere close to me, it's all I can do to maintain control. He has NO idea what's going on inside me, or what kind of pheromones he's putting out! I nearly drool every time I get a whiff of him. It's way sexier than any cologne or perfume, and it just ramps me up something awful. I'm trying hard not to flirt, but to hear India tell it, I'm doin' it anyway. Dammit.

Then again, Omega suddenly realized, *while Romeo, bless him, seems clueless, Echo...doesn't. I've told him, several times, about the pheromones, about how I'm struggling, and he looks like he gets it, but he still seems to want to...stay close. Not just close, but like right next to me. I...wonder.*

Omega let her mind drift back to the time they spent in the hot tub at Echo's weekend house.

* * *

"No. I'm not afraid of you, Meg," Echo had said. "Not at all. There are really only two things in the universe that truly scare me, though, and both of 'em have to do with you. Okay, well, maybe three, and the third one has to do with Ma."

"You're afraid of losing her, now that you got her back," Omega had determined.

"Bingo. But the other two things are: one—I'm honestly afraid of you getting yourself killed, and two—I don't want to do anything, or have any-

thing happen, that would send, or drive, you away from me...from being beside me."

"Aw," she had murmured, realizing he had meant it; his face held an earnest, sincere expression that told her he had just opened himself up to her, revealing a part of his innermost being, his private thoughts...to her, about her.

"So I really am trying to avoid upsetting you by the physiological responses I can't control, baby," he had added. "As far as whether or not I'd wanna go there with you, have you looked in the mirror lately? You're a beautiful, intelligent, talented woman, honey. And damn strong, damn tough, and damn resourceful. Granted, certain persons to whom we alluded earlier are too closed-minded to see it, but otherwise, I think there aren't too many straight, unattached males who wouldn't be interested, Meg, given half a chance and some encouragement."

Then, moments later, he had added, "When certain people sound off their big fat damn mouths, remember that your partner thinks you're hot stuff." He had grinned, that mischievous, infectious grin that she secretly adored. "And he's the one that counts, anyway, right?"

* * *

He thinks I'm hot stuff, Omega considered, as she turned away from the beach house and headed back down the beach, toward the point. *As well as beautiful, intelligent and talented. And alla that was in reference to 'the guy bits.' Which had got active that morning. While I was curled up in the hammock with him, asleep. Fairly wrapped around him, at that.*

She clambered up on a large boulder, which would be on the edge of the surf at high tide in a few hours, and gazed out to sea, thinking hard.

Maybe...maybe the whole 'active guy bits' thing wasn't as general as he let on? she wondered. *Maybe things got active because it was ME lying there, wrapped halfway around him? Could Ace actually be interested? But then if he was, why hasn't he, I dunno, SAID something? Done something? Asked me out on a proper date, or, or talked about us going deeper with the relationship, or...*

She pondered that conundrum for a while. *Well, there's a couple of possibilities, as far as I can see. Either he only recently realized it...which is possible, given that it's only been—what? since the spring?—that he seemed to have gotten over Chase. Maybe he finally got past that relation-*

ship, and realized he had somebody with him who might make a good, um, companion, in more ways than he had thought about, up to that point.

Or, she continued speculating, *maybe it has something to do with the partnership itself. Maybe he thought it would be, I dunno, unprofessional or something. Because surely he knew I was interested...didn't he? Well, maybe not. He's not omniscient, and I HAVE worked really hard at not letting on, because I thought it would squick him out instead of turning him on...*

OOO! The thought suddenly hit. *What if he really DIDN'T know I was interested, and THAT was the problem? Because he didn't wanna risk the partnership? We ARE the top team in the Agency, heads of Alpha Line and all. I mean, that was actually one of MY considerations, for keeping quiet about how I felt. And he and I are enough alike that he might have viewed it the same way!*

Huh. So maybe, just maybe, Ace is interested in me after all. Oh, that would be so wonderful, Omega thought, smiling dreamily to herself. *And... if he is, it might be possible to resolve the problem we got right now with the relationship. Because if we, um,* Omega felt her face flame with embarrassment over the thought despite being all alone, *if we become lovers, then not only would I be happy, and maybe he would be happy too, it would kinda... vent...some of the junk I got churning around inside, with the whole drive to mate an' shit. Not with the guy Slug had in mind, of course, but forget THAT, anyway.*

We'd have to be REALLY careful about not having kids, I guess; I don't know if my genetics alone are a sufficient condition to generate a next-generation assassin or not. Omega shivered in dread. *That would be horrible, for our own children to kill their father. No. I couldn't take that. No kids, not under these conditions. So the birth control India gave me stays in effect. For the rest of my life, I guess. Dammit. I love kids, and I'd love to have HIS kids. Then again, who knows what Slug did to THAT, or how said kids might turn out; they might not even remotely resemble human. So... yeah. No kids. Oh well.*

She picked up several pebbles she found on top of her rock perch, and juggled them in her palm for a few moments, staring down at them without truly seeing them, thinking...briefly remembering Echo's hand, holding several moon shells as he offered them to her. Abruptly a montage of recent events—holding hands as they walked along the beach, even without anyone watching; Echo flinging Wright across her bedroom before sitting on him and beating him into unconsciousness after finding him in bed with Omega; kissing her forehead...several times; cuddling her in the hammock and stroking her hair and back as she vented all the pain, the humiliation, the horror; reaching into her mind, then gritting his teeth and hanging on, determined to share the source of that horror, just so she would have some-one who understood, someone she could lean on fully—all this, and more, flashed through her mind's eye. Omega began to seriously consider just how deep her partner's affections ran.

Wow. He really cares. It could still be only a best-friends thing, an' probably is, but what if it's not? What if it's more? Or what if it could BECOME more? Maybe this could work, after all, she decided. *It'll speed things up a lot, especially over what I would be more comfortable with. It basically means we'd become lovers right off, and...* she shrugged, *work out the details of the relationship as we go. But I guess there's a certain amount of that sorta thing that goes on in any permanent romantic relationship. And it isn't like we just met last week, anyway. We've been together over a year and a half now. For all intents and purposes, we've had merged quarters from...from the time Slug first attacked me; the back door is rarely closed any more. Yeah. If he's really interested, I think this will work. And I have plenty of evidence that he might be. All circumstantial, but still. Though I suppose at least some of it is just because we're best friends, and as he pointed out, his instinct is to try to help me, soothe me, whatever it is that I need at the time. All the same, that's not a half-bad foundation on which to build a...well, it isn't 'marriage' until the Ennead gets off their collective asses and approves an amendment to our charter, but...yeah.*

Omega took the pebbles and, one by one, tossed them into the surf, watching the ripples they made overcome by incoming waves. Said waves were now—finally—soothing her, somewhere deep within, much to her re-lief, though she suspected that it had as much to do with her conclusions regarding Echo as to any rhythmic sounds. Still, she felt better, more in control of her life, than she had been only a little while before. *I've got options I didn't have before,* she realized. *And that...helps. I get to make a choice, at least of sorts.*

"So," she declared to the ocean, "how do we get this started?"

That was when it hit her.

Oh shit! If everything I just worked out is correct, then he doesn't KNOW I'm interested! Which means I have to let him know. Which means...I have to make the first move. Aw, damn. I'm not gonna be allowed to do ANY of this in an old-fashioned manner, am I? No courtship and dating, no letting him make the first move, no romantic overtures. Just, 'Look. You can have me if you want me. But it means we gotta pretty much jump into bed together an' get busy. Think you can handle that?' As Fox would say, 'Oy vey. That's meshuginah!' Damn, damn, damn. If ever there was a man that I'd prefer made the first move, it's Echo. Omega smeared a hand down her face. *But of COURSE I'll have to basically throw myself at him.*

Momma, Daddy, I am...SO sorry. This isn't how you brought me up, and it is NOT how I would want it to go down, given my druthers. But I'm running out of options, here. It's this, by deliberate choice, or going there anyway when I finally lose control. Because I'm getting so tired. The constant sense of Mark—or, well, his programming—trying to get past my telepathic block, trying to get into my mind and seduce me; the hormones, that India's medscanner shows still increasing—how the hell much can that shit go up before everything hoses inside me, anyhow?—the memories of the abduction; waking up and finding Mark, naked in bed with me, just as he rips off my pajama top with the intent to rape me...running over a significant chunk of the globe, in a desperate effort to get away from him... trying to get off-planet, only to feel like I'm getting my insides ripped out...

She drew a deep breath, then let it out in a long sigh.

Too much stress. I can't keep this up indefinitely, and I think 'indefinitely' is getting awful damn close. I'm gonna lose it, probably sooner than later. At least, if I do it now, while I still have a little bit of control, it won't be quite so humiliating as waiting until the hormones take over and I lose all sense of anything except throwing him down and jumping on top of him. Which is likely to end up with ME getting flung across the room.

* * *

Pebbles expended, Omega got up and began a slow meander back toward the beach house.

I might as well try this tonight, she decided. *At least I'll know, one way or another. I'll wait until India and Romeo go to bed, then find Ace, and... and do what? I gotta figure out how I'm gonna approach this. I need to give him an out, in case I've read this all wrong, and be delicate and discreet enough that I at least maintain some sense of self-respect and, and maybe a little dignity. I hope. How the hell am I gonna...?*

She sighed, then bent and picked up a shell.

* * *

Omega spent most of the remainder of the day wandering the beach alone, evidently lost in thought. She skipped lunch entirely, and Echo did not try to go find her, as she had made it plain to him that she wanted— needed—to be alone; but to his relief, at India's insistent urging, Omega came in for a quiet dinner with the others at the patio table on the deck, though she kept her distance, and said little.

But I'm starting to understand why, at least a little bit, he realized, as he watched her surreptitiously. *Especially after that little primer India gave us guys over lunch. It opened up a lotta questions that I didn't get to have answered, but I'm starting to grasp the gist of things, at least. I don't like it—any of it—but I don't know what to do about it. At least, not yet. And I'm sure Meg hates it even worse. Judging by what India said over lunch, Meg's medical condition is continuing to deteriorate, which I wasn't expecting. I thought that, well, that the way she was at my place in Ipswich was pretty much the way it was, and she was handling that reasonably well. But I was wrong. She's getting worse, and she's struggling...and to hear India tell it, losing. Never mind the potential medical risks, if this shit keeps ramping up the way India says! It could KILL Meg. Which I guess means that I've got some decisions to make, coming up pretty soon now.* He sighed. *And dammit, I don't like any of my options. DAMN Slug to the bottom level of hell!*

Shortly after dinner, Romeo and India decided to retire early, after making sure Omega had medication to get her through the night.

Huh, Echo thought, watching the pair flirt subtly as they made their way to their bedroom. *I guess I know what they're gonna do. I hope they remember to close the window, so we can't hear! I wonder if Meg is affecting them somehow, or if they're just picking up on her increasingly seductive behavior, and it's giving 'em ideas. I...oh! The pheromones! We've really only talked much about how Meg responds to OURS. But she has to be putting them out, too. And if those pheromones are responding to her hormonal shit-storm, then...wow. In which case, Romeo and India may be reacting to 'em, and completely subconsciously. Or maybe,* he decided, wry, *I just have no clue what goes on in their quarters behind closed doors, and this is noth-*

ing unusual. He stifled a snort of bleak amusement.

Omega, too, disappeared into her room, so rather than risk bothering her in her current vulnerable state, Echo retrieved a book from his gear, turned on a lamp in the common area as the sun went down, and sat down on the couch to read.

"Echo?" Omega's voice filtered through the vagaries of the book's plot to his conscious awareness.

"Hm?" he answered without looking up.

"If you want your partner...back, you've got it, Ace. But I thought I'd better show you what you're letting yourself in for." The couch gave slightly next to Echo as Omega sat down beside him, and automatically, he glanced up.

"Damn," he whispered involuntarily. Echo's eyes widened and darkened as the pupils dilated—he knew they did, because the dim room got a lot brighter; his nostrils flared slightly, and he caught his breath. The book slid to the floor, forgotten.

Omega sat close beside him, almost but not quite nestled into his side, wrapped only in clinging black silk and lace; bare skin was visible through the openings in the lace. She had unbraided and brushed her hair, and the shining platinum tresses cascaded down her shoulders and back. The sapphire eyes appeared lit from within.

She met his gaze steadily, withstanding his scrutiny silently. Omega maintained a demure, reserved posture, even when Echo extended his hand and lightly fingered the silver hair, letting the back of his hand gently brush her soft cheek.

* * *

In her turn, Omega watched Echo's reactions, studying his expressions. As her observant eyes noted his nostrils flaring repeatedly, she extended her own hand to run a featherlight fingertip fondly down the bridge of his nose to its tip, and he closed his eyes for a brief moment at the sensuality of her touch, exhaling slightly.

"You see, Echo?" Omega said, keeping her voice soft. "Pheromones work both ways. But you're not even aware of 'em, only how your body responds to them. It's completely and purely involuntary. And I can't turn mine off. I can't turn ME off. When I've been keeping you at a distance, it's because I've been trying to protect you, not me. This is what you'll have to deal with, every minute of every day, if Bet, India, and the others fail. But if that's what you want...if you're okay with that...here I am."

* * *

"Meg...what do YOU want?" Echo asked in a low voice. *Is she really... offering herself to me? Does she want us to become lovers?* he wondered. *Is she asking...to become MY lover?*

The blue eyes met the brown ones steadily.

"I would've thought that was obvious."

Echo's breath caught again as his deepest dream faced him, offering to come true, and he raised his other hand, plunging his fingers into the silken hair to cradle her head in his hands. His head bent over hers.

But there was one more question that had to be asked.

"Is it just because I'm...available?" he whispered.

* * *

"...Yes and no," she murmured. She loved him, without doubt; however, that was not the matter under discussion, at least in this instance. But she was hesitant to give him the honest answer, knowing it would hurt him, even as Echo instinctively buried his face in her hair, breathing deep of the subtle fragrance that rose from her body. "I...I can't help it, Echo. My body would react the same if it was Romeo, or Mu, or...or Mark sitting here with me."

She felt him stiffen slightly at her brutal honesty, and she plunged on, trying not to dwell on the emotions she now knew—because of the shift in his pheromones—were coursing through him.

He wants me, she realized. *Right now, he does want to sleep with me, but how much of that is even real? Most of it is probably the pheromones. I'm putting out so much now, I can almost feel my skin releasing 'em, at this point.*

"But...but I...still have some control," she told him, rushing through the rest of the explanation as best she could. "Echo, I...I'm closer to you than to anybody else, anywhere on this world or any other, and...and I trust you. If...it's gonna happen, I...I mean, you would be...the best...at least I know you'd look after me, treat me right, no matter what happened..." she stopped as he raised his head then to gaze into her eyes. "Echo...it's your call."

Echo studied the azure eyes, and this time Omega dropped her gaze, unable to withstand his scrutiny. *I'm throwing myself at him,* she thought in utter humiliation, feeling her face heat. *In the worst possible way. But...if he walks away, if he breaks up the partnership, you might as well shoot me through the heart, or the head. So I'm not sure I have any other choice. Not any more. Maybe...after what he said, up in Massachusetts...maybe we can make it work. Please, God, help us make it work.*

"This isn't really how you want it to happen, is it, Meg?" he said softly.

"No," she whispered, ashamed.

"How, then?"

"You know me better than anyone, Echo," she murmured huskily. "You know I resent feeling driven to it. Hate feeling that I've involuntarily driven the man I'm...with...to it. You." She paused, and dared to throw a single, shy glance his way; he sat watching her, his hands still buried in her hair, his attention fixed on her, on her words. "You know I'm...old-fashioned. I guess that's considered ridiculous these days, but..." Omega paused again, waiting for reassurance from the man beside her, but Echo sat watching her silently, listening intently. The dark, dilated eyes were disconcerting, their gaze intent on her face. "Anyway, I...I'd rather...take it slower...not," she glanced down, "just jump into...into bed right off. Build the relationship. And when the time is right, it's a mutual decision, a permanent decision, me and...whoever; you, if...if you wanted, based on love and what Romeo would call, 'the C word,' not just—raging hormones. That's how I'd like it to be. But somehow, things never seem to work out the way I'd like. And now I don't really have that choice."

Omega stole another look at Echo through veiled lashes. His hands were still buried in her hair; his eyes searched her face with an intensity she had never seen in him before.

"So you can have your partner back, Echo," she offered, "whether India and Bet and the others can come up with any solutions or not. If you even want me back under these conditions. I haven't forgotten about...about Chase; I know you still miss her, even if she is...well. I know you said you were past that, but I...still remember that she held a place in your heart. And I don't want to lose you, in any sense. So...here I am. You can have me. Completely and totally, and in every meaning of the word. I just...had to show you what you were getting yourself into, first. You decide."

Echo silently dropped his hands, still looking at the beautiful, pale face of his partner.

Then, with a sudden effort, he stood, strode rapidly across the room, into the hall, and through his bedroom door, closing it behind him. To Omega's sensitive ears came the faint clicking sound of a door locking.

* * *

A shocked Omega stared after him, now white-faced and dizzy; as she heard the lock engage on his door, she suddenly flushed scarlet, her face burning with shame and mortification. Rejection slammed through her like a megatsunami, unstoppable and just as devastating.

Well, I screwed that up, the thought flitted through her mind. *I guess I totally misread everything up in Ipswich, too. He was only trying to be nice, trying to boost my self-esteem and make me feel better about myself. And I just threw myself at him...like the slut some of the other agents think I am. Maybe, now, they're right. And now...it's all over. He's never gonna wanna work with me again, after this.*

Hanging her head in humiliation and self-disgust so intense she could barely keep from throwing up, she saw the forgotten book lying on the floor at her feet. Contemplating it forlornly for long moments, Omega eventually leaned over and picked it up.

"*Cyrano de Bergerac*—apropos, somehow," she murmured to herself in a choked voice, as tears sprang to her eyes and she fought them down, along with the bile that tried to rise in her throat. "Cyrano, count your blessings—at least you were human."

Omega stood and switched off the lamp. She moved silently to Echo's door and laid the book on the floor beside it.

"I guess the scientific definition was the correct one, after all, huh, Echo?" she murmured, and the slight sounds of movement from the other side of the door, as if someone were pacing, suddenly ceased. Then she entered her own bedroom, closing and locking the door behind her.

* * *

Had there been an observer at The Beach, he might have heard sounds suspiciously like soft, lonely weeping from somewhere in the beach house, late into the night; whether male or female might have been more difficult to ascertain.

But it didn't matter; there was no one to hear.

298

Chapter 10

An exhausted Omega finally slept deeply and late under the influence of India's medication, which the considerate physician had left on Omega's bedside table, along with instructions on dosage.

When she eventually got up the next morning, Echo was already standing in the common area of the beach house in his black flight suit.

"Meg, something's come up at Headquarters," he told his partner. "Fox called me this morning to tell me about it. It's that whole thing with Alpha Seven—remember that? It turns out Tare never told Yankee he was going on sabbatical, let alone why, and Yankee's kinda gone over the top. Fox tried to sit him down and explain, but he's not havin' it. As the department chief, I need to get involved. So I'm afraid I have to go back for a little while."

"Oh, damn. What a mess! Do you want me to come, too? Assistant chief an' all," Omega offered, half-turning toward her bedroom to fetch her kit and get into her flight suit. Echo's normally-impassive face became even more inscrutable.

* * *

"...No, Meg," Echo told her, keeping a tight rein on his emotions; the fact that he had come very near to taking his partner up on her offer the night before, especially given how he already felt about her, was creating a maelstrom in the Agent's mind and heart.

And now I gotta go off and leave her, dammit, he thought, struggling to keep the pain off his features. *That's bound to go over like the proverbial lead balloon in the current situation. I may well have lost her, despite anything I can do. Especially after...last night.*

"That would defeat the whole purpose of our bringing you here, baby," he continued aloud. "As long as you stay here, you're safe; Wright can't get to you. Stay here, baby; be safe. Romeo and India are staying with you. I'll be back as soon as I can."

Omega paused, and Echo saw her face flush slightly as she glanced down, unable to meet his eyes. "Echo, are you going back to look for another—"

"No." Echo kept his voice decisive and firm, brooking no contradiction.

* * *

"I...okay," Omega responded, doubtful. She shot him a concerned glance.

"What's wrong?" Echo asked, as Romeo and India moved to flank Omega, offering silent support.

"I've...got a funny feeling about this," Omega said, confused.

"One of your hunches?" India asked, glancing anxiously at the men.

"Sort of, yeah. Do you have to go, Echo?" Omega responded, expression growing more and more worried. "I really...for some reason, I..." She moved to him, laid her palms on his chest, looked up into his eyes, pleading, and whispered, "Don't go. Please."

Echo looked down at her for a long moment, his expression unreadable. Then he glanced past her at Romeo and India for a split-second, and turned away slowly, seeming very reluctant.

"I'm sorry, Meg," he said quietly. "I have to get back. Fox is expecting me." He left the beach house swiftly.

A little while later, they heard the roar of jet engines, and Omega went to the door in time to see a black dart streak away.

* * *

A lonely Omega, bereft of her closest companion and confidante, mostly moped around the rest of the day, afraid to get too near Romeo and feeling like a fifth wheel despite Romeo's and India's best efforts to get her involved in their activities.

By evening, Omega was grateful that Echo had insisted on re-applying her sunscreen the day before, despite her protests—reverting to absent-minded scientist, she had neglected it this day, and India had to treat the red, painful skin.

"Get some sleep, girlfriend," India told Omega, administering a mild analgesic. "You'll feel better in the morning. Romeo and I moved our bedroom to be closer to you, what with Echo gone, so we're right across the hall now. Yell if you need anything, and we'll come running, I promise."

"Thanks, India." Omega hugged the other woman. "This is just an outrageous predicament. Sometimes I feel like the original hard-luck kid. I appreciate everything y'all are doing for me. I hope y'all know that."

"We do, Meg. That's what we're all about, helping out. Besides, family, ya know, sis." India smiled. "See you in the morning."

"Good night."

* * *

The following morning, India shook Omega awake. "Meg, wake up. Wake up, honey. It's urgent."

Omega jerked awake with a start at the painful grip on her inflamed shoulders. "Ooo! Ooo! Sunburn—sunburn!"

"Oooch! Sorry; I forgot. Meg, honey, you've gotta wake up."

"I'm awake already. What is it?" Omega sat up and saw Romeo standing in the bedroom doorway.

"Honey, Headquarters just notified us—there's been an accident..." India said softly.

"Somethin' went wrong with the T-Bird, Meg," Romeo said in a low tone. "Echo crashed."

"WHAT?!" Horrified, Omega automatically leaped from the bed, then self-consciously reached for her robe, throwing it on over her nightshirt as she stammered, "But...but...he bailed, right?"

"It was over a populated area, Meg," India murmured, in pain. "And of course our jets aren't...standard. Echo rode it down...to steer it away..."

"In his last transmission," Romeo said quietly, gently, "he said to tell you...he was sorry he'd...have to stand you up..."

* * *

The blonde Agent now experienced the final, staggering emotional blow in a long string of gut-wrenching events. The sunburned face went blank, the blue eyes empty, in shock. Omega laid back down on the bed, and silently curled up in a ball.

Romeo and India glanced at each other, a hint of fear appearing in their expressions.

"Meg? Meg?" India said, laying a gentle hand on the stunned Agent's shoulder. No response was forthcoming. "Meg, say something."

"Go away."

* * *

Omega lay in the bed, unmoving, for a long time. She clutched a pillow to her chest and huddled around it, as if it might be the body of her dead partner, somehow come back to her. The empty blue eyes gazed at nothing, her mind refusing to accept this last, devastating calamity. One part of that mind kept expecting Echo to call her name, then knock on the door to her room and come in. But she knew, realistically, that would not happen— would never happen again, now.

For the time being, most conscious thought had fled, and she simply lay where she was, existing. After several hours, her body began to protest the unaccustomed inactivity, and operating on instinct, she rose, stretched, and entered the bathroom. There, she relieved herself and got a drink of water at the sink, then came back out into the bedroom...operating on a kind of autopilot.

A knock at the door made her heart leap...until India called softly, "Meg? Meg, Romeo has breakfast ready. Do you want to come eat with us?"

Some part of Omega's brain registered that she was expected to respond, but her body didn't seem to want to obey that particular imperative. The very thought of food in those moments caused her gut to churn, threatening to purge the water she had just drunk. So she ignored the inquiry and turned toward the window.

"Meg? Honey? Are you there? Are you okay?"

Omega managed to force out a grunt that time.

"Do you want breakfast?"

"No," Omega said clearly.

There was a pause, then soft footsteps retreated from the door.

Omega dragged a chair over to the window and sat down, staring out... ...Seeing nothing.

* * *

"I'm worried, honey," India told Romeo. "I...knew she'd be upset, but...I had no idea she'd react like this."

"She's reactin' like Echo would, I think," Romeo decided. "Not 'cause she's tryin' t' imitate 'im, but 'cause she's so much like him in a lotta ways."

"I always wondered about that. Do you think that's something Slug did, making her like him, so they'd bond?"

"Nah. I talked t' Echo about that once, 'bout a month ago. Turns out he an' Meg had already talked about it. She was afraid o' that, too, but he was convinced that they were alike 'cause they were alike. He says he's always been able t' see a diff'rence b'tween th' programmin' an' Meg's natural personality. I think he's prob'ly right."

"You said Meg was afraid of it. Was he able to convince her?"

"Yeah, he was. Siddown an' let's eat. I'll put some stuff by f'r Meg if she comes out."

"But...I'm here to look after her medically. I feel like I should be in there, making sure she eats, making sure she drinks, taking care of her, maybe sedating her..."

"Let 'er 'lone, baby. She's hurtin' bad. You know how she barfs up her toes if she gets really upset 'bout something. An' this is a hella damn big something. You go pushin' food an' water on 'er now, it's just gonna make 'er sick. She don't want anything right now. She's too upset." Romeo shrugged as he handed India a plate with a large serving of breakfast casserole. "She's prob'ly still tryin' t' come t' grips with it; it doesn't seem real to 'er yet."

"But I can't let her get dehydrated..."

"She ain't gonna get dehydrated. Relax. It'll be okay. All the bedrooms got bathrooms. She gets thirsty, she'll get a drink o' water. An' prob'ly won't even hardly realize she did it. Calm down. You can't get in there 'less she lets you in, anyway. Echo f'rgot t' undo th' security he set up; I got a call in f'r Fox t' help us out with that. But until 'e does, if she don't want you in there, you ain't gettin' in."

* * *

Omega sat in the cushioned wicker rocking chair, the same one in which Echo had sat and talked to her, the night she had had all the nightmares. The faintest whiff of his scent came to her nose, and she swallowed hard, caressing the arm of the rocker with her fingers, wishing it was his arm. She blinked away tears, and stared out the window.

"It's all over," she murmured, as she gazed out at the sunny sky and blue surf, feeling resentful of the beauty that she could not share with the man she had loved. "I...I've got nothing left. I can't believe...after all the missions, all the stuff that's happened, the aliens we've fought, the perps we've caught...and the T-Bird, the aircraft he loved so much, is what turned on him and killed him. It's...not fair. And I never even had the chance to tell him I loved him." Then she shrugged. "Maybe it's better that way. In the end, he wasn't interested after all."

She sighed, and debated getting up to pace, but found she didn't care enough to bother. *After all,* she thought, *I've lost the man I loved enough to die for, to die trying to protect. The man I'd hoped, one way or another, to spend my life with...even if it proved to be nothing but a platonic friendship and partnership. I'd have stuck by his side until my dying breath, if he'd asked. But he's the one that's...* She broke off, unable to formulate the thought as yet. *Nothing matters any more.*

Her mind drifted, random memories of her partner surfacing: Echo laughing, giving her instruction as a rookie agent, teaching her how to fly a spacecraft, learning how to set up a telescope from her. Sitting across the table from her at their favorite restaurant, sharing a huge slice of cheesecake. Sitting beside her in the stands at the stadium to watch their favorite baseball team play. Walking hand in hand along the beach outside his beach house.

All gone now, she thought. *The only thing I have left is work...and I'm not sure that's enough any more. Never mind the fact that every single task I do for the Agency will remind me of him. I'm not sure if I can stand it. Not after everything else that's gone down. Not after being systematically stripped of every other thing I ever cared about. Even my own humanity. Only the creature is left now.*

I'm proud that he died being heroic—but he was always a hero to me. It just seems utterly absurd that so simple a thing is what killed him, when we've been in so many worse positions. The youngest and toughest of the Originals is gone. I guess that just leaves Fox, out of all of the Originals. Mr. Badass, the Alpha Line chief, died due to an equipment malfunction, not through any intrigue, or a perp getting revenge, or the mission from hell, or anything like that. The T-Bird broke, that's all. I wonder what the other Alpha Line Agents are gonna do, when they hear the news.

All at once, she sat up straight.

"Oh shit," she murmured. "Ace left some unfinished business...and I was his assistant chief. That leaves...ME...in charge of the department. Damn, damn, damn. I don't wanna...but I gotta. People are depending on me. For a little while longer, I guess."

* * *

I don't really want to do this, Omega thought, getting out her cell phone. *I just...don't. It shouldn't be me doing it, it should be Echo. But*

304

he's...gone. And now it's up to me.

Omega drew a deep breath, then let it out in a sigh, biting her lip until it oozed blood. She wiped the back of her hand across the wound, then wiped her hand on her shirt, heedless of staining.

She activated her phone and hit a particular speed-dial number.

* * *

Alpha Seven was in Fox's office when the call came in on Fox's personal-issue cell phone. He answered it in speaker mode, as was his automatic response when in his office.

"Fox here."

"Hi, Fox. It's Omega," came the subdued response.

"Oh, great," Yankee muttered. "Just what I need."

"Shush!" Tare hissed, jerking a finger across his throat with one hand, and smacking him in the shoulder with the back of the other. "Aren't you in enough trouble?!"

"Omega," Fox responded, surprised. "I...didn't expect to hear from you."

"Well, I thought maybe...seeing as how I'm the de facto head of Alpha Line now, I'd better...check in and, and see about things."

"WHAT?!" Tare and Yankee both exclaimed, horrified. "What happened to Echo?" Tare added.

"I have Alpha Seven in my office at the moment, Omega," Fox noted. "That was them you heard, just now."

"Oh, right. Well, guys, you know I'm off in seclusion because of the situation with Wright. So Echo was coming back in the T-bird to see about helping with your sitch, and...something went...wrong. It...it went down."

"He, he's in Medical, though, right? He bailed, an' he's gonna be okay?" Yankee asked, sitting upright in shock.

"...No. Alpha Two told me he...rode it down...to keep it away from... population centers." Omega's voice was raw, and cracked at the end.

"Oh, damn," Tare whispered, aghast. "Omega, I'm...so sorry."

"Me too," Yankee said simply, face paling with the additional grief.

There was silence on the line, and the three Agents knew she was struggling to remain professional.

"Anyway," she said after several moments, voice rough, "you guys are one of the reasons I thought I'd better check in. I've pulled up the files, Fox,

305

and I understand what went down."

"Do you have any comments, tekhter?" Fox wondered.

"As a matter of fact, I do, Fox. As the acting head of Alpha Line until such time as you formally appoint a successor for Echo, AND as the person under protection at the time of the event, not to mention as an Agent who...who just lost...her partner," it was obvious to the three assembled that Omega choked those words out, "I'd like...to request clemency, Fox." They all imagined her shaking her head, rueful. "We already lost an important member of Alpha Line. We don't need to lose another department member if we can help it. Especially given what was going on inside Yankee when it all happened."

"Explain," Fox said, shooting a glance at Alpha Seven, both of whom looked confused.

"Fox, were you ever a field agent? Did you ever have a partner?"

"No, Omega, I wasn't, and I didn't. I was head of Diplomacy when I was promoted into the Directorship. Before that, I was head of Lord Entiyti's security detail. His personal bodyguard." Fox shrugged. "Even when I worked for the Mossad, I was...a bit of a loner. I was never assigned a partner, as such. That wasn't the way my group operated."

"That's what I figured. So you won't be familiar with the bond that can develop between partners in a field team," Omega explained. "Yankee, it's my understanding that Tare left on a medical sabbatical, but didn't tell you?"

* * *

"Right," Yankee said, dropping his pained gaze to the floor. "We'd... had some arguments in recent weeks. I...didn't know what was going down. I didn't know if he was sick, or, or dying, or if he just decided he hated my guts, or...what."

"I'm sorry, Yank," Tare murmured, contrite. "I thought someone else was gonna pass word..."

* * *

"He means me," Fox sighed. "I fully intended to call you in as soon as Tare was gone...but then Wright was brought in, and that whole carnival funhouse thing started, and...the next thing I knew, you were already on guard duty WITHOUT Tare, and...well." Fox shook his head. "I should have known better than to promise to do something as important as that; as

Director, my entire schedule can get overturned in a heartbeat, if an emergency comes up. I need to delegate more, I guess. But things like that... they ARE important, and it makes me feel like drek to shuffle it off on a subordinate."

"But why didn't Tare tell me himself?!" The pain in Yankee's voice and face was palpable.

"I was too upset," Tare choked out. His face crumpled, and he put it in his hands. "I saw your attitude deteriorating, Yank, and I knew sooner or later, something was gonna happen, something bad. An' I didn't wanna be around to see it go down...and now it has."

"And this is my point, Fox," Omega's quiet voice interjected. "What happened...it wasn't truly dereliction of duty. There were two factors in play that caused it...neither of which was Yankee's fault."

"Explain, tekhter."

"One factor was Mark Wright's altered mental capacities," Omega explained. "He was modified to be able to go unnoticed, to influence humans' minds not to see him."

"You've been talking to India about it."

"No; why?"

Fox blinked.

"Because she proposed the same thing."

"Oh. Well, I can confirm it, then."

"What?! How?"

"Through the mental link. I know he had that ability. Even I had to pay really close attention to keep up with him."

"Do you have that ability?"

"No; evidently Slug thought he'd already given me the perfect cover by inserting me into the Agency. Woulda been useful a few times, on assignment, but...no."

"All right," Fox murmured, as Alpha Seven listened in shock. "What is the other factor in this whole debacle, in the core of which Yankee found himself?"

"The other factor was psychological distraction, rather than telepathic, Fox. It was honest, genuine, heartfelt concern for his partner, and a corresponding kind of panicked agitation probably amounting almost to obsession to know what was wrong, what had happened...and what he might do to fix it. Dear God, I know what THAT feels like, after the shapeshifter shot Echo last Christmas. Not to mention the way we got beat up in the space-ship crash in the spring. I thought I was gonna lose him, both times. And now I have," she added, her voice growing harsh and rising an octave. "And it hurts about as much as anything I've ever experienced in my life. So now Tare has to watch, to lose a partner himself, as Yankee gets thrown out? No. That's not fair to either of 'em, Fox. As I did in the hearing where they became Alpha Line Agents—and let me add, they've been good Agents—I respectfully request clemency."

"Omega," Fox said, "there are certain specifications for dereliction."

"I know. But again, I don't think this was true dereliction."

"What would you have me do, tekhter?"

"You're asking for my recommendation?"

"I am, tekhter."

"So—what—you're required to brain-bleach?"

"Yes."

"But under certain conditions, brain-bleached memories can be re-trieved and re-downloaded later, right?"

"They can."

"Then overlay the 'dereliction' judgement with a 'mitigating circum-stances' ruling. And do everything you can to make this one of those special brain-bleaching conditions, Fox," Omega decided. "Then, after Yankee has been out of the Agency for, oh, six months, a year...bring him back. Re-install his memories and reinstate him. Make the punishment a probation, not an expulsion."

"That...might just work, tekhter..."

* * *

"Um, can I ask something?" Yankee murmured. "I'm sorry to inter-rupt..."

"Sure, Yankee," Omega said immediately, sounding almost—almost—normal. "Whatcha need?"

"Fox keeps calling you 'tekhter.' What does that mean?"

"It's Yiddish for 'daughter,'" Fox answered, meeting Yankee's eyes; the hazel eyes looked sad. "Omega has been...very lonely...at times in the Agency. She's assembled an approximation of a family around herself to try to help alleviate that loneliness. Somewhere along the way, I found I had been appropriated as the father figure. Since Echo is—was—my oldest living human friend, and I not infrequently called him 'zun,' or son, it seemed logical..."

"Oh, okay," Yankee murmured, comprehending. "Omega, you get... lonely?"

"Yeah, Yankee. I do. And I guess...it's gonna get worse."

"Is it because of what Slug did to you...?"

"Yes and no," she replied. "Let's just say that he made sure that...that there isn't anybody on the outside for me to go home to."

"Ohmigaw," Tare whispered, shocked. "Your birth family? Your whole birth family?"

"Yeah. All gone. Couple that with some natural disasters in my youth, tornadoes an' shit? Well, I got one distant cousin that I barely even know, I only met once years ago, and who wouldn't know me from a fence post. And that's it. Listen, Yankee," Omega added, "I want you to know something. I get why you don't care for me much. Aside from the whole thing last Christmas, which I understand hurt your ego, but I didn't know what else to do..."

"Yeah. I shouldn't have done that," Yankee admitted. "To be honest, I barely remember it. I was...pretty out of it."

"I know you were, and I know why—cold meds make me pretty loopy under normal conditions!—and I'm sorry for anything I did which might have mixed signals for you."

"Given everything the shape-shifter had been feeding us," Yankee confessed, "I'm not sure you could have done anything that wouldn't have fed into that whole ball o' shit, Omega. I was just...gullible."

"Well, there's more to it than that, isn't there? I mean, when you look at me, you see something unnatural, a being that was created and programmed for destruction. And I know you gotta wonder if all of that has been turned around, or if it's still buried, latent, someplace inside me. I know, because I wonder all that, too."

Tare and Yankee gaped at the phone on Fox's desk, then at Fox himself. Fox sighed in a kind of melancholy, then nodded silent confirmation of what Omega was saying. Both members of Alpha Seven winced.

"And I get that you hate the unnaturalness of it, and that you wonder if you can trust me," she continued. "Don't feel bad; I hate it worse. A lot worse."

"You...do?" Yankee breathed.

"Yeah. Like, every time I look in the mirror. Every day. You have no idea what it's like to feel as if your body has...betrayed you. And be thankful for that lack of knowledge. I'm not who, or even what, I thought I was, when I first came into the Agency. And I still haven't come to grips with that. I don't know if I ever will."

"Why haven't you had it...'fixed,' then?" Tare asked, puzzled. "I mean, we got this regen procedure now..."

"Oh geez, have I thought about it," Omega answered. "I came really close to it when Doron worked on me after the Cortian incident. But I talked with him before he put me in the regen pod...if so rushed a discussion can have normal conversation terms applied; I mean, I was dying...because by that time, I'd begun to see how certain of my 'enhancements,' let's call 'em, were helping Echo and Alpha Line. I wanted to tell Doron which ones I wanted to keep—which ones were useful—and get rid of everything else." She paused, and the cell phone's speaker fell silent.

* * *

"Except," Fox murmured, urging her on, realizing the two men with him needed to hear what happened next.

"...Except Doron explained that it didn't work quite that neatly," Omega continued. "I didn't get to pick and choose. It was all...or nothing."

"Oh wow," Yankee mumbled.

"So, since by that time, some of my own personal weirdness had been the reason others—like Echo—were still alive at that point, I decided that the best thing for the department, for the Agency, was for me to keep 'em, the enhancements, I mean," she declared. "Not the best thing for me, necessarily, because I still hate it. But the best thing for the people around me. The problem is," she added, "that the ramifications won't settle down and go away. There's always some new...SOMEthing...like Mark Wright, f'r instance...that keeps cropping up to haunt me. To make my life difficult, and keep me from forgetting, even for five minutes, what I am. And what I am... is not human. Not any more. And I'm not even any other defined species; I'm kind of a kluged-together...creature. A thing. And I know it. I don't like it, but I know it."

"You know Zebra does not agree with that assessment, tekhter."

"I know. But Zebra doesn't have to live with it every moment of every day, either."

"Damn," was all Yankee knew to say.

"What he said," Tare agreed. "Omega, I can't speak for Yank. But...I'm sorry for my reactions that have caused you pain. I didn't mean to. I...have been intimidated as hell by you, and, and I didn't know HOW to react."

"Echo told me as much, a while back," Omega said. "Something about...you'd told him to? Right before your sabbatical?"

"Oh, good. I wasn't sure he'd mentioned it yet," Tare murmured. "Yes, I told him to tell you. In a way, it's kind of an ass-backwards compliment, because you're so damn impressive."

"Really?" Yankee said. "Because, when you get right down to it, that's...the biggest part of it for me, too. And...it scares me, sorta."

"Why, Yankee?" Fox asked. "Why does it scare you?"

"Because if it happened to me," Omega tried, "who else might it happen to?"

"Exactly," Yankee admitted, shamefaced. "I mean, look...we already got suckered by the shape-shifter. That felt like an incredible betrayal, in so many ways. But what if somebody abducted me, or Tare, and, and 'modified' us like that? Programmed us? We could have a huge loose cannon go off inside the Agency. And it would be US!"

"Well, it can't happen like THAT, ever again," Fox determined, "because Omega saw the potential for that, as soon as she came back to us after HER little sabbatical to consider the matter and get her head on straight, right after it happened. And with her ongoing help in determining what to look for, now Medical screens all new candidates for such things, AND verifies, at each physical, that our current agents have not been subjected to such atrocities, unbeknownst to them. Up to and including psychological analysis by a Deltiri counselor, if it is deemed necessary."

"Really?" Tare replied. "Wow, Omega. I...dunno what to say. You've been looking out for everybody, all along."

"She has," Fox agreed. "Even to the detriment of herself, her own being."

"I know what to say," Yankee declared. "Thank you."

There was a long silence. Finally Omega's voice choked, "You're welcome."

And the line went dead.

* * *

After several moments of respectful silence, Fox spoke.

"Well, gentlemen, Omega has offered a workable compromise, I believe. If that is acceptable."

"Nothing about the situation is 'acceptable,' from my perspective," Yankee sighed. "I didn't mean to screw up, Fox. And it wasn't 'just' because it was her we were protecting. She was my department's assistant chief, and she's our chief now, it looks like. Have I had an attitude problem, where she's concerned? Yeah. But...but after all that," he waved a hand at Fox's cell phone, "maybe...maybe all I really needed to do was...to sit down and have a long talk with her."

"She's not that easy to have a talk to, about this sorta shit," Tare pointed out.

"No. But she's a lot like Echo, in that," Yankee noted. "Or, well, like Echo WAS. So I understand that much. And if she's been in that kinda pain, with next to nobody to share it with—"

"She has no one, really, to share it with," Fox observed. "A scant handful of staffers in Medical—two, perhaps three—have been the only people on Earth, or anywhere else, who know the full extent of what was done to her. Them, and the Arcturan ambassador, who deprogrammed her. She would tell no one else; she was too...ashamed. Not even I know very much; I've allowed a medical privacy veil to remain over most of it."

"Aw shit," Yankee breathed. "An' my attitude only made it worse."

"If it helps, know that you're not the only one," Fox said. "There are others."

"Scant comfort," Yankee noted. "I guess I got some thinking to do about her, and try to get it done before the brain bleaching. Hey—what about Echo? How much did he know?"

"Echo had...managed to coax some of it out of her, a good bit just recently actually, and had hopes of one day understanding it all. But..." Fox shrugged.

"Yeah," Tare agreed sadly. "That's moot, now."

They were silent, pondering recent events.

"So. We have a probationary period for Yankee to work out, I suppose," Fox concluded.

"Fox, about that," Tare said, "I want to amend it, please."

"Let's hear it, zun."

"You called him 'zun,' too," Yankee observed.

"Yes," Fox agreed. "Don't think that my 'family' is limited only to a few 'special' Agents, gentlemen." He quirked his fingers as he said the word, as if making quotation marks. "By now, I assume you've read the more complete historical section of the Alpha Line Agent's handbook, so you know that I'm...a good bit older than I appear." Both members of Alpha Seven nodded. "And as I was an integral part of setting up this Agency, with instructions from no less a one than Lord Entiyti, it has a great deal of meaning to me. Each and every one of you is, to some extent, one of my 'children.'"

"That...thank you, Fox," Yankee murmured.

"Yeah," Tare agreed. Fox nodded acknowledgement.

"Now, Tare, you had an amendment to the probation to propose."

"Yes, sir. Yankee and I have made some enemies of our own, over the years," Tare pointed out. "Perps that wanna get back at us, shit like that. They're not as nasty as Slug was, but it won't do to ignore 'em, either. Whatever you set up for Yank's probation, I want to go undercover, as... as his roommate, or best friend, or...something. Get me in close. I want to watch over him and make sure nobody gets to him, while he's brain-bleached."

"Aw," Yankee breathed, deeply affected. "Tare, man, that's..."

"A good plan," Fox said, voice gentle, "by a good friend." He turned. "Tare, escort your partner back to confinement, while I run this up the flag-pole and see if I can't get it approved."

* * *

Omega refused to come out of her room all day. Nor did she accept any food that Alpha Two tried to bring to her door, or let them in, even for India to check her out.

"But Meg," India had protested from the hall, "I'm trying to take care of you. I'm supposed to be your medic through all this."

"No," was all Omega had answered.

Late that night, after Romeo and India had gone to bed, they heard the door of the beach house open and close, as well as several beeps as the household security system reset itself, and got up to investigate.

Omega's bedroom was empty. The door stood open. Inside, the bed

313

remained unmade; the wicker rocker sat in front of the picture window, facing outward. A used glass sat on the end table beside it, a few dribbles of water inside.

"Well, at least she's taking in water," India observed.

"India, hon', c'mere," Romeo called softly, and India moved to his side. He pointed out the window.

The former astronomer and one-time astronaut sat on the beach in the moonlight, staring out at the deep blackness of the ocean under a spectacular starry, dark sky.

But she never once looked up.

* * *

Omega was still sitting on the beach the next morning when Romeo and India came down for a swim. Alpha Two glanced at each other, then walked over to the grieving Agent.

"Meg?" Romeo said, kneeling beside her. "You been here all night?"

"Yeah, jun-Romeo," Omega responded, correcting her mode of address in mid-word, to something more neutral than one of Echo's nicknames for the other man. "I...had some thinking to do."

India and Romeo exchanged another glance.

"'Bout what?" Romeo wondered.

Omega shrugged.

"Does it matter now?" she murmured.

"Meg," India said softly, laying a light hand on the still-reddened shoulder, "I know you two were close. It's gotta be rough to...lose a partner. Echo...was a special man. We'll...we'll all miss him. But...you've gotta pull it together, girlfriend; you've gotta keep going. Echo would want you to."

The blonde Agent shook her head in disbelief, rolling her eyes heavenward. Then she shot a hard, pained look at the other woman, shaking the hand off her shoulder in annoyance.

"That's a moot point now, isn't it?"

India was taken aback. Romeo motioned her away, and they left Omega to her bleak musings as they headed toward the surf.

"Let 'er alone f'r awhile," Romeo advised his partner quietly. "She jus' needs to get it out. You think she's cried for 'im yet?"

"I don't think so," India answered, considering.

"Uh-huh. I didn' think so, either. You know who she reminds me of real strong now?"

"Echo?"

"Yeah."

"Damn. That means she's internalizing everything."

"Yup."

"Which means she may NOT cry."

"That's...possible, I s'pose."

"We've got to do something."

"We gotta give it time, India," Romeo advised. "I've seen this with my old SEAL team buddies, when we lost somebody. You can't press this; it's gotta happen in 'er own time. Be cool, baby. Be patient. There ain't anything we can do for her now, 'cept just be here."

* * *

Omega spent the day on the beach. India managed to coax her into the shade, to avoid making her sunburn worse, and Romeo talked her into eating a little lunch, though it wasn't much—a couple of bites, at best. Afterward, he approached his own partner curiously.

"She's not reactin' to me, India. You s'pose—?"

"She's not reacting to anything, Romeo. Dammit, she lost her partner. The best friend she had in the world."

"I wonder..." Romeo muttered to himself, glancing at the stoic woman down on the beach.

"Wonder what?"

"I'm...not sure. Maybe...maybe that's not all Echo was. Not to her, anyways."

"As long as they've been together?" India pointed out. "If there was that kind of interest there, I think one or the other of 'em would have acted on it, by now."

"Maybe so," Romeo said.

But he still watched the woman on the beach, thinking.

* * *

That night, Omega came to Romeo and India. "Guys—I want to go back for the funeral. To say goodbye. No matter what."

The couple looked at each other.

"Meg, there isn't going to be a funeral," India said softly. Omega paled.

"It...was that bad? The crash?"

315

Romeo and India stared at each other for a long moment, wondering what to say to her.

"Pretty lady," Romeo tried, "when Fox called with...the news, he said there'd be a...whaddaya call 'em?"

"Memorial service," India supplied.

"Yeah. After this sitch with Wright gets resolved," Romeo continued. "That way, you c'n be there."

Omega turned away, jaw tightening, face hard.

"Then to hell with it," she muttered under her breath, and went into her room.

A few seconds later, Alpha Two heard the sounds of locks engaging.

* * *

The next morning, Romeo and India banged on the locked door. "Meg! Wake up! Bet called! There's good news!"

The security disengaged, and Omega opened the door.

She looked haggard and pale, despite the remnants of her sunburn; it suddenly struck Alpha Two that, for the second night in a row, Omega had likely not slept, or even attempted to do so. The fact that sleep had been elusive and greatly disturbed in the nights preceding was not helping matters.

"What?" she asked, voice flat.

"Zz'r'p and the other Deltiri have deprogrammed Wright! He's in a regeneration pod, being returned to normal right now. In a few days, he'll come out, be brain-bleached, and sent home. It's over," India told her friend.

"I know," Omega answered...with Echo's characteristic enigmatic response.

"What?!"

"I felt the telepathic link go down late yesterday," Omega explained. "With Echo...gone...Mark wasn't...needed any more. His programming switched off. I knew Zz'r'p was poised, waiting for that opportunity, and I felt him start on Mark just before the telepathic link collapsed. I'm glad for Mark. Yes...it's over." Omega's tone was strained.

"Fox sent another T-38, Meg," Romeo said quietly. "We can go home now."

"All right. I'll get ready."

* * *

"South Pacific, huh?" the lone pilot of the black T-38 remarked to her

316

wingmen as they crossed the Pacific Ocean. "Leave it to the Agency to have a facility there. And leave it to Echo to know about it."

"Not bad, huh, pretty lady?" the other pilot remarked. "Echo has good taste."

"Had."

"Uh, please repeat?"

"Had. Echo HAD good taste."

"Uh. Yeah. Sorry."

"There's the West Coast. Coming up on Sea-Tac. I have the tower beacon."

"Roger that," Romeo replied. "I copy tower beacon too. Not far now. We're headed home."

"You got that right, hot shot," Omega radioed.

Abruptly, the lead plane diverted away from an east-northeast heading, to a flight path well south of east.

"Meg?! Where are you goin'??" Romeo exclaimed, startled. "That ain't th' way home."

"Not for y'all. But it is for me," Omega responded. "Listen up. My last order as acting chief of Alpha Line in Echo's demise is to designate Alpha Two as Alpha One's replacement. Tell Fox that Alpha One no longer exists, and Agent Omega is 'retired.' He knows he can trust me to...keep a secret, brain-bleacher or no. I'll leave the T-38 in Atlanta."

"Meg! Wait!" India called.

"See ya around, y'all. Or not." There was a click as the comm was switched off. The afterburners kicked in, and the black jet disappeared in the distance.

* * *

Nearly a week later, Ann Ramey entered a certain farmhouse outside Huntsville, Alabama, somewhat breathless after carrying the last heavy load of boxed and crated astronomical equipment to the barn.

"There," she said to herself. "I think I'll go upstairs and get my hat, then go for a walk with a glass of iced tea, catch my breath and cool off. That stuff was heavier than I remember. Maybe I can go figure out which fields I can plant with what this fall...take in a few horses to board..."

She was halfway up the stairs when she heard the authoritative voice.

"Omega."

The lightly-tanned platinum blonde woman in black jeans and black-and-white plaid work shirt stopped dead without turning.

"Agent Omega doesn't exist any more, Fox. She's 'retired.' She sent word, remember?"

"Dr. Megan McAllister, then."

"She's gone, too. Vanished in west Texas without a trace several years ago. The woman who lives here these days is a reclusive distant cousin of Dr. McAllister's, Ann Ramey. Now...please leave."

"Meg, please talk to us." India's pleading voice finally convinced her to turn. Fox, Romeo, and India stood together in the foyer, looking up the staircase at her.

* * *

"We wantcha to come back with us, pretty lady," Romeo said softly, looking up at his one-time colleague. "Y'r family misses you."

"Nice try, Romeo." Her drawn, somewhat pale face showed no expression whatsoever. "But I have no family, not any more. I can't handle the pain of those kinds of close relationships. I'm staying here. I've had enough. More than enough."

"But...we thought...what happened to the 'family,' Meg?" India asked, trying to hide the hurt.

"Oh, India," she sighed painfully. "I still care. That's the problem. I could handle everything fine before Mark...no, before Slug's version of Mark...bollixed up my insides. Mark is almost back to normal by now, I should think; I expect Zebra will be decanting him in the next few days, if she hasn't already. But I'm not." She dragged the back of her hand across a perspiring forehead. "I dunno why, but I didn't go back to normal when the link with Mark collapsed. Oh, the telepathy seems to have gone back to its usual levels, not that it was ever bumped up very much with respect to anyone but Mark. But I'm still...hyped up and hormonal. And I just can't handle the heightened intensity of emotion, of response, and stay in the Agency—or any non-isolated—environment." Another sigh. "And Echo was my...my stabilizer. My anchor. Even before my biochem wacked out. Always so cool, so everything-under-control. He made it easy to be his partner, if I'm honest with myself. But when I...lost Echo, I lost a lot more than 'just' a partner. I'm gonna miss you, Ace. So bad." Her eyes were distant, unseeing. "So no, y'all. I'm not coming back. I can't. I'm gonna stay

318

right here, where I can isolate myself, and become a...a hermit, or something. It's the only thing I know to do."

* * *

The three Agents exchanged wordless glances, and after a moment, the object of their errand turned to continue upstairs.

"We brought someone along to try to change your mind, Omega," Fox said then, gesturing through the screen door. "At least hear us out." With a resigned sigh, 'Ann Ramey' turned, folded her arms, and waited, grim of face.

Unexpectedly, a tall, rugged, handsome, dark-haired man in a black Suit stepped through the screen door, a warm smile on his face.

"Hi, Meg," the familiar, deep-timbred voice said, as Echo gave her his brightest smile. He held out his arms, welcoming her to come into them.

Before anyone could even move, the trim, athletic blonde collapsed and slid to the foot of the stairs, where she lay crumpled, unmoving, unconscious.

* * *

Dimly, the 'retired' Agent felt herself carried upstairs.

"Shit, India!" she felt the vibration of Echo's voice in his chest against her cheek, "Meg's burning up." She was laid carefully on blessedly cool sheets.

Echo's voice...ECHO'S voice!

"...Trying to find out...just a minute..." India seemed to fade in and out.

* * *

Omega was in the cockpit of the T-38 when everything started to red-line. She wrestled with the controls uselessly as the aircraft went down.

Fire exploded around her as the jet impacted. She could feel the heat of the flames on her skin. She was burning alive.

No...no...not me. Echo... Omega was badly confused.

* * *

"Damn, India! One-oh-four and climbing!"

Echo?? That's Echo's voice. But...but he's...

"I see it...got to bring it down...brain damage..." *India.*

"Can you do anything?" *Fox's voice now.*

"I'll try...no sign of infection..."

"Am I dead, too, then?"

319

* * *

The four Division One Agents looked at each other, startled at Omega's slurred, puzzled question.

"By HaShem..." Fox murmured, concerned. "What did that mean?"

"No telling. She's delirious," India remarked. "Her fever's dangerously high."

"She doesn't believe I'm alive," Echo realized, crouching beside the bed to talk to the semi-conscious woman. "Meg, it's Echo. I'm sorry, baby. I didn't mean to give you such a bad shock. I'm not dead, Meg. Everything's gonna be fine, honey. I'm here. I'm really here."

Echo took the moist washcloth Romeo brought and began sponging her face, neck, and arms in an effort to cool down his hallucinatory partner. Meanwhile, India rapidly ran scan after scan with her medical instruments.

"That's it!" India suddenly exclaimed. "This woman is damn near impossible to keep down!"

"What?!" the three men asked simultaneously.

"It's her biochemistry! Remember how she said she was still struggling with the hormones? And how she looked all hot and sweaty? Her body is finally trying to re-establish itself at normal levels, and even out all of the hormonal stuff that Slug's tinkering induced," India explained. "Think of it as...as burning off the excess hormones, I guess. The grandmother of all hot flashes! Massive adrenal surge, the whole works. Now that the telepathic contact is broken, the hormonal stimulus must be gone, too. Wright's went back to normal within minutes. But for Meg, given the female hormone cycle, it apparently took a while for it all to kick in and drop down, like she mentioned earlier. It's not the way I would have expected it to work, given what I know about endocrinology—but admittedly, I'm not a specialist. So who knows what Slug's tinkering did? Anyway, I know what to do for her now."

"What, then?" Romeo asked.

"I've got to walk a tightrope," India answered. "I have to let the fever do its job with her biochem, accelerating her metabolic processes, but keep her cool enough not to fry her brains." India started removing Omega's work boots. "Romeo, go bring me a pan of cool water and some more washcloths."

"You got it!"

* * *

Romeo was back in a few minutes with the requested items. "Thanks, honey," India said, and took the cloths, tossed them into the water, then set the pan on the bedside table. "Now you guys get out of here."

Fox and Romeo exited the room, but Echo stayed by the bed.

"India, you'll need help."

"Yeah, I could use a hand..." India glanced up into Echo's concerned brown eyes, and pondered the situation for a moment, trying to decide what to do. She remembered how the two had spent days together, just the two of them, crashed on a protoplanet, keeping each other alive, even with Echo deathly ill and essentially immobile...and made her decision. "Well, you've already seen her a few times in a bikini, and she doesn't have to know, I guess. You get her shirt off, I'll get her jeans."

"Consider it done."

* * *

Several hours later, a worn-out India led an equally-drained Echo downstairs. "She's sleeping comfortably, and according to the medscanner, she's back to normal," India told the waiting men, pacing in the central hallway.

"Fever?" Romeo asked.

"Gone," Echo replied.

"Biochem?" Fox pressed.

"Tranquil as a summer breeze." India smiled.

"Th' house won't be f'r long, when she wakes up," Romeo remarked, making a face. "We got some big-time explainin' to do, guys. She's gonna be pissed."

"And with good reason," Fox averred.

"Yeah," India agreed. "We hurt her badly."

"Did any of you notice her room?" Echo asked very quietly.

"Yeah," Romeo answered, his face sad. "You couldn't hardly tell it was hers anymore. Got rid o' everything t' make her even think of space."

"Did Echo's 'death' do that to her?" Fox wondered.

"Well, I think it was at least the straw that broke the camel's back," India observed. "She was already under a tremendous amount of physical and emotional stress. We may need to see about getting her some counseling after this...assuming we can convince her to come back."

"What do you mean?" Fox wondered. "How do you know that?"

"She spent most of her time just thinking, after we told her Echo was dead. She didn't want to talk, didn't want to eat, didn't want to even see us. She sat in her room, or on the beach, lost in thought. Now I'm beginning to believe she must have been busy creating a new persona for her 'retirement,' one where she wouldn't be reminded of...everything." India sighed. "But it had to be done. We had to do what we did."

"It was really a brilliant idea, India." Fox nodded. "You and Bet worked it out quite nicely, between you. If Wright believed Echo dead, the need for assassin offspring was obviated, and his programming could be switched off—would likely switch itself off, with no need for us to force it. Once that happened, we could deprogram him without interference or risk to him, Omega, or the telepaths, return his genetics to normal human configuration in the regeneration process, brain-bleach him, and send him home."

"But Meg had to believe I was dead, or Wright would know it through the link," Echo added. "That was the...difficult part. Damn, how I hated to do that. She'd been through so much shit already, with this whole mess with Wright."

* * *

"Well, at least that explains why," a soft voice came from above and behind them. They turned to see a weary, robe-wrapped Omega sitting on one of the top stairs, watching and listening. "But it doesn't explain how the people I trust most in the universe could...violate that trust so. Or how I can regain that lost faith in them. You lied to me. All of you. With no compunctions. No hesitation."

"Strictly speaking," Fox murmured, "I didn't, since I didn't talk to you."

"Oh, really? I seem to recall a phone conversation, with Alpha Seven in the room, Fox." Omega glared at him. Fox started in surprise; he had temporarily forgotten that particular incident.

For once, just once, one of his Agents stared Fox down.

The only one of the four who could meet the reproachful blue eyes was Echo, and his own eyes were full of pain.

"If you don't know how, if you really believe deceiving you came easily to any of us, then you're not as...perceptive...as I always thought you were, Meg," he answered in a low voice.

"Maybe...I just need to hear it." She held out an entreating hand.

There was a pause, while the others considered.

"Omega," Fox finally said, "we couldn't let this go on forever, our four top Agents sitting isolated, barricaded on an island in the South Pacific. But we simply would not let Wright get to you! We take care of our own, Omega. You're a member of Division One; you're my adoptive daughter, as nearly as I have one—"

"You're fam'ly, Meg," Romeo interrupted. "Whether you wanna be or not, now."

"We care about you, sis," India added firmly.

"We weren't going to let anything happen to you, tekhter, if it was in our power to prevent," Fox added. "We couldn't, and live with ourselves. But we had to put an end to it. The sooner, the better; India indicated to us how much you were beginning to struggle even to maintain a semblance of normalcy. We didn't want to wait until your willpower failed, and you were broken."

"And then Echo remembered what you told him in Massachusetts," India noted.

"Huh? What did I tell him that pertained to this?" Omega wondered, confused. "I don't think I said anything that..."

"Yeah, you did," Echo declared. "Remember when you told me that Wright tried to come after me, when the hover mattress flipped and I got knocked loopy? Near as I can remember, you said something like, '...if he'd succeeded in killing you, it would have ended the mission altogether, and maybe even shut down his programming. 'Cause there wouldn't be any need for another generation of assassins, if you're dead.'"

"Ooo. Yeah, I do remember that," Omega decided.

"And that's what clinched it for us," India noted. "You, yourself, fig-ured out that if Echo was dead, there wasn't a need for the...mating...to oc-cur. And you had to have realized that, based on your telepathic interactions with Wright. There's no other way you COULD have known."

"Obviously we couldn't, and wouldn't, actually kill Echo," Fox ob-served.

"But that didn't mean we couldn't make it LOOK like 'e was dead," Romeo added. "Way we figured it, if we could convince you, it would con-vince Wright. Then the whole thing 'ud collapse, an' once Wright was back

323

t' normal, we let you know that Echo's okay, an' we all go home."

"Which is why we're here now," India appended, and the others nodded. "It...just took a little while to get Wright to a place where we all thought it was safe, and then a little longer to verify where you went..."

"And that you were still here," Fox amended. "After you shooed off the caretakers, that is."

"Was it extreme?" Echo finished for them. "Yes. But you were at the end of your rope, we were out of ideas, and it was our last gamble, Meg. We went from bridge to poker. A high-stakes bluff. And it paid off." He paused, then shrugged. "Actually, I'm really kinda surprised it worked. As well as you know me, as well as you read me, with your enhanced senses and the way all of that had been heightened by the link with Wright, I was sure you'd see through my...'poker face.'"

"Yeah. When you started getting those 'feelings' that something was wrong," India reminded her, "all three of us about had cows, as Romeo put it."

"...I had to gamble on your state of mind being sufficiently distracted by all the...biochemistry." Echo sighed. "And then clear out, before you could figure anything else out."

The house fell silent again.

* * *

Finally Omega stood and padded barefoot down the stairs. She headed into the kitchen, with the others trailing behind. She opened the refrigerator and got out a big pitcher of iced tea. She poured five tall glasses and put them around the table, then sat down and sipped from one.

The others slowly took places at the table.

Echo sat down last, in the position the others had left open for him, beside Omega.

"So what's been happening at Headquarters?" Omega asked.

* * *

"...And meanwhile, they're shipping Tt'l'k back to Deltir," India said, "in the Arcturan equivalent of a strait jacket, I gathered. Zebra told me he deteriorated fast, under the stress of Echo's report, the reprimand from Zz'r'p, and the ensuing investigation into why he did what he did."

"So he was mentally ill?" Omega wondered, surprised.

"Apparently so," Fox confirmed. "I had a little talk with Zz'r'p the day before yesterday, which was the day they took Tt'l'k to the Area 51 Spaceport, to ship him back home. So you don't have to worry about him any more, Omega; he's no longer planetside. And Zz'r'p sends profuse apologies, tekhter—to you and Echo, both. He was at the Hong Kong Office, helping with an interrogation of a rogue Froon, when this all started going down. He's informed me he plans to stay closer to Headquarters from now on; he's tired of being in the wrong place at the wrong time when his 'star pupil' needs him, he said."

"But they needed him, too," Omega murmured.

"He plans to have another assistant sent from Deltir, and he said HE... or she, we're not sure yet which...can do the 'away jobs,'" Fox explained. "Only this time they're going to do a more thorough screening job for the position. He's even working out a checklist for that. One that includes EXTENSIVE experience in interrogations AND negotiation."

"Which will definitely help prevent another recurrence of a mentally-not-right Arcturan mind-forcing somebody," Echo grumbled. "There's interrogation, and then there's mind rape."

"The line can be fine, but it was definitely crossed in this instance," Fox averred. "With BOTH members of Alpha One, even if only one of you could sense it."

"Yeah," Omega agreed, subdued. "I...I know this is gonna sound bad, but...after what he did, I'm glad Tt'l'k is getting sent home, though I'm sorry about...about the..." Omega paused. Then she scowled. "No. I'm gonna be honest, with myself and with y'all. I think he deserved what he got. He always had an attitude problem, from the time he arrived on Earth."

"Ya know, he did, didn't 'e?" Romeo noted. "Tt'l'k had a weird concept o' humans an' Earth from the get-go, like Meg said. India, babe, you don't s'pose he was goin' off even then?"

"No," India disagreed. "Zebra and I both went back and looked over his medical records, and confirmed that there was no sign of Mr'd'k-P'rr'l syndrome at that time. It's been a sudden and rapid onset—not even his last physical showed up anything, according to Zarnix. No one's quite sure why it hit so fast, which is another reason for sending him home, so specialists can examine and treat him."

"Better for him and us," Fox decided.

"You know one reason for that attitude, don't you?" Omega asked. "A lot of that was directed at me, because I was born human and yet I had the whole telepathic thing goin', which he thought was just plain wrong, on lotsa levels."

"Wait, Meg," Echo stopped her. "How did you know that?! I never heard Tt'l'k say anything..."

"I know. YOU didn't. Nobody else did, either. He never said it out loud," Omega informed her partner, then tapped her temple. "But he made subtle...jabs...at me, telepathically, whenever I consulted or trained with Zz'r'p in the embassy...which was one reason I tried to have Zz'r'p come by our quarters, or placed a vidcall, or...whatever. Even when he didn't say anything, Tt'l'k would fairly radiate disapproval. I talked to Zz'r'p about it a couple of times, and he told me Tt'l'k was jealous of the attention I got from Zz'r'p and the other Arcturans. He reprimanded him a couple of times, which only made Tt'l'k worse."

"Shit," Echo grumbled. "I didn't know anything about that."

"Nor did I," Fox noted, in some displeasure. "And you realize that that factors into the events in my office?"

"Hm. You're right," Echo agreed, scowling briefly. "Tt'l'k resented Meg, and that situation gave him the perfect opportunity to make her look as bad as possible in front of the people she cared about most. To utterly humiliate her."

"Damn," India muttered, angered. "You two have a point."

"I believe, Echo, we should possibly amend our earlier report," Fox concluded.

"Agreed," Echo said, frowning.

"So...no. I'm not sorry for him," Omega declared. "I know I should be, but I'm not. 'Cause I'm tired of being the butt of people's jokes, foul temperaments, and general snarky attitudes!"

"Speaking of snarky attitudes," Echo noted, "Fox, do you want to fill Meg in on Alpha Seven, or shall I?"

* * *

"...And so that's how matters resolved with Alpha Seven," Fox explained. "I ran your recommendation up the flagpole, Omega, after clandestinely getting Echo's take on it..."

"I thought it was a great idea, Meg," Echo averred. "Especially since you made Yankee start understanding your perspective on things."

"And given the several 'mitigating circumstances' you laid out, and your ongoing refusal to press charges, Omega, even the Ennead had no qualms accepting a modified punishment," Fox finished. "Considering the mental anguish and psychological damage the situation had caused to Yankee AND Tare, they were even willing to waive convening a formal tribunal. But given their own backgrounds with some vengeful criminals, Tare insisted on going undercover to protect his partner during his suspension. So Alpha Seven is still on the rosters, but off the active duty list, for the time being, at least." He drew a deep breath. "Depending on how that goes, they may...or may not...ever come back."

"But at least the option is open," Echo added.

Omega sighed.

"Hey, wha's wrong, pretty lady?" Romeo wondered. "I'd 'a thought you woulda been glad t' get 'em off your back. Yankee 'uz always snarkin' 'bout you."

"She understood why," Fox explained. "She told us so, the day she called in as the Alpha Line Chief."

"Which I guess I wasn't, really, after all," Omega noted. "I'm just... glad..." Abruptly she choked, and took a big sip of her iced tea, in an effort to open her throat. When that didn't work, and she had to struggle rather alarmingly to force the fluid past the constriction in her throat, she set the glass down, rested her elbows on the tabletop, and put her face in her hands. Moments later, something glittered as it fell between her fingers and splashed, wet, on the table.

"Hey, now," Echo said, keeping his voice soft and low. "It's okay, baby. I'm okay. I'm here, we're still partners, you're better. Wright's being fixed and sent home; he'll never bug you again. You ensured Alpha Seven had options left open. It's over. We're all here and okay. Everything's gonna be all right. It's all right now." He eased an arm around her shoulders, rubbing his hand across her back as he did, and she turned into his chest and began to cry softly.

Fox took one look at the situation, and glanced at India, who pressed her lips together, offered a concerned frown, then jabbed her finger in the direction of the door to the hall. Fox, India, and Romeo eased back from the table and rose.

"Echo, we're going to give you and Omega a little private time to vent and reconnect," Fox murmured.

"Yeah, man, y'all relax. We got y'r backs," Romeo said quietly.

"Call me if you need me," India added.

"...Sorry," Echo's chest noted. "Gimme a minute..."

"Hush that," Fox ordered, but gently. "You've been through hell, tekhter. And..." The Director shrugged. "I think perhaps we owe you this. And more beside, but this will do, for now."

"Thanks, guys," Echo said, and the blonde head in his chest nodded agreement.

As the trio exited the kitchen, Echo eased his arms around his partner.

Chapter 11

A week later, back at Headquarters, Mu slipped into the break room and slid into the chair across the table from Omega, after discreetly signaling the Hypothenamoids congregated there. The bean-shaped, coffee-loving insectoid aliens grudgingly cleared out as Mu said cheerfully, "Hi, Meg! You're back."

"Oh," Omega said blankly, looking up from her prepackaged Danish. "Hi, Mu."

Mu surveyed her for a moment.

"I love the tan. Tell Echo he did a good job."

"Okay, um, thanks...good job at what?" Omega asked, puzzled. "He's good at pretty much anything he sets his mind to."

"Taking care of you."

"Oh." Omega blushed, and Mu studied her quizzically. "Yeah. That's what...partners...are for." She placed deliberate emphasis on the word. Then she downed the last of her coffee, shoving the disposable cup aside.

"Want some more coffee?" Mu asked, getting up to get a cup for himself.

"Yeah, thanks; my sleep cycle is still a little wonked, so I could do with the extra caffeine about now. Lotsa cream, no sugar. No, no, not the powdered junk. That's nothing but pure sugar and some white coloring. I think it's nasty. So does Echo. There should be some real cream in the fridge. Echo put some in there, this morning."

"Oh, there it is. I got it." Mu poured the hot beverages, then sat back down, handing a cup to his companion. "So how about dinner and a movie tonight?"

"Oh! Um, okay, I guess," Omega replied, a bit diffident.

"You sound...not too sure."

"I guess I'm...just surprised you still want to go out," she hedged, unwilling to tell him that she was still working to get her head together, or that Echo and Fox, not to mention India, were pressing her to obtain some counseling. *And I'm not sure WHAT I want any more,* she added mentally... but did not say. *Never mind what I might, one day, be able to HAVE...or not. Apparently 'not,' though.*

"Of course I do. You're gorgeous, smart, and totally cool, honey. What time do you get off duty?"

"Alpha One's shift ends at 26:00 D1," Omega answered.

"Okay, I'll swing by your quarters around 27:00. Will that work?" Mu asked.

"Sure. I'll be ready."

* * *

That evening at about 26:45 D1, Omega emerged from her bedroom, straight into her partner's unanticipated appraisal.

"Hmmm," Echo murmured thoughtfully—and mildly suggestively—while standing in the back door and surveying the blonde Agent.

Omega was stylishly, if casually, dressed in slim black jeans and white silk blouse, open at the throat. Her feet were encased in black patent pumps. The shining mane was upswept and twisted; glittering diamond earrings cascaded from her earlobes.

"...What's this all about?" Echo finished, leaning against the doorframe and folding his arms.

"Oh, um," Omega glanced away, "I forgot to tell you. Mu's taking me out tonight."

"Oh," Echo said, voice somewhat flat. "I guess I'm on my own for dinner, then."

"Isn't your mom back?"

"Not yet. She'll be at the Ranch until Angamar gets back. However long it takes."

"Oh. I just thought Angamar would have been back by now."

"Nope. Where are you two going?"

"He said something about dinner and a movie."

"Well, hell, you and I do that all the time."

"Yeah, that's true," she admitted, a bit prim, "but there's a difference between a couple of friends and co-workers grabbing a bite and catching a movie together, and...and a man asking a woman out."

Echo absorbed that.

"If you say so," he decided. "Are you looking forward to it?"

"Well, the truth is, I'm a little nervous."

"Nervous? You?"

"Yup."

"Why? Do you want everything to go well that badly?"

330

"I want it to go well, yeah, but—"

"You're a hopeless romantic at heart, aren't you, Meg?" Echo remarked softly, watching her.

"Yeah. At least, I'd like to be," she said quietly. "I never seem to ever get much chance to practice."

"You...didn't seem out of practice to me," he said in a low tone.

"Echo, I...I'm sorry about that," Omega began, feeling herself flushing under the golden suntan. Her partner eyed her.

"Why?" he wondered.

"You have to ask?!" she exclaimed, shocked.

"No. I meant, why me?"

"Again," Omega reiterated, more quietly this time, "you have to ask?"

"Yeah. You pushed Mu away."

"I pushed you away, too. Or tried. You wouldn't be pushed away," Omega noted.

"You still haven't answered the question," Echo pointed out. Omega sighed.

"Is there a man on the planet I'm closer to, more comfortable with, or trust more? I knew you'd never...abuse the situation. Just like you told me up in Massachusetts. And you didn't." She paused and turned away, fighting down humiliation. "I'm...sorry I offended you."

* * *

Echo straightened up and pushed away from the doorframe, startled.

"Is that what you think?! I—" But before Echo could say anything further, he was interrupted by a knock at Omega's door. "Dammit, his timing sucks...for me," he muttered under his breath as Omega went to let Mu into her quarters.

"Hi, Meg," Mu greeted his date. "Wow, you look great. Ready to go?"

"Mmm, let me think..." she pondered. Echo watched, amused, as Omega patted pockets. "Winchester & Tesla...*carte noir*...brain-bleacher... goggle-glasses. Yep. I'm ready."

"Meg," Mu said, exasperated, "it's a date, not a mission."

"I'm still trying to figure out where she's hiding all that in those jeans," Echo deadpanned, neglecting to say anything about the possibility of multiple warp pockets inserted in strategic locations; it was, after all, something of a trade secret for the Alpha One team. Mu grinned in appreciative agreement. Omega ignored the remark with good humor.

"I know it's a date," she replied to Mu. "But I'm still an Alpha Line Agent. The number two man in the department, no less."

"Well, so to speak," the two men commented simultaneously, and Omega chuckled.

"I can tell I'm gonna have to keep the two of y'all separated if I don't want you gangin' up on me," she said, and grinned. "Thanks, guys. That's... some much-needed ego boo right now. All right, Mu, I'm ready. Let's go." As the pair headed out the door, Omega called over her shoulder, "See you later, Ace. Don't wait up!"

The door closed behind them, and a suddenly-serious Echo stood staring at it for a long time.

He never bothered to eat dinner.

* * *

Mu took Omega to Quan Lunpe, an upscale authentic Thai restaurant.

"This is my favorite restaurant in New York," he told her with a smile, as the maître d' seated them at a table in the corner. "Do you trust me to order for you, Meg?"

"What did you have in mind?"

"I was thinking, for the first course, tom yung goong; it's a spicy soup with shrimp, if you're not allergic to shellfish. For an entrée, I thought I'd order you geng kheaw wan gai, a Thai green curry," he explained. "Dessert can be some flavor of sticky rice; they have a bunch of variants here. How does that sound?"

"Um, no offense, Mu, but I dunno," Omega murmured. "Isn't most Thai food kinda...spicy?"

"Well, yeah, that's sorta the point," Mu said with a grin.

"I...might have a little trouble with it right now," Omega admitted, putting a light hand to her belly. "After all the, uh, the carnival ride I've had for a life lately, Echo's even had to tone down on some of his Tex-Mex recipes..."

"Oh! Ooo, geez, I never thought about that," Mu murmured, concerned. "Isn't that a little unusual for you, though? I mean, the way you ate back in Dallas, I thought you had a cast-iron, asbestos-lined gut."

"Normally, I would," she offered him a rueful smile. "I love spicy foods generally, and the menu you selected sounds really good. But...well, think about all the, um, the biochemistry. India said it threw my entire system off. I've got specific orders from the medlab to eat very mild foods, with lots of protein, until everything gets back to normal."

"But I thought...you'd said your, uh, 'biochemistry' WAS back to normal..."

"Oh, it is," Omega explained. "All the, the hormones an' junk, are back to normal levels. But it was wonked for so long and so bad that my other systems went way outta whack. Never mind the stress levels. The most obvious, and most annoying, casualty seems to be the digestive system."

"Well...crap. As it were." Mu offered her a teasing grin, and she laughed.

"Something like, yeah," she agreed. "But if memory serves regarding those particular dishes, I wouldn't make it through the movie on your proposed menu. Could we...maybe pick out something really mild for me? You're welcome to eat a spicier menu if you want, but..."

"That's not a problem, honey," Mu said, nodding. "Zeta doesn't care for really spicy stuff just on principle; she's the agent they're looking at partnering me with. So I already know some good stuff we can order off the menu that'll work for you. And I'd sorta figured on us sharing the dishes; it's sexier that way, I think. I might just order the mixed vegetable thing for a side, 'cause it tends to be spicy, and then we can...lessee. You said lotsa protein, right?"

"Yeah."

"Okay, then let's go with moo daeng for an entrée," Mu decided. "That's pork with a sweet, non-spicy sauce, and a touch of garlic. Will that work?"

"Yeah, that sounds good," Omega told him.

"We can tell 'em to leave out the garlic, if you want."

"No; just a touch should be okay. And I'm really sorry."

"All right. It's no big deal, honey; I want you to enjoy the evening, not spend half of it in the ladies' room, sick. How about this? We can have basic spring rolls for an appetizer; plain steamed white rice for a side, along with my vegetable dish, which YOU need to stay away from," he told her, and grinned. She chuckled, and he continued, "Then some sorta flavored sticky rice for dessert. Do you like mango?"

"Yes!"

"The mango sticky rice, then. Does that sound better?"

"Much. And..." Omega shrugged. "Again, sorry for the complication."

"No problem. Relax, Meg. We can check out the spicier dishes some other time, when you're better recovered from...everything."

"Okay."

"Do you drink?"

"I've been known to, yes." She offered him a mischievous smile, and he grinned.

"Okay. Thai beer, plum wine, regular wine...they have a couple brands of good sake here, though it's a Japanese drink...or maybe a cocktail? Ooo, I bet you'd like a milk punch! It's kind of like iced tea, but made with coconut milk and...rum, I think."

"That sounds nice!"

"A couple of milk punches it is, then," Mu said, and smiled.

* * *

They chatted and joked their way through the meal. Mu occasionally told her off-color jokes, and made light-hearted innuendoes that left Omega somewhat uncomfortable, given her recent difficulties, but she tried to laugh anyway. *He's only trying to be sexy with me. I don't want to make him self-conscious,* she thought, *and I do want to see what he's like in his off-duty life. He wasn't part of my whole support team through the mess with Mark, so he probably hasn't got a clue about what-all it did to me. Not really. And I...don't think I can tell him. Not now. I can't talk about it yet. Not...to somebody who doesn't already know. I can barely talk about it to the ones who DO know.*

They finished sharing a large serving of sticky rice with mango slices and mango syrup, then Mu called for the check and paid.

"Now for a good flick," he said, escorting Omega to his waiting vehicle.

* * *

Mu was younger than Echo; he was even a year or two younger than Omega, in actuality. And while Echo liked sleek, sporty cars, he had had sufficient time in the Agency to get the matter out of his system, and settle in with a vehicle whose appearance he liked, but which didn't unduly stand out. Echo then quenched his need for speed by hot-rodding the already-enhanced Corvette. The result was, in Omega's considered opinion, a subtle, classy, sexy ride.

Mu, on the other hand, was new to the Agency, and still enamored of the entire *I can have any car I want, and it'll do more than anything else on—or off—the road* mentality. Consequently, he had chosen a high-end sports car to have modified to Agency specifications: a Lamborghini Huracan. The sleek black machine, with its passive cloaking and morph ability, looked to Omega more like something that should be at a spaceport than on the streets of New York, and she found herself moderately uncomfortable with the attention from passers-by, as Mu helped her into the low-slung passenger seat.

"Ready?" he asked with a smile, as he buckled into the driver's seat and pressed the start button.

"Yep."

"Strap in, baby! Here we go!"

And they were off with a roar.

* * *

"Okay, so we got our choice of that latest in the horror franchise, or a romantic comedy," Mu noted, studying the marquee board at the movie theater...which was not the one she and Echo usually frequented.

Great, Omega thought, trying not to pull a face. *I don't really care for either genre. I'm more into action-adventure, science fiction, or fantasy... like Echo. Agh. I'm on a date with another man; I gotta try to stop thinking about Echo every other second! It isn't like he's ever gonna ask me out, not like this. Not after...that last night at The Beach. Still and all, I've been through my own personal nightmare lately, so maybe...eh. I wonder what Mu wants to see.*

"What did you have in mind?" Omega wondered aloud.

"Well, I've always kinda enjoyed horror movies for, um, serious dates," he said with a mischievous grin. "When my girl lets out a little scream, then huddles into my chest, I like it." He shrugged, and the grin got wider. "Not that I expect that to be easy, with present company!"

Lovely, she thought, heart sinking. *That means he picked a doozy. No. I just don't think I can—*

"Oh shit!" Mu exclaimed, and palmed his face. "No, that won't be good for you, honey. I'm sorry; I wasn't thinking. With the...'mission'...you were just on, you need something a LOT more light-hearted than that damn horror flick. You haven't laughed, or even smiled, as much as I'm used to seeing from you, not tonight. Are you okay?"

"Yeah, I'm okay. I'm just...yeah, you're right," Omega confessed. "I'm still working on...I dunno." She shrugged. "It's...hard to explain...unless you were there," she tried. "But no, I don't think I'm in the mood for a horror movie. I kinda just got done living one."

"Right. We'll see the romantic comedy," Mu decided. "I think you need to laugh a little, for a change."

"Okay. That'll work."

"Good."

* * *

Much later, Mu and Omega arrived back at her front door, laughing and chatting.

"Thanks, Mu," Omega smiled, making it as warm as she could. "I had...fun." *Not as much fun as if Echo and I had gone out,* she considered, *but I never see him checking out my butt when he thinks I'm not looking, either. That was a nice ego boost, I'll admit.*

"Then how about inviting me in for a drink before I go home?" Mu slipped his arms around her waist.

"Okay. That sounds like a plan," she said, pulling away gently before leading the way in. "What would you like?"

* * *

"What have you got?" Mu asked, noting the open back door and the dark apartment beyond without comment. Omega went into the kitchen and Mu moved to the black leather couch, surveying it for size, before sitting down.

"Mm, not much in the way of alcohol, I'm afraid. I'm not a big drinker. A Guinness, some chocolate stout, a couple German beers, some Zinfandel. If you want something harder, Echo might have something; I could go over and fetch it. I'm sure he wouldn't mind."

"Nah, it's good. I'll take one of the German beers."

"Okay." A few minutes later, Omega came out with Mu's beer in a chilled stein, and a mug of chocolate stout for herself. "Here you go." She joined Mu on the couch. "So what did you think of the movie?"

"Hm? Oh, I enjoyed it," Mu said. Unassuming, he slipped his arm around her shoulders in an affectionate, familiar gesture as they sipped their drinks. "It was funny, especially when the leading man fell outta the tree. But mostly I enjoyed the company."

* * *

"Thanks." Omega smiled, somewhat shy.

"'Pretty lady,'" Mu murmured in her ear, taking the drinks and setting them aside, "why don't you go close the connecting door?"

"Why?"

"We don't want to disturb your partner, now, do we?"

"How do you figure on disturbing Echo?" Omega asked rather bluntly, growing uncomfortable. Mu smiled gently, a dark, velvety, smoldering light in his eyes.

"Because...I'd really like to stay with you tonight, Meg. And I...don't want to be interrupted. I want to be able to concentrate on you." He worked his fingers up into her hair as he spoke, freeing it from its upswept twist before she could react, and it tumbled down around her shoulders. "I missed you while you were gone, Meg. I kept up with what was happening, how you were doing. I even went to Fox and volunteered to lead the search for Wright when he went missing...several times, as it turned out. It worried me. A lot." He gazed into the wide blue eyes. "Has anyone told you lately what a drop-dead beautiful woman you are?" Mu breathed.

"N-no...not...real recently..."

* * *

Before Omega could say anything more, Mu's lips had covered hers in a long, slow kiss. She stiffened, then gradually relaxed as Mu drew her ever so gently closer, careful, after everything that had happened to her, not to frighten her.

"I won't hurt you," he murmured against her lips. "I swear I won't. I know what you've been through."

At last Mu ended the kiss and raised his head. Omega dropped her gaze, blushing. He smiled.

"Go close the door, Meg," he said softly.

"Mu, I...I think you've—" Omega began.

* * *

"I'll save you the trouble, Meg." The couple on the couch looked up to see an impassive Echo standing in the back door. "Don't bother getting up."

Echo closed the door, and Omega listened in dismay to the soft click of

337

the security locks engaging. *Oh no,* she thought, heart sinking as a kind of flashback hit and, once again, a sense of rejection inundated her. *Not again. Just like at The Beach. Only...I wonder what he saw, and what he thought about what he saw.*

Mu sat looking from the closed door to a dumbstruck Omega.

"Why do I have the feeling more happened there than I saw?" he wondered, bemused. "Never mind. Where were we?" he dismissed the incident with a warm smile, drawing Omega close again.

"Mu...please." Omega gently disentangled herself. Mu stared at her.

"Meg—what's wrong?"

"What I was about to say before Echo...closed the door," Omega began, trying her best to resume a normal demeanor, never mind train of thought, "was that you've...kinda gotten the wrong impression, and I'm sorry. This is...going too fast for me, Mu," she tried to explain. "Recent events notwithstanding, I'm not...I don't..."

"Aha, I get it. Old-fashioned Southern lady, huh?" he suddenly caught on, and she nodded. "Okay, Meg, honey. I can respect that. I'm sorry, too; I never meant to push you, especially after all the stress of those 'recent events.' We'll call it a night, then."

She blinked, startled at his immediate understanding and acceptance. Mu stood, and Omega followed him to the door. There, he turned.

"Our schedules will synch up again in two days. Want to go out again?"

Omega risked a quick glance at the back door, and closed her eyes for a moment, tucking her head, as if shy. *HE'S sure not interested,* she thought. *No matter how much I wish he was, Echo is never gonna be interested, not the way I thought—hoped—he might. If I'm gonna have a relationship, it'll have to be with someone else. And Mu seems...nice. I mean, wouldn't it be cool to have a mate living here, AND a best friend next door? The question is...am I willing to settle? I guess the only way to find out is to try.*

"Sure." She nodded affirmation.

Mu leaned forward and kissed Omega's forehead gently, but as he did so, he glanced thoughtfully over her head, back into the apartment.

"All right, Meg. See you in a couple of days."

* * *

After Mu left, Omega pondered his goodbye kiss. *Echo kissed me on the forehead in the exact same place several times, up in Ipswich,* she realized. *It isn't anything especially sexy; it's just affectionate. So why did Echo's leave me almost wobbly-kneed, but Mu's...didn't?*

Giving up on that line of inquiry, she went to the back door and knocked.

"He's gone, Ace," she called, waiting for the door to open, its accustomed state.

But nothing happened, and eventually Omega turned off the lights and went to bed.

* * *

After closing the back door, Echo closeted himself in his bedroom, in deep pain. *I've lost her,* he thought, despairing. *I waited too long, and I've lost her. And Mu is over there right now, seducing her into letting him go to bed with her. Not that it looked like she minded that much. Hell, maybe that's what she meant, that night at The Beach—it was him she really wanted, not me. Maybe...maybe I need to dissolve the defined partnership anyway. Step aside and let her be happy. And maybe I need to just...retire, after that. I could forget, that way. Maybe. I dunno if anything could make me forget Meg. But a retirement brain-bleaching stands the best chance, I think. Except then I lose Ma, too, 'cause she's enjoying working for the Agency now. Well, shit.*

He paced the floor of his bedroom.

Okay, maybe I stay with the Agency, and just retire to the Ranch, he considered. *Joe can go home and marry his girlfriend...at least somebody ends up with who they want...and I'll talk Ma into transferring there permanently, and we'll run it together. I guess I should ask her.*

He sighed, then pulled out his cell phone, hitting a particular speed dial. When the other end of the connection answered, he held it to his ear.

"Ma?" he murmured into the phone. "It's Alex. I know it's late, but...I... really could use some advice...and there's not many people I can talk to about this..."

* * *

"No, no, no," Dihl declared. "I can't believe that for one minute. Not that partner of yours."

"Ma, he's over there right now," Echo explained. "She'd already taken her hair down, and they were kissing like...like I only wish I could kiss her." He sighed. "He told her to close the back door—you know, the one between

339

our apartments—'cause he didn't want the 'subsequent events' to disturb me! He flatly told her that he wanted to spend the night, and she didn't even protest, Ma," Echo said, miserable. "I've...lost her."

"Son, I want you to do something for me, right now," Dihl said, stern.

"What?"

"Do you have the back door closed?"

"And locked," Echo all but growled. "Meg may accept him, but I don't know this Mu well enough to give him access to my home, especially if I'm asleep."

"That's more like my Apache warrior. Go unlock that door, open it, and go into her quarters," Dihl all but ordered. "I want to see if your assumptions are right, or if you're exhausted and letting matters get you down. After all, you were on guard for her for...how long did that whole situation run? How much actual rest have you really gotten in the last couple of weeks, son?"

"Eh," Echo said, and sighed. "It wasn't so bad at first. But as Meg's condition deteriorated, so did my sleep. I...got damn worried."

"And since you brought her back to Headquarters?"

"It's...a little better. But I'm still awfully worried about her. She needs counseling, and I'm telling her to get it, India's telling her, Fox is telling her, but...she won't."

"Give her time, son. She likely won't because she feels...humiliated by it all. And it's still too close; it would be hard for her to talk about it to anyone, least of all someone she considers a stranger. Is it affecting your sleep and rest, your worry?"

"Some, yeah. Okay, a fair amount, I guess."

"So your objectivity is compromised. You're worn out, and not thinking straight."

"Maybe," he admitted then. "All right, I'll...go see if...if Mu is in the bedroom with her."

"Which proof will be if her bedroom door is shut, yes? You told me that she always left it open if you were welcome to come in and check on her in the night, didn't you?"

"Yeah, maybe," Echo said, exiting his bedroom and going to the back door. A quick murmur to A.T.L.A.S.S., the household computer, unlocked it. He eased it open.

Omega's side of the back door was still wide open. Her quarters were darkened and silent, and he stepped just inside the back door, letting his eyes adjust, before looking around.

To his left, he saw a door archway, faintly filled with a soft orange glow. *Her nightlight,* he realized. *The bedroom door IS open. But did they leave it that way 'cause they already knew the back door was shut?* He held the phone to his lips and breathed, "Ma, don't say a word until I tell you."

"Understood, Alex."

Echo tiptoed over to the bedroom door. It stood wide open.

If Mu stayed over, he thought, *he's either an unpleasantly fast lover, or they were both too tired for 'extracurricular activities.' This makes no sense. Unless he's not there. I hope Meg will forgive me for what I'm about to do. 'Cause I have to know.*

Remaining just outside the threshold, Echo leaned forward and peered inside, just for a moment. He blinked several times, trying to get his eyes to dark-adapt.

I can't tell for sure, he decided, *but I think there's only one body in the bed. And it's too small to be Mu.* Tentative relief washed through him. *I think she must have sent him away, after all. That means I still might have a chance.*

He tiptoed back to his bedroom.

* * *

"That is what I fully expected, son," Dihl told him, after he finished describing what he'd seen, she had asked several pointed questions, and he had filled her in on what he felt Omega would be comfortable with Dihl knowing. "And I feel sure that your tired eyes did not deceive you, and that she was indeed alone in the bed. It may well be time for you to make your move, however. If she has accepted a date from him, it is likely because she no longer believes there is a chance with YOU. Especially after...what just occurred. Whereas, you tell me, Mu was open and accepting of what just happened, or as much as she was willing to tell him."

"So was I."

"But you had to...refuse her...at The Beach. Knowing her, she likely interprets that as NOT accepting."

"Hm. Yeah, good point. And some comments she's made tend to support that, except every time I try to discuss it with her, to explain, we get

341

interrupted. So...I need to do something. But...I...got nothing."

"Oh, of course you do, son," Dihl said, exasperated. "You're just too tired to think straight, after all you've been through—since I have been working on Omega's genetic problem, Zebra kept me apprised of matters, and even consulted with me a couple of times, so I already know what you both have been through! If you cannot think, will you allow me to help, by giving you ideas and instructions?"

"I...kinda think that might be good, about now," Echo admitted, smearing his hand over his weary face and up into his hair with a sigh. "'Cause yeah, I am pretty tired, when you get down to it. Once we get our desks dug out from under, I might see if Fox will give Alpha One an extra day off, to try to play catch-up on our sleep."

"I think that is an excellent notion, son, and I will 'put a bug' in Zebra's ear about it, to help matters along. All right. Tomorrow, you are going to make breakfast for two, and you are going to pull out all the stops. For tonight, here is what you need to do to prepare..."

* * *

The next morning, Omega woke to the aromatic smell of coffee with chicory. Sleepily she got up and wandered into the bathroom, where she washed her face, brushed her teeth and hair, and threw on her black silk robe.

I still feel beat up, even two weeks after though it's been, she thought, staring at herself in the mirror. *Damn, but that whole mess with Mark took it out of me. Part of me thinks that Echo an' Fox are right, and I oughta get counseling. But I just don't see...too many people knew about that whole mess as it was. Too many people...who now know just what I am. Never mind the whole 'in heat' aspect of it. If I have to tell a counselor enough about it for him or her to understand it sufficient to advise me, then I gotta tell 'em EVERYthing. And I just don't think I can. I can't face it. I still haven't told Echo some of that shit. I can't...I can't even choke it out to Zebra, and she already knows all of it.*

She sighed, uncertain what to do. Finally, she shoved it into a corner of her mind and determined to face the more immediate Gorgon—an Echo who, last night, had seemed upset about having to close the back door. *Though exactly why, I'm not sure,* she considered.

Then she meandered into her living area.

* * *

The back door was open once again. The coffee aroma she had smelled earlier was drifting through it, along with a faint sizzling sound.

"Meg? Is that you?" she heard a call.

"Who else would it be, Echo?" she asked softly, moving to the back door. Echo stuck his head out of his kitchen; he looked a little uncertain.

"I...thought maybe...I mean, I wasn't sure..." He looked away. "I, uh, I got worried about you last night, so I DID, um, go check to make sure you were okay. But I didn't go into your bedroom, just in case you...weren't alone. I didn't want..."

"Aw," Omega murmured, touched and concerned. "Did you have a flashback to the Cortian thing?"

* * *

"No. Like I told you a few days ago, I think I got that one under control. This was more about...you having nightmares after...Wright. And I thought, if Mu was there, but he didn't know about some of that...well, I thought it could be bad." *Which is true,* he told himself. *I really WAS concerned about that, and it would have been bad. It's just that it wasn't the only reason I checked. Or even the main reason.*

"Oh. No." Omega shook her head. "It's okay. I asked him to slow down."

"And?"

"He said okay, and went home."

"So you're still seeing him?"

"Yeah, I guess so. We're going out again tomorrow night."

"Oh." Echo stifled the disappointment and brought out a platter of scrambled eggs and bacon in one hand, and a basket of homemade biscuits in the other. "Well, come get breakfast, baby. I'll get the pot of coffee."

* * *

"Mmm, this takes me way back—all the way to my childhood!" Omega said enthusiastically, sitting down at Echo's table. "My all-time favorite breakfast. Simple and filling. The only thing missing is the—" Echo leaned over her shoulder and sat a jar in front of her, "honey for the biscuits..." She grinned in delight, staring at the jar of honey. "You think of everything, Ace."

"By now, I know what you like." Echo shrugged. He joined her at the

343

table, and they started eating companionably. After a few minutes, Echo said, "Meg, listen, I...wanted to tell you something."

"What?" Omega looked up.

* * *

"I didn't want you thinking you offended me in the safehouse on the island—The Beach, I mean. You know what I mean. Yesterday, I got India to give me a little detailed medical briefing on the entire situation, something I wanted to do but never really got the chance while it was all going down. I managed a little bit during the whole mess, but there was a lot more I felt like I needed to know. See, I dug into the technical, scientific aspects of it as much as I could while it was all happening, and yesterday, I asked a shit-ton of questions."

"Oh," Omega murmured. Echo watched as she paled, and bit his lip before continuing.

"Since I was there to see most of it go down, there weren't a whole lotta things that she refused to discuss, for privacy's sake, but I also tried not to go THERE about it, either. In other words, we tried to preserve your privacy as much as we could, while still ensuring I had enough understanding to grasp exactly how things were affecting you, and what I did right or wrong, in trying to support you."

* * *

"Oh," she reiterated, deciding he had been more unsure of himself and his responses than he had let on at the time. "Well, um, you pretty much did everything right, Ace. And there were things you had to do, whether it was easy on me or not; I understand, and understood, that. I just...there were times when...when it was hard, is all...I mean..."

"Shh, Meg; hush, baby," Echo told her, voice and manner gentle, face open. "It's okay. I understand. I've got a much better idea now of what you were really going through, and frankly, not only am I NOT offended, I'm... honored that you...trusted me like that. And no, I haven't told India or anybody about it; it's none of their business."

A certain amount of relief washed through her at that, not that she had actually expected him to tell anyone. *Still, if he thought it was needful, to illustrate how far gone I was or something, maybe,* she thought. *I dunno. Knowing him, probably not, but I can see where it could happen. But it didn't. Only...there's something else I need to know, something that I don't understand.*

"Then why did...did you get up and leave so suddenly, if you weren't offended?" Omega asked, staring at her plate, appetite gone for the moment.

* * *

"Meg," Echo said quietly, watching her and seeing the pain—and sense of rejection—she was trying hard to hide, "I was trying my damnedest to live up to your trust in me. Whatever comes of our relationship, I realized you didn't really want it to happen the way it was going down at that point. You were doing it because you felt trapped, so I was trying to do what I promised you days before—I refused to take advantage of the situation. If it's gonna happen, then it needs to happen the way we both want it, not because one of us feels forced to it. But it was...hard. I guess I probably coulda done it better, and not hurt you so much in the doing, but...well. I didn't exactly have a whole lotta time to plan it."

He paused to study her face and make sure she comprehended, and she nodded acknowledgement of his remarks, so he continued.

"Look, I don't...express myself very much; you know that. That leads some people to think there's nothing to express. But I'm not a machine. I'm as human as you are. No, I don't think your scientific definition is correct, and I never will," he added, as she glanced intently at him. "And, like you pointed out, pheromones work both ways. I think you must have been pumping 'em out by the gigaton that night! I'm not sure, but I think I might actually have smelled some of yours, when...when you and I...talked...on the couch, that last night. Something sure smelled drool-worthy, anyway. Let me tell you, though, it was damn hard to get up and walk away, baby. Harder than you'll ever know. You...well, Mu and Romeo aren't the only guys around here who think you're a 'pretty lady,' you know." He felt his face grow warm at the admission. *But I gotta start getting a few things in there, otherwise Mu is gonna walk off with her,* he decided.

"Aw," Omega murmured, her cheeks flushing delightfully.

"Remember what I told you in the hot tub at my beach house?"

"Yeah. You said, any time somebody made me feel bad about myself, I should remember that my partner thought I was hot stuff, and his was the only opinion that counted."

"Thinks."

"Huh?"

"You quoted me in past tense. My opinion isn't past tense, it's present tense. I THINK you're hot stuff."

"Oh." She blushed again, offering him a slight smile.

"I have to admit, though, the mixed signals I'd been getting from you—which was partly my own fault, since I was encouraging you to 'be normal' and you were trying, because it's what you thought I wanted—had me more confused about the truth of your situation than I'd thought. When I really realized what was happening, and how you felt about it—which only fully started to occur in those moments...well. I decided you'd be better off if I put some distance between us—like you'd been asking me to do for the previous several days. Which request suddenly made an awful damn lot of sense then. And which is also what triggered me to have that talk with India once we got home; it raised a lot of questions in my mind, and I needed answers. I wanted to make sure that...well, that I knew how to respond to you about certain things, without accidentally...making like Alpha Seven, or something. See, I know you're still trying to get a grip on everything, and probably will, for quite a while to come. And I wanna help, not make it worse."

"Oh." Omega stole a glance at him; he watched her, wondering what it meant. "So you're not..."

"It's okay, Meg. We're good, you and me. And just between you and me, I don't see that ever changing. No matter how close our relationship may get."

"But...but the whole reason I came to you that night was...you were talking about breaking up the partnership, and..."

Echo drew a deep breath.

"I'm not entirely sure I even meant that," he admitted. "Some part of me was already working on a smaller version of the bluff that India and Bet devised, I think, though theirs was way more go-for-broke. But what I was really trying to get across was that we couldn't function as Alpha Line field agents as it stood. What I was more likely to have done, if matters didn't resolve, was to simply give up the field work and run Alpha Line from my desk. Just to try to keep Alpha One intact...if I could." He shook his head. "There's no replacing you, baby. And there never will be." He offered her a half-smile. "We're good. In every sense of the word."

Echo saw Omega's discomfort leave, and nodded to himself. *Good. I got through to her, and she understands. Maybe not how important she is to me, not fully, not yet. But that's gonna change, if I got any say about it. But now she knows how I felt, and what I was trying to do at The Beach—to give her what she wanted, the WAY she wanted it. Not all helter-skelter because the situation forced it, but the whole, committed, in-this-for-the-long-haul thing.*

"All right, Ace. That's good," she said, more cheerfully then. "So's breakfast, by the way. I guess that means I'm in charge of dinner tonight?"

"Yep. It's your turn." Echo grinned.

"Oookay. Hey, you never have showed me how to make that chicken Marengo stuff!"

"Only because somebody I know has been hip-deep in would-be lovers," Echo retorted, blunt.

"When it rains, it pours. That's no excuse!" She grinned; Echo was pleased to see it—Mu hadn't been the only one to notice her more subdued mood since she had returned to Headquarters.

"What? Had you rather I'd take a baseball bat to 'em? That was the only way I could get to you at times," Echo teased. "And damn, did I consider it—several times!"

"It's definitely made for a change of pace," Omega admitted, sobering. "I'm not used to it. I keep waiting for the other shoe to drop..."

* * *

It dropped the very next day. Alpha One and Alpha Two stood on one of the catwalks overlooking the Core the subsequent afternoon, having what India termed a 'post-mortem' of recent events.

"...So Wright's been brain-bleached and sent back home; everything's back to normal, where he's concerned. All things considered," India said, "Wright just wanted to forget and get back to his life as quietly as possible. Did you know he had a fiancée? Poor man. I think he couldn't bring himself to face you, Meg. He asked Bet to relay a message, though. So Bet asked me to pass it to you."

"What was it?" Omega asked quietly.

"He said to tell you—and Echo—he was sorry, terribly sorry. He couldn't help it, and he couldn't find a way to stop it—no matter what he did, no matter how hard he tried. He said he already knew you understood, but wanted you to hear it anyway. But he...didn't know if Echo would." The

347

physician-Agent paused. "Do you understand, Echo?" India asked, curious.

"After everything that's happened," Echo remarked, apparently expressionless to everyone except Omega, who saw the thoughtful, compassionate look in his dark eyes, "I understand a helluva lot better than he thinks."

"Good, I guess," India decided.

"Yeah," Omega averred, "it is."

* * *

Echo gazed out over the Core, leaning his forearms on the rail, as the others continued to chat lightheartedly. Then he stiffened, ever so slightly.

"Hey, pretty lady!" Romeo grinned, pointing. "Someone's lookin' for ya."

"Mu," Omega murmured, spotting the former Secret Service agent as he entered the Core. She turned and walked off the end of the catwalk, down the wall, and over to the other agent. India, Romeo, and Echo observed the inaudible conversation.

* * *

Omega smiled as she walked up, but a somber Mu didn't return it. He spoke to her hesitantly, earnestly, and the smile on her face faded slowly.

Mu asked a question, then waited silently.

Omega nodded, then glanced down.

Mu leaned forward slightly, asking another question, and Omega glanced up at him quickly, a bright smile on her face which only the watching Agents realized was false. She made a dismissing motion with one hand. Mu looked skeptical for a moment, and Omega grinned, brushing the air with her fingertips in a universal *go on—get out of here* gesture.

Mu turned to go, but he glanced up at the catwalk for a moment, searching out a particular pair of brown eyes; he nodded at Echo, who raised an eyebrow over dark, narrowed eyes.

As Mu's back receded across the Core, the grin on Omega's face vanished, momentarily replaced by the loneliness and pain of one more rejection even as her shoulders slumped in discouragement, then she sighed and shrugged to herself.

Raising her head, Omega glanced around—and spotted her three companions watching. Her body went rigid, and she averted her flushing face; they comprehended that she had realized they were witness to the entire scene. They saw her sigh, then look back up at them with a lopsided, rueful excuse for a grin...which didn't reach her eyes. Omega held her hand out, palm up, in an *Oh well, what can I say?* gesture, then she turned and left the Core.

"Damn," Romeo murmured, saddened.

"Poor Meg," India said softly. "You know, Romeo, Meg felt bad for us when she found out about our marriage dilemma. But at least I've got you. Nobody wants her."

"'S a damn shame, too," Romeo observed. "Th' pretty lady's got one o' the biggest, most affectionate hearts I've ever seen, even if she does try her damnedest t' keep it hid."

"That's only to protect it, Romeo," India remarked, and he nodded agreement.

"When she finds th' right man—"

"If she ever does," India sighed.

"Well, shit, India, give the pretty lady some hope. When she does, it'll be one helluva romance." Romeo grinned. "Don'tcha think, Echo?"

"Mmm," Echo responded, still looking absently across the huge room, lost in thought.

"Well, come on, Romeo," India said. "The shift's over. Let's go home."

"Okay. See ya later, Echo."

* * *

Echo glanced over his shoulder at the departing Agents, nodded acknowledgement, then resumed his thoughtful contemplation. He stood there silently for quite some time.

Finally he nodded to himself, the corners of his mouth turning up almost imperceptibly, then his jaw fixed in determination.

Echo turned and strode out of the Core.

* * *

When Echo entered his quarters and walked by the back door, he automatically glanced through to see what his partner was doing. Omega slouched on the couch in jeans and t-shirt, TV remote in hand, channel surfing aimlessly. Silently, surreptitiously, he watched her sigh and toss the remote on the coffee table, then pick up a book and try to lose herself in its pages.

After a moment, she laid it in her lap, held up her hands, and studied them, as if she could find the answers to her isolation there. At last, she picked up her book and attempted to resume reading.

Echo nodded again, more decidedly this time, and moved on without a sound, pulling his cell phone from his pocket.

* * *

A comfortable Omega sprawled on her couch, finally absorbed in her book, when she heard Echo's voice from the back door.

"Ready to go out tonight?"

"Oh." Omega tossed her reply over her shoulder without looking, trying to sound nonchalant. "I thought you saw what happened in the Core. Mu...called it off. I guess he...changed his mind. All things considered, I'm not really surprised, I guess."

"I know. I saw."

She put her book down and stared straight ahead at the wall to hide the pain in her eyes.

"Then don't you think it was sorta cruel to bring up the subject—"

She broke off as she felt something tucked into her hair behind her ear. Omega put up a hand and explored it with delicate, sensitive fingertips. It was a blossom from the flowering plant Romeo had once given Echo—a stargazer lily, the same type his old girlfriend had liked so much, and which Omega had once confessed to liking, as well. Omega sat up and turned toward her partner, who had showered and changed into a fresh Suit.

"Thanks, Echo; that was sweet," Omega told him with a sad smile. "But you put it behind the wrong ear. Single, unattached women wear flowers behind the other ear." She located the stem to move it to the other side, but Echo swiftly covered her hand with his own.

"Leave it alone. I put it exactly where I intended to. It looks...good there."

Omega blinked at him, confused.

"Go get ready to go out, Meg." Echo pointed at her bedroom.

"But Echo, I told you, Mu isn't taking me out."

"I know. I...thought maybe you...might like to go out with me instead."

* * *

Echo withstood Omega's startled scrutiny, the barest hint of uncertainty in his eyes and stance, waiting patiently for her answer. He watched her fingers creep back up to the blossom he'd tucked into her hair, her expression thoughtful, as her sensitive fingers explored it, almost caressing.

Then Omega's entire face lit up with a smile.

Only Echo's dark brown eyes responded, flashing in an answering smile as Omega replied, standing.

"Yes, Echo. I'd like that...very much."

Author's Notes

There are, as always, the usual suspects to thank: my husband, Darrell Osborn, and my parents, Steve and Colene Gannaway. There is also my editor, Courtney Galloway, who provided excellent and varied points of view for looking at the story, and some fascinating discussions about perception of characterization. That assistance has been especially true for this book, because my mom had a stroke during its production, and my world rather tilted on its ear there, at least for a while.

We are reaching the culmination of the Alpha One character arc. This book begins a kind of trilogy within the series, which taken all together provides said character arc's climax, so be patient and read through to the end, and I think you'll approve. And be aware, I've done my due research with friends who have been through experiences similar to what Omega is going through, and they tell me my depictions are realistic. Hang on tight! The roller coaster is departing the station! Enjoy the ride!

~Stephanie Osborn
Huntsville, AL
April 2018

About the Author

Stephanie Osborn is a former payload flight controller, a veteran of over twenty years of working in the civilian space program, as well as various military space defense programs. She has worked on numerous Space Shuttle flights and the International Space Station, and counts the training of astronauts on her resumé. Of those astronauts she trained, one was Kalpana Chawla, a member of the crew lost in the *Columbia* disaster.

She holds graduate and undergraduate degrees in four sciences: Astronomy, Physics, Chemistry, and Mathematics, and she is "fluent" in several more, including Geology and Anatomy. She obtained her various degrees from Austin Peay State University in Clarksville, TN and Vanderbilt University in Nashville, TN.

Stephanie is currently retired from space work. She now happily "passes it forward," teaching math and science via numerous media including radio, podcasting, and public speaking, as well as working with SIGMA, the science fiction think tank, while writing science fiction mysteries based on her knowledge, experience, and travels.

For more, go to http://www.stephanie-osborn.com/.

A sneak peek at *Phantoms*, Book 8 of the Division One series, by Stephanie Osborn!

"...Wow. That's...bizarre. So there seems to be a real, live 'theater phantom' plaguing the production?" Omega verified. "Talk about life imitating art."

"Yes," Michael answered. "The way I figure it, whoever is doing it was likely inspired by the plot of the show, so he or she is deliberately paralleling events. And it falls under the jurisdiction of Division One because there is such a preponderance of offworlders in the cast and crew. Especially the crew."

"And you want Meg to step into the female lead to try to lure the phantom into the open?" Echo asked.

"Exactly."

"Why? It's an awfully dramatic tactic," Echo pressed. "And what about the understudy?"

"It's...it's getting dangerous, Echo," Michael finally admitted. "Two nights ago, the chandelier really did fall. Do you know how heavy that thing is, with all the rigging? An experienced Division One Agent in the role is more likely to...survive...than poor Sofia. OR Kate. In fact, Kate, the understudy, is so frightened that she's taken a temporary leave from the company, under the guise of a 'family emergency.'"

There was a long, towering silence.

"So all you really want is to use Meg as bait," a grim Echo finally declared.

"Well...yes. I suppose so, in a way..."

"No."

"But, Echo—"

"No, Michael," Echo reiterated, reserved and formal. "You want to put my partner in position as a target, where she can't defend herself adequately, and I can't get close enough to do it for her. That's unacceptable."

"Echo, we've got to help," a concerned Omega said earnestly.

"And we will. But not at the risk of you becoming a permanent part of the stage," Echo answered, relenting slightly. "Come on. Let's go talk to Fox. I'll be in touch, Mike."

The two Agents stood and exited the restaurant. Michael noticed Echo's splayed hand resting lightly—familiarly, almost possessively—on the smooth, bare skin between Omega's shoulder blades, exposed by her formal evening gown, and raised an eyebrow in surprise.

* * *

"Echo, you know I've got to do it," Omega said from the passenger seat of the Corvette as it took them back to Headquarters after their formal date. "If that sort of stuff keeps up, Sofia doesn't stand a chance. She's not trained to run a gauntlet, Echo. I am."

"Yes, you are. But—"

"I should be able to step into the role with only a couple of brush- up rehearsals. And Michael can coach me through the rest."

"True. But—"

"Besides, Sofia has fans, a family. An entire show depending on her. On the other hand, if something happens to me, it isn't like there's anybody to miss me."

The Corvette was silent. Then a pale Echo, staring straight ahead through the windshield, said in a low voice, "What am I?"

"What?"

"Do you really think I wouldn't even notice if something...happened to you?"

"No," she responded softly, touched. "But...let's face it, Echo. I'm your third partner. There are other Division One agents. Other partners. There's nothing special about me. Recombinant genetics notwithstanding."

"Damn," Echo said, face nearly white, a strange look in his milk chocolate eyes, "you do think I'm a heartless son of a bitch, don't you?"

"No, Echo, no!" Omega exclaimed, shocked that she had just done the one thing she had thought impossible for her to do: deeply hurt Echo. "I don't mean it like that at all! I'm just trying to be...practical. You know it's true—"

"No, I don't. Have you forgotten about the defined partnership we've got? Alpha One is us, baby. You and me. No substitutes. No replacements."

"—And you know there's a job to do," she said, pretending to ignore his statement. "You're a professional, Echo. The consummate Agent. To

355

many in the Agency, you're the definition of what an Alpha Line Agent should be. Hell, you're the definition of an agent, period."

"Including you?"

"Including me. ESPECIALLY including me. And if anybody should know, it's me. You trained me. So...I know what I have to do, Echo."

Echo mulled over their situation.

"I seem to recall, once upon a time, you doing everything in your power to keep me from going on a mission that you knew was likely to get me killed," he pointed out.

"Or enslaved." Omega nodded. "And I recall your refusing to be dissuaded because there was a job to do."

The interior of the vehicle was silent for long moments.

"I don't like it, Meg."

"Neither did I, Echo. Neither did I."

"All right." Echo sighed. "Let's learn from that earlier experience, you and me, and make sure we communicate and work together through all this mess. Deal?"

"To the best of my ability. Deal."

"Okay. What do you want me to do?"

"Well, assuming Fox approves it—it really is way higher-profile than any agent has ever done before, and he might not—then you're gonna have to work closer with me than we've ever worked in our entire partnership," Omega told him. "Because what you told Sir Michael was right: I am gonna be basically defenseless up there. We'll need nonverbal signals..."

"We need the exact layout of the stage and sets."

"Yes, and we'll need to develop strategies intended to work around, and with, the layout," Omega added.

"And I need to watch you like a hawk," Echo finished.

Don't miss any of these highly entertaining SF/F books by Stephanie Osborn!

The *Division One* series by Stephanie Osborn:
Alpha and Omega
A Small Medium At Large
A Very UnCONventional Christmas
Tour de Force
Trojan Horse
Texas Rangers
Definition and Alignment
Coming soon:
Phantoms
Head Games
Break, Break, Houston

Alpha   and   Omega   (ISBN: 978-0-9982888-0-2   e-book/978-0-9982888-1-9 print) by Stephanie Osborn

Dr. Megan McAllister was already a pretty unusual human—NASA astronomer, professional astronomer, polymath—when she encountered the man in the black Suit that night in west Texas. What Division One Agent Echo didn't know, when he recruited her to the Agency, was that she was even more special.

But he'd find out, soon enough.

Stephanie Osborn, aka the Interstellar Woman of Mystery, former rocket scientist and author of acclaimed science fiction mysteries, goes back to the urban legend of the unique group of men and women who show up at UFO sightings, alien abductions, etc. and make things...disappear...to craft her vision of the universe we don't know about. Her new series, Division One, chronicles this universe through the eyes of recruit Megan McAllister, aka Omega, and her experienced partner, Echo, as they handle everything from lost alien children to extraterrestrial assassination attempts and more.

[First book in the *Division One* series]

* * *

A Small Medium At Large (ISBN: 978-0-9982888-2-6 ebook/978-0-9982888-3-3 print) by Stephanie Osborn

What if Sir Arthur Conan Doyle was right all along, and Harry Houdini really DID do his illusions, not through sleight of hand, but via noncorporeal means? More, what if he could do this because...he wasn't human?

Ari Ho'd'ni, Glu'g'ik son of the Special Steward of the Royal House of Va'du'sha'ā, better known to modern humans as an alien Gray from the ninth planet of Zeta Reticuli A, fled his homeworld with the rest of his family during a time of impending global civil war. With them, they brought a unique device which, in its absence, ultimately caused the failure of the uprisings and the collapse of the imperial regime. Consequently Va'du'sha'ā has been at peace for more than a century. What is the F'al, and why has a rebel faction sent a special agent to Earth to retrieve it?

It falls to the premier team in the Pan-Galactic Law Enforcement and Immigration Administration, Division One—the Alpha One team, known to their friends as Agents Echo and Omega—to find out...or die trying.

[Second book in the *Division One* series]

* * *

A Very UnCONventional Christmas (ISBN: 978-0-9982888-4-0 ebook/978-0-9982888-5-7 print) by Stephanie Osborn

It's Christmas in NYC, but for Alpha Line it's anything but a Silent Night: The Agency has a mole, leaking classified information to toy manufacturers and film producers alike, and the Agents are in danger of losing their anonymity. To complicate matters, the Prime Minister of Lambda Andromedae III, complete with entourage, has arrived to negotiate a new trade agreement with Earth. Worse, the more paranoid Division One field agents look at Omega's recent history with the Agency and suspect they have identified the mole!

Simultaneously, the discovery of a grim countdown in the most incongruous place possible—the Christmas tree at Rockefeller Center—augers the threat of horrific events on Christmas Eve itself.

Meanwhile, Omega is struggling to adjust to her very first Christmas in the Agency, made more difficult by the exposure of parts of her past long hidden from her conscious mind.

Will Omega be able to refute the accusations, or be punished for crimes she did not commit? Will the internal conspiracy expose the Agency? Or will efforts to thwart it see Echo—and Fox—caught up in the accusations as well? What is the meaning of the countdown to Christmas Eve, and will any of Alpha Line survive it? [Third book in the *Division One* series]

* * *

Tour de Force (ISBN: 978-0-9982888-6-4 ebook/978-0-9982888-7-1 print) by Stephanie Osborn

Alpha One is participating in Omega's very first First Contact diplomatic operation. Unfortunately, it's going to split up the team—the Cortians, a race from the Sagittarius Dwarf Galaxy, have stringent requirements, and that narrows down the list of "candidate exchange students" to...Echo. ONLY Echo. PGLEIA's top Division One Agent, the man being groomed to be the next Director...and Omega's partner. A plum assignment, for the pick of the crop.

But Omega doesn't see it that way, though she can't—or won't—explain why. She is determined to stop the mission from going forward. At any cost.

Why is Omega trying to scuttle a diplomatic mission? What is she seeing that more experienced Agents aren't? Why won't the others listen? Is something bigger, more menacing, happening to her—to them? Will— CAN—Alpha One survive? [Fourth book in the *Division One* series]

* * *

Trojan Horse (ISBN: 978-0-9982888-9-5 ebook/978-1-947530-00-3 print) by Stephanie Osborn

After returning the healer Doron to his homeworld of Edeptis, Echo takes Omega on a training run to make her a PGLEIA-certified starship pilot—celestial navigation, extra-vehicular activity, emergency repair, planetary surveys, you name it. And he secretly delights in seeing Omega's joy at finally fulfilling a childhood dream.

But when the Cortians show on the scene, intending to take Alpha One into custody for crimes against the Cortian Amalgam, the resulting dogfight severely damages the *Trojan Horse*, causing it to crash on a primitive protoplanet. Both Echo and Omega are badly injured, and it will take both of them working together to survive in the wreckage, while more Cortian vessels search for them overhead, and Fox and the rest of Alpha Line try to fight their way through to rescue their friends and colleagues. [Fifth book in the *Division One* series]

* * *

Texas Rangers (ISBN: 978-1-947530-01-0 ebook/978-1-947530-02-7 print) by Stephanie Osborn

It's time for Alpha One to take a vacation! Traveling to the Ranch, a field station in western Texas near the famed Pecos River, the pair relax and unwind, riding horseback, picnicking, and generally having fun...

...Until they discover a team of alien assassins—the original JFK hit team, no less—sneaking across the landscape and headed to Dallas, to take out the current President on a campaign junket!

Meanwhile, back at Headquarters and unknown to him, Echo's estranged mother—who believed him killed years before, when he entered the Agency—lies unconscious in a regeneration pod, while the medlab staff, led by Zebra, works frantically to save her life: Shortly before their vacation, Omega discovered that Naalin Bryant had developed a particularly virulent form of cancer.

Can Alpha One infiltrate the assassin team without being killed? Can Alpha Line stop the assassination of the U.S. President? And can Zebra save Echo's mother's life and return her to her son, or will Echo lose one—or both—of the two women who mean the world to him? [Sixth book in the *Division One* series]

* * *

Definition and Alignment (ISBN: ebook/ print) by Stephanie Osborn

When another enhanced human, Mark Wright, unexpectedly shows up at the Agency, Alpha One discovers that they still aren't done with Slug's machinations and levels of planning: Wright is there for Omega, and the NEXT generation of assassins will be GENETICALLY programmed to kill Echo! Thus begins a bizarre, inverted manhunt as the telepathically-brainwashed Wright chases Alpha One across the planet, using the pre-programmed mental link that Omega can't fully block, to follow her anywhere Echo can take her... [Seventh book in the *Division One* series]

* * *

The *Burnout* series by Stephanie Osborn
The Fetish
Burnout: The mystery of Space Shuttle STS-281

360

Coming soon:
Escape Velocity

The Fetish (ASIN: B007YATGG8) by Stephanie Osborn

In *Burnout: The mystery of Space Shuttle STS-281*, Dr. Mike Anders buys a small spaceman fetish from a Zuni elder at a trading post. But there's a story behind this little lapis spaceman carving. What is it, and how did it come to be?

* * *

Burnout: The mystery of Space Shuttle STS-281 (ISBN: 1-60619-200-0) by Stephanie Osborn

How do you react when you discover the next shuttle disaster has happened...right on schedule?

Burnout is a SF mystery about a Space Shuttle disaster that turns out to be no accident. As the true scope of the disaster is uncovered by the principle investigators, "Crash" Murphy and Dr. Mike Anders, they find themselves running for their lives as friends, lovers and coworkers involved in the investigation perish around them.

* * *

Sherlock Holmes: Gentleman Aegis series by Stephanie Osborn:
Sherlock Holmes and the Mummy's Curse
Coming soon:
Sherlock Holmes in the Wild Hunt
Sherlock Holmes and the Tournament of Shadows

Sherlock Holmes and the Mummy's Curse (ISBN: 1-51888-312-5) by Stephanie Osborn

Holmes and Watson. Two names linked by mystery and danger from the beginning.

Within the first year of their friendship and while both are young men, Holmes and Watson are still finding their way in the world, with all the troubles that such young men usually have: Financial straits, troubles of the female persuasion, hazings, misunderstandings between friends, and more. Watson's Afghan wounds are still tender, his health not yet fully recovered, and there can be no consideration of his beginning a new practice as yet. Holmes, in his turn, is still struggling to found the new profession of consulting detective. Not yet truly established in London, let alone with the reputations they will one day possess, they are between cases and at loose ends when Holmes' old professor of archaeology contacts him.

Professor Willingham Whitesell makes an appeal to Holmes' unusual skill set and a request. Holmes is to bring Watson to serve as the dig team's physician and come to Egypt at once to translate hieroglyphics for his prestigious archaeological dig. There in the wilds of the Egyptian desert, plagued by heat, dust, drought and cobras, the team hopes to find the very first Pharaoh. Instead, they find something very different... (First book in the Gentleman Aegis series)

Sherlock Holmes and the Mummy's Curse is a Silver Falchion Award winner.

* * *

The *Displaced Detective* series by Stephanie Osborn:
The Case of the Displaced Detective: The Arrival
The Case of the Displaced Detective: At Speed
The Case of the Cosmological Killer: The Rendlesham Incident
The Case of the Cosmological Killer: Endings and Beginnings
A Case of Spontaneous Combustion
Fear in the French Quarter

The Case of the Displaced Detective: The Arrival by Stephanie Osborn is a SF mystery in which brilliant hyperspatial physicist, Dr. Skye Chadwick, discovers there are alternate realities, often populated by those we consider only literary characters. Can Chadwick help Holmes come up to speed in modern investigative techniques in time to stop the spies? Will Holmes be able to thrive in our modern world? Is Chadwick now Holmes' new "Watson"—or more?

And what happens next? [First book in the *Displaced Detective* series]
* * *

The Case of the Displaced Detective: At Speed by Stephanie Osborn
Having foiled sabotage of Project: Tesseract by an unknown spy ring, Sherlock Holmes and Dr. Skye Chadwick face the next challenge. How do they find the members of this diabolical spy ring when they do not even know what the ring is trying to accomplish? And how can they do it when Skye is recovering from no less than two nigh-fatal wounds?

362

Can they work out the intricacies of their relationship? Can they determine the reason the spy ring is after the tesseract? And—most importantly—can they stop it? [Second book in the *Displaced Detective* series]

* * *

The Case of the Cosmological Killer: The Rendlesham Incident by Stephanie Osborn

In 1980, RAF Bentwaters and Woodbridge were plagued by UFO sightings that were never solved. Now, McFarlane, a resident of Suffolk has died of fright during a new UFO encounter. On holiday in London, Sherlock Holmes and Skye Chadwick-Holmes are called upon by Her Majesty's Secret Service to investigate the death.

What is the UFO? Why does Skye find it familiar? Who—or what—killed McFarlane?

And how can the pair do what even Her Majesty's Secret Service could not? [Third book in the *Displaced Detective* series]

* * *

The Case of the Cosmological Killer: Endings and Beginnings by Stephanie Osborn

After the revelations in *The Rendlesham Incident*, Holmes and Skye find they have not one, but two, very serious problems facing them. Not only did their "UFO victim" most emphatically NOT die from a close encounter, he was dying twice over—from completely unrelated causes. Holmes must now find the murderers before they find the secret of the McFarlane farm. And to add to their problems, another continuum—containing another Skye and Holmes—has approached Skye for help to stop the collapse of their own spacetime, a collapse that could take Skye with it, should she happen to be in their tesseract core when it occurs. [Fourth book in the *Displaced Detective* series]

* * *

A Case of Spontaneous Combustion by Stephanie Osborn

When an entire village west of London is wiped out in an apparent case of mass spontaneous combustion, Her Majesty's Secret Service contacts The Holmes Agency to investigate. Once in London, Holmes looks into the horror that is now Stonegrange. His investigations take him into a dangerous undercover assignment in search of a possible terror ring, though he cannot determine how a human agency could have caused the disaster.

Meanwhile, alone in Colorado, Skye is forced to battle raging wildfires and tame a wild mustang stallion, all while believing that her husband has abandoned her. Who—or what—caused the horror in Stonegrange? Will Holmes find his way safely through the metaphorical minefield that is modern Middle Eastern politics? Will this predicament seriously damage—even destroy—the couple's relationship? And can Holmes stop the terrorists before they unleash their outré weapon again? [Fifth book in the *Displaced Detective* series]

* * *

Fear in the French Quarter by Stephanie Osborn revolves around a jaunt by no less than Sherlock Holmes himself—brought to the modern day from an alternate universe's Victorian era by his continuum parallel, who is now his wife, Dr. Skye Chadwick-Holmes—to famed New Orleans for both business and pleasure. There, the detective couple investigates ghostly apparitions, strange disappearances, mystic phenomena, and challenge threats to the very universe they call home.

It was supposed to be a working holiday for Skye and Sherlock, along with their friend, the modern day version of Doctor Watson—some federal training that also gave them the chance to explore New Orleans, as the ghosts of the French Quarter become exponentially more active. When the couple uncovers an imminently catastrophic cause, whose epicenter lies squarely in the middle of Le Vieux Carré, they must race against time to stop it before the whole thing breaks wide open—and more than one universe is destroyed. [Sixth book in the *Displaced Detective* series]

.